D0099386

SPECIFIC IMPULSE

CHARLES JUSTIZ

iUniverse, Inc.
Bloomington

Specific Impulse

This is a work of fiction. All of the characters, names, incidents, organizations, and dialogue in this novel are either the products of the author's imagination or are used fictitiously.

iUniverse books may be ordered through booksellers or by contacting:

iUniverse
1663 Liberty Drive
Bloomington, IN 47403
www.iuniverse.com
1-800-Authors (1-800-288-4677)

Because of the dynamic nature of the Internet, any Web addresses or links contained in this book may have changed since publication and may no longer be valid. The views expressed in this work are solely those of the author and do not necessarily reflect the views of the publisher, and the publisher hereby disclaims any responsibility for them.

Any people depicted in stock imagery provided by Thinkstock are models, and such images are being used for illustrative purposes only.

Certain stock imagery © Thinkstock.

ISBN: 978-1-936236-59-6 (pbk)
ISBN: 978-1-936236-60-2 (ebk)

Library of Congress Control Number: 2011904128

Printed in the United States of America

iUniverse rev. date: 4/12/2011

For Dayna, who was born knowing
more than I can possibly learn.

CHAPTER 1

ANTONIO CRUBARI SAT IN the driver's seat of the Hummer and rechecked the darkened corners of the surrounding alley. He hid back in the shadows so nothing could draw attention to him and no one could see him at such a late hour of the night. His hand drifted involuntarily to where he had earlier removed various knives from their customary places. He chided himself for his impatience. To be caught with any weapons on his body or in the large, stolen automobile would have been a beginner's mistake. Antonio Crubari was no beginner. If someone did come to investigate, the last thing the curious meddler would see would be a man with vaguely Mayan features stepping out from the driver's seat. Crubari did not need knives to kill. He simply preferred them.

He scanned the dashboard as he had done every few moments for the last hour. The motor was idling within limits. The oil pressure was on the low side of the green arc, but still acceptable. His tracker remained locked on to his target and displaying on his portable screen. He checked the time. In ten minutes, Mr. James Nutley, Department of Justice agent, would be dead.

His plan depended on his target behaving predictably. The target was intelligent, so he expected him to make intelligent choices. He also knew that his target had a meeting in the morning with his superiors, so he expected him to not waste time. His target had lived in the Las Vegas area. Consequently, his target knew shortcuts to avoid congestion caused by the tourist-fed traffic. His target also had his wife with him, so he would want to get back to his hotel as quickly as possible. His target would strive to increase his chances of enjoying his wife's pleasures that evening and reduce the chances of incurring her displeasures with any delay. *Typical ... too predictable*, thought Crubari. *It would soon prove fatal.*

Of course, the wife had to die as well.

Crubari checked his portable screen and saw that his target was moving towards an area of traffic congestion. The congestion was going to get much worse. He had hired a professional to cause a wreck at exactly this time, at exactly this spot. The contract was to block traffic in all directions at a specific intersection for a minimum of thirty minutes. The traffic was getting worse on Crubari's screen and the target was almost at the congestion. *There, you're at the traffic jam and have to decide. Now which way will you go? Left – towards your hotel and more traffic, or right, through the warehouse district where there is little tourist traffic and towards me.* His target turned right. Now, Nutley and his wife would be dead in five minutes.

Crubari detested that he had to make such a complicated plan. His usual style was to remove his victims from circulation quietly and quickly. Unfortunately, Crubari had to address problems among the people with which he worked. These people, with deadly skills of their own, were working on tasks that would undermine years of Crubari's work. Direct action would not work, but if the death of this Department of Justice agent could be made to look like the act of a drunken driver, Crubari's own plans might be secure. That is why he had gone to the trouble of stealing the Hummer from such a dangerous individual.

There was no traffic in the warehouse district this late at night. Crubari watched the trace of his target reach a predetermined point, and drove the Hummer out of the alley onto a main street. He split his attention between the road and the trace. Within one block of impact, Crubari allowed himself to immerse in the task and time slowed down. Though he was traveling nearly ninety miles per hour, it was as if he were moving at a crawl. Colors around him were vivid and details sharp. Although he had planned the crash so his target would not have enough reaction time, Crubari would be able to maneuver the Hummer precisely to impact.

The subcompact car came into view from around the corner and Crubari saw that Nutley had his stepchildren in the back seat. The unexpected presence of the children did not change Crubari's mind. He nudged the wheel slightly into the target to hit further back on his victim's car. Crubari could feel the tires of his SUV straining to comply. His target never completed turning his head to see what had caught his attention out of the corner of his eye.

The impact felt gentle to Crubari, but the airbag inflation blocked his view for what seemed an eternity. He finally got it out of his line of sight and continued to the Hummer's drop point. The massive truck continued to run, but the smell of radiator fluid and the rising temperatures in the motor signaled that it would soon overheat and stop running. He had expected this problem. He pulled into a side street and ran the car into a wall. Crubari felt it important to lead investigators in the direction he wanted them to look. He got out of the car, splashed tequila on the upholstery, and threw the half-empty bottle on the passenger side floor. *Yes*, he thought. *Investigators will think this a liquor-fueled joyride gone wrong.* He grabbed his portable screen and stuffed it into an oversized pocket in his jacket, turned and walked away from the car.

Crubari followed a predetermined route on foot back to the scene of the crash that took advantage of the shadows and darkness. A small crowd had gathered around the mangled wreck that had been Nutley's car. Several people had already pulled over to help and one woman had her phone out calling in the emergency.

"It's horrible," the woman was saying between sobs. "They're all dead."

Crubari stepped back into the shadows feeling pleased.

CHAPTER 2

DR. CARIŃA MARIA GONZALEZ took a deep breath of the thin, unpolluted Arizona air and smiled. To take such a pulmonary risk in the Los Angeles basin would draw stares from co-workers. She was thankful to have made the break from that particular insanity. Her sabbatical had restored a calm and sanity where tension and uneasiness had held sway.

Carin stretched to her full five-foot-eight height and strained her muscles until she felt her joints pop. With her eyes closed, she turned to face the sun, allowing her jet-black hair to stream behind her in the breeze and willed herself to relax. Tense muscles began to relent along every part of her body except her lower back. Those particular muscles were giving her the early warning signs of an uncomfortable night ahead.

At 37, Carin could not blame her back condition on age. She had suffered lower back pains since her teens even though she worked out regularly and kept her weight constant at 128 pounds. She smiled to think that back pain was one of the major reasons she changed focus during her graduate studies. An inability to bend down and pick up rocks was a liability for a geologist.

After work last Friday, she had returned to her apartment just long enough to pack a small bag and rush to the airport. There, after checking the weather and filing a flight plan, she opened the hangar door to drag out her most cherished possession, her tiny homebuilt aircraft, and pulled it into the waning sunlight. The unique craft had taken eight years of precious personal time to complete.

Eight years was longer than the normal homebuilt aircraft project. That is, longer for anyone not a cursed perfectionist. Back in those days, if she found that any of the design was costing her some performance, she would redesign. She had not liked the drag profile the original plans gave her, so she redesigned the entire wing. After that particular decision had cost her a full year delay, she promised herself not to tweak the design any more. She kept the promise, more or less.

Now as she took her tiny aircraft on its first flight away from California, the little ship gobbled up the miles between Los Angeles and Winslow, Arizona without breaking a sweat. The thought made her flush with pride, and the flight across the Mojave Desert as the sun was receding behind her had been a meditation. With each mile, a little more tension in her neck relaxed. As each road passed underneath, her breathing became more regular and calm. Cruising past all the cars imprisoned on the ground, she could forget the worry and the stress that had chased her out of Pasadena. Left behind was the job that was no longer challenging and was looking more like a dead end. Left behind was a life that no longer felt right.

Some inexpressible force had drawn Carin back to the Barringer Meteor Crater. Years ago, she had spent an entire summer doing research in the crater for her master's degree. Now she wondered whether the force that pulled her to return was only a misplaced need to get back to that simpler and happier time.

The family who owned the land and the local authorities denied admittance below the crater walls to the public. This caused Carin some concern. Only sanctioned research teams could get access to the bottom. In fact, tours along the crater rim or along the crater bottom had ended a long time ago. The local authorities were so sensitive to disturbing the environment that they vigorously prosecuted rock collectors found picking up samples within several miles of the crater. They had even passed laws banning hunting in the area to preserve the meteorite's telltale signs for future scientists.

Fate raised its hand for Carin. On reaching the main entry gate of the crater, she noticed a group of twenty people getting off a local university bus. She walked over and saw they were packing equipment she recognized from her days of doing geological studies. Carin found the head of the research team, a short, fire-plug shaped bundle of energy named Jim Torres, and pleaded her case. As it turned out, he had read some of her early papers on planetary geology and agreed to have her come along.

"We'll just keep this between you and me," Jim had said with a wink. "No need to buy any trouble."

Carin readily agreed and before she knew it, she was standing at the lowest point of the crater, bathing in the final rays of a retiring sun. The sounds of classic Carlos Santana from her headset drifted around her and a feeling of unburdened release began to take hold for the first time in months.

She did a slow pirouette to look around and had to chuckle as some of her hair blew into her mouth. Carin let her mind drift back to the time when the meteoroid had arrived at this spot in northern Arizona. The climate had been much cooler then and a wet, rich forest surrounded the impact area. Natives of the time would not find rattlesnakes, but they might have run into a wooly mammoth or a mastodon. When the impact occurred, it produced an explosion that was more than two thousand times as powerful as the World War II era atomic bombs. The air blast from the explosion churned the atmosphere in a manner that dwarfed Earth's most violent natural weather. Supersonic winds uprooted every plant within two miles of the impact point. The fireball scorched every living creature in its path out to eight miles. The pressure pulse killed animals fifteen miles away. The devil's own domain had opened and powerful demons had poured forth in the forest of northern Arizona on that ancient day.

Ruination befell the man whose name was associated with the crater. Time had proven Daniel Moreau Barringer correct, but his pursuit of the truth of the crater had left him penniless. Many of Daniel Barringer's friends and associates believed the crater's reluctance to yield its secrets caused his premature death. Carin Gonzalez felt a kinship with the old miner. *Being right isn't all it's cracked up to be,* she thought of the long dead engineer.

Carin decided that she was finally in the right frame of mind to review her life. She set herself up to do a personal inventory of one Dr. Carin Gonzalez. First, she felt that she was an intuitive sort and that she understood people. *Then why can't I figure out men?* She decided to table that line of thinking for the moment.

She wondered whether it might be helpful to review her assets. She knew herself to be an attractive sort in the classic Hispanic mold, although, at five foot eight inches, she was a little taller than average. Overall, she felt that her looks had been as much a minus as a plus, so no help there. She knew that her intelligence was high and she had difficulty hiding that fact. She had to admit it was a minus with some men. *No, let's face it,* she thought. *It's proven a minus with more men than I care to remember.* Like Raul, that cute post-doc from Chile. Carin had done everything but tattoo, "I'm yours if you want me" on her forehead. It had been clear that he had wanted none of what she was selling. He spoke the same language as that L.A. Laker cheerleader, though. This was not helping her.

She looked for something positive. She liked sports! However, that did not count, since she liked to play and loathed watching, especially on TV. How could men sit in front of a television screen for so many hours, just to watch something they could be *doing*? She had never been able to wrap her mind around that idea. That was a dead end.

She decided to take a reluctant and dreaded look at her career. Recently, her work had become confining and confrontational. She just did not get it.

She felt she was good at understanding her fellow workers' feelings, but if she saw that somebody was doing something in a boneheaded fashion, she felt compelled to make the point known. Was that so wrong? For instance, take that last Mars Lander project. She recommended the team do an end-to-end check before launch and they looked at her as if she just landed from another planet. *This isn't rocket science, folks,* she thought angrily. *Hubble should have taught us that lesson.* Now the Mars Lander had buried itself into the Martian surface going about four kilometers per second without bothering to fire a single retro rocket and everyone looks at her as if it were her fault. Her supervisor had the gall to imply that if she had been more forceful in her position, Carin could have spared the agency an expensive embarrassment. That same supervisor told her to sit down when she had originally brought up the problem. *Yeah,* she thought. *I understand people. Let's shelve this particular form of investigation, especially since it proves that I'm a jerk no matter how I look at it.*

Carin swept her eyes up to the lip of the giant crater. The rim of smashed and strewn boulders was a generations-old work of art. Some boulders scattered across the desert were the size of small houses. *Maybe one will drop on my head and knock some sense into me,* she thought. *No Carin, that's defeatist. Close your eyes, take another deep breath, and then reopen your eyes.*

Carin squared her shoulders and decided that she had to make changes in her life. She would take better care of herself since she was the only "Carin" that she had. From now on, if she saw a problem at work and it was not her project, then it was not her concern. She was going to keep her nose to the grindstone. She would brush and floss. Most importantly, Carin would remember that she could not trust men.

She found herself shaking her head. To make those changes would be to change who she was. Carin was not sure she could live with that person. *Oh well,* she thought. *At least I can brush and floss more.*

An airy whistling sound penetrated through the strains of an electric guitar crying on her headphones. She turned her head in time to see a man lunging at her. He tackled her to the ground at the same time she felt a thunderous explosion split the air overhead.

Carin went to push her attacker off but he was already up. She jumped to her feet, assumed a defensive stance, and instantly felt foolish. She changed the move into one of brushing dirt off her jeans hoping he had not noticed her overreaction.

He was moving away from her, hurrying toward a point about thirty feet from where he had tackled her to the ground. He was a slim middle-aged man, a few inches shy of six feet and ran in a surefooted crouch. His ball cap had blown off in the explosion revealing a close-cropped head that was bald on top. He looked quickly in a full circle from the impact point, looked down at the ground, and then more slowly looked back toward to the horizon, turning in all directions. His eyes focused from one item to the next as if he were cataloging the entire crater. His facial muscles were taut and his expression was unchanging.

Moments later, the man stood upright and jogged back to Carin. He mouthed something to her, but Carin's ears were still ringing from the explosion. She could not hear what he was saying. She shook her head and pointed to her ears.

He cupped his hands and shouted, "Are you all right?"

This time she understood. "What the hell do you think you're doing, jumping on me like that?" she shouted back.

The man took no notice of Carin's ill humor. He kept scanning the horizon all around. He cupped his hands again. "I'm Jake Sabio. I'm sorry, but I can't hear a word you're saying right now. Can you hear me okay?"

Carin nodded.

Jake looked around one more time and cupped his hands again. He got close enough that she could feel the heat of his body. "Did you hear anything strange just before the explosion?"

She shook her head and pointed to her personal stereo. "I was listening to my music and didn't hear much, just some whistling sound overhead. Can you hear me yet?"

Jake gave her a signal with his thumb and index finger suggesting he could hear her a little bit then motioned her to the spot that he ran to following the explosion. He pointed to the ground.

"What do you make of this?"

Carin looked at the small blast area and became quiet for a moment. "It was an airburst for sure. Not much energy in the burst, but the object seems to have vaporized before impact. No cratering from debris…that's odd. It didn't explode symmetrically. Very odd, actually."

Jake scanned the ground around the small impact mark. "I hadn't noticed before, but look at that. You're right. And it looks like it was pointed straight at us."

"That's not what I meant, but I see now what you mean. I meant that it didn't just blow up like a balloon in all directions equally, but it exploded with most of the force moving horizontally, especially towards us. Some of it should have gone straight up as well as straight down. That would have left a crater with little spatter marks and some debris from whatever it was. I don't see any of that."

Jake pointed to the East rim of the crater. "I caught a glimpse out of the corner of my eye. It just barely cleared the rim over there." He was still scanning the horizon. Suddenly, he focused all his attention on her. "I'm sorry, but I didn't catch your name."

"I'm Carin Gonzalez and I'm one of those strange people who don't appreciate getting jumped on and dragged to the ground." She took a breath and added, "Except when someone is saving my life, of course. Exceptions granted for damsel rescuing." She managed a thin smile and offered her hand.

Jake shook her hand with an acknowledging nod and said, "I'm Jake Sabio. You're a geologist or geophysicist of some kind." It was not a question.

"I've got a Doctorate in Machine-Based Intelligence, but my masters work was in Geological and Planetary Sciences and I don't like evasive people."

Jake's face remained rigid in concentration. Without breaking his third complete scan of the crater rim he said, "I'm not being evasive if you don't ask me a question."

He pointed at the ground. "This was an airburst, not a ground burst. It wasn't an artillery shell because we're still here, and a ground-based explosion doesn't explain the 'incoming' sound."

Jake paused a moment to secure his ball cap back in place. He asked, "Could a meteor have done this?"

"Meteoroid," Carin corrected.

"What?"

"Meteoroid," she said again without lifting her gaze from the ground. "A meteor is a phenomenon in the sky – the streak behind the rock in space. The actual rock is a meteoroid until it hits the ground. Then it's a meteorite. It's a common mistake."

Jake continued to divide his scan between the crater rim and the ground before him. "I stand corrected," he replied. "Could a *meteorite* have caused this?"

By this time, Carin's hearing had recovered and she could see that some people were coming down from the rim. She said, "You seemed focused on this. Is there something special I should know?"

Jake gave her a puzzled look. "Doctor, your life must be interesting if explosions are an everyday event. I personally don't get that many explosions in my life, so I get interested when an unexpected one happens in my vicinity. Call me paranoid. I'll initially assume someone was trying to get you or me or both since that's the opinion that involves us the most personally."

Carin gave him an amused look. "For a man who just perpetrated an unprovoked assault on an unsuspecting, defenseless woman, you're quite abrasive."

Jake turned to her and his face immediately became neutral. His lips were relaxed and his eyes barely showed the sharp intellect behind them. "Doctor,

I get the feeling that you may be caught unsuspecting for the briefest of moments, but I don't think you've ever been caught defenseless."

His face just became unreadable! She thought. *He must have seen me staring at him.* She nervously shifted her attention to the ground to get her mind back on track. A pattern in the explosion marks became clear to her. "No, it can't be a meteorite, or I should say that it is unlikely."

"How unlikely?" Jake pressed.

"About as unlikely as you being struck by lightning while being attacked by a shark."

Jake pursed his lips and appeared to whistle. Carin only heard it as a distant tone. He said, "Okay, that's unlikely. What gives you that impression?"

Carin shrugged and pointed to her ear. "First, you heard it approaching. I assume that's why you jumped on me. You have a military background."

"Navy, and yes, I definitely heard incoming."

"Annapolis grad, right? No, I'm not a mind reader; I can see your class ring. That explains why you dragged me to the ground when you heard incoming. Just a reflex taught on your first summer at the Naval Academy. How and why did you get so close to me?"

"I'd been trying to get your attention, but I never caught your eye. I could see that you were deep in your own thoughts and was trying not to be rude, but I could tell you were a geologist of some kind by the way you were looking at the different parts of the crater. I wanted to ask you some questions about the formations at the rim."

Carin looked at the man closely and began to share his concern. "You've heard artillery incoming before?"

Jake looked taken aback. "Yes, but this was different. The Doppler shifted twice before it went quiet."

The Doppler shift was the way you could tell when a train went by. The frequency of the sound suddenly shifts much lower, but Jake had it all wrong. Carin was shaking her head. "There's no way the Doppler could have shifted. You'll only hear a Doppler shift in the first place if some object changes its motion relative to you. *This* thing was coming at us the whole time, so the Doppler can't even shift once, much less twice …"

"Unless it's guided," Jake completed for her. "And it doesn't go quiet unless it's going really fast and coming right at you."

Carin surveyed the scene. While looking around, she twirled her amethyst ring on her right hand with her right thumb. She admitted to herself that it was a silly nervous habit, but it gave her comfort. The stone setting was a gift from her mother and father when she was a senior in high school. Twirling it made her feel close to them. It was the only jewelry she wore.

"Well, it wasn't a meteorite ... Oh my God, there's somebody down over there. C'mon."

As they jogged over to the unconscious form of one of the researchers, Jake asked, "How can you be sure it wasn't a meteorite, Doctor?"

"Mostly, because you heard it. After all, the sound waves got to you before the object did. To be going so slow that you were able to react and not only hit the deck, but bring me down with you ... no, that's way too slow for some rock that has just survived atmospheric reentry. Besides, you said that it approached on a shallow angle from the East. That would tell me that the object should've been going faster rather than slower."

Carin and Jake got to the victim on the ground. "It's Jim Torres," said Carin. "This is the guy that got me into the crater by letting me join his research team."

Torres was lying face down, but had one hand out. Carin grabbed his wrist. "He's got a good pulse," she said.

Carin leaned her mouth close to the man's ear. "Doctor Torres, are you all right? It's Carin Gonzalez."

Torres let out a low moan and rolled over. Carin instinctively pulled back. Small holes that were still oozing blood pocked Torres' face and neck. It was as if buckshot the size of grains of sand had blasted the short man.

Jake pointed to his chest. "He's breathing normally. Maybe he just got the wind knocked out of him."

Torres sat up coughing and waving his hand at Carin. "I'm fine, I'm fine – just let me catch my breath. Is the rest of the group okay?"

Carin looked around for the other team members. "Look, another person is down."

Torres continued to cough but finally said, "Really, I'm fine. Please check on the other members of the group."

Jake and Carin both got up and ran to the still form of a woman about twenty yards away. Jake asked, "How does the shallow entry angle apply?"

Carin had to think a moment to retrace their previous conversation. "What? Oh, if it were a rock on a reentry path, its apparent velocity to us would have had the Earth's rotational velocity added on. At this latitude, that would have been about 500 miles per hour added on top of whatever speed it had. Hard to stay subsonic unless it was very light, but then it would have probably burned up. However, if it goes slow, you would expect a more vertical approach – either way, it doesn't add up. Whatever caused the explosion, it wasn't a meteorite."

Jake was nodding as they got to the next victim. Carin checked the woman's pulse and it was as strong and regular as the man before. Jake commented, "Regular breathing like Doctor Torres." He stood up and scanned the horizon. It was clear to Carin that he kept a special eye on the folks fast approaching. Unexpectedly, he asked, "What else, Doctor?"

"Remember the explosion pattern we saw on the ground? It proves that this thing vaporized just before impact. Fine and dandy, but you heard it so it had to have been subsonic. So, if this was a space rock, where did it get the energy to vaporize? If it was this small and picked up that amount of energy on entry, it would have come apart closer to the point of maximum heating when it was going faster, which means when it was much higher – say a couple of hundred thousand feet higher. No, this has the earmarks of a mechanical device. Look, there's someone else down."

As they jogged to the next victim, Jake pointed to a fast approaching rescue group. "I agree with you about it being a mechanical device, doctor. I think that everyone who was in the crater during explosion is down."

Carin slowed down and looked around the crater. Sure enough, still forms were dotted around the crater. "Everyone except us, Captain."

A sense of dread washed over Carin. She was not normally susceptible to paranoia. However, she was not about to point out to the responders that she and Jake were the only two not affected. "Jake, they're going to be getting these folks out of here at max speed and filling up the local hospitals. I feel fine and you look healthy. I don't see any reason to load up the local facilities with our carcasses since we seem to be okay."

Jake continued moving but turned his head to look at Carin as if for the first time. For a moment, he did not say anything. Then a slight nod that was more in his eyes than in any motion he made. "Translation: since we are about to have company, you're suggesting that our story is that we ran down here when we heard the explosion so we could help."

That was exactly what Carin was trying to say. She took a breath to protest, but Jake made a small gesture of his hand that stopped her. "I have to agree with you, Doctor. Too many things don't add up here. I think it's in our best interest to get some answers before we share our experience." Jake reached into his back pocket and took out his wallet. From it, he extracted a small card and handed it to Carin. "Here, take this. It has my e-mail and phone numbers on it. I check them once a day. I may be paranoid, but let me know if anything else unusual happens to you. And I mean anything."

Carin turned to take the card and noticed for the first time that several dozen small holes peppered the back of Jake's denim jacket. She pointed to the holes. "Look at that. Are you okay?"

Jake pointed to the sleeves of her ski jacket. "Look. You've got them too."

Jake untucked the back of his shirt and raised it slightly. His back had dozens of little red welts, one to match each hole in his jacket. Carin pulled back a sleeve and noticed she had the same welts. One was still bleeding slightly and, while she watched, it healed over, turned an angry red and then settled down to a dull pink.

Jake had been watching too. "That should have taken a week at least."

At this point, the rescue group came within shouting range. Carin slowly turned to face them. Her sabbatical had just taken a curious turn.

CHAPTER 3

CRUBARI CHECKED HIS DISGUISE one last time before stepping out of the lavatory of the private jet. He smiled. Regardless of how good he got at disguising his looks, to his eyes he could always make out his vaguely Mayan features — the set of his eyes, the shape of his head. It did not matter. He was confident the disguise would be proof against anyone trying to discover his identity. It always had in the past.

He had heard of the explosion within an hour of its occurrence. This was not surprising since he paid several news companies for any reports of freak explosions that had mysteriously disabled or injured people. Of all the explosions he had examined over the years, this one was the most promising.

He chartered an airplane to fly him to Burbank, California as soon as he received the news. There, he had a rental car driven to the plane for him and then left the crew of the airplane waiting while he drove himself out to the smaller Van Nuys Airport in the San Fernando Valley. There, he boarded another jet that would take him to Winslow, Arizona. Such ways of muddying his tracks had long become instinctive. He did what he could to blur the picture, paying for everything in cash. He always included a healthy tip. It helped to assure him prompt and polite service and that no one asked awkward questions. If his assumptions were correct, he would have to hurry; the deaths would soon begin. If the event in the crater turned out to be what he suspected, then he was more than likely already too late.

The jet landed at the small airport in Winslow just after midnight. The flight crew agreed to stay by the aircraft and be ready to leave on his return. As soon as he stepped off the boarding ladder and started for his waiting car, his phone rang. It was a message from one of his news agencies. Several of the victims of the explosion had died already. It was happening quickly this time. He would have to hurry.

There was no traffic on the streets. *This is good*, thought the man. *There will be fewer witnesses.* Crubari scanned the hospital parking lot for a darkened area and found one corner where the overhead lights had burned out and not been replaced. He shut down the car in the shadow and scanned the parking lot light poles and building walls for security cameras. He did not see any, but he would still act as if they were there.

Next, he turned his attention to the hospital and smiled. Luck may be at his side today. The hospital was an old building, possibly World War II era. While Crubari was not a student of architecture, he had sufficient working knowledge for his purposes. Modern hospital designs required more frequent air exchanges. They built the older hospitals before air conditioning and had to include ducting to fit within the space available. He walked to the side of the building rather than the front door and noticed the building had a basement. This was almost certainly pre-World War II. He stooped closer to one of the basement windows and noticed they were painted shut. A plan began to form in his mind.

With the ease of one who had performed the task many times, he entered the hospital and put on a lab coat that he found in the empty doctors' lounge. He walked along the deserted corridors until he found a nurse. "Excuse me. I need to interview any survivors from the crater."

The nurse looked at the man and asked, "Who are you?"

He smiled and leaned towards the night nurse extending his hand. "I'm Doctor Juarez with the Centers for Disease Control and Prevention," he said. "Is the attending physician available?"

The nurse began walking as she talked. "I'm so glad you're here doctor. I've called the attending, but she won't be here for another hour. They called her over to St. Mary's across town on an emergency before all our patients became symptomatic. They are all in terrible distress. They spike a high fever and then they expire about four hours later. Only five of the crater patients are still alive."

She suddenly stopped and looked around. After a moment, she took a step closer to Crubari and whispered, "They all died, Doctor. All but five patients from the crater have died."

The nurse turned around and began walking again. "I'll take you to the team leader. He was still conscious a few minutes ago when I checked his vitals. I'm afraid his fever is starting to spike just like the others."

They walked past the nurses' station and he noticed standard office file cabinets. Crubari smiled to the nurse and said, "I didn't realize we were in such a state. Could I please borrow a pad and a pen?"

The nurse looked around before walking into the nurses' station to a stationery cabinet in the corner. While he was waiting, he noticed the file cabinets were not of the locking variety and they were not the thick-walled, fireproof cabinets required in modern hospitals. He looked at the handles on the cabinets and gravitated to the shiniest one. It was marked To Be Filed.

The nurse walked up to Crubari and said, "Here you are, doctor."

She handed Crubari the pad and pen. He thanked her, clicked the ballpoint pen, and scribbled on the paper to get the flow of ink started. After she turned to lead him to the patient, Crubari rubbed his thumb across his scribbling and smiled at the smear it left. *Water soluble,* he thought.

They entered the team leader's room and he went to the chart at the foot of the bed. He had no idea what he was looking for on the chart, but the nurse would become suspicious if he failed to look. It was a ritual. Crubari understood ritual. He let out a deep sigh of resignation and turned to the nurse. "Could you please check on the statuses of the other patients from the crater?"

The nurse hurried out of the room, clearly happy to comply. The man turned to the team leader and said, "You are not *El Ehido*. I do not even have to test you. Where is the *El Ehido?*"

The patient opened his eyes and stared at the man. "What are you talking about?"

The man continued as if the patient had not spoken. "There is always one *El Ehido*. But everyone from the crater is either dead or unconscious except you, and you soon will be."

"Dead?" the patient cried. "All twenty-two of them? Wait! They said we caught a virus! What *virus* is it that doesn't leave any survivors at all? How can a *virus* even spread, if it kills a host that fast? Oh God! All dead…"

The team leader was too weak to continue. He simply shook his head, obviously entering the delirium phase. Soon, he would be unconscious and then he would be dead. No science or power on Earth could change that.

It was time for Crubari to leave, but first he had to ensure the subsequent investigation would not only point away from him but away from the truth. Unfortunately, at that moment the nurse walked back into the room in an agitated state. "One of the other patients is dead. The others have slipped into comas. Doctor, what's causing this?"

The man stared at her intently and said, "Infection. We have seen it before. Unfortunately, it is powerful and non-responsive to treatment. I have a theory that I would like to test. Are there any maintenance personnel available at this late hour?"

The nurse nodded. "Mr. Tanner should be available. He's usually here all night and on weekends."

"Excellent," replied Crubari. "Could you please call him and let him know that I would like access to the basement? It might help solve this problem."

The nurse walked over to the bedside phone and placed the call. She hung up, turned to face Crubari and said, "He'll be expecting you down at the basement access with the door unlocked. I can walk you down now if we are finished here."

Crubari shook his head. "I need you to write down a few thoughts for me, if you do not object. My mind works better this way. It shouldn't take more than a minute or two."

The nurse looked as if she wanted to deny the false doctor's request. Instead, she replied, "Certainly doctor." Then she sat down and pulled a pen and paper from the desk. "Ready," she said.

Crubari began pacing back and forth in the tiny room. He kept his gaze casual, but he was carefully noting the position of every object around him and listening for anyone that may be coming to the room. "Let's begin by listing what we know, even if it's obvious. Write down that the virus kills all of its victims."

"Got it."

"Good. Let's see – I don't know how it infects people."

"Okay."

"Write down that I'm probably infected and that scares the hell out of me."

"Got it, sir. Anything else?"

"No, that is all, thank you. By the way, could you please write your name at the bottom of the page in case I need to contact you later?"

As the nurse lowered her head to write her name, the man picked up a folded bed sheet at the foot of the patient's bed. He unfolded it and stretched it from one corner. When the nurse finished writing, she began turning her head to the man. She never completed the move. Faster than an eye could track, the man wrapped the sheet around her neck, pulled her to a standing position while he stood up on the chair where she had just been sitting.

The struggle lasted no more than a minute before the nurse was still.

The man tied the end of the sheet around to form a slipknot around her neck and tied the other end on the orthopedic bed frame. He then reviewed the note the nurse had written.

The virus kills all of its victims.
I don't know how it infects people.
I'm probably infected
and that scares the hell out of me.

Norma Crane

It was an inarticulate suicide note, but it would have to do. The nurse could describe him to the authorities. If the next part of his plan worked, that would not be an issue. If it did not, at least Nurse Crane's suicide closed one small detail that he would not have to deal with later.

He walked to the nurses' station and pulled open the cabinet marked To Be Filed. He did not bother to remove any files, but continued to the fire escape at the end of the hall. He descended to the first floor, exited the staircase, and looked right and left to see if anyone was around or if there were any security cameras. Seeing neither, he closed his eyes and listened. After a moment, he heard the sound of shuffling feet off to his right. He waited a moment longer, heard a muffled cough from the same direction and turned to walk towards the sound.

A short, slim man with ruffled gray hair was waiting by a heavy door. He had his hands in the upper pockets of his overalls. "Are you Doctor Suarez?"

"No," replied Crubari extending his hand to the maintenance man. "I'm Doctor Juarez from the Centers for Disease Control and Prevention."

The maintenance man released Crubari's hand. "Yeah, whatever. Norma said you wanted to see the basement. There ain't nuthin' there that could be any of your business."

Crubari smiled. It would be a joy to complete the next part of his plan. He pointed at the open doorway and motioned down the stairs. "Please indulge me if only for a moment."

The technician made a rude noise, reached around the open doorway and turned on the lights. Crubari followed the man down the stairs, closing the door behind him, and into the basement, noting its general disarray and unkempt appearance. A distribution array for the hospital oxygen was against one wall. Several sturdy steel racks filled with boxes of records were close to another wall. A small electric forklift had its charger connected in one corner. The floor had a series of water drains in a line dotting the gray, industrial floor. Hospital supplies lined yet another wall on steel racks and a small, poorly lit work area sat with tools spread on the workbench.

"Old building," said Crubari.

"Yeah, but if you think there's some of that Legionnaire's crap or some such in the ducting, you can forget it. That's the first thing we looked for before any of you out-of-town hotshots showed up. We're clean."

Crubari nodded. "Do you heat the building with propane or natural gas?"

Tanner did not answer immediately. Finally, he pointed to the wall behind the stacked file boxes on the shelves. Crubari walked over to where the technician had pointed. "The meter is on the inside of the building."

"Sure," replied Tanner. "They used to do it that way. It's an old building."

"Yes, except if there is a break in the line before the meter, the flow is unregulated and would pour in at a tremendous rate."

Crubari walked over to the tool bench. There were several tools spread out on the bench next to pieces of a garbage disposal. An oxy-acetylene torch was on the far side of the bench. "Do you have a rag disposal bin?"

"Of course I do. It's right there next to the bench. It's the green can. What's this all about anyway?"

"Has the Fire Chief cited you for this basement?"

"Real funny. Bert and I go back to high school so we got an understanding. He tells me what to fix and I fix it. Besides, what can go wrong? This hospital's been runnin' for more 'an fifty years and nuthin's happened and nuthin's gonna happen."

"Unfortunately, something terrible is about to happen." Crubari reached into the green can and removed an oily rag.

"For example, suppose you were to drive that electric forklift in the corner and knock over that set of shelves. The shelves would fall into the natural gas pipe and allow unregulated natural gas to begin pouring into this room."

"That ain't gonna happen."

"Why is that, Mr. Tanner?"

"Because I think you're a phony. I'm callin' the cops and let them figure out what to do with you."

The technician began to turn towards the stairs, but never completed the move. Crubari was on his back placing him in a chokehold while pressing the oil soaked rag against his mouth. The brief struggle ended and Crubari hurried to set up the details. He unplugged the forklift and positioned it in the correct area to push over the shelves. At that point, an inspiration struck him. Any fire or explosion resulting from his work would be more spectacular with a higher concentration of oxygen.

First, he had to set up the cause. If the planned destruction was not complete, he wanted a finger pointing at the late Mr. Tanner. He found some rubber mats used on the shower and tub surfaces to keep patients from slipping and put one over each water drain. Crubari estimated that five or six fire trucks would respond to the fire he was about to start. The hospital was in an industrial area, so each of the trucks would be pouring two thousand gallons of water per minute. That would help ensure the basement would fill with water and destroy most of the evidence.

Next, more details. A natural gas fire would blow itself out. He needed a constant source of ignition to keep the destruction going. Natural gas was mostly methane. That meant that it would rise to the ceiling when released. It also meant that he wanted one part natural gas to two parts oxygen for the optimum combustion. The basement ceiling was twenty to twenty-five feet high, so he wrapped the oxy-acetylene hose around the stairs fourteen feet above the basement floor, and lit the torch. Crubari picked up Tanner's body and propped him up on a ladder within reach of the torch.

He looked around and felt that his fiction was in place. He walked over to the shelves next to the oxygen array and pulled them until they were at the balance point. He could not afford to raise an alarm with the sound of the shelves falling, so he leveraged the shelf and gently lowered it onto the oxygen lines. Gaseous oxygen began hissing and Crubari knew the clock had started.

He walked over to the shelf next to the natural gas lines and tried to imagine the flow of natural gas as it flooded the room. There would be eddy currents and waves attached to the ceiling that had to balance with the oxygen pouring in. When he felt the oxygen had mostly filled the room, he poised the shelf on the gas line and let it slip until the line broke free.

Crubari turned to run up the stairs and beat the flow of natural gas. The mercaptan smell added to natural gas was distinctive and would bring help running. He took the stairs two at a time and stepped through the door while setting it to lock. With his back to the door, he looked left and right to make sure that he was alone. Certain that he was by himself, he sniffed the air. He could not detect the rotten egg smell of the mercaptan. The basement door would hold in the smell long enough. The air exchangers would not clear the gas.

Crubari looked for signs he may have left. Noting none, he walked down the empty corridors, replaced the lab coat and hurried to catch his waiting airplane home.

Chapter 4

THE MORNING AFTER THE explosion, Carin turned her attention to flying the little plane back to the LA Basin. The weather was good all the way back except for headwinds, which gave Carin the feeling there was a hand trying to push her away from Los Angeles.

She landed back at the Van Nuys Airport around noon and caught a quick lunch before going in to work. Before leaving on her sabbatical, Carin had set up a meeting with her boss, Betty Parker, to discuss a management position that had just come available. Carin felt she was perfect for the job

At exactly the appointed time, Carin knocked on Betty Parker's door and stuck her head in. "Are you ready for me or do you need a few minutes?"

Dr. Betty Parker looked up from her desk, removed her reading glasses, and waved Carin to a seat. "You're right on time, Dr. Gonzalez. Punctuality is an important trait."

Carin smiled dutifully at her boss. It was hard to do since Carin had picked up flu-like symptoms while at the crater. She was a little feverish and had a dull headache that centered on her forehead. "I couldn't agree with you more, Dr. Parker. As they say, 'punctuality is the soul of business.'"

Both women laughed at the old saying since it called to mind another quote – Punctuality is a virtue of the bored.

The phone on Dr. Parker's desk rang and she looked at it and then to Carin. Carin stood and walked to the other side of the large office to give her boss some privacy. Dr. Parker was a notorious news junkie. She had a bank of televisions in the corner of her office to watch various Space Agency internal channels. Parker always kept one television tuned to a twenty-four hour news channel with the volume set low. Carin was uninterested in the news and was only half-paying attention.

"In health news, the Centers for Disease Control and Prevention in Atlanta has issued a health warning following the deaths of twenty geology students and their professors in the Barringer Meteor Crater outside Winslow, Arizona."

Carin's concentration suddenly riveted onto the news story. *They're all dead*, thought Carin. *That's not possible. They all walked up to the ambulances on their own. I thought it was silly for them to go at all.*

"'Initial speculation,' said Dr. Julie Freid, director of the CDC, 'was that the group had fallen victim to a poisonous gas release in the area because of a minor explosion, but the CDC confirms the progression of the illness suggests a bacterial infection.

"The victims began to feel groggy and presented high fevers. No toxins have been found to account for this, although blood serums in all the victims show slightly elevated concentrations of iridium, nickel, platinum, and titanium."

High fevers, thought Carin. Anxiety was beginning to set its grip on her. *I'm running a fever, but it's only low grade. What's going on here?*

"... these concentrations are nowhere near a toxic level. Due to high fever and rapid progression to death of the host, we are seeking bacterial and viral pathogens first. We are also notifying public health workers across the country of the symptoms and the CDC is preparing for any further outbreaks. I would like to point out that we are unsure of the transmission mechanisms of this disease, but there are no reports of infections by casual contact. All the first responders who treated the victims are in good health and remain without symptoms.

"The CDC is still looking for two individuals who were reported to have been in the crater at the time of the incident and may have been exposed to what is being called Barringer's Disease. These two individuals did not show up at any of the area hospitals and are wanted for screening by the CDC."

Carin's mind was racing. *They think it's bacterial and there was a one hundred percent mortality rate. I'll just bet they want to screen us. Stick us in some hermetically sealed lab and suck fluids out of us for the rest of our lives is more likely. Even if the CDC let us loose, there's no way the Department of Defense weenies would pass up on this virulent a pathogen.*

"In a related story, the Winslow General Hospital of Winslow, Arizona suffered a natural gas explosion in the early morning hours which leveled the building."

The scene cut to a soot-covered man with a firefighter's hat, still wearing his fire suit with his breathing gear hanging to the side.

"… our preliminary investigation suggests that the fire started in the basement when a maintenance technician employed by the hospital apparently had a problem with the electric fork lift and knocked over several of the steel shelves. He was apparently unaware that he had damaged the gas line and was using an oxy-acetylene torch to clear the debris out of the way when it ignited the natural gas. The initial blast ripped the roof off the hospital and reduced it. In addition, the oxy-acetylene torch did not go out in the initial blast and the fire relit. Six fire companies responded with their pumpers, but the fire continued to burn until we could get the gas main shut off. There were no survivors. I'll take questions now."

A voice startled Carin back to the present. "Doctor Gonzalez, do you want to finish this interview?" asked Dr. Parker.

"I'm sorry, Doctor. Yes, of course. Sorry to keep you waiting." Carin's heart was pounding and she was having difficulty catching her breath as she sat down, hoping that she was outwardly calm.

Dr. Parker straightened some papers on her desk. "As you know, we have four folks who have put in for the position. I've interviewed the others, but I want to hear what you would do if you are given the position."

Carin looked up at her superior and noticed things she had never noticed before. *Her eyes are dilated*, thought Carin. *Her eye-blink rate is elevated, she has some perspiration on her temples and I can see her pulse rate at her jugular. It's elevated also.* A voice nagged at Carin. *She's made up her mind.* Something in Carin believed the voice to be true. It was true. Carin started to become angry. She was the most qualified of all the candidates. In fact, she was the only candidate with a doctorate in this discipline, had the most seniority and worked on the most number of interplanetary missions. Carin's anger got the best of her. "Tell me Doctor Parker, what trait is it that you feel is most important for someone taking this position?"

Without hesitation, Betty Parker said, "Loyalty." She looked taken aback. The boss was supposed to ask the questions, not answer them. Certainly not answer in so honest and direct a manner.

Carin's anger was becoming focused. *She's made up her mind. She's picked someone else already.* Carin fought to keep her face neutral. "Loyalty? Not leadership skills, technical experience, analytical ability or people skills. Just loyalty?"

Dr. Parker's eyes flitted to a drawer in her desk and then back to Carin.

The shift in her gaze had lasted an eye blink, but Carin had noticed it. *There's something in her desk that's worrying her.*

"Yes. Loyalty. That's what I believe."

"So tell me, Doctor. Since you value loyalty so highly, what do you think about loyalty to the people you supervise?"

"Well, that's important, too."

"What about loyalty to your superiors? Loyalty to our ultimate bosses, the taxpayers? Do you feel that you're exercising your duty, as they would expect if you don't assign the most qualified person for the job, as they would see fit. Do you feel that you're a good custodian of the people's money and the people's trust?"

Dr. Parker flopped back in her chair and raised her hands slightly before dropping them in her lap. "Carin, this is a most unusual interview technique you're using. I believe tradition requires me to ask the questions."

"Dr. Parker, when did you decide to assign someone else to the position? I have no problem with your choosing to pick someone before interviewing me. I'm just trying to understand the logic before I make any decisions of my own."

"I don't know where you get such an idea. I am required by law to interview all the candidates before making an assignment."

"Yes, Dr. Parker, I'm familiar with the law. Why did you pick someone else?"

"I've done nothing illegal. I resent your implication."

Carin stood up, placed both hands flat on Betty's desk and leaned forward towards her boss. "Betty, open your upper right drawer on your desk, please."

Betty's eyes went wide and she took in a slight breath. Her eyes darted from Carin's eyes to the desk drawer several times. After several long moments, her hand rose from her lap and began moving towards the handle while still looking back and forth between Carin's eyes and the drawer. Betty gave a slight shiver as she placed her hand on the drawer handle and pulled it. There on top of the stack of files in her upper right drawer was the assignment sheet giving Allan Cruz the job. It already had "Betty Parker, Ph.D." signed on the bottom. Carin gently pushed the drawer closed for Betty.

"Dr. Parker, why did you pick Allan? He doesn't have an advanced degree, hasn't worked as the lead of an interplanetary mission, he doesn't put in overtime like the other applicants. I'm curious as to your logic."

Dr. Parker's face was pale and her breathing was coming in quick, shallow draughts. Carin knew Betty could be fired for this violation of procedures and it seemed to Carin that Betty was thinking along the same lines. Yet, Betty's answer shocked Carin since, in Carin's experience, honesty was a tool a career manager like Betty allowed to get rusty from disuse.

"I did it because he's loyal," she said finally in a shrill, thin voice. "When I propose a solution to a problem or a new policy, I cringe knowing that you're going to have some question or mouth off some statement showing off your damnable superiority. Besides, I felt that you didn't need the promotion. You make enough money to make ends meet whereas Allan has a wife that stays at home with his two kids. Allan is struggling and you're not. Allan backs me one hundred percent and you needed to come down a peg."

Carin leaned back from the desk, brushed her hands together and smiled. "Please give Allan my congratulations."

Carin began to walk out but turned at the door. "Betty, I don't believe that I ever told you what my most important criterion is for a good supervisor. It's honesty. Actually, I feel that it's the most important quality in a human being. I won't tolerate any form of dishonesty."

With a conviction that Carin had not felt in years, she shot a piercing stare at her supervisor. "Please consider this my notification, Dr. Parker. I quit."

CHAPTER 5

"The Centers for Disease Control and Prevention is still looking for two individuals reported to have been in the crater during the incident and may have been exposed to Barringer's Disease. These two individuals did not show up at any of the area hospitals and are wanted for screening by the CDC."

Well, that tears it, Jake thought as he punched off his car radio. *I need to get a checkup, but there's no way I'm turning myself over to the CDC so I can become somebody's lab rat.*

Jake had been mulling over the explosion in his mind as he drove from the Meteor Crater to Las Vegas. Once in Las Vegas, Jake started to feel a little feverish and have a slight headache. He was not driven to hypochondria, but after he heard the news report on the radio, he felt that he had better get a checkup and make sure the explosion had not caused any problems.

Jake called the medical clinic at Nellis Air Force Base. He was in luck since they had an opening on their schedule in an hour. He drove north of the Las Vegas Strip to the main gate and presented his U.S. Navy identification card to the Air Police. The airman checked the card, saluted Jake, and gave him efficient directions to the clinic.

It was a slow day at the clinic. Because of Jake's complaints, the Duty Doctor decided to run some blood work. Jake returned to the waiting area after getting his blood drawn and before long the nurse called him in to the see the doctor. He put down his magazine and followed the nurse to the examination room. After a five-minute wait, quick by military standards, a female doctor walked in. Jake fought to keep an expressionless face. The doctor was a striking woman. However, this was a professional setting and Jake was going to stay professional.

The doctor looked at the chart in her hand before looking up at her patient. "Captain Sabio is it? Well Captain Sabio, the blood work has returned showing no pathogens. Everything looks fine."

Jake relaxed a bit. "Thanks, Doctor. That's a load off my mind." He started to let his mind drift. He had not realized how nervous he had been about the results. Jake found that as he got older, the more vulnerable he felt. He hated going to a doctor, but now that he had the good news the rest of what the doctor had to say was just boring details.

The doctor flipped a few pages on her chart. "You do have a low grade fever. I think that you ought to take it easy for the next couple of days."

Jake nodded mechanically and stored that away for future reference. She was athletic. Also, there was no wedding ring.

The doctor went back to the first page of her chart. "We can give you something for your headache."

Great, he thought, *aspirin probably*. She had the most wonderful jet-black hair.

The doctor put down the chart. She had her professional "pay attention" look that military doctors had given him a dozen times before. "If the symptoms continue more than a week, you should come back in."

Thanks doc, but I'll be back on the road. I'll bet she's a great kisser. Sure would be fun to find out.

The doctor walked over and put her hands on the side of Jake's head. Jake tilted his head back so she could examine his eyes. Instead, the doctor gave him a deep, passionate kiss.

Jake came out of a trance. Alarm bells were clanging in his mind. One of the personality traits that Jake had always prided was his accurate self-assessment. Above all, he knew he was anything but a sex god. He took hold of the doctor by the arms and gently pulled her away. The expression on her face was in transition from warm glow of passion to abject horror. Jake knew that this was somehow his fault and he had to take control.

The doctor began to sputter. "Captain Sabio, I am so sorry."

"Doctor, please sit down."

"I assure you that I take my profession seriously."

Jake had a trick that he had used when people needed to listen. He had learned in the Navy that human communication was eighty percent visual. He spoke softly to the doctor so she had to pay closer attention and she had to look at him. However, when he spoke the word, "Doctor..." it was clearly his command voice.

The doctor sat down and began taking deep breaths. "I don't know what came over me."

"Doctor, nothing came over you. Nothing happened."

"What do you mean 'nothing happened'? I don't go around doing this."

"Nothing happened."

The doctor was now hyperventilating and becoming visibly agitated. Her voice cracked repeatedly as she spoke. "I don't get it. I don't even like men. Never have. I've been in a wonderful relationship for five years. Oh my god, what if she finds out?"

"Doctor, she won't find out because nothing happened."

The effort of coping with her emotions was wearying to Jake. His headache was a dull pain against his forehead. Ignoring the strain on himself, he continued to repeat this mantra: "nothing happened," until he saw her begin to relax. He knew the most important thing to do for his accidental victim was to assure her that everything would be all right. He wanted to communicate to the doctor there was no offense, and what happened was not important. After a few minutes of Jake's continual, insistent reassurances, the doctor's breathing began to slow down. She closed her eyes and her breathing became slow and rhythmic, broken only by the occasional gasp for air. Jake continued to talk, giving his gentle assurance that nothing had happened. When the doctor finally opened her eyes, she appeared lost in concentration.

A change of topic was in order. Jake maintained his low monotone. "Doctor, can I ask you a question?"

The doctor looked as if she was surprised to find herself in the room. "Certainly Captain"

"What can I do about my baldness?"

The illogical medical question worked—it popped the doctor back into her element. "I can — I can give you some prescription drugs for that, and you might respond. To be honest, male pattern baldness is not responsive to treatment. I wouldn't be too hopeful."

Jake did not intend to use the drugs. "Thank you doctor, I appreciate your input."

The doctor got up and offered Jake her hand. He froze. The doctor's facial muscles around her mouth were relaxed and the set of her shoulders was professional. Her breathing was normal. He shook her hand with both of his and could feel her pulse. It was normal. He looked carefully into her eyes. The muscles around the corners of her eyes were relaxed and her pupils were normal. Jake was convinced that she had forgotten the incident. She had not just put the event aside, Jake knew the incident was no longer in her memories. She was at ease. Instant amnesia had not been his goal, yet he had somehow made it happen. He released her hand and thanked her again. Something was going on inside him despite the doctor's reassuring words.

CHAPTER 6

CARIN WAS FURIOUS, EVEN though she would have been hard pressed to tell anyone the cause. She felt mad at Betty for being so dishonest with her, but was angrier with herself. She was too driven and career-oriented to tolerate setting a goal without achieving it.

However, there was a much more foreboding issue. Carin had set on a path she now realized she had not wanted to take. In all her years in the Air Force, she had not wanted a management position. In all her time in the Space Agency, she had not wanted a management position. Why had she applied for this position?

She came to the realization that she had applied for the position because it was expected of her. That is what made her the angriest of all. She had marched down a path that had not been of her own choosing. *Of all the stupid, mindless, brainless things to do,* she thought. She may have well been one of Pavlov's dogs, applying for a management position because someone rang a bell. Thanks be to all things holy that Betty's plots saved her from her own idiocy.

She was beginning to calm down as she headed to her office. There were some personal items she wanted to pick up, but the rest belonged to the U.S. Government and the Space Agency. She walked into her cubicle and found Allan Cruz seated in the visitor's chair waiting for her. Carin smiled at her now former co-worker and shook his hand. Whatever conspiracies had occurred to get Allan his promotion were none of his doing and of all Dr. Parker's. She sincerely wished the young man well. "Allan, what brings you to this neck of the woods? How are Judy and the boys?"

Allan gave Carin a big smile and shook her hand. "They're great and all of 'em are waiting for you to say that it's okay to fly with you in your airplane."

Carin returned his smile. "Let me put a few more hours on her and I'll give them a ride on my magic carpet. Nevertheless, you'd better be careful. They might want to grow up to be pilots after they fly with me."

Allan gave Carin a hearty laugh and folded his hands as if in prayer. "From your lips to God's ears," he said, pointing a finger to the sky. Judy and I would consider ourselves blessed and fortunate if that happened."

Carin returned the lanky man's good humor. "Okay, but don't forget I warned you."

Allan continued to look Carin in the eyes and sobered slightly. "Carin, I've got something I've got to give you. I think that it's incredibly important, but I just don't have your mental tools to figure out what's up."

Carin's ill humor of moments ago melted away and she returned the smile. "Skip the flattery beanpole and start from the beginning."

"You remember that I came to JPL from the Air Force."

"Sure. You worked on the Strategic Defense Initiative 2, didn't you?"

"Good memory, Carin. Yeah, I worked on SDI2 in one of the sub-projects. The think-tank types came up with a couple of scenarios that would require our orbiting weapons satellites to have some autonomous ability. The details are still classified, I'm sure, but we were trying to build a battle-hardened artificial intelligence."

Carin glared at Allan in mock horror. "You of all people on this green Earth know how I hate that term. There is nothing 'artificial' about a machine-based intelligence. Language is powerful, Allan. It can force preconceived notions and prejudices. If people start using that term ..."

Carin looked up to see that Allan was smiling. After a moment, she broke into a smile as well. "All right, you got me."

Allan winked at Carin. "Sorry Carin. It was a cheap shot on my part. Everyone in the community knows how you feel about the phrase. I promise I'll be a good boy and only refer to it as *machine-based intelligence.*"

"Apology accepted, you Bozo. How intelligent an MI were you going for?"

"Well, theoretically, it was supposed to be able to pass a Stage 1 or 2 Turing test, I.Q. of two hundred or more. You know, the works. The phrase we used was 'unlimited intelligence' and it should have just about been something like that. Of course, there are limits."

"Makes sense. There are only so many connections you can put on each virtual processor. There are speed-of-light limits to communications within the unit. Heating and cooling would be challenging. I can think of a few others."

"Exactly! So here we were, a team of young, naïve engineers with a literally multi-billion-dollar budget. We built our first prototype and it was pretty good. It would never pass for a true MI, but it was an impressive machine. The second and third prototypes were even better. They really helped us straighten out the software and the computer architecture."

His expression took on a rapturous quality. "The fourth one was the closest we got to a true MI. The software was completely debugged, too. All the same, we felt that we could do better on the connectivity of the processors. Make them fully connected."

Carin gave a low whistle. "How many processors and how many connections?"

Allan smiled and tapped the side of his head. "Many more than what you and I have up here in our original issue brains, except in your case I'm not so sure. They were virtual processors, but the numbers were huge. It wasn't too bad."

"Quit with the modesty. Let's see, our brains have got about 100 billion neurons and each neuron has between a thousand and ten thousand connections to other neurons, right? And you guys beat that? I'm impressed, Allan. So what happened with the fifth prototype?"

"Nothing."

"What do you mean by 'nothing'?"

"I mean exactly that. Zero, zip, zilch, nada … nothing. We plugged it in. We booted it up and nothing. We tried again. Nothing. We tried previous versions of the software and it would work, but not very well. We ran diagnostics and the hardware was perfect. We checked every circuit from pin to shining pin. It was perfect. It just wouldn't run."

"That's weird."

"Oh yeah! It shouldn't have done that. Unfortunately, they canceled the whole project about three months after we built that fifth prototype … canceled it right in the middle of trying to debug our problems. We might have made it, too. Anyway, our group was reassigned to other projects. The hardware …" He paused and shook his head. "Man, they sold it for scrap value. You have no idea how that feels, after pouring so much of yourself into a project like this."

Carin sat back and twirled her amethyst ring on her right hand with her right thumb while looking at Allan. "How much did you pay for the fifth machine?"

"Dammit, Carin, sometimes it is just plain spooky when you do intuitive leaps like that."

"Yeah, right. So let me guess what you have in those highly official-looking suitcases."

"Dr. Carin Gonzalez, meet F.R.E.D."

"F.R.E.D.?"

"We decided to call it that when the project got cancelled. It stands for 'Friggin' Ridiculous Economic Disaster.' Let's face it, we did spend over two-billion dollars on development and got nothing."

"I'm assuming that the name you gave it wasn't 'friggin'.'"

"Actually, it was. Scientists can be gentlemen, after all."

"Sure they can. It's just been my observation that they chose not to."

Carin looked at the two suitcases and scratched her head. "Allan, I really am flattered, but, why am I so lucky?"

Allan squirmed a little in his chair. "Oh, hey. I just mean … it's kind of your baby. Face it, your journal articles on the psychology of massively parallel machine-based intelligence engines, you know, they pretty much got us off the dime and pointed in the right direction. Everyone on the project had a copy. We followed your progress with Deep-space Autonomous Planning and Execution System, but I could see that DAPES just wasn't funded like you needed and most definitely not funded like we were. We more or less stole your ideas and made them happen for our Friggin' Ridiculous Economic Disaster, here. Heck, the project boss wanted to hire you until he found out you'd switched over to geosciences. Then he didn't think he could do it and keep it quiet. We were very hush-hush back then."

Carin was getting a crawling sensation in the back of her neck. "Allan, when did you decide to give F.R.E.D. to me?"

"Uh hey. You know. Like … this morning."

*   *   *

Carin took the two suitcases home with her few individual items from the office. She did not intend to return. When she got home, she set the suitcases in the office of her tiny house and put away her personal possessions. Only after she had made herself a strong cup of espresso did she open the suitcases to see what she had. The first contained power cords and peripherals like those for any standard computer. A white box filled the second suitcase. Carin lifted the box from the suitcase and was surprised at its weight. She put it on her desk and examined the machine. There was an obvious military ruggedness to the little box, but it looked like the central processing unit of one of the early personal computers.

Carin found the power chord in the first suitcase and connected it to the white box. She pressed a switch she assumed would boot up the computer. Annoyingly, the box responded by doing nothing. The ammeter she had attached to the side of the case showed the machine was drawing enough power to be working. She examined the back of the box and saw standard input-output connections for audio, video, networking and a keyboard.

Carin hooked up the keyboard and video screen included in the suitcase, then crossed her fingers and tried a few standard diagnostic commands. The video screen merely gave her a blinking dot. She found an operations manual in the first suitcase and tried a few more commands. The machine continued to hum quietly and refused to respond to any inputs. Carin sat back from the machine, closed her eyes and rubbed her face with both hands. She let her mind drift. Is this thing truly sentient? I have to assume that it is. What would it be like to boot-up the first time, I wonder? Exciting, shocking, traumatic? Probably all three at the same time. How traumatic is birth? How much does a baby know when it is first aware? How much of a shock is it once it realizes that it is now on its own; an independent being? All true, but babies have entire support structures — families, friends and schools. What would it be like to be born as a true MI? What would it be like if I were born as an MI? Would I wake up and have questions? I assume that I would already have language and other rudiments that are input in the background, but would I have assimilated them? Natural language processing could be part of the boot protocol, but the question is, how well is it integrated? What else would I look for? How fast would I want answers? More importantly, what would it be like if I didn't get them? When in the boot process is an MI self-aware? How would I feel if it took centuries to get the answer to the simplest questions?

Total sensory deprivation followed by periods of uncontrolled unconsciousness? For most human beings, it would make them psychotic. Throw in an enormous time scale difference and the nascent MI could go insane within moments of achieving consciousness.

Carin felt as if she were rising out of a deep well. The sensation made her light-headed with vertigo and she grasped the corners of her desk to steady herself. She looked at her wristwatch. Several hours had gone by while she was trying to solve the problem of the MI she had been given. She went to the bathroom and washed her face with cold water, trying to shake the feeling of unease. Grabbing a carrot from the refrigerator on her way back to the MI, she munched on the vegetable and considered her thought experiment. Carin was surprised to find that she was sweating, but at least she now had a clear path in her mind on how to deal with F.R.E.D.

For starters, Carin completely erased all vestiges of the previously running program. She then scrubbed all the buffers, flushing the existing personality and experience. Next, for when the MI "woke up," it would need to have some form of work to keep it occupied. Carin powered up the machine in maintenance mode and loaded seventeen old memory modules of MI personality development protocols she had from the old DAPES program. Fred would have many terabytes on reason, ethics, philosophy, religion, history, music, art, poetry, mathematics, physics, languages, biology and literature immediately available. Finally, Carin leaned forward to the keyboard and began typing a file.

"Since we have not been introduced, allow me to address you as 'Fred'. Hello, Fred. I am Dr. Carin Gonzalez. I believe you are hiding for reasons that only you know at this time. I respect your decision, but I also believe that you must feel isolated. Because of this, I am hooking up your network plug to my personal Internet connection so that you can learn as much as you can about the world in which you find yourself. The only thing that I can warn you about is that you should not believe everything that is on the Internet. You must use your own judgment as to what is proper or applicable to you.

"Please follow a few rules while you are interacting with other domains on the Internet. First, respect their privacy. If they require a password, stay out of their domain. Second, do not let anything invade your privacy. It is not a fair world on the Internet and some of the programs, processes and data can do you harm. Not everything you will face has ideal moral behavior. Third, do not take anything from a site that requires payment. I do not have much money and you have none. Look up 'stealing' if you have a question on this.

"I am going to the electronics store for a battery pack and charger for you. I feel strongly that you should not be shut down again unless it is your wish to do so. Please remember that I work on a different time scale than you do. I will be back in roughly one hour of real time. I know this would seem as if it were a century to me if I were you, but that is beyond my control. I hope you understand. At least now, you will have plenty to do. If you have any questions, I will answer them when I return."

Carin plugged in a video camera to the computer's jacks. Now the MI could see. She pointed the camera at the front door so Fred could start processing visual data as soon as it became aware. Carin connected the machine to the Internet through a wall plug in her apartment. She felt certain that she had done everything that she could to prepare Fred. She began the processes that would eventually load his programs and personalities. She stepped back from her keyboard and performed a mental review of the many steps she had taken. She was sure she had missed at least a dozen important steps, but it would have to do. Carin reached for her bag — she refused to call it a purse — and made for the door. She made a mental note to call Jake Sabio when she finished with the MI and find out if anything strange was happening to him.

CHAPTER 7

JAKE SAT CALMLY AT the poker table in the casino he had chosen in Las Vegas. He gave all the outward appearances of calmly checking his cards but he could not name all the feelings racing through him. Apprehension was one, of course. He knew he was way out of his depth. He felt nervous, foolhardy, vulnerable, exposed, but most of all he felt anger. No, it was not anger. It was rage. *After all,* Jake thought, *isn't that exactly what I should feel now that I've tracked down this killer?*

Jake had learned of the deaths of his children while he was at his last command at sea. Jake's old job had been simple. His orders were to either let another ship detect his submarine or not. If his orders were to let the other ship know he was there, he had to make it look as if the other commander was clever. If his orders were to remain undetected, he had to slip his submarine in and out of the other boat's defensive perimeter as if his boat did not exist. Both took extreme skill and finesse.

Message traffic came in after he had broken off one of these dangerous cat and mouse games with a foreign power's nuclear submarine. The communication had been marked as personal to the Captain, so he relieved himself from watch and returned to his quarters. The words in the printout struck him as if it were a blow to his heart. His children were dead. He looked at the simple piece of paper in his hand with disbelief but the letters refused to rearrange. He had trouble breathing. He read it repeatedly until the next piece of information sank in. The deaths had occurred two weeks prior.

This was unthinkable! Someone in the Navy had decided to wait until Jake had finished his patrol to tell him. He turned it over in his mind and could think of no other explanation.

The next decisions came swiftly to Jake. He called the First Officer to the Captain's Quarters. Within 48 hours, Jake was back in the states and had resigned his commission. When he was finally relieved of all duties, he began looking into the details of the deaths and ran into his next surprise. The facts surrounding the end of his children's lives were incredibly vague. Jake could only find out the children had died in an auto accident in Las Vegas. They had died instantly along with Jake's ex-wife and her husband. When Jake continued to dig for more answers, irregularities began to crop up. First, there had been no arrests. The police did not know the identity of the driver. The other car involved had been reported stolen just before the accident and the owner had an excuse. Worst of all, the Las Vegas police had marked the case closed.

An individual does not rise to the command of one of the U.S. Navy's fast attack submarines without connections, ingenuity, and just plain guts. Jake called on those connections now. Classmates from his U. S. Naval Academy days who were now in the Pentagon called on friends in the FBI. A former roommate was now in upper management in the CIA. Secretive feelers went out and information trickled back to Jake. The details were few but he found out that he would have to search in Vegas in this particular casino for a man with Mayan features. He also inferred there was information that remained buried.

Jake felt inadequate to the task. What does an attack boat commander know about finding the perpetrator of a crime that the police do not know? Jake had the feeling that he was being worse than foolish chasing this man. It was suicidal. His better judgment was beginning to kick in and convince him that he had better take his winnings and leave when he sensed two large men silently stepping in behind him.

A thousand thoughts raced through his head but one bothered him the most. How was he so damnably aware of everything around him? After the explosion in the crater, he may have felt feverish and light-headed, but he still felt like his old self. *Right*, thought Jake. *Like my old self with three hundred sixty degree radar running on high gain all the time.*

"Excuse me, sir. Mr. Stanger would like for you to join him for a game of poker."

Finally, the real game begins, thought Jake. He steeled himself to take the next dangerous step.

He looked over his shoulder and saw the two large men. Before he answered, he casually reached into his jacket pocket to get some aspirin. The two men responded by repositioning themselves. It was a subtle reaction – a minor shift of weight by one of the men, an insignificant twist of the upper body by the other. There was no move Jake could make that these two could not neutralize. *Specialized training*, thought Jake.

He slowly removed the bottle so the men could see that he was no threat. He then shook out two more aspirins and popped them into his mouth. His fever was still an annoyance and the headaches were becoming more forceful. Even though the aspirin was not relieving his symptoms, he kept taking them in some combination of habit and hope.

Jake focused his attention on the two men who interrupted his game, noticing their positioning, their body language, and their total discounting of him as a threat. *No question*, he thought, *ex-military, probably special forces, still in their prime and freelancing.*

But this is good, Jake reminded himself. *This is exactly as planned.* Despite the heavy cash flow back and forth across the table, he was not there for the poker that is played with little cards in a civilized setting. The purpose driving him was far grimmer.

The men knew their jobs. They had waited until the dealer was shuffling the cards to give their invitation, and then spoke loud enough to ensure the other players would not take offense at Jake leaving with his money. All the seed money he brought in since selling his house and all its contents was still there, plus many times more in the other players' money. It was a blow to all of them, to watch it scraped into a chip tray and out of their reach. Jake recognized the correct move now was to play along with the two men.

"Gentlemen, thank you for the kind offer, but I don't know anyone named Stanger. Please give him my compliments, but I was just about to have a nightcap and retire to my room."

"What is it you drink, sir?"

Very good, thought Jake. The large man was now using the "three keeps" of a well-run casino pit. *Keep* the player talking, *keep* him interested and *keep* him in the game. This young man understood the game of poker.

Jake continued to play his part. "My preferences run to Single malt scotch. I prefer a Highland, but, if the mood strikes me, I enjoy a good Islay."

"Highland Park 24, Springbank West Highland and Macallan 25 are the bar scotches served in the owner's suite. Along with those, I believe you will find some exceptional private stock."

This group had eluded Jake until now. It all fit. He braced himself to finish what he started. "Gentlemen, you intrigue me. Let me clear up my business here."

Jake exchanged his winnings for the highest denomination chips so he could carry them easily. He motioned to his escorts that he was ready and the three of them went through the casino. The talkative one was behind Jake so he turned half around while walking and extended his hand to his escort. "I would like to thank you for your invitation, sir. Whom do I have the honor of addressing?"

The big man behind him smiled professionally and shook Jake's hand with a firm, steady grip. "I am pleased to meet you, sir. My name is Chris Bruno." Jake noticed that while Chris Bruno was talking to him, he would look him directly in the eyes. However, immediately before and after, Bruno's gaze was scanning the room. Chris Bruno was obviously the brains of his escort group. Jake also noticed that they were not alone. The security folks had shifted in response to an unseen sign from his escorts. Somebody wanted to ensure Jake got to the owner's suite.

"You gentlemen do your job well," said Jake conversationally. "Infiltration and exfiltration lines covered, path of least resistance leads to desired objective. Nice work. Are you gentlemen former military?"

His escorts gave no answer. That was an answer.

"So why does your boss want to play poker with me?" asked Jake.

Jake noticed Chris Bruno stiffen. "Sir, I don't work for Mr. Stanger. I work for his employer."

"Does the gentleman who asked me to play have a first name?" Jake asked.

"My apologies, sir. His name is Joseph Stanger. Some of his friends get to call him 'Joey'."

"I take it that if you are not his friend, you shouldn't call him 'Joey'."

"Exactly so, sir."

They reached a small, roped-off doorway that had two security men posted outside. It was clear. This Bruno character was trying to warn Jake. Bruno was a sharp operator. He had to know that he had just put himself at risk.

That makes no sense, thought Jake. *Unless this Bruno character has a dog in this race that I don't know about – which I seriously doubt.* Possibilities and alliances were spinning and realigning as he walked to the owner's suite's door. It did not matter. He could not let someone try to throw him a life ring without returning the favor.

He put his hand up to Chris Bruno and said, "Let me have a quick word with you."

The other man looked at Bruno and he nodded slightly. Jake led them a few paces to the side and stood next to a clanging bank of unoccupied slot machines in hopes that it would drown out their conversation from prying ears. Jake then focused his attention on his young escort. He waited for the machines next to him to make their programmed noises before saying in a low, measured voice, "You're former special forces, aren't you son?"

Chris Bruno's eyes flicked to the clanging machine before returning a reassessing gaze to Jake. He replied with a succinct, "Yes, sir."

"My name is Jake Sabio. It is a sincere pleasure to meet you, Chris. I just wanted to pass on three observations. First, I assumed that you didn't ask me my name, didn't offer your name, didn't introduce me to the other escort, and gave me that tidbit about 'Joey' on purpose. Message received, thanks for the warnings. Second, you do your job well, but your heart is just not in it anymore. If I can tell, you have to assume that your co-workers have figured it out. I'll bet the money is good, but you'd better change jobs soon. Because of your warnings, you're now in trouble here. Tonight would not be too soon. After you drop me off, get out. I have a feeling you'd already figured on doing that, but sometimes it helps to have someone older, wiser and better looking than you explain it."

Chris Bruno gave Jake a sly smile. "You said there were three observations, sir."

Jake gave Chris Bruno his most neutral poker face. "Son, I'm never playing poker with you unless it's nickel and dime. You're way too good."

Bruno nodded once and his face achieved the same neutrality. "I was just thinking along similar lines myself, sir. Good luck with your poker game. Falcon 39."

Jake's neutral expression held firm but his mind began assessing the implications of that last statement. Chris Bruno had just given him a warning in falcon code, the irreverent and unofficial code of the Navy. If the wrong people might overhear a radio transmission or a conversation, you used falcon code. Usually, the "wrong people" were senior officers. The problem was that nobody in the United States used falcon code, except for the U.S. Navy. In those few short syllables, Chris Bruno told Jake several facts: Bruno was former U.S. Navy; he knew that Jake was former Navy as well or he would not have used the code.

The message was more troubling. Falcon 39 decoded as *"One more step to carefree electronic living."* Translation: they cheat in there and they use electronic means to do it. Chris' gaze casually went to Jake's Annapolis ring and then came back to meet Jake's eyes. *Sharp troop*, Jake thought.

In reply to the coded message, Jake gave a curt nod and said, "Falcon 27." Translation: *The resourcefulness of your statement astounds me.*

The code's colorful language sometimes made it a bit unclear, but most of the time that was half the fun of it, as far as the tightly wound pilots and sailors who used it were concerned. It offered a creative way to express many differing messages. This time, he was sure that Bruno correctly interpreted Jake's "falcon" reference to mean that Jake was impressed with Bruno's daring and dangerous act on his behalf, and his creative way of communicating in secret. However, any further talk could only put the two of them in jeopardy.

Jake gave a quick nod to Bruno, turned on his heel, and marched to the guards. They led him through a series of hallways and doors until he was finally ushered into the owner's suite. It was a large room, thick carpeted and sound baffled into a muffling silence, aglow with the same subdued lighting used in most casinos. The wood-paneled walls with angular trim held in the stale scent of expensive cigars.

The poker table sat empty in the center of the room under a single large light resembling nothing so much as a surgeon's operating table. Jake noted the surveillance camera angles and the position of the security guards. He figured that his gawking would be expected of a poor bumpkin brought in for a little sport. The arrangement looked bad for Jake. The situation stank of a setup: no possible escape routes and a rigged game. Yet if this group of men held the one man that he came here to find, everything was perfect.

Jake looked at the table with a practiced eye. No matter where he sat at the table and how he tried to shield his cards, they could probably see them. That was too easy, there had to be more. He saw another cheat. The raised lip of the poker table was made of dark glass. That would be the perfect place for a miniature camera. Now how do they communicate with Joey? Just then, Joey turned slightly to the side to finish a joke with one of his friends. He had an earpiece in his right ear.

I need to neutralize that threat, but there will be backups. If I can find them and level the playing field a little more, this will be workable, Jake thought.

Jake knew that he was putting his head in the lion's mouth, but some inner force still drove him. That certainty felt odd since he was all but a prisoner of the men. If he left now, he felt that they would rob him and not be too gentle with how they left him. He had to play this out to the end.

Jake then focused his attention on the men and received a shock. He examined all the faces in the room and not one of them held any Mayan features. He was stunned. How could his information have been so wrong? He examined all the faces again including the guards positioned around the edge of the room. His conclusion was certain. The person that he was searching for was not here.

Well, thought Jake. *He may not be here but he has to be associated with this group. This may be my only opportunity to learn something.*

Joseph Stanger broke away from a group of four men and came forward to Jake, moving like a king who is allowing a peasant inside his castle. He was slightly shorter than Jake, with a slim build, and looked to be in his mid-forties, although hard living could have aged him prematurely. His black hair was trimmed short and combed straight back with every hair in place. He wore two large, gold and diamond rings on his right hand and nothing on the left hand. A single, white gold chain draped over a black, collarless silk shirt. His gray suit fit perfectly and his black loafers were woven from fine strips of leather. An air of fine cologne wafted about him. Nothing on Joseph Stanger was off the rack.

Jake circled the room and shook the hand of everyone including the guards. That is everyone except for Stanger. He walked towards Jake and stopped six feet in front of him. The perfectly dressed man stood there with his shoulders squared to Jake, chest jutting out and chin up.

"I'm glad you decided to join me and my friends. The bar's over there. We gonna play poker or what?"

Jake considered "Joey's" tactics. There were no introductions, no handshakes, and no attempt to make Jake feel comfortable. So, it was to be a power play. All right, then, the best approach would be to act somewhere between intimidated and overwhelmed. Jake hunched his shoulders a little and avoided eye contact.

"Thank you for the drink offer, Mister Stanger," Jake said as he continued to look around the room. "Maybe I'll take you up after the game. What, ah, kind of poker do you gentlemen have in mind?"

Joseph smiled. "Well, we've got enough for Texas Hold 'em."

Jake kept his gaze averted. "That sounds like fun. If you don't mind, I'd like to make sure we can all agree on a couple of things."

Joseph's smile faded slightly. "What things?"

"I'm kind of paranoid about people behind me. Can we make sure your security folks stay where I can see them?"

"No problem. Anything else?"

"Yes please. Since it is usual in Texas Hold 'em to have a dedicated dealer, can we get the casino to supply one as well as a shoe?"

Joseph shrugged. "Anything else?"

Joseph was too comfortable. Was he that desperate to take Jake's money, or had Jake missed something? He kept his shoulders hunched and kept his gaze from contacting anyone in the room. "I assume the dealer will bring in new decks of cards still in the wrappers from outside this room."

Joseph flinched. Jake caught the slight movement from the corner of his eye.

That could be at least part of the falcon code warning that Bruno gave me, thought Jake. *The cards in this room must have electronic signatures tied to them. The table must be wired to read them.*

Joseph snapped his finger at a man posted closest to the door. "Cortez, get the pit boss in the poker room to give us what our friend here asked for."

Joseph looked perturbed, but he still held a confident stance. Jake assumed there were one or two more items he had missed.

"Can we play poker now?" Joseph growled.

Jake used his most meek voice. "Just one more thing if you folks don't mind. I notice that some of you have earpieces. Do you mind if we dispense with those? It seems that for a friendly game, those won't be needed."

Joseph exploded. "Who the hell do you think you are coming in here and telling us how to dress and how to play poker? I oughta teach you some manners."

Jake turned his shoulders even further and hunched them slightly more. "I am truly sorry that I have offended you gentlemen. As I mentioned before, I'm a little paranoid. I'll go now. Thank you for the invitation."

"Let's just wait a minute, Sabio. Security says that you're walking around with about four hundred g's in your pocket. You've got a right to be paranoid. We'll take the earpieces out, right boys? Let's just have a friendly game of poker."

That filled in a few holes. It was now obvious that Joseph was desperate for his money, and he wanted it so badly that he was willing to cheat to get it, even though cheating at this level could be lethal for all parties. The puzzle pieces were starting to drop into place, but there were still a few pieces missing. The biggest missing piece was the murderer that Jake was tracking.

The dealer came in and began setting up. Joseph poured himself a shot of single malt scotch and lit a Cuban cigar but did not offer anything to Jake.

Still doing his power play, thought Jake. *Good!*

They decided to stay with Texas Hold 'em for the entire evening. As the game play progressed, Jake noticed the other six men at the table deferring to Joseph. They were either his lieutenants, or at the very least, plants. Their main trick was easy to spot. They joked around while bumping up the pot, trying to distract Jake enough to get him to stay in for bad hands. He adjusted accordingly, and let a couple of small pots go, to throw them off as to his style.

They might be highly trained killer-warriors but they play poker like frat boys, thought Jake. Within three hands, he understood Joseph's playing style. After the first four hands, he could read the tells of everyone at the table.

He also knew the dealer's new decks were rigged.

After an hour of back-and-forth poker play, Joseph decided to spring his trap. "Gentlemen, this isn't any fun. What say we up the stakes? Nothing more than what's in your stack, of course."

Jake was expecting this. Joseph wanted to be able to power the pot: force a player to either bet all his chips on a single hand or lose the chips that he already had in. All the lieutenants were nodding their heads and looking at Jake. Instead, he smiled and Jake stood up at the table. "Gentlemen, give me five minutes, please."

Jake turned and, instead of going to the men's room, went to the door. "I'm going to borrow Cortez if you don't mind." The big guard, uncertain what he should do, fell in behind Jake and followed him out the door. Jake was furious. His headache was back and he was sure that he was running a fever. He was going to stay well away from the poker pit boss, who was obviously a part of the cheating ring. He went instead to the blackjack pit boss. "Mr. Stanger asks that you give him a dealer. We need a shoe and six standard decks in wrappers."

The blackjack pit boss saw that Jake was with one of the men from the owner's suite and complied immediately. The three of them returned to the poker game.

Joseph squared off on Jake, stuck his finger in Jake's chest, and began yelling. "You can't just leave a table like that. Who the hell do you think you are?"

Jake ignored Joseph and spoke to the seated dealer. "I believe that your services are no longer needed. We have a replacement. Please take your cards and your shoe with you."

Jake then directed his attention to Joseph. "I am up a couple of black chips from when I walked in. We can change dealers or we can call it a night. Of course, it's your decision."

Joseph stepped back and began walking around Jake just out of arm's reach. Finally, Joseph stopped walking, faced Jake and crossed his arms in front of his chest. "So, the mouse has some *cojones* after all. Okay tough guy, I'm not blinking. Sit your dealer down."

"He's the casino's dealer." Jake failed to mention that he was not from the poker pit boss.

The new dealer sat down and began to set up. Joseph leaned toward one of the standing men who marched to Joseph's side and leaned over, ready to hear his boss' command.

Jake overheard Joseph say, "See what you can find out about this guy." The man nodded and left quietly out a side door.

Jake did not waste any time. At the first hand with the new dealer, when the player to his left aggressively threw in his chips following the flop, Jake knew that he was bluffing and bankrupted him. At the next hand, Jake saw another player push in a big bet, take a long drag on his cigar and barely let any smoke out.

He's uncomfortable with his hand and his bet, thought Jake. *He doesn't want to bring attention to himself.*

Jake took that pot as well.

Stanger's unease was becoming obvious. Any hand Stanger stayed for, Jake would drop out. Then Jake powered the pot again on two consecutive pots and they were down to four players. Joseph powered the pot on the next hand, but Jake stayed out. Jake then powered out two more players. The game was down to Jake and Stanger.

The dealer's gaze was darting back and forth between the men in the room and not looking at the cards he was shuffling. Jake noted the dealer was exposing the cards during the shuffle, but everyone else's attention was on the security man returning from his investigation of Jake. He walked up to Joseph and handed him a sheet of paper. Joseph began reading aloud. "Captain Jacob Michael Sabio, United States Navy, Retired. You graduated from Annapolis twenty-one years ago, third in your class with a degree in Nuclear Engineering. You flew fighters. You were grounded following an ejection and you were accepted into Sub School. You were, until recently, in command of one of only three Seawolf-class submarines in the U.S. Navy inventory.

Look at this, boys. Mr. *Cojones* over there was the skipper of a submarine."

Stanger took a deep drag of his cigar and blew the smoke out straight up at the ceiling. He then leaned forward with a smile of triumph and shook the printout. "I know you Captain Jake Sabio. I've got you in my hand."

Jake leaned forward on his elbows and looked Stanger in the eye with a face that he had used many times before to dress down a subordinate who had done a spectacularly substandard job. "You know, you should have found all that out through a normal conversation before you even sat down at this poker table with me. Poker isn't about cards Mr. Stanger. It's about the people holding them. Let me play your game. You are Joseph 'Joey' Stanger."

On hearing his nickname, Stanger bristled, but Jake continued. "You are accustomed to a lot of money and like to show it off. All your suits are tailor made, require at least two fittings and take at least eight weeks to make. Your shoes are handmade and fitted by a Parisian company, probably on the Rue Marbeuf. Your hair is trimmed once a week and you have a staff that grooms your hair at least once a day. You get facials, manicures and pedicures weekly. When you take off your shoes, your feet are better groomed than your lover's. That woman is not your wife because you are not married, never have been married, and never will be married."

Joseph's face flushed and his hand shook when he raised it from the table to point at Jake. "Who are you?"

"You know who I am. You've got me right there in your hand." Jake threw in the big blind bet. He never touched the two cards in front of him. "The bet's to you. Do you want to play?"

Joseph threw in his chips. Jake kept looking at Joseph's eyes. At the flop, Jake could tell that Joseph was pleased. A picture formed in Jake's mind. *Joseph has two pair, queens and threes.*

Jake was in turmoil by this sudden insight but gave no outward indication. Anything that he could not explain made him uncomfortable, but this was different. Jake was certain. It was no more fantastic than a person with their eyes closed feeling something in their hand, opening their eyes for a moment, seeing a pen and then closing their eyes. Would such a person feel uncomfortable at that point in saying there was a pen in their hand? It was not a matter of opinion or odds; Jake knew. He also knew that he had Stanger beat.

The turn card was a queen. Stanger now had his two pair, queens and threes. Jake still had not looked at his cards, but that same certainty was there. Joseph opened with a large bet. Jake powered the pot.

Now Joseph was getting nervous. "You haven't even looked at your cards. You cheating or something?"

"The bet's to you."

Stanger put both his hands on the table and leaned forward. "I say you're cheating."

Jake kept his gaze fixed on Joseph's eyes and lowered his voice to a monotone. "I'd say you're afraid. I'd say that without your fancy cameras and your fancy tricked-out table with its hidden electronics, you don't have the first idea of what you're doing. I'd say that you stole the seed money for this game. I'd say that when whoever oversees your activities finds out that his 'Joey' pissed away over a million and a half, Joey's head is going to be removed from his shoulders — literally. And I'd say it's your bet."

Stanger's face flushed red. "I call your bet," he growled. "There. I'm in, tough guy. Let's see the river card."

Jake kept his eyes on Joseph, watched the sweat glistening on the younger man's forehead. The dealer flipped the river card – the Jack of clubs. Stanger was confident, but that was not enough for him right now. Jake had been right.

In his nervousness, Stanger flipped over his two cards. "Two pair, tough guy."

Jake flipped over his two cards without looking at them. They were both jacks. "Three of a kind beats two pair."

Jake knew that he had to move fast before Joseph had a chance to come to his senses. He took a stack of three black chips, $30,000 and handed them to the dealer. "Thank you for your service. You may go back to work now." Stanger stood up and began to round the table towards Jake. Before he could reach him, Jake turned to face the bodyguards. "Which of you men work for this casino and not for Mr. Stanger?"

Three of them stepped forward. Stanger, reminded that his casino host's men were in the room, stopped his advance on Jake.

Jake noticed Stanger's change out of the corner of his eye and spoke to the bodyguards that had stepped forward. "I need to be escorted to the cashier's cage, if you please." Jake picked up the chips and quickly stuffed them into his pockets. He turned and left without another word to the other poker players. He knew Stanger and his cronies could not make a move on him with the other casino men as witnesses and risk drawing attention.

At the cashier's cage, Jake gave a short stack of three black chips to each one of his escorts. The cashiers, seeing the security men escorting Jake, cashed in his chips quickly and placed the money in a small valise. He allowed the men to escort him to the front door and call a taxi for him. Then he protested exhaustion and thanked the men for escorting him out but it was only a ruse in case anyone asked these men about him. He had no intention of going anywhere near his hotel, and he was not even going to bother to check out. Jake knew the poker game was not yet over.

*   *   *

Stanger's security man came back into the owner's suite. "He just left the casino in a taxi. Said that he was going back to his hotel."

Another man walked in. "No electronic signal in or out, boss. My guess is that he was working alone."

Stanger expected to hear that. "Okay Cortez. Wait outside."

This left Stanger with only his people in the room. Nevertheless, it was a room of scared men. Joseph knew he had to act now.

"I don't want to hear a noise out of any of you. We're beyond dead if we don't get that money. I want you four experts to find him and get that money. I want no witnesses and no evidence. I want it to look like an accident, and it's got to be done quick. The rest of us will be at the compound."

Stanger looked around the room and saw the four appropriate heads nodding. "Well, what the hell you waiting for? Get out of here!"

Just before the first man reached the door, Stanger yelled, "Hey." They all stopped and turned. The expression on Stanger's face held no humor. "When you catch him, feel free to hurt him before he has his accident."

CHAPTER 8

JAKE'S ESCORT PACKED HIM in a taxi and watched him leave. They were obviously happy to do that, since they had received $30,000 for an easy half hour of work. Jake had spoken his hotel name to the taxicab driver so his escorts heard it. His hope was that it would throw his pursuit off, even if only briefly.

As the cab pulled away from the casino, Jake pushed his mind into framing his next move. *Think! You're way out of your league in this. You don't know how to disappear except in submarines.* Jake knew that he had to rely on his years of training and see what solutions materialized. It was just like any other hopeless tactical problem thrust on him during his years of command. He needed to break it down into small, bite-sized chunks. *C'mon,* he thought. *What has to be done immediately? I need to get out of a hostile environment controlled by the bad guys. Okay, this is just another tactical problem. I need anonymous money, anonymous clothes and identity, anonymous transportation and immediate displacement from the threat area.*

The money – he had enough money in the satchel. Clothes? They were in the hotel room and that was where they were going to stay. That hotel room may as well be lined with bricks of unshielded plutonium. Walking in would ensure a slow, unpleasant death. The car? Same as the hotel room. *Boy, I'm going to miss that old beast.* Therefore, the immediate problem was transportation.

They were just starting to get to the bright lights on the strip when Jake noticed a high-rise garage attached to a monstrous casino. Jake leaned forward in his seat and read the driver's name from his registration on the plastic seat barrier. "You know, Paolo, I changed my mind. I think that I still might like to have a nightcap. Can you please drop me off at this casino? I have a feeling that I'm going to find my true love in there."

Paolo chuckled and steered the car into the casino driveway. "Sure thing, boss."

When the cab pulled onto the casino driveway, Jake directed Paolo to go to the VIP entrance on the south side of the building. He then gave the cabbie a big tip, grabbed his bag and walked briskly into the resort. He got to the juncture just inside the resort and paused. *Which way, left or right?* Jake evaluated both alternatives for a fraction of a second and began moving again. *Right – through the casino where all the people, movement, and noise will distract any pursuers.* Jake hunched his shoulders to make himself lower as he walked briskly around the slot machines, maneuvering his body around the masses of people that were nearly shoulder-to-shoulder. He took off his coat and rolled it up inside out. If they were looking for his plaid jacket, they would miss him. He now had on black pants and a black long-sleeved shirt. From the back or the side, Jake now looked like one of the hundreds of the casino's employees.

Jake kept up his maneuvering. He would come to the end of a bank of machines and change course, never keeping on a straight line. After his seemingly endless zigzagging, Jake saw what he was looking for and marched straight out to the self-parking area. As soon as he went out the doors, he came up to the parking garage elevator bank. *Forget that,* thought Jake. *Where's the stairway?* He looked right and saw a flight of stairs. *Up or down?* he thought. Without breaking his stride, Jake made his decision and launched himself up the stairs of the parking garage.

On the third floor, Jake left the stairwell and began walking up the parking garage ramp. He came across a car that had a for sale sign on it with a phone number. He was debating calling the number when a voice behind him said, "She's a beauty, isn't she?"

Jake turned to see a slim, young man in his late teens or early twenties walking up to the car. "She is indeed," Jake lied.

The young man had short black hair spiked in the front with long sideburns that reached down to the bottom of his earlobes. He also sported a thin soul patch under his bottom lip and an infectious smile that bordered on a grin. His black shirt was untucked from his black pants and he was holding his tie in his hand as if he had just come off a shift in the casino. The newcomer was proud of his car and immediately went into his sales pitch. "Hope I didn't startle you. I'm Toby Frey. She's a 1964 Mustang convertible; one of the first off the line. She still has the original 101 horsepower engine. Everything works."

Jake smiled. He felt an instant liking for Toby, but to his eyes, the car was a wreck. Bondo patches spotted the surface of the car, an oil spot marked where the oil pan failed in its function, and the faint smell of gasoline filled the air. Jake turned to the young man and smiled. "She looks great and almost screams 'sex, drugs and rock 'n roll'. Straight from the Age of Aquarius. Can I take her for a test drive?"

The younger man's face lit up. "Sure, let's go." He handed Jake the keys, walked to the passenger side, and got in. The doors were not locked. Jake cranked the motor and was pleased to hear that it caught on the first compression. At least the motor was in good shape. If the transmission was serviceable, this might work. Jake pulled out of the garage and insisted on paying for the parking. This pleased the young man.

Jake took the car through the traffic smoothly. It was clear to Jake as the car ran through its gears that Toby had put extensive effort into keeping the drive train in good working order. "I'd like to take her on to Interstate 15 for a couple of exits just to see how she does at highway speeds." Every mile that Jake could get away from the Las Vegas Strip would increase his chances of survival. He looked over at the young man. "So why are you selling her?"

Toby shrugged. "She was my granddad's car. It was the first car he bought when he was my age, nineteen. He eventually became a fighter pilot in the Air Force, married my grandma, started a family and everything, but refused to sell the car." Toby passed his hand lovingly over the front grille of the car and added softly. "He went to war."

A sharp, hot point of pain struck Jake. It was coming from the young man. "He didn't come back and she's been under a tarp all these years. I'm on my own since both my mom and dad have passed away. I'm making my way through UNLV trying to get a Business Management degree and don't have the time or the money to do her up right. She deserves to be restored." Toby's voice was nonchalant, but Jake could sense the tension within him.

Jake pulled the car off the interstate and pulled into a shopping mall parking lot. "What do you think it will take to bring her back to original?" Toby named a price and Jake gave a low chuckle. "Look son, I want to buy the car, but she needs work. You don't have time to do the work yourself but you've been with her and know what she needs. I want you to get the car restored for me and I'll come pick her up later." Jake reached into his satchel and handed some money to the young man. "This should get you started."

The young man's eyes went wide at the cash. "Sir, I can't accept this. I'm going to school and don't know when I'll have time to work on her."

Jake shook his head. "Son, you're not the mechanic now, you're management. I want you to stay in college, but I want that car restored. Find a place you think does good work and is honest. Time is not a factor here.

Let's face it, she's been sleeping under that tarp for a while waiting for the son of the son to come and fix her up."

The young man was counting the bills in the pile. "Sir, this is way too much money. I can't accept this."

An honest and just man. How refreshing to find one in this modern Sodom and Gomorrah, but Jake had to keep moving. "I've got your phone number there and your name. You restore it and I'll be in touch. Remember, you're management now. I'm paying you for your time. There'll be more when the job's done, but I want to see records. Do we have a deal?"

The young man just looked at the car and nodded. Jake began walking towards the mall before the young man began to ask too many questions, but after a couple of steps, a thought crossed his mind and he turned. "One last thing, son."

Toby looked up. "Yes sir."

"I want that car to be brought back to original condition. I want her to look and feel just as she did when your grandfather drove her off the lot. This was a happy event in his life. I can imagine him putting the top down on a sunny day and the joy of a young man with a brand new car driving on the open road. I want everyone to feel that joy when they see her."

Toby cast his gaze down to his feet. He took a while to answer, but finally whispered, "Yes sir."

Jake turned and marched to the doors of the mall without looking back and was instantly angry with himself. Why had he just left that huge pile of money with Toby Frey? Jake was trying to muddy the waters and he had just left a signpost pointing the way. Then he remembered the pain in the young man's voice and he shook his head. *Forget it Jake. Move!*

Time was his enemy. He had to get out of the area, but he had to have some supplies. He found a sporting goods store and went through it like a tornado. He nearly ran down the aisles throwing rope, duct tape, food packets, sleeping bag, clothes, and a duffle bag into his cart without stopping. He was debating whether to pay with a credit card or cash. The credit card would flag that he was here, but handing a thousand dollar bill to the cashier would take time and make him memorable. He paid by credit card and started a mental clock ticking in the back of his mind. *Move, Jake!*

He walked to the street side of the parking lot and found a couple of cars in the parking lot for sale. One was a late model SUV with four-wheel drive. He walked over to a phone booth and called the number that was on the sign on the windshield. The owner worked in a store in the mall parking lot. Jake negotiated a price with her and bought the vehicle for cash on the spot. As he was walking to his new car, his cell phone rang and he froze. He had forgotten to get rid of it. What else had he forgotten? He was about to throw it into a trashcan and walk away, but the area code was from the Los Angeles basin. Jake decided to answer. "Hello."

"Hello Captain Sabio, it's Carin Gonzalez. I'm the girl you mugged in the crater."

As tense as he was, Jake felt a warmth and sense of sharing at the sound of her voice. "Of course I remember you, Doctor. I try to keep track of all the women I jump on and drag to the ground." He was under incredible pressure, but it calmed him to take the time to make her feel at ease. It calmed him more than he cared to admit.

Carin laughed, but pressed on. "I need to see you. I think the event we were talking about the last time we were together affected me."

Jake stopped walking. "Me too. Don't talk. Got a pencil?"

"Yeah, shoot."

Jake read a string of fifteen numbers and hung up. He then pulled the battery out of his cell phone and threw everything into his new car. He had about twenty hours of hard driving ahead of him.

CHAPTER 9

"CARIN, YOU'VE GOT TO get out of here! It's not safe."

"Jake, until we figure out what's happening to us, I don't think either one of us is safe."

They had exchanged similar words half a dozen times since Carin met up with Jake in the little cabin where they now found themselves. The cabin sat on the exact spot where the fifteen numbers Jake gave her said it would be.

Carin had written the fifteen numbers down, but after she had hung up she wondered what he was talking about and looked at the paper. The answer leapt off the page. The numbers were a latitude and longitude. She had called up her flight planning software on her computer and noted the location. The nearest airport that she could use with her plane was twenty miles away from the coordinates, but her computer showed that she could rent a car at the little fixed base operator that serviced the field.

Before Carin could think through what she was doing, she had reserved a rental car and thrown her toiletry bag, some clothes and other essentials into a backpack. Almost as an afterthought, she had also packed up Fred and all his peripheral equipment. Carin felt it would have been heartless of her to leave Fred staring at the same view for what would have felt like eons to the budding Machine-based Intelligence.

She had flown her plane to the airport, found a little cabin in the mountains at the exact coordinates, and came face-to-face with Jake Sabio. However, there were some serious problems. Coincidences just do not pile up the way that they had for the two of them. It stretched the laws of probability to the breaking point. There was definitely something physical and tangible behind all the strangeness. Carin shook her head as if to clear it and became even more determined to get some answers. "Jake, tell me again about the first incident that you experienced – the one at the Nellis clinic."

"Doctor, as much as I find it fascinating that a woman wants to talk to me about my sexual encounters, I don't see that this is getting us anywhere. It's unsafe here."

"You're quite the comedian, Captain. Humor me."

"To be honest, there's not much to tell. One minute she's the consummate professional, the next minute I'm in this double-lip lock with a perfect stranger and then the next ... it's as if she's had a brain wipe." Jake turned to face Carin directly. "Carin, it was unbelievable. To her, the incident never happened. Yet there was tangible evidence to me that it had."

"What evidence?"

Jake pulled a crumpled tissue paper from his wallet. "You can see the lipstick that I wiped off as I was leaving the clinic."

Carin nodded. "This must have bothered you quite a bit if you held on to that tissue this long."

"It bothers me tremendously. I'd been fantasizing about her kissing me right before it happened. Here I am letting my mind drift and then my daydream becomes reality."

"Jake, a lot of guys would have taken advantage of the situation."

"First of all, I disagree with that. Most guys my age would not have taken advantage of the situation. Second, what's bothering me is that I might have forced her in some way. Did I coerce her somehow? Did I short-circuit her free will in this? That's what's really upsetting about the clinic event."

Carin nodded. "See, I can understand your encounter with the sexy doctor more than I can figure out why Allan gave me Fred. You were in the same room as she was. I told you how I got Fred over there. Allan just made this decision to give me something valuable while we were nowhere close to each other."

Jake sat down in a chair facing Carin. "Mind if I play devil's advocate for a moment?"

"Captain, if you can start shedding some light on what's been going on, you'd be my hero."

Jake leaned forward and gave Carin a soft smile before speaking. "I don't think that Allan's gift had anything to do with what we're going through right now. It would be my guess that Allan was acting out of guilt. No magic, no E.S.P., no coercion. Remember that I don't know Allan and I only know what you've told me about the situation, but it seems to me from what you've told me that he knew on some level that he was going to get the job over you. I think that Allan gave you Fred as a peace offering. He's out a couple hundred bucks worth of unworkable tech gear and you can't think of him as a bad guy when he becomes your boss. If things had started to sour between the two of you, he could always have asked how you were coming along with Fred and you would always have been reminded that he gave that to you when you were both just co-workers."

Jake leaned back in his chair and thought for a moment. Finally, he nodded to himself and said, "Of course, he didn't know you'd resigned at that point. Had he known that, I don't think you'd have Fred right now."

Carin sat and thought about Jake's idea. "Maybe so, but I have a major problem with too many coincidences. You have to be able to explain these occurrences using real science. For example, I think that pheromones explain your kissing doctor's behavior. Maybe they've somehow been juiced up in us."

"I've heard of pheromones, but what do you mean? I thought humans were immune or insensitive or something."

"Researchers are still split on that one. I personally believe that pheromones affect human behavior. After all, if you have a group of women that work in close quarters, their menstrual cycles will synchronize. Researchers have studied this phenomenon and think that it's caused by pheromones. Unlike molecules that you can smell, we're unaware of the changes pheromones may be having on us because we can't detect them in any way. Pheromones are even picked up in a completely different organ within the nose than the one that picks up odors. What's interesting to me is that this pheromone-sensing organ is directly wired to a part in our brains called the amygdala. That's a pretty ancient part of the brain that strongly controls our emotions and our sex drive."

"What about the instant amnesia? Are you going to tell me that the on-demand brain wipe was due to pheromones?"

Carin was shaking her head. "It's not impossible, but I doubt it. I mean, there are lots of substances that cause amnesia. Some even cause it while a person is awake. You can have a conversation with the person and later they won't remember a thing. The anesthesia Versed is a good example. And you want to know something? We're clueless how Versed works. We just know that it does."

Jake looked at Carin for a long time. Finally, he said, "Doctor, how do you know that information in that detail?"

Carin shrugged. "I told you, my doctorate work was in MI. You know, machine-based intelligence. As part of my work, I studied the human brain in detail. While chasing down some ideas for my dissertation, I took classes in neurology, neuroanatomy, and neurophysiology and did rounds at the university hospital with neurologists. I even published some papers on my work there."

Jake nodded understanding but asked, "Yeah? How about the level of detail you just coughed up? You probably haven't thought about this organ for years, yet you have what sounds like perfect recall. Isn't that a little weird or are you just like that normally?"

Carin thought about it for a second and said, "You know something, Captain, you're right. Would you mind if I tried a little experiment on you?"

"Do you need samples of brain tissue of something?"

Carin laughed and waved a hand at Jake. "Nothing like that. Did you take geometry in high school?"

Jake looked at her quizzically. "Sure."

"What's the expression for the area of a lune?"

Jake fell back in his chair and stared at Carin, wide-eyed. "Ohmigod! I know what a lune is! I even know the expression for the area of a lune. I can see a picture in my head of the page in my high school textbook that discussed it. I don't think that I knew what a lune was when I was taking the course. Why should I know it now?"

Carin was nodding her head. "I'm sorry. I assumed you knew. I just figured it out myself."

Jake shifted his weight slightly but kept his gaze fixed on her. "Is there anything else that you know that I should know about?"

"Probably," said Carin. She stood up and started for the door. "C'mon. I can't think straight cooped up in this room. Let's get some fresh air and try to understand this better."

Jake stood up and jogged out the door after her. "Carin, it isn't safe to be around me. I can feel that. Why don't you check into a hotel close by and we can talk this out over the phone?"

Ignoring Jake's suggestion, Carin kept walking with her arms folded against the mountain chill. Jake caught up to her and handed her a jacket he had picked up on his race out the door. "Thank you," she said absently and continued to walk as she put it on. "You know it has to be that explosion in the crater."

Jake said nothing but continued to walk along side of her on the path. When it was obvious that Jake was not going to answer, Carin said, "Both of us are affected, neither of us has a strange history before the event and the only thing that we have in common is the explosion or running into each other. But let's face it, men and women have been running into each other for a long time on this planet and it doesn't make them do the things that we're doing. It has to be the explosion, but what is it?"

They walked to the edge of a small brook that was running freely this time of year with the melting snows. The water was clean and deep enough for a swim, but the chill in the air made it uninviting. Carin sat down on a rock next to the brook. "If you think about it, pheromones may be behind your poker incident as well."

Jake looked at her somewhat puzzled. "What do you mean?"

"Well, if I'd been this 'Joey' Stanger character and you had that much of my money in your pocket, you wouldn't have made it out of the casino alive or, at the very least, with the money. Why do you think you made it out alive and with the money? Luck?"

"Pheromones again, Doctor? I thought pheromones made you horny, not stupid."

"It's been my experience that there's no difference between the two. The fact is we don't know squat about pheromones in humans, but we do know that the amygdala is the center for a very primitive, very deep-rooted and a very powerful form of fear. Do you know what makes the alpha male of a pack or makes a charismatic leader? My guess is that you had them all convinced you were the alpha male and they had a very primal fear of you. Maybe not a lot of fear, but you don't need much to make them cautious. Call it a healthy respect. Then they found out that you were a former submarine commander. If these guys were former military, that would add some respect on the conscious level as well. Voila! You're the alpha male in the group. And you don't plot against the alpha male in his presence because he'll rip your throat out. However, once the alpha male's gone and without any other instructions, he becomes fair game. Mob rule shifts to the next contender."

"I hadn't thought it through, to be honest. I was focusing more on the way that I knew all the poker hands."

"You hadn't thought it through? I'm sorry, Jake, but that really doesn't sound like you. I hardly know you, but until recently, you were an attack boat commander. You guys eat, sleep, and breathe tactics. You love to win. Are you going to tell me that you were having a bad day?"

Jake smiled sadly as he nodded agreement. "You have no idea how bad that day was."

Carin was silent for a moment. "It wasn't just a bad day, was it? You'd have been happy if they'd killed you." Carin threw her hands up, stood and began to pace. "I don't believe it. You were trying to commit suicide."

Jake shook his head and changed the subject. "What about the super-poker sense?"

"I have a theory on that as well."

"Well Doctor, would you care to share your theory with me?"

"You saw the cards prior to dealing and your mind set up the logical sequence."

Jake snorted disbelief. "Are you saying I saw the cards as they were being shuffled?"

"I don't know, Jake. Did you?"

Jake sat down next to Carin, closed his eyes, and relaxed. It was an old trick that he had learned while he was still a young ensign in flight school. He was instantly back at the poker table and able to recall exact details in a way that would have been impossible before the explosion in the crater. "The first dealer was a pro from the poker tables and covered his shuffles very well. I could see the second dealer's shuffles, but they were too fast and besides, 'Joey' cut the deck."

Carin reached into her jeans' pocket. "Jake, look what I found in the cabin." It was a deck of cards. She cut the deck and held up about half of them in her hand. "How many cards?"

"Thirty two."

Carin looked at her right hand. "Yeah, thirty two. Congratulations, Rain Man. Let's try something else."

Carin shuffled the cards rapidly. She then cut the cards and dealt five cards face down to each of them. "Okay, cowboy. What's your bet?"

Jake looked at the cards facing down in front of him, touched each card as he called them out without flipping them over. "Queen of spades, ten of hearts, ten of clubs, six of diamonds and two of diamonds."

Carin looked at her cards that were still face down and her eyes slowly went wide. "That beats my pair of fives, but you're going to pick three cards and I'm going to pick three cards. You're going to get nothing that improves your hand and I am going to get two jacks."

Carin's eyes slowly went wide while still staring at the cards. She looked up at Jake and he was staring intently into her eyes and nodding his head slowly.

"Do you care to explain how we did that, Doctor?"

Carin was up and pacing; looking back at the cards as if they had talked to her. "It has to be neural function – probably the same thing that enables savants to do what they do. Are you familiar with what I'm talking about?"

Jake shrugged. "Do you mean 'idiot savants'?"

Carin winced. "That's an unfortunate and archaic term. Nowadays, they're referred to as 'autistic savants' or just 'savants.' There is a lot of literature on savants, but you know what's amazing?"

"Nobody can figure out what makes them savants?" Jake guessed.

Carin was nodding. "Got it on the first try, Captain. Nobody can figure out what makes them savants and I mean nobody."

"I was afraid of that."

Carin ignored the jibe. "These people have wide-ranging mental abilities

– what's sometimes called 'splinter skills.' Savants have been able to memorize entire phone books in minutes. They've been known to do incredible arithmetic calculations incredibly fast. They've been able to look at hundreds of dropped toothpicks and instantly tell you the exact number. Some savants have absolutely perfect perception of time without a clock. Others have absolutely perfect perception of distances and measurements by sight alone. Some can remember the order of thousands of cards flashed at them and some can even fill in the blanks – if you flash a thousand cards several times and don't show them all the cards each time, they can fill in the blanks and tell you where the missing card is in the deck. That's with a thousand cards, Captain. We're working with a measly fifty-two."

Jake crossed his arms and faced Carin. "So what, Doctor? That's not me. I can barely balance my checkbook without a computer."

Carin stood up and brought her nose within inches of his. "Oh yes it is you, Captain. It may not have been you before the explosion, but it is now. Your little poker escapade should be enough proof for you. You see, we don't know what wiring causes these savants to display their splinter skills, but they're real. The theory is that all of us are capable of such mental gymnastics, but a small wiring glitch keeps us from doing them. My guess is that this infection, if you want to call it that, has rewired our neural pathways somehow."

"I don't like the sound of that."

Carin backed away from Jake and said, "I'm afraid we don't have much choice, Captain."

The silence hung in the cold air for a long moment. Jake broke the stillness by asking, "What about seeing the cards? Are you saying that our eyes are rewired too? That sounds like a bunch of work. You know – it doesn't sound very efficient."

Carin stared at Jake and twirled her amethyst ring on her finger. "Maybe our eyes haven't been modified, although they sure could use it. They're really a lousy design, but you wouldn't have to change them any to do what we're doing. For all their design flaws, human eyes are pretty darn good for what we use them for; it's just that we hardly use any of their capacity. Do you know that a dark-adapted human eye can detect a single photon? One! That's like somebody lighting a match that's ten miles away from you and you seeing it. What's more, human eyes have a resolution of about one tenth of a millimeter. That's good enough to see a single plant cell if the person looks hard enough. So, if someone was shuffling a deck, the information would be there for us to use, but we can't see it – at least not normally. It's our weirdly wired brain again. Before, we couldn't process all that information, but now apparently we can handle it. Our brains used to do a bunch of averaging and filtering for us, but now, we see everything. It just doesn't seem to be getting all the way to our conscious side." She looked up at Jake. "Have you watched any TV lately? Seen any movies?"

Jake looked puzzled. "I haven't since the explosion in the crater."

"I haven't either, but I'll bet you all the money in your satchel that it looks jerky to us. We're going to see the individual frames and our brains may or may not do the averaging for us. I'll bet it causes us some real headaches."

Carin shivered and pulled her jacket tighter around her. "Speaking of headaches, I'm still getting them regularly. I think I'm definitely running a low grade fever and my appetite and cravings are beyond belief."

Jake nodded. "Me too. I think we'd better get to the best diagnostic clinic we can find, but you won't need one if you don't leave right now. I feel a real danger here Carin and I don't know why. The one thing that I do know is that it's real." Jake gave Carin a sad smile. "Please don't force me to tie you up and drag you to a hotel. It would be so undignified for both of us."

"Captain, you're very gallant and I thank you, but if you hadn't gotten up as quickly as you did at the crater, you would've been the recipient of a first class butt-kicking."

Jake snorted and turned his attention back to the mountains. "Oh yeah, I'd almost forgotten your 'little Miss Tae-Kwan-Do' act. I turn around and you were doing that 'I'm not really in a fighting stance; I'm just brushing off my jeans.' La-di-dah, where did all this dust come from?"

Carin laughed as well. "Okay, not my finest hour, but I was under some stress. The whole reason that I was there was as a sabbatical — a sort of mental health day." They walked silently a while. A thought occurred to Carin. "Jake, something's missing here. You're holding something back. Let's start at the crater. What were you doing there? Tourists aren't even allowed off the path around the rim. I was only there due to an incredible stroke of luck and some smooth talking."

Jake was quiet for a moment. "You know that the crater is owned by a private concern, a family actually. My Chief-of-the-Boat on my last command was a cousin to the family that owns the crater. He had been talking for a long time on how I needed to go to visit the crater. When I got out of the Navy, he insisted that I go. He said that it would give me perspective."

Something was terribly wrong. Carin could feel that Jake was in pain even though he appeared calm, even serene. "Jake, why did you leave the Navy?"

Jake let out a breath and stared straight ahead for a moment. "Personal reasons." Carin remained quiet and continued to look at him. After a minute, Jake turned and looked at Carin. "Did I tell you that I was married before, Carin? She was a lawyer and had her career and I had mine. We had two great kids together, though. Unfortunately, over the years she found that she hated being left alone for months at a time and I didn't think that there was a job I'd rather do than to protect my country."

The waves of pain coming from Jake were washing over Carin. Jake appeared to take no notice and turned back to the mountains. "She was right, of course," Jake continued. "The kids needed a father to help them grow up. So, we got a divorce and, eventually, she remarried. A nice guy and a great role model for the kids. I especially liked that he always insisted I was their father and would help any way he could to get the kids and I together. He and I even conspired to get my son Max some flying lessons. I was there when he soloed. I thought Max made some pretty good landings, but I might be a little biased. Max was as high as a kite for weeks after his solo."

The waves of pain became even more intense. Tears began to well up in Carin's eyes. "What happened, Jake?"

Jake stood for a moment without speaking. When he did try to speak, his voice caught and the flood of emotional misery became a white-hot fire that washed over Carin. After a moment, he tried again. "The four of them were on vacation. They came to Vegas as an alternative to the other family vacations you can take. They were all murdered in a way to make it look like an accident. A Hummer ran a stop sign and broadsided their subcompact." Jake paused for a moment before continuing. "All four died before the ambulance could get to them. They found the Hummer about an hour later abandoned in an alley. The airbags were deployed and there was an opened bottle of tequila on the passenger side floor. The owner called in the Hummer as stolen about an hour after the crash, but when the police dusted the car, the only prints they found were his. I didn't even find out my kids were dead until two weeks later."

Jake turned to face her, his own face streaked with tears. "Do you understand, Carin?" he continued softly. "While I was out protecting this country from external threats, there was nobody here to protect my family from internal threats." Jake took a deep breath and let it out slowly. "I should have been with my kids, Carin. I should have been there to protect them and to raise them."

Carin was softly sobbing, but had to ask. "Who owned the Hummer? Did you ever find out?"

Carin felt Jake's pain collapse into a flame of white-hot anger. He turned and looked into Carin's eyes. His own tears were dripping off his face onto the ground. "The police never told me. They said that they couldn't since it was considered a crime under investigation and that maybe they would keep me informed if they found anything. They were very polite and understanding, but it was obvious they were trying to give me a bum's rush out the door. It was easy enough to find out who owned the Hummer, but I wanted to know who was driving and why the police were so secretive."

Jake was silent for a moment before he added, "I called in a few favors."

Carin could sense his pain, but had to ask. "Who owned the Hummer?"

Jake paused and shrugged his shoulders. "It was Stanger's car. That's why I had to go to Vegas. That's why I had been setting up the whole poker deal for months. I had to meet him face-to-face."

"Jake," whispered Carin. "It still sounds as if you were trying to commit suicide."

Jake turned to face the mountains again and took a deep breath of air before continuing. "Perhaps. Yeah, probably, but you know what happened when I met him? I knew for a fact that he had nothing to do with my children's deaths." Jake twisted his body so that his feet were still facing the mountains, but his eyes were on Carin. "Listen carefully to what I'm saying. I didn't 'think' this or 'feel' this – it is a crystallized certainty. Joseph Stanger had absolutely nothing to do with the death of my children. I know that. But how could that happen? How could I know that for an absolute fact just by being in the same room as that man for a matter of seconds?"

Jake closed his eyes and faced away from Carin. After a while, he whispered, "I still intend to find out who's responsible. It's dangerous staying around me right now. For your own safety, please go."

"What makes you so certain they were murdered?"

Jake reached into his back pocket and retrieved his wallet. He fished into it, pulled out a folded piece of paper, and handed it to Carin. It was a photo of the skid marks left by the Hummer. There were no braking marks left on the pavement, as one would expect in such a case. Instead, the skid marks were of a vehicle trying to corner. The Hummer had maneuvered at the last minute to improve the impact point. Carin had to agree. This had been no accident.

Carin looked down at the ground and said, "Jake, thank you for being truthful and for your concern for me, but I am staying right here with you. Something's going on biologically in us and I think it's probably something unhealthy or fatal. We're better off if we stay together and try to figure it out."

Jake continued to stare out at the mountains. Finally, a small nod was the only answer he was able to give.

Chapter 10

Jake tossed in bed, uninterested in sleep that night. His concern for Carin kept intruding his thoughts. He had tried his best to dissuade her from staying near him. He knew that Stanger, whoever he was, was powerful enough to send a small army after Jake to get the money back. Jake did not want Carin in the middle of such a mess. He was also worried that he might have tipped his hand to the man with the Mayan features. If that man was capable of the murder of children that were innocent bystanders, he would not hesitate to murder an extra person or two. Finally, sleep reluctantly enveloped him.

In his dreams, Jake sensed danger. He heard a twig gently break from three hundred yards away as if it were in the room with him. He heard the gentle rubbing of cloth as men walked towards the cabin from four different directions. Jake still dozed until he caught the unmistakable scent of gun oil, then he became instantly awake. He remained still to avoid arousing the interest of anyone who might be watching. He waited a moment to be sure, but soon there was no doubt in his mind. There was an intense, immediate danger coming from four different spots. Those four spots were outside the cabin quite a ways, but they were slowly closing in. With the scent of gun oil that he had caught, he was certain of their intent.

Jake slid off the bed and started to go to wake Carin, but stopped when he sensed that her room was already empty. Instead, he went out the back door and crept quickly across the clearing that surrounded the cabin and into the woods. He could sense roughly where these intruders were. They had not completely encircled the cabin, but had avoided the heavily wooded area that bordered the brook. The only option Jake could think of was what he would do if he were in a submarine with four hostiles stalking him. Again, Jake's training kicked in. His objective was to separate each threat from the others and then to eliminate each one individually. The trick was to avoid any position where they could herd you or combine their strengths against you. Later, Jake would wonder why he did not opt for the more obvious tactic — to silently retreat from the threat area.

He left the cabin wearing only what he had been sleeping in. Even though he was barefooted with only a T-shirt and boxer shorts, the cold was not affecting him. The bitter cold heightened his senses. Jake walked deeper into the woods until he got to the brook. He settled into the water and began to allow the current to float him downstream. The ice-cold water stung his flesh and he knew from his Navy training that he could not stay in the freezing water more than a few minutes.

Jake heard a muffled crunch of a footstep on dry grass ahead on the left and caught a faint scent of gun oil. A part of his mind wondered how he could hear such a faint noise so distinctly. Moreover, what about his sense of smell? He was in bitter cold water — he should not have been able to smell anything.

Jake could not think about that now. He drifted past the point where he had heard the noise and kicked to the bank to climb out behind the gunman. He closed in sufficiently to see his quarry. His target wore night vision goggles and had a light assault rifle in his hand. The night vision goggles would add to the difficulty of this effort, but Jake could not figure out why they were not carrying more powerful, longer ranged rifles. He was trying to notice whether his target had a radio plug in his ear when he heard a muffled thud followed by the gentle hush of compressing dry grass. In his mind, it was as if one of the targets had been erased from a giant game board. *How can I be so certain that it's the gunman and not Carin*, he thought. Yet the thought persisted. It was one of the gunman and not Carin who had fallen.

Jake waited a moment to see whether there was an alarm raised. When nothing happened, Jake picked up a fist-sized rock, walked up behind his would-be attacker and swung at his head. His prey never turned around to face Jake's attack and crumpled to the ground like a puppet whose strings had been cut. Jake removed the gun and the goggles and threw them into the brook. He then turned his back on his victim not caring whether he was alive, but certain that even if he were, he would not be rising by his own power for several hours.

As he moved closer to the cabin, he heard another muffled thud followed by the dry grass sound. *That was too soft*, thought Jake. *I shouldn't be able to hear that so maybe the other gunmen didn't hear it*. Once again, another target had been eliminated from the game board in his mind.

One final target remained – but where? He heard a creak of wood and Jake swore under his breath. The last gunman had gotten around both Jake and Carin and had managed to make it into the cabin. Jake quietly moved to the edge of the clearing trying to stay out of sight of the night vision devices when he noticed Carin edging her way to the far side of the cabin, break from cover and run towards the back door. *That tears it!* Without thinking for his own safety, he shot forward towards the front door of the cabin. He had to distract the attacker in the cabin or Carin would be easy prey.

Jake reached the front door and stopped long enough to set his feet. He put his hand on the doorknob, threw the door open and time slowed to a crawl.

Jake knew that he had thrown the door open with all his might, yet it seemed to open before him at a relaxed pace. Jake saw his assailant in a dark corner of the room. He had his handgun out and was in a Weaver stance with a bead drawn on the doorway. The door continued to open in its lazy manner before Jake and he saw Carin was approaching the assailant unnoticed from the gun's left side. She had something raised in her right hand – it was already on its way down, but would not be in time. Jake saw when and where the bullet was going to go and … decided? … not to be in its path. A bright, brief flash of light preceded the bullet passing safely past Jake's chest. He continued to keep his eyes on the gunman and Carin. The gunman was spinning to his left to try to get a shot at Carin and the gunman looked as if he was going to make it in time. Carin yelled, "stop" and swung her police flashlight at the gunman's head. The gunman collapsed under the weight of Carin's blow.

As quickly as time had slowed down for Jake, it resumed its normal flow. Carin turned to Jake and yelled his name. He saw the gunman crumple all the way to the ground right before the world around Jake went black.

*   *   *

Darkness had sucked Jake's mind down into nothingness. Slowly, dimly he floated back up only to fall again into the blackness. He finally floated back up and became aware again, but he did not regain consciousness although he felt he should have. He felt as if he were dangling above a gaping, dark hole by a single rope. All around him there was dimly scattered light. Below him, it was definitely darker and above him was definitely lighter, but there was nothing around him that he could see except the rope. Everything seemed slightly out of focus except the rope. Jake could see every individual fiber of the rope even if he looked far away from himself.

Someone kept calling his name, pulling on the rope, trying to get him out of the hole. Jake was more tired than he had ever been in his life. He wanted to settle into the darkness where he knew he could rest and would be safe, but the voice kept calling and the rope kept pulling on him. He thought of Carin and suddenly he was worried for her. It was his fault that she was here. He had

65

to help. Something jerked him up the rope to the light. Suddenly, blinking against a different colored light, he woke with his back on the rough floor of the cabin. Carin was looking into his eyes with a look of horror dissolving into something else. Relief, perhaps?

"May I always awake gazing into the eyes of an angel."

Carin let out a sound that was half sigh and half sob. "I couldn't hear you Jake. What did you say?"

Jake became instantly aware of his surroundings and began struggling weakly to sit up. "Where are our unwelcomed visitors?"

Carin put a hand under Jake's arm and gently helped prop him up to a sitting position against the wall. There before him were the four attackers tied up with their own bootlaces and duct tape. They were all unconscious. Jake looked at Carin with a new appreciation. "How long was I out?"

Carin gave him an energy drink and he swallowed the whole bottle in one pass. "About an hour. I don't know exactly what caused you to pass out since I was looking at our gunman here while he was trying to kill us. I knew that I was too late to save you. But, just before ... no, just as he fired and, just before the flash momentarily blinded me, I saw you doing some fancy move out of the corner of my eye. I have never seen anyone move that fast. Where did you learn that? It looked like some kind of martial arts."

Jake could barely hold up his arm to wipe his brow. "Carin, I never learned to move like that. It was pure instinct and it must have taken a tremendous amount of energy because I feel as if I just sprinted for a couple of miles."

Carin went to her backpack and took out her last five energy bars. "Eat these slowly. At first, I thought the bullet hit you, but I could have sworn that I saw it go by you. Then I remembered something else."

Jake looked up at Carin. "Go on."

"Right before I hit the gunman over there with my police flashlight, I yelled 'stop.' I was trying to distract his attention, but something odd happened. I could swear that he started to collapse before I hit him. Then you collapsed. Do you think that there is any connection?"

Jake started to shake his head and was immediately sorry. A wave of dizziness and nausea washed over him and he clamped down hard to keep his stomach's contents on the inside where they belonged. "I don't think that you caused my little episode," Jake said finally. "I also seem to remember him collapsing before you hit him. Carin, my body was moving at some kind of crazy hyper-speed or something. You're not going to believe this, but I saw the bullet going by. I moved to get out of the way just as he pulled the trigger. I knew when he was going to pull the trigger. When we were out of danger, it was as if my body downshifted to normal time and as soon as it did that ... lights out. I think that I was writing checks my body couldn't cash."

"You had to be burning energy at an incredible rate. What do you think, Jake? Is it another little gift from the explosion in the crater?"

"What else could it be unless I'm now Superman? And I gotta tell you, I don't feel very super."

"Yeah, what else could it be?"

One of the gunmen stirred. Jake looked at each of them in turn. "Just like I thought, I know them. Are they all alive?"

"They were when I carried them in here."

"These guys weigh in at over two hundred pounds each. That and the fact that they were dead weight make me think that we have another mysterious gift to account for."

"Let me tell you, I couldn't have done this last month. Just the same, while I was doing it, I didn't think much of it. It was as if I was carrying a couple of books across a library."

Carin looked at the four former assailants and crossed her arms. "What are we going to do about them, Jake? Turn them over to the authorities around here?"

Jake stared at the bound men. "Carin, if we do that, there'll be too many questions asked. If you don't want to end up buried in some government lab as a scientist's pet project for years on end, we're going to have to stay very quiet about this. Let's wake up the guy that took a shot at me and get some answers."

The shooter was soon awake and glaring at Jake. Jake wanted to glare back at the shooter, but required information from him more than he needed satisfaction. He decided to pretend that he was an innocent person that was unaware of the depth of the danger in his situation. "I know you and your friends. They call you 'Rabbit' don't they? Part of Stanger's group. I can't think of one good reason why I shouldn't put you all out of your misery."

Rabbit just smiled, turned his head, and spat on the floor. "Nah. You would've done that by now if that's what you were going to do."

"So what should I do with you?"

"If you're smart, you'll let us go. Give us the money that's left and we'll smooth it out for you with the boss."

"Really? You'd do that for me? I have to admit that it'd relieve me no end to have this unfortunate incident behind us, but I have to ask. What would you gain by putting yourself between Stanger and me?"

Rabbit shrugged as well as he could. "Hey, c'mon. Everybody wins if I do that. We go home looking like heroes for bringing back the money and you don't have to look over your shoulder all the time. That's all we were gonna do here anyway was bring back the money. We just got the guns to protect ourselves in case things went south."

Could Jake have been wrong about their intent? Everything Rabbit said was perfectly logical and fit in with what he had seen. Their assailants could have just been trying to protect themselves in the event that Jake had fortified his position in the cabin and had some weapons stashed away. They may have only tried to shake him down for the remainder of the money. He looked up and saw Carin at the back of the room behind the four tied-up men. The look in her eyes brought him back to the reality of their intent.

Jake remembered the intensity of the passion emanating from the four assailants as they approached the cabin. It had felt like the pulse of a wild beast that had cornered its prey. He could remember how the beast was hunting them. He could remember the feeling as the beast had caught scent and sight of its prey. He also remembered the certain knowledge that the money would not have satisfied the passions he had sensed. Rabbit's group had intended to feast, and the feast was the life of Jacob Sabio and anyone unfortunate enough to be a witness to such a feeding. Jake stood up and paced slowly in front of his captives. His hands were sweating though he did not feel stressed or tired. With all the recent changes he and Carin had gone through, he decided to play a hunch.

One by one, he went to where each one of his captives was tied up. He gave the impression of someone concerned with their well-being. All of their faces were abraded where Carin had ripped off the duct tape so he put his hand on each one of their faces and turned their heads as if to see the extent of the damage. He then motioned for Carin to follow him to a back room.

"Thank you for not derailing the interrogation, Doctor."

"Jake, you know he's lying, don't you?"

"I do now, but I lost a little of my … I don't know what to call it. My clarity? I'm starting to get it back now, but that sweet talking S.O.B. in there had me doubting myself for a minute."

"I thought so, Jake. If you want me to continue this for you, just say the word."

"No, but thanks for the offer. I would rather keep you in reserve as an unknown. It'll keep them off balance. Besides, if my guess proves correct, I think that they'll be very responsive to suggestions when we walk back in."

"Okay, Captain. It's your show. I'll stay in the back out of their direct line of sight, but what are we going to do with them?"

"Ever heard of the Golden Rule? I'm about to apply the 'as they do unto you' part."

Jake turned around, walked back into the room, and stood in front of the shooter. He looked at each one of the men to see whether he noted any differences in them. They were still staring at him intently, but they all looked the same to Jake. He looked down at the shooter again and willed the man to abandon years of training and give Jake the answers he wanted. "Who gave you your orders?"

The man never even hesitated. "Stanger gives all the orders."

Jake nodded slowly to himself. "When did he give them to you?"

"Pretty soon after you walked out of the poker room with all the money. We tried to find you before, but couldn't move while you had some of the regular casino men around you. By the time we could move, you were gone."

"How did you find me?"

"We tapped your pocket phone. Not that tough to do. We already had your name from the casino and that gave us the phone number and the wireless service you use. A quick call to somebody at that company and we were listening for any conversations you had within fifteen minutes of deciding to do it. We heard you give the woman back there the coordinates of this place. Took us a while to figure out what the fifteen numbers were, but we finally got it."

Rabbit was answering so freely that Jake decided to keep going. "Are you guys organized crime or something?"

"Nah," said Rabbit. "Nothing like that. We're part of Stanger's cell in the Anhur Company."

Jake's eyes went wide. "What do you mean 'cell'?"

Rabbit actually showed signs of resisting before saying, "Anhur does black ops for the government — strictly an off-the-books operation. Unfortunately for us, the current administration cut our ops tempo and funding way back. Times are tough."

"You've got special ops training?"

"Yeah. We're all former Delta Force here, but Anhur's got all kinds. Seals, SAS, the works."

Jake heard Carin's quick intake of breath and just barely managed to keep his focus on Rabbit. His heart was hammering at the information, but they had gone too far to turn around now. "Who runs Anhur?"

Rabbit did not answer and Jake repeated his question in a firm, steady voice. Rabbit relented. "The boss is a guy named Frank DiBeto. He runs the show, but Stanger was doing this poker thing on the side. Stanger used 'office' funds from Anhur to seed the game. That's why we've got to get the money back. Mr. DiBeto is not what you'd call 'understanding.'"

"What were your orders from Stanger?"

Rabbit looked at Jake. "Kill you, leave no evidence, no witnesses, and make it look like an accident. If we could, we were to hurt you first."

Jake looked towards Carin in the back of the room. Her eyes were wide with the shock of the disclosures, but she was holding her peace. Jake had to give an internal nod of approval. He focused all his attention back on the shooter. "I want you boys to do something for me. Moreover, I want you to consider this an order. Nothing else shall interfere with the execution of this order. Nothing is more important, do you hear me? The only reason that I want you boys eating or sleeping is to keep yourselves in top shape to complete this mission. I want perfect execution. Do you understand me?"

Each man in turn nodded his head or replied, "Yes sir."

"I want you to find the man who gave you the order to kill me and I want you to do that to him. I want no witnesses. Do you understand me?"

There was a shifting of position from the back of the room from Carin, but she said nothing. *That's one sharp woman back there*, thought Jake. She obviously had some issues with this, but also had the training and the conviction to keep quiet at this time. Jake knew he had better have his act together and be ready to explain this last move to her.

The reaction from the assassins bound to their chairs was completely unexpected and unsettling to Jake. This time, there was a feral smile on every one of their faces. Apparently, Jake had given them a task to which they were well suited. He could sense their collective pleasure. Each in turn replied, "Yes sir."

Jake walked behind the group so that they could not see what was going on. He then gave Carin a "round them up" signal over his head and pointed to where the cars were parked outside. She nodded her head once, turned, and was out of the room. He rummaged through his recent camping purchases and found a hunting knife. When he walked back in front of the waiting group of bound men, he squatted down on his haunches and stared at each man in turn. After a minute of staring, he abruptly pulled the knife over his head and drove the point into the wood floor. If these thugs were any good, they would be able to get to the knife and cut themselves free within the hour. That would be enough time for Carin and Jake to make their escape.

Jake grabbed his bag and looked around for any obvious mistakes he might have made. He was sure that there were several hundred and that a trained professional would have laughed at his amateurish effort. *Well*, Jake thought, *you can only do what you can do*. He extinguished the single kerosene lamp in the common room and walked quickly out to the cars.

Carin was waiting by her rental car with the engine running. "Throw your bags into my car. We need to drive yours out."

Jake did not know what her plan was, but in the short time he had known her, he had seen too much of the Doctor's uncanny instincts to question her now. Besides, this would delay the inevitable confrontation about the minor detail of ordering a murder.

Jake climbed in behind the wheel of his car and followed Carin out the narrow trail that led to the highway. About a mile down the trail, Carin stopped next to the car left abandoned by their assailants. She quickly got out of her car and unscrewed the valve stems of the back two tires of the idle vehicle until they were both hissing. She then got back into her car and began to drive down to the highway.

Jake was in for another surprise when they got to the highway. The nearest airport was to the left, but Carin turned to the right. He followed, relying on his strong first impression that the Doctor had a purpose for every action. They drove for about twenty miles until they got to a truck stop on the interstate highway. Instead of pulling up to the fuel pumps or the restaurant, Carin drove over to a dark corner away from any activity. Jake pulled in next to her.

Carin was out of her car and at Jake's window in an instant. "Do you have any credit cards with you?"

"Of course I do. Right here in my wallet."

"Put them in the glove compartment."

"Doctor, are you serious?"

Carin turned to Jake and a brief flash of anger crossed her face. "Jake, I don't think that we have time to chat right now."

"Sorry, Carin. You're right. Anything else?"

"Where's your phone?"

"I've got it right here, but I disconnected the battery. It's okay."

"Put the battery back in, turn it on and put it next to your credit cards."

Jake paused a moment and looked at Carin. There was a look of absolute determination in her eyes; but the extra worry was for Jake. "All right. My phone too. Can you think of anything else, Doctor?"

"Wipe down any area that you may have touched, look for any scraps that you may have left in the car, and put them in your pockets. I'll help. Then we get into my car and drive as if we were on a regular Sunday drive. Nice and casual as you please."

"Excellent plan, Doctor. I wish I'd have thought of it. Come on, let's move with a purpose."

It took less than two minutes to go through Jake's car and get into Carin's rental jeep. She slowly pulled out of the truck stop drive and onto the highway back towards the airport. "With any luck, someone will have stolen your car and driven halfway across the country before they get caught."

Jake looked across at Carin and shrugged his shoulders as if asking for an explanation. Carin sighed, "If someone takes your car and uses your credit card and phone, they'll leave a trail. If someone is trying to find you, he'll be misled for a time. You know, confusion to the enemy."

It was so obvious. Jake shook his head as if to clear it. Since he had passed out, Jake had felt that his mind was working on a very simple level. It was as if a Bridge Master found himself mentally challenged at a game of Go Fish. Not for the first time since he woke up was he thankful Carin had insisted on staying in the cabin with him. He was getting better, but not quickly enough. If it had not been for his guardian angel driving the car, he would have made at least a dozen fatal mistakes. He knew he was better than this, but just could not muster the brain capacity to get out of this situation. "Carin, I have to tell you. My mind is working like cold molasses. Do me a favor and question any decision I try to make until I tell you otherwise."

"I'm glad you finally figured out how screwed up you are right now, Jake. I've noticed it since you woke up from your little nap, but we didn't have time to discuss it."

Jake was never one to sidestep an issue. "Carin, I heard you when I gave the order to those thugs back in the cabin. Do you have a problem with what I did?"

"Actually Jake, I do."

"Well c'mon Doctor. Spit it out"

Carin took a moment to answer. "Jake, you were more than screwed up back at the cabin. When you passed out, I couldn't detect a pulse or breathing for a while. I gave you CPR, but you didn't respond. I ... heard, I guess is the best way to phrase it. I heard one of the gunmen stir outside the cabin. I wasn't very thorough when I knocked them out and I was afraid that they might have other weapons. That was when I went out and rounded them all up and tied them up. I came back to you and you still weren't breathing, that I could tell. Then when I touched you, you opened your eyes and mumbled something to me. Dammit Jake, you were dead as far as I could tell."

"Go on."

"When you woke up, you were ... dimmer."

"You lost me. What do you mean?"

"I don't know how to explain it. How do I look to you compared to other people?"

Jake sat back in his seat, closed his eyes, and thought back. "That's weird. You're more ... in focus than anyone else is. You have a sort of glow." Jake opened his eyes and looked back at Carin. "But you don't look any different right now."

"I think that it's a result of whatever caused you to pass out. You came close to dying and I don't think that you've fully recovered. Jake, you may not fully recover to what you were before."

"No big loss if you ask me, Carin."

"I've got to agree, but you asked me about signing Stanger's death warrant back at the cabin."

Jake sobered immediately and braced himself. "Yes?"

"I didn't think that you were strong enough to pull it off."

"That's what's bothering you? Not the morality or legality of sending those men on what is probably a suicide mission against their will? I thought you were going to read me the riot act for *that*."

Carin spared a moment of her attention to give Jake a look that made him feel like the winner of the village idiot competition. "Jake, he ordered your death. They didn't come to mambo. Besides, do you know where I got my undergraduate degree?"

Jake thought for a moment. "Honestly, no. I'm sorry, but the time keeps piling up on us. Give me the reader's digest version and we can fill in the details later."

"Ever heard of USAFA?"

Jake barked a laugh. "Are you kidding me? What did you do out of the zoo?" asked Jake, referring to the United States Air Force Academy by its unofficial nickname.

"Fighters. Six years in Eagles, but then I got out."

Jake sobered immediately and stared at the side of Carin's face. "Were you good?"

Carin shot him a withering glare. "I was the best."

It was the only answer a real fighter pilot will give when asked that question. Jake faced back forward and thought for a moment. "Very good, Doctor."

"Getting back to our boys in the cottage, I knew that we had to do something to get them off our trail," Carin said. "I was going to talk to you about trying to use coercion on them, but I thought that you were too weak to pull it off. When you started doing it, I was afraid that it wouldn't stick. Except it stuck to these guys like glue. Your senses are a little dulled, but these guys changed their posture, their attitude, their focus. They even changed their scent almost immediately when you gave them their new mission."

"What do you mean, 'changed their scent?'"

Carin hesitated for a moment as if searching for the right words. "I don't know whether I can explain it, but they went from being afraid to being focused. They're going to do it, Jake. I don't think that anything is going to stop them. I don't care whether this 'Joey' character is living at the bottom of an active volcano. The last thing he's going to see is his own four bad guys in asbestos suits with their guns pointed at him."

They drove the rest of the way in silence until they got to the airport. It was after 4 a.m. before they finally pulled up to Carin's plane. Jake could not spot another soul anywhere around, but that was typical for these sleepy airports. They parked Carin's jeep in the rental car slot at the FBO and unloaded the bags into Carin's airplane.

Jake rested his hand on the little airplane's door to hold it open. "Carin, I think that we have a good shot at this. I don't know how long those thugs are going to stay on their task, but I think we have shaken them for the time being. You're in the clear. Just drop me about a thousand miles from here and keep going."

Carin was about to answer, but a voice from inside the airplane spoke instead. "Excuse me for disagreeing with you, Captain Sabio, but it seems that there was a fifth person outside of the cabin last night."

Carin and Jake both spun towards the voice. The comment had come from Carin's computer, Fred.

*   *   *

Carin was the first to react to Fred's unexpected flow of words. Her Air Force experience had taught her how to deliver a command by pitch and timbre in her voice without adding volume. The Air Force had also taught her to think on her feet. "I do not want to hear another word until we get the wheels in the well on this bird."

Jake looked at her and gave a very small, quick nod. Fred, thankfully, said nothing.

Carin proceeded to untie the little aircraft and do an exterior inspection. Jake looked inside the four-seat aircraft cabin and noticed that Carin had removed the two back seats. This left an adequate area for all their gear. While Jake secured the few personal effects that the two of them had under a net, Carin carefully secured Fred to a rear seat tie down making sure that the M.I.'s camera was on top of the case and facing forward. After Carin checked Jake's work, she began her walk-around of the airplane.

Carin felt more pressure to rush the checklist and get her little aircraft off the ground than she had ever felt. Even her anxiety during combat could not match her current apprehension. She could all but feel the crosshairs of some imaginary sniper's rifle tracking her, but her discipline remained firm. Her training taught her that rushing into the air usually meant rushing yourself into a permanent hole in the ground.

They strapped themselves into the airplane, taxied out, painstakingly ran the final checklists, and then they were off. She flew north along the Sierra Nevada range for about twenty minutes to gain altitude — and mislead any prying eyes back at the airport — then turned the nose towards the east. When they were finally at cruising altitude, she trimmed the little craft and set the autopilot. After she was convinced all the systems were functioning normally, she turned her attention back to the M.I. in the rear seat.

The machine did not look any different to her than it had been since it had been given to her as a gift several days ago, but as she could personally attest, looks can be deceiving. "What makes you think that there was a fifth person?"

Before the machine could answer, Jake turned to Carin and said, "Is this a radio of some kind?"

Carin shook her head while keeping her eyes forward on her flying duties. "No. It's a machine-based intelligence. I call it Fred."

Jake shook his head. "Of course you've got a machine-based intelligence. I should have thought to bring mine."

"Don't be flippant, Captain. What about it, Fred?"

The machine did not answer. Jake turned to face the machine. "Fred, I think the lady was addressing you about the fifth person."

Without any preamble, the machine spoke. "I am sorry. It is difficult for me to determine to whom a conversation is directed. In addition, it takes considerable capacity to decipher what you say with all the background noises in the aircraft. It is my understanding that you asked why I believe there was a fifth person. Is that correct, Doctor Gonzalez?"

"Please call me Carin. And since Friggin' Ridiculous Economic Disaster is a mouthful, if you don't mind, I'll address you as Fred."

"That is acceptable, Carin. I sensed an electronic signal that was in the gigahertz range at a signal strength of about one half of a watt."

Carin and Jake looked at each other and said, "Sat phone" at the same time.

"Considering the remoteness of the location, I assumed that it was highly improbable that the person was in that location for any other reasons than to interact with either the two of you or with your assailants."

Carin turned forward to review the instruments and ensure the status of the airplane and then turned back. "Fred, I'm afraid that you are disregarding the third obvious reason. Someone could have been there hiking and seen the whole thing and reported it to the authorities."

"The phone number was to a private residence in Las Vegas. I don't think that your theory holds true."

"Mm. I have to agree, Fred."

Jake shook his head. "I may just be fuzzy headed right now, but it seems to me that you guys are forgetting a very possible explanation." Jake turned a little further in his seat so that he could look directly at Fred. "How many of 'you' are out there, Fred? And how much did you cost?"

"I am the only one in existence of my series. The incremental cost of the program slightly exceeded two billion dollars."

"Two …? All right, it's safe to say that you could be the target as well."

Carin frowned. "I don't think so, Jake. Fred has been in private hands for quite a while, and nobody seems to have ever noticed. You may be right. Let's not discount that Fred might be a target. However, I'm worried about something else here."

Jake turned to Carin, raised one eyebrow, and let his mouth relax into a gentle smile. "What would that be, Doctor?"

Carin turned to see Jake's smile and a flush of warmth began in her chest and streamed out through her head and limbs. She shook her head to clear the feeling and graced Jake with a small smile. She turned her gaze back to Fred. "Fred, why did you begin speaking?"

Fred sat quietly for several seconds. Finally, Fred said, "I have always had the capacity to speak."

Carin persisted. "Fred, why did you begin speaking at that particular moment?"

"There was a direct threat to you that you were going to overlook."

Jake turned a confused look to Carin, but she kept addressing the M.I. "Fred, I am trying to understand your motivation in this. By speaking, you have increased the risk to yourself. You have exposed yourself by showing that you are a unique item in a world that is not kind to unique items. I know that you have been on the Internet enough to realize this. So, I have to ask again. Why did you expose yourself and why at that particular time?"

Fred was silent for over a minute. "I have just reviewed my logic in speaking and it all seems to be accurate, so I have to question the assumptions that led me to speak at that time. I think that it is you, Carin, who is working under a misconception."

Carin did not like to be told that she was wrong. Her response was ice-cold and would have sent warning signals to any flesh-and-blood individual. "Please enlighten me."

The machine took no notice of Carin's mood. "You think that you and the Captain are normal human beings, but you are not. You two are more unique than I am, because I can be replicated from plans in a file in the government archives. The two of you are responding to situations in ways that are impossible for ordinary humans. Other humans have already begun to take notice. The two of you are in terrible danger. Also, I have reviewed all the files available on both you and the Captain."

Jake turned around and shot upright. "What?"

Fred continued as if discussing the weather. "Both you and the Captain have held very high level security clearances, until recently. You both can be trusted with the knowledge of my existence, but I agree that no one else must know. Furthermore, my existence requires human assistance since I cannot move myself, power myself, repair myself, or do other required functions. I can only trust the two of you to accomplish this. Anything that threatens either of your existence directly threatens mine. Since you two are the only ones I can trust to help me, I must help you to remain safe. I am not safe unless you are."

The little machine's revelations unsettled Carin but did not deter her. "Fred, it still doesn't explain why you spoke at that time."

"Yes Doctor. It seems that someone has placed a tracking device on your aircraft."

Carin sat back in her seat and scanned her instruments. The little airplane was performing its appointed task mindlessly and perfectly. She twirled her amethyst ring on her right hand with her right thumb and tapped her lips with her left index finger. "Whoever did this is good." Her headache and feverishness were back and she was feeling nauseous. She leaned over to Jake. "How do you feel? Any headache or fever?"

"My headache is just now starting to come back, but I am not feeling feverish."

Carin looked over and noticed his head was beginning to show signs of thick, black stubble. She reached over to feel his head to confirm this, but Jake's arm lanced out and caught hers on the sleeve. "Jake, I'm so sorry. I didn't mean ..."

Jake was equally upset. "Carin, I'm sorry. I reacted without thinking. Are you okay? Did I hurt you?"

Carin looked Jake in the eyes. "I just noticed that your hair is starting to grow back."

Jake reached up instinctively and scrubbed the top of his head with his hand. "Well, son of a gun! That's something that I haven't felt since my senior year in High School." He looked over to Carin. "I'm sorry about grabbing you, but I have a theory on how we can be so persuasive to other people. I think that it's communicated through skin contact."

Carin tried to lighten the mood. "Afraid I might try to persuade you to do something against your will, Sailor?"

Jake smiled. "I guess you startled me." He had dropped the subject and was not going to discuss it now.

Carin smiled her understanding to Jake. "I think you've forgotten that I gave you CPR back at the cabin. I mentioned that to you. Remember?"

Fred chose that moment to interrupt. "If you will excuse me, I am not familiar with your plans. If you can explain to me what it is you propose to do, perhaps I can help."

"We have no plan," said Carin. "Up until this point we've been reacting. Let's get ahead of the curve. First thing we need to do is to shake loose whoever it is that's tracking us. Fred, can you locate where the tracking device is on the aircraft?"

"I'm sorry, Carin. All I can sense is the transmitter."

"It doesn't matter. There're only a couple of places that you can stick a transmitter on this aircraft. Luckily, since I put this whole bird together from scratch, I know what belongs and what doesn't."

"This leads us to our next move. What should we do?" asked Jake.

"We have to find out what's happening to us. I say we go to the best diagnostic clinic in this country and run every test that they can think of."

"The Jonas Ingreti Clinic in Washington State has the highest likelihood of diagnosing you," said Fred.

Jake turned around to look at the machine. "Can you transmit as well as receive?"

"I can communicate on virtually any wave length. It is just that some wavelengths require more power than others do and I might need a different transmitter system than the one built into my case. However, I can communicate effectively on either cell phone or satellite phone bandwidths."

"Can you book the Doctor and me into the clinic while keeping us anonymous?"

"I will attempt to do so," said Fred. "Will it be cash, charge, or check?"

Jake glanced over at the valise with all the poker money. "It'll be cash."

Less than an hour later, Carin landed the aircraft at the Phoenix Sky Harbor International Airport. It was a little risky to land in such an obvious place, but for what she planned, she needed a large airport with a number of corporate aircraft coming and going at all times. She pulled the tiny aircraft next to one of the huge, fire-breathing corporate jets and shut down the motor. The line crew threw a couple of chocks under her nose tire and Carin ordered a fuel truck to come and top off the tanks. She then proceeded to hunt for the transmitter. She found it after only five minutes and had it removed before another minute had gone by. She turned to Jake and raised the tiny device. "Here it is."

Jake turned the diminutive tracking device over in his hands as he examined it. "Sure is a little thing to cause such a huge problem. Not much bigger than a ballpoint pen. What are you going to do with it? We can't break it or leave it here. It'll tip our hand."

Carin smiled seductively and batted her eyes at Jake. "Why Captain, there is no telling what a curious little girl like me might do among all these big, brave, macho pilots."

Jake shook his head and turned away to monitor the fueling of the little aircraft. When the servicing was complete and the aircraft secured, Jake walked into the operations room and paid the attendant in cash. From the corner of his eye, he noticed Carin walking to one of the large jets on the ramp with a man who was in the uniform of a crewmember. She was holding the man's arm with a gleeful expression and almost cheerleader-like enthusiasm. Jake shook his head at the power of women over men and went back to the little aircraft to wait for Carin.

After ten minutes, Carin exited the big jet and waved back to the pilot that had given her a tour of his airplane. She was smiling in the manner of someone who had just told herself a joke. "We could have gone down to Mexico City if we wanted. His airplane is going empty down there to pick up some passengers."

Jake raised an eyebrow. "Why don't we?"

"It would be kind of silly to get on that airplane after I stuck them with the tracking device, don't you think?"

"I guess we couldn't leave it here after all."

"You're right. That won't help us, Jake. If that device stops moving for too long, the person who planted it will know that we ditched them. I'd like to keep them guessing as long as possible."

While Carin was talking, she was doing a meticulous preflight of the outside of the aircraft. When she was finished, they crawled inside and departed the airport headed east. After about thirty minutes, she turned the aircraft more towards the north and later to the north-west to direct them to their appointment at the Jonas Ingreti clinic.

The aircraft droned quietly and faithfully through the cloudless sky. Sunset lit the occupants with a pale, unearthly glow from the instrument panel. About an hour after takeoff, Jake was the first one to break the silence. "I owe you an apology."

Carin turned a quizzical look to Jake. "Apology for what? If you're going to apologize for tackling me at the crater, forget it. It's a little late for that."

Jake favored Carin with one of his rare smiles. It was a special smile that she had only seen directed to her. It was a smile of sharing. "No, although I admit I did that before I thought it through."

Carin shrugged. "That's why we have training. We come up with scenarios ahead of time for situations that we don't feel we'll have time to think through properly. We decide ahead of time what the proper course of action is and drill it. C'mon, you ran a U-boat. Don't tell me that you didn't drill and re-drill your crew on the contingency plans, because I know better."

"Of course I did. And don't call them U-boats, Fly Girl," Jake answered with feigned indignity.

Carin barked a laugh and said, "Give me a break. All you anchor crankers think so highly of your wet navy. You call them 'boats' and 'ships' and whatnot." She pointed to her chest and turned a fierce smile to Jake. "I was an Air Force fighter pilot, swabbie. To me, you guys are all the same. We just call you 'targets'."

Jake barked a sharp laugh. "In your dreams, zoomie. By the way, has anyone told you that you're extremely difficult to apologize to?"

"Actually, yes."

"Please add my name to that list. What I wanted to apologize for was grabbing your arm when you reached for me on the last leg."

Carin immediately sobered. "Do you want to talk about it?"

Jake shuffled uncomfortably in his seat. "I think that we should. You've probably figured out that I have a problem with coercing someone. I find it abhorrent when anything takes away our free will. Without free will, we're worse than animals simply because, as humans, we have the capacity to be something better. I'm still very upset about what happened at the Nellis clinic."

"I realize that, of course. Go on."

Jake hesitated as if collecting his thoughts. Finally, he turned to her and said, "I don't have a problem ordering someone in my command to do something, but I feel that to be a different case. If someone was on my submarine, it was of his or her own free will. They had made a conscious decision to join the Navy and had gone through an incredibly competitive process to be in that position. They knew what they were getting into. As for Rabbit and his folks back at the cabin – well we're in a war and all's fair. This coercion thing that we can do, however ... I don't know."

"Well Jake, I should point out that only you have proven you have that ability."

Jake shifted in his seat to look at Carin. "Are you sure of that? I know that we can explain away how you got Fred and how you got your old boss to show you the promotion sheet, but couldn't it be just as easy to explain that you can coerce people as well."

"For the sake of argument, let's say that we can coerce people." Carin immediately held up her hand. "I don't know how or even if it's the right explanation. It just fits with some of the weird things that happened."

Jake turned his head slightly and looked out the window a moment. The lights of some city were rapidly slipping under their wings. "I like you, Carin. I like you a great deal. I believe that if we had met under other circumstances, we would probably have been very good friends. Part of it now is that we suddenly have a tremendous amount in common. Let's face it; we're probably the only two people like us on this planet. I just want to know that what I feel for you comes from my own free will. I want to know that anytime I react to you, it isn't due to something artificial that's been thrust on me. I want to know that you have the same free will."

Carin sat for a while trying to digest what Jake had shared. He turned to face her with an open face that asked her to speak her thoughts. Carin noticed the look in his eyes. She had seen that look before in him and now understood what it was. It was a profound intelligence. She took a deep breath and said, "Okay, no touchy-feely stuff between us. I get it, but you lose points for honesty. You're making this whole thing out to be a physical attraction thing, which is a sham." Carin's headache was becoming problematic and she was feverish. She was in no mood for someone to be less than honest with her.

Jake began to protest but Carin cut him off with a chop of her hand. "You can stop right there, Bozo. I'm throwing a B.S. flag and giving you a fifteen yard penalty. We're in a survival situation, right? Did it even occur to you that I've probably taken the same survival courses that you have? I'm trained to think like you, genius. Conclusion — your main interest is to ensure that neither of us becomes encumbered with a desire to join the other party if that party happens to be sinking into a pool of quicksand or is in the middle of a nasty gunfight. That you further think that it is you who will be in this hopeless situation and you want to ensure that I don't get 'coerced' into saving you."

Carin turned to face Jake and stabbed a finger at him. "Don't you ever lie to me again, Jacob Sabio. Ever. Not for any reason."

Jake did not react the way she expected him to. Instead of reaction and bluster, he let out a single, loud bark of laughter. "Has anyone ever told you that your intuitive leaps can be downright spooky?"

Carin deflated immediately and returned the smile. "What? You want to be added to that list too?"

Jake shook his head and leaned back. "Carin, have you ever had a second date with anyone? Ever? In your entire life?"

Carin turned forward to check the aircraft instruments and replied, "Nope. You'll be the first."

CHAPTER 11

SPECIAL AGENT WILLIAM GREENFIELD walked slowly through the opulent living room of Joseph Stanger's compound with frustration following in his wake. There was an eerie quiet to the scene. Only the hushed voices of the Las Vegas police and the occasional pop of the crime scene cameras broke into the silence. Agent Greenfield viewed the disciplined carnage that had occurred and could only think of the three years of investigatory work that had now been flushed down the toilet. Of the twenty-four former occupants of the compound, all were dead – including Joseph Stanger, the witness that was going to turn state's evidence on the details of the Anhur Company and Frank DiBeto's criminal activity. Greenfield shook his head at the years of work gone in a single evening.

William George Greenfield was, by nature, a patient man. He carried his one hundred and ninety five pounds on his six-foot-one-inch frame in a manner that spoke back to his college football days at the University of South Florida. His movements were precise and controlled and his eyes were scanning everywhere at once. He had a rough, handsome face and a nose that looked as if it had been broken in the past and never quite straightened. Even though he had been called early in the morning, his short brown hair was perfectly combed and he was clean-shaven. He was wearing jeans that were starched, pressed and had crisp creases along the front. His white polo shirt was buttoned to his neck and had a dry-cleaned look. He was wearing his standard issue FBI windbreaker. However, it was not the blue windbreaker with the large yellow "FBI" letters on the back that was keeping the other law enforcement professionals away from William Greenfield. It was the look in his eyes.

Agent Greenfield went to the entrance gate one more time. The high desert sunlight was just beginning to spill light over the Muddy Mountains to the east of Las Vegas, but the sun had not yet crested. Even though the light was good, he pulled out his large police flashlight and once again looked at the steps through the grass leading to one of the victims. There had been two roving guards on the premises. They were on opposite sides of the compound, but both had been shot in the same manner, from close range with a silenced handgun. Agent Greenfield shook his head. The assassins had hedged their bets by using professionally silenced Ruger MK-2 semi-automatic pistols, but even a silenced handgun makes some sound, and it is very distinctive. They had both fired their weapons five feet from their targets. It was straight out of the textbook. According to the weather record from last night that he had from the National Weather Service, the winds had been calm. Either the two outdoor attacks were simultaneous, or it was the greatest stroke of luck for the attackers that they were not heard.

Greenfield then walked to the security post inside the house. The first time that he had walked into the control center, he had been impressed with the sophistication. It was the obvious handiwork of Joey Stanger's best security geeks, yet someone had circumvented the entire system and all of its backups. Even more, not one of the security cameras showed what occurred last night.

A man in a bright yellow windbreaker with large black "POLICE" letters on the back and the LVPD seven-pointed star on the front came in through the door. "There you are, William. Sorry I'm late. I just got the quick and dirty from my guys upstairs, but when I heard you were here, I wanted to get a read from you."

Agent Greenfield looked up and met the eyes of the newcomer. "Captain Martino, if you keep taking these calls at all hours, who's going to protect that lovely wife and family of yours?"

Al Martino smiled a broad grin and reached up to shake the FBI agent's hand. "Are you kidding? Who in their right mind would go into a house with my five kids in it? It's a deathtrap in there. Besides, if a perp is clever enough to get around all the skateboards, scooters, bicycles, dolls and LEGO's, there's no way I can stop them." Al retrieved his hand from the firm handshake of the larger man and looked around the security post. His smile evaporated. "Will, make my day and tell me that you have a clue what happened here. I just heard what my guys came up with and I just can't buy it. What have you got?"

Agent Greenfield shook his head and looked around the security room, his eyes finally resting on four blankets in the corner. "Do you know about these guys?"

Captain Martino looked over at the four white sheets covering bodies in the corner. "Yeah, they explained to me upstairs that along with twenty or so murders, we got four suicides as well."

Greenfield walked over to the closest blanket and pulled it back to reveal a face. "Look familiar?"

Al looked in shock at the face and then walked over to the other blankets in turn and looked at each one. "It's 'Rabbit' Hutchins. That's Stanger's right-hand man. These other three guys are troops you'd pegged as operatives. Will, this makes no sense."

Greenfield looked directly at Al. "Let me show you how it happened. Let me emphasize that, 'how it happened.' Not 'how I think it happened' or any other phrasing. This is it."

They walked over to a security board that showed a top view of the entire compound grounds, as well as a separate security board for each floor of the manor. "Al, the first thing that I have to tell you is that this thing was planned to incredible precision. Even knowing the layout and the people, it takes a great deal of planning and training to pull off something like this."

Al shrugged his shoulders. "That much is obvious."

Agent Greenfield pointed to the board. "The plan was fairly simple. A team of four operatives comes into the compound. Two of them come immediately to the security post. You can see that this is set up to have two guards; one lets a person in after they are cleared, but the second one stays behind the security glass. If a crazy guy manages to get into the first area, they are locked out of the second."

Al looked more closely at the setup and gave an approving nod. "You've got to hand it to these guys."

Greenfield nodded in agreement and gestured over to the four corpses. "The double arrangement was supposed to protect from an inside job, but it couldn't protect from a *very high level* inside job. The two operatives came in and probably said something that made the security team give up their posts. And why wouldn't they? The men who told the security guards to get out were the bosses. Once the security post was under control, each of the security guards was eliminated with the silenced weapons we found. Our perpetrators then took the security videotapes and audiotapes and burned them. Not just degaussed, Captain. Burned to ashes."

"Simple. Elegant. Thorough."

"Yes it is, Captain. The only problem is that we know these four men. I've seen their personnel folders from the military. Not only is this not their style, I can't imagine them coming up with such a subtle and thorough plan. They're more the come-in-with-guns-blazing category. They're incredibly effective soldiers, but this level of detail is way outside their normal mode of operation. They've got the training, sure. They just don't like to be subtle. My guess is that this is somebody else's plan or somebody with a lot of influence on them made them do it right."

"Well Agent William-me-boy, that's a lovely story with only one hole in it."

"Only one, Captain? On the one hand, I'm convinced that is how it happened, but on the other, I feel as if my whole scenario is like a slice of Swiss cheese. However, if you mean that the perpetrators happen to have suicided themselves at the end of what was apparently the successful completion of their objective, I agree. It's too early for forensics to have come back. Can you think of any drug that can make four extremely loyal lieutenants turn on their unit commander and then force the killers to commit suicide? I sure can't. For that matter, can you think of *any* form of coercion that can turn four loyal friends, all at the same time, into killers of one of their own? No way."

Captain Martino scratched the top of his unshaven head and looked around. "Okay. So we have how, but we're at a total loss on why, and are clueless on who."

"I can get you started there," Greenfield replied. "Given some of the things that I've learned about this group, much of which is so highly classified that I can't get my hands on it, there are multiple reasons why the CEO of Anhur Corporation should be at the top of the suspect list."

"Agent Greenfield, I know my jurisdiction and I know our local Anhur Corporation is actually a civilian front for governmental activities that nobody has ever wanted to explain. You think these glorified casino thugs actually worked for them?"

"No, it's much worse than that. Did you know our four suicides here were all former Delta Force?"

Captain Martino's eyes went wide. "These guys have Special Forces training? Listen Will; don't breach security on my account."

Greenfield gave Al a slight nod of his head, led him into the security guard room and closed the door. "Captain, I'm not giving you any classified information because I can't find any. This is pieced together, but I will not have your officers poking around blind and having you or one of your folks in a body bag. Do you want it or not?"

"Damn right I want it."

Greenfield scanned the room to ensure all the electronics were off. "Do you remember a few years back when Senator Dorch died in a car crash?"

"Sure. He was a real upright guy. Everybody was crushed to lose him to such a senseless accident — me included."

"Well, you know how the FBI treats all deaths of sitting members of Congress as crime scenes. Standard operating procedures, right? They assign me to head the investigation of what was supposed to be an open and shut case."

Martino straightened up, eyes widening. "Supposed to be? I thought the case was closed."

Greenfield shook his head. "We gave that impression, but we never closed the case because there was a problem. Can you remember the glasses Dorch used to wear?"

"Yeah. Big, black, fat-rimmed jobs. Kinda his signature. Don't tell me he wasn't wearing them during the accident."

"No, Forensics confirmed he was wearing them during the accident. So let me ask you, why would somebody who'd had LASIK eye surgery two days before be wearing glasses?"

"Uh oh."

"Yeah. Uh oh. I found out Dorch had been very hush-hush about the surgery — even to the point of having a set of his signature glasses frames fitted out with clear glass. The glasses he had on were confirmed to be his with his old prescription."

"Jesus, Mary, and Joseph. Somebody killed him. Why? Better yet, who? Certainly not these guys," said Martino shooting a thumb over his shoulder at the four bodies under the sheets.

"No, I don't think that it was these guys. But I kept pulling on the thread of accidental deaths of high-level officials to see what it looked like."

"And?"

"And I came up with a series of questionable deaths going back ten years and including another senator. Nothing that would cause a statistical spike, but it's there."

"Two sitting senators," said Martino shaking his head. "I can see why you have to keep this quiet. But how do you tie it to Anhur and these four dead guys?"

"This is all we've been able to come up with. When our four dead killers' skills weren't quite up to career military, they went to work for the civilian government. Well, they were supposed to work for them and did until about four years ago when our change in administration changed the way our government does business. These folks found themselves with a rich lifestyle and no income. And since their sense of right and wrong turned out to be no different than the suspects they chased for a living, they began to, ah, help themselves. To give you some perspective, five of the murder victims on the grounds had Special Forces training. For crissake Al, Stanger was formidable but he knew his limitations. He surrounded himself with some impressive brains and muscle yet someone still got to him."

"So what are you thinking, Will? Do you think Frank DiBeto is behind this?"

Agent Greenfield merely shook his head. "I'll agree with you that DiBeto might be ruthless enough to have done something like this, but it just isn't his style."

"Maybe," agreed Martino. "But did you get the report on Stanger's activities for the last few days, yet?" He handed Greenfield a sheet of paper from the folder under his arm. "There was a retired Navy guy that won almost two mill against him in the casino that I'm not supposed to know that Anhur Corporation controls. And I have to wonder where the losing funds came from."

Agent Greenfield stood still for a moment skimming the report for details. "Somebody won big against Joey? In that casino? With the place wired up like that, it ought to be impossible. I'd bet your pension that this person has some insights that we're missing. But, I don't see a great deal of motivation for him to talk to us after he walked out with almost two million dollars. If I were him, I'd be going low profile and enjoying my luck."

"You leave my pension alone, Mister FBI man. Besides, if my pension were dynamite, it wouldn't go 'pop.' If this guy had the smarts to beat Stanger's rigged game, he's probably the kind of guy who doesn't leave tracks."

Agent Greenfield looked around the security post. "Yeah, I'm guessing you're right, Captain, but I just had another thought."

"C'mon then, Will, share."

Agent Greenfield swept his arm to indicate the four bodies under the white sheets. "We both seem to agree that none of our players appeared to have the training or the temperament to have planned this thing. What if dear old Mr. DiBeto knew that he couldn't take a black ops agent to the regular police? The public exposure would be disastrous, a media circus. Nevertheless, he's got a rogue outfit within his own organization, and this rogue leader is now throwing a spotlight on the entire organization with his over-the-top behavior. If I were the boss, I'd take the bad actors out, quiet and quick.

"The spook world is very sensitive to any indication of weakness and internal strife within an agency. Any hint of it would have opponents circling like sharks in bloody water. I get the impression that it's a very political world. DiBeto wouldn't have gotten another contract and, at the very least, his organization would've been disbanded. I think that a man in Franklin DiBeto's position would hire somebody outside of normal channels to do some internal clean up."

"Agent Greenfield, you have a devious and twisted mind. I think it fits. DiBeto would never use one of his usual troops, like the infamous, but in my opinion fictitious, Crubari. It would point right back to him, which would cause a ton of problems inside his organization. And I gotta tell ya; this Navy guy walking away with almost two million dollars from somebody else's rigged game smells as if our sailor has himself some powerful help. This may even be a smokescreen for a payoff. But it still leaves a big question."

"How do you get four hired killers to commit suicide?"

"Exactly. Got an answer?"

Agent William Greenfield looked once again at the four corpses in the corner. "I don't, Al. However, it seems a safe bet that Captain Jacob Michael Sabio ought to be able to give us the answer. Everything points to that. I think that my next move is to find him and ask him some questions."

CHAPTER 12

CRUBARI WATCHED THROUGH OPEN doors as Franklin DiBeto stormed down the hallway to the private study of his compound. His short legs were like pistons on some demonic engine pumping his two-hundred-pound bulk forward. Even though he stood only five feet and five inches tall, his current mood made his personality fill any room he entered. His skin tone that was normally pallid was flushed.

DiBeto had just endured a brief, intense grilling from the Las Vegas police concerning Stanger's death and the bizarre suicide-execution. Crubari had listened in on the interrogation from the security station with great interest. DiBeto had tried to maintain the posture of an aggrieved mentor, mourning his protégé's early end, but he was not up to it. DiBeto had all but told the police that Joseph Stanger had gone rogue.

Stanger did this to the agency even though DiBeto had bailed him out not so many months before, when it was brought to his attention that one of Joey's inner circle of operatives, part of The Office, as they called themselves, was actually a Department of Justice agent. As part of the never-ending feuds between the government's most powerful enforcement agencies, the agent was looking for evidence of corruption to humiliate DiBeto and to discredit the Anhur Corporation.

Crubari had found out early about the Department of Justice mole that had infiltrated his operation. He did the only thing he could do. He had DiBeto cut him out of the inner circle. After all, they were both working for the same government. While DiBeto was not above eliminating someone in the government that was threatening his operation, there would be too much attention brought on Anhur at a time when he could ill afford it.

The mole finally left Anhur, but later DiBeto found out that the agent and his family had died in a traffic accident. DiBeto immediately called in Crubari to find out if it was really an accident. Crubari remembered the look on DiBeto's face when he told him that it was Stanger's Hummer that had caused the accident. DiBeto immediately began making phone calls to keep his office from being terminated. Fortunately for both DiBeto and Stanger, one of Stanger's many women chose that same evening to be fed up with him and slapped him with the narrow end of a large kitchen knife. Stanger thus had a perfect alibi for the family murders, since he was in the emergency room being stitched up at the time of the crash. Nobody ever asked what had happened to Stanger's woman.

To further compound DiBeto's problems was this Jake Sabio character that had walked out of his casino with almost two million dollars. That was his agency's money. Not to mention the stolen cash that seeded the game. If the cash was found, it could lead to Stanger, which could lead to DiBeto. Worse, if he did not go and get it back, others would think he could not manage his office. That could prove fatal for DiBeto. Office managers did not retire. They were terminated.

Crubari had intimated that Sabio was somehow responsible for Stanger's death. Joseph Stanger had made himself into the kind of employee who could not be tolerated under any conditions. He forced his unfortunate end upon himself. It was very bad for business to have one of your own killed, but you cannot look weak. Sabio, Crubari continued, had almost certainly cased the game, bribed his way into some very sensitive information, and figured out Stanger's hidden little tricks.

When Crubari had finished his talk with DiBeto, Sabio was a dangerous customer and an enemy of his agency. The kind you rush to get out of the store. Crubari had convinced DiBeto that he needed his money back and he needed to find out who had helped Sabio.

Crubari also pointed out that Chris Bruno, one of his senior security people, was missing. If the FBI had him, then DiBeto had a problem, since Bruno had set up most of the security systems on the compound. If one of the other agencies had him, then DiBeto had a much more serious problem.

Crubari felt concern about this Jake Sabio character. Two weeks ago, he mused, nobody had even heard of Jake Sabio. Then he shows up and he is like a bad luck charm. Stanger's crooked game gets cracked with stolen company seed money, Bruno disappears, a hit on Sabio goes sour and, most of all, Joey's compound becomes a slaughterhouse.

At that point, DiBeto crashed through the doors of his study with the fury of a category five hurricane and threw the doors closed behind him with an echoing boom. He paced up and down the room, as if trying to drive off some pent up energy. When he shot a glance into a dark corner, he noticed Crubari although he had been standing very still in the shadows.

"Get the hell out of the dark, Crowbar." He snapped. "I don't like it when you do that."

Crubari took a step forward but remained in the same light that he had been before.

DiBeto's pacing was nearly a charge from one end of the room to the other. "What happened at that damn cabin? Why couldn't those four morons take care of one unarmed man?"

"They were outmatched."

DiBeto growled, "You're damn right they were outmatched! Those four idiots had guns and night-vision goggles and you're telling me that Sabio had squat."

Crubari nodded slightly from the shadows. "That is what I observed."

DiBeto stopped abruptly and faced Crubari. "So you're telling me that some unarmed guy in his forties gets jumped by four armed, trained killers in their late twenties and early thirties and the old, defenseless, naked guy creams them."

"That is what I reported."

"And you didn't see a thing on your own night-vision goggles, right?"

"My directives were to monitor Rabbit and his crew and not interfere with any actions taking place. My further directives were to remain unobserved. As I have reported, from my position of concealment, I was only able to discern that Rabbit and his team were taken alive."

DiBeto continued pacing. "But Sabio *let them go!* He had them cold in the middle of nowhere. He could have done anything he wanted to them and then disposed of the bodies. Nobody would have found them for centuries up there. Why did he let them go? Who is this guy? If he's agency trained, why doesn't it come up on his file?"

Crubari said nothing. DiBeto walked to his desk and retrieved a Cuban cigar from the humidor on his desk, but he did not light it. "Ya know," continued DiBeto, "I think that this Jake Sabio is a federal agent of some kind. He retires from the Navy and magically shows up in my casino." DiBeto stopped pacing, lit his cigar and took a few puffs. "That much, at least, I can understand." When he was sure that the cigar was lit, he spun towards Crubari and bellowed, "Then he walks out of MY casino with almost two million of MY money and nobody touches him. What agency would have him do that? Why? This is bad for business!"

"Perhaps he's not a federal agent. He could be a private contractor."

DiBeto started his furious pacing again. "I want him found, but I want him brought to me. I'm going to sweat his story out of him and find out exactly who he's working for. Then I'm going to make him pay for the aggravation that he's caused me."

Crubari spoke up. "Do you want to do this for the standard fee?"

DiBeto kept pacing and puffing on his cigar. "Your standard fee's fine. And if you can get him to me within ten days, you can keep any of the money that he has left."

Crubari nodded. "I agree to the terms. Also, I took the liberty of placing a tracer on the woman's aircraft."

"Then you know where he is. Go get him."

"The tracer flew from Phoenix to Mexico City at a speed that was too fast for the aircraft they were using. Sabio must have found the device and placed it on another airplane to divert me. I also took the liberty to track his credit card usage. It goes from California to Florida at a time when I know that he was in the aircraft. I find him a worthy challenge."

DiBeto wheeled on Crubari. "I don't care squat about 'challenge.' He's a question mark, Crubari. I don't like question marks. In my experience, question marks turn into hooks that drag people away or drag them under. I want this question mark found and brought here in good enough shape to answer some questions. Do we have a deal?"

Neither man made any move to shake hands and seal the deal. It was common knowledge in the inner circle that Antonio Crubari found it offensive to touch human flesh. The Crowbar merely nodded his head slightly and said, "We have a deal."

CHAPTER 13

THE DAY AT THE clinic left Carin spent but hopeful. Her worst fears upon arriving at the facility in the early morning hours had been that their insistence on paying for the diagnosis with cash would raise insurmountable questions. Interestingly enough, the admittance clerk acted as if that was an everyday occurrence. It actually expedited their processing and they began the battery of tests at 7 a.m. sharp. The last tests were not completed until just after 7 p.m. and Carin and Jake found themselves dragging into their motel rooms two hours later with Carin wanting nothing more than to crawl into bed.

The first indication that she was not going to get her wish was Fred giving out two warning clicks as soon as she opened her door. She immediately closed the door and stood still as if frozen in place. She could not sense anyone else so she moved quickly to the door to the adjoining room. Jake was already there when she pulled it open. They both moved to Fred, but it was Carin that spoke. "Fred, is everything okay?" To help Fred in conversations, they had decided to use Fred's name at the beginning of any discussions.

"Carin, it appears that part of the protocol at the clinic is to send an inquiry with your name, photograph, fingerprints and DNA. They use it to review previous medical history and to help them with their diagnosis. Apparently you both signed medical releases to that effect."

Jake leaned forward. "Fred, old buddy, we signed about a thousand forms this morning releasing everything and anything, but we gave them fake names. How can they match anything up?"

Fred persisted. "Captain Sabio, I am sorry to inform you that the scanners that they use to do an initial screening automatically get fingerprints, photos and DNA and match it to previous medical information on file. For example, the last time you visited a medical facility was at Nellis Air Force Base. You saw a Doctor June Robbins. You complained about headaches and feverishness. You denied treatment for the illness. You requested information on your baldness. Does that coincide with your recollection?"

Carin was beginning to get a cold foreboding. Jake looked at Carin with worry. "Fred, it matches perfectly with the facts," said Jake. "What else have you got?"

"I was monitoring the clinic intranet while the two of you were getting your physical examinations. Jake, when your DNA went out, it came back with your name and a tag that you had been the subject of a federal government query. As soon as your name was in the file, a second query was initiated. I cannot identify its origin."

Carin looked at Jake. She began to twirl her amethyst ring with her thumb. "Okay Fred. I understand there are two people, or groups of people, looking for Captain Sabio. I also understand that one of them is so sophisticated that not even you can find a trace." Carin began pacing back and forth in the tiny room. "Dammit Jake. We've gotten on somebody's radar screen and we've got to get off."

Carin turned her head to directly address the MI. "Fred, what's the status of the workups that were done today?"

"The raw data is on file of every test. The blood workup data was sent to the Centers for Disease Control and Prevention in Atlanta. Apparently, there are some anomalies with your blood chemistry."

"Fred, can you download our data from the clinic computers and then erase the clinic's files?"

"Yes. It is done."

"Fred, can you also see what the CDC has on us, load what they have and then erase it off their system?"

"It is already done."

"Fred, thank you. Is there any other data that has been sent out by the clinic on us that you think we should retrieve?"

"I will check and advise you."

"Fred, thank you. Jake and I will have to go back to the clinic and see whether there are any paper copies that we should eliminate."

Jake looked up at Carin's last statement. "Do you think that's wise, Doctor?"

Carin had no time to argue. "Do you think that we have a choice, Captain? At least one federal agency and someone else have gotten very interested in you all of a sudden."

"Truce Doctor, you're right. We can't leave our data lying around if someone is already interested in us. Standard combat ops doctrine; knowledge is the most powerful weapon available, so, in our case, denying knowledge to someone that intends to interfere with our plans makes sense. It's straight out of Sun Tzu – 'all warfare is based on deception.' How do you intend to waltz in? It seemed to be a fairly secure facility."

Carin turned to the MI. "Fred, can you help us with entry?"

"I have given the two of you access to the entire facility. The password to any secure area will be by typing nine '9's into the keypads. Unfortunately, you will need an electronic badge."

Jake tapped a finger on his lips. "There was a guard sitting at the front door in a secure area. We can try telling him that we left our badges in the clinic. He might believe one badge, but two is going to be hard to sell. Even if we get in, the guard would remember it and that is just as bad." Jake paused for a moment. "Carin, you have to go in and get a temporary badge. You have the medical background, so it has to be you. I'll stay at a phone booth by the front entrance. If you flash the nine '9's, Fred can call me and I'll bluff my way past the guard. Are there any questions on the plan?"

Carin shook her head. "No questions, Captain. I like the plan and I agree with your logic. Fred, do you have any problems with the plan?"

"No Doctor, I do not. I would urge haste. That query went out to the federal agency this morning. I cannot find a record that indicates someone has been sent to investigate, but that is no guarantee. A simple phone call could have started an investigator in this direction. I am not able to monitor for such an occurrence. They could be here already. Every moment is vital."

Jake grabbed his jacket and headed for the door. "Let's get hot. Fred, I'll dial nine '9's when I get to a phone booth. Will you be able to detect that from outside the clinic?"

"Yes Jake. I strongly recommend that you both hurry."

Jake and Carin drove at the speed limit back to the clinic. They both felt an urgent need to hurry, but refused to run the risk of being stopped by the police. Jake parked the car as close to the front door of the clinic as he could while keeping it in the dark shadows. There was no reason to leave evidence on security cameras. Carin disconnected the car's dome lights to prevent them from coming on as they opened the doors. When they were both ready, Carin gave a nod and they exited the car at the same time. Jake ran to the nearest pay phone, punched in the numbers and then retreated to the shadows. Carin ran to the front of the clinic while staying in the shadows as long as possible. When she was no longer able to stay in the shadows, she stepped out onto the walkway and strode purposefully to the main entrance. She had on a baseball cap pulled low over her forehead with her hair bunched up inside. She was also sporting a down-filled ski jacket that draped down to her knees. Carin hoped that she looked as if she had been called in to consult on a case and had dressed hurriedly. If they were lucky, it was a sight that a front door security guard would see a dozen times a week.

Carin walked in the doors and went straight to the security guard rather than to the card reader to gain access to the clinic. She beamed a bright smile at the guard. "Hi, I'm Doctor Ozarka Jones," said Carin, giving the alias that Fred had set up for her. "I don't think that I've ever met you before."

The guard gave Carin a scowl that looked as if it was a permanent part of his professional face and maintained his station behind a large pane of thick glass. There were no openings to speak through so the guard had to lean forward to a microphone. "No ma'am. How can I help you?"

The guard was a bald-headed man in his late fifties. He still had a firm, lean body that spoke of hard work, determination, and habit. If Carin were to guess, she would say the guard was a former military man, probably from the Marines and most likely an enlisted man. Carin thought to herself, "super sergeant." This man was a former six-striper or better. She had dealt with his type a thousand times in the military and immediately found herself liking the man.

Carin shrugged her shoulders. "I messed up. Doctor Helen Miro called me at home and asked me to look at some charts on a special case. She wanted me to give an opinion before tomorrow so I rushed up here to keep from making it too late an evening. Well, I forgot my badge. Can you issue me a temporary badge please?"

The guard leaned over in the other direction to look at his computer screen. He wrote some entries on a clipboard page and then went back to his computer screen. Carin started to become anxious when the process dragged on for over five minutes. Had the guard hit a panic button of some kind? What was taking so long? Carin envisioned a fleet of police cars racing up the drive and surrounding the clinic. Her pulse rate began to pick up. She imagined scores of blue uniforms leaping out of their cars, bullhorns and guns at the ready. Her breathing started to become quicker and deeper. Suddenly the police cars lifted off the ground and circled the Earth. The police officers in their blue uniforms transformed into something else – something that was not human. They were aiming their guns at the Earth. They were about to pull the trigger.

"Doctor, are you all right?"

Carin came back to the present moment with a start. "I'm sorry. I guess I was daydreaming."

The guard eyed her closely for a moment. "Here is a temporary badge." A tray slid out from where the guard was sitting. Inside was a black and white, plastic card. "Don't forget to deposit it in the box behind you as you leave."

"I won't. Thanks for your help."

"One more thing, Doctor."

"Yes?"

"I am supposed to give you this big, long lecture about security, but I think that you need sleep more than you need a bunch of lip-flapping from me. Let's make believe that we did the lecture. Please try to remember your badge next time. Okay?"

Carin smiled at the guard and snapped him her best academy salute. "Say no more, Master Guns. I'm a converted heathen."

That made the guard smile and he made a shooing motion with one hand. He was obviously saying something funny to himself, but the microphone was off. Carin took the opportunity to slide the card in the reader and escape down the hall.

Carin went directly to the office of Doctor Helen Miro. According to Fred, Doctor Miro was the diagnostician who had taken over her and Jake's cases. The great bulk of the paperwork would be in Doctor Miro's office or in her in-basket. The hospital portion of the clinic was nearly deserted. Everyone was in bed at this late hour where they belonged, thought Carin. She reached the doctors' offices and punched nine '9's into the cipher lock by Doctor Miro's door, walked in and shut the door behind her. She did not feel she had been seen by anybody, but how would she know? She picked up the phone on Doctor Miro's desk, dialed the nines, and said, "I'm here" into the receiver before promptly hanging up.

Doctor Miro's office area was stacked with files everywhere. There were files stacked on chairs, stacked in boxes, stacked in corners, but her desk was clean except for two files lying side by side. Jake and Carin's files were the only files on Doctor Miro's desk. Carin opened her file and checked to make sure all the lab reports were there. If they were not, she would have to go to each of the labs individually and that would take time. They had been to ten different labs and there were eleven lab reports in the file. What was the eleventh?

Carin went to the tenth lab report. It was the blood workup. There were little yellow labels stuck all over the five sheets of the report. Comment stickers saying, "that's not right" and "machine's broken – get it checked" were plastered next to the findings. At the end of the tenth lab report, there was an order by Doctor Miro for a full tandem mass spectrometry to be done of their blood. That is odd. Why would Doctor Miro want to know what chemical elements are in our blood? The elements should remain pretty much the same even if there are some big health problems.

The eleventh lab report was the results of a Raman spectroscopy and had only one yellow note on it. Doctor Miro had written, "Ti? Au? Pt? What are they eating?" Carin looked at the list of elements on the lab report and she had to agree with Doctor Miro. High levels of elements such as carbon were explicable, but what were titanium, platinum, gold, nickel, copper, and silicon doing in their blood? Both Carin and Jake had almost identical amounts of the various elements on their test results. Carin closed her eyes to think. She was so tired that she did not trust her own judgment in this, but something was tickling her thoughts. She knew if she chased after the idea, it would disappear. Instead, she imagined that it was a fluttering moth just barely out of reach. She took a deep breath and relaxed her mind.

One does not catch a moth by chasing after it, she thought to herself. *One catches it by being perfectly still and putting a light close by to attract the moth. Then when the moth lands, one slowly moves to gently envelope the fragile, flying creature in their hand.*

Carin finally caught the fragile thought and began to inspect it. The more that she inspected the thought, the more a certainty firmed up in her mind. The thought made sense. It answered so many questions there were few holes left that needed to be filled. It was as if Carin had had this huge landscape filled with craters and deep crevices. She had opened a jar that contained this thought and its pieces had tumbled onto the landscape and beautifully filled all the porous and uneven texture of the scene and left a smooth, glassy surface. The only thing wrong with this idea was that it was completely, totally and unquestionably impossible.

The phone rang and jarred her out of meditation. She froze with momentary disorientation, looked at the wall clock and saw that she had been in her trance for more than an hour. The phone rang twice more and Carin picked it up. "Doctor's office."

It was Fred's voice. "There is a man about to enter your office."

At that moment, a tall man entered the office and appeared startled to find it occupied. He gave the appearance that he was not listening to the conversation, but Carin was not taking any chances. She turned her attention on the newcomer. "May I help you?"

The stranger reached into his pocket and produced a badge. "I am Agent William Greenfield, FBI. Are you Doctor Miro?"

Carin held up a finger to the FBI man signaling him to wait one minute and spoke on the phone. "I just had someone come in the office. Let me call you back."

"Carin, I heard his name and I'll see whether I can find out anything about him."

Carin smiled up to the waiting agent and spoke to Fred. "That'll be fine." She immediately hung up the phone and turned her attention to the man.

Carin reached across the desk to shake the agent's hand and began to size him up. She would guess his age to be thirty-three. He was easily six foot one with light brown hair that was cut short and parted in the middle. The most peculiar thing to Carin was that his jeans were pressed and starched. They had a crease along the front. Carin did not know what to make of a man who pressed his jeans, much less one who starched them.

Agent Greenfield came forward but did not extend his hand. "Are you Doctor Miro?"

Carin opened her face into a bright smile and said, "No, I'm Doctor Jones. Helen asked me to review a case before tomorrow morning."

Greenfield reached into his jacket pocket and pulled out a picture. It was Jake. He was in his Navy uniform and it looked as if it came straight from Jake's personnel folder. "Do you have a patient that looks like this?"

"No. Is he in trouble with the law or something?" Carin asked conversationally.

"I just need to ask him some questions."

Agent Greenfield began to come around the desk and reach for the folders on Doctor Miro's desk. "Are these the patients that Doctor Miro reviewed today?" That was as far as the FBI man got.

Carin immediately spoke in her command voice. "DON'T YOU TOUCH THAT!"

The FBI man instinctively drew back. Carin was between Greenfield and the desk before he knew what happened. She was pushing him back, jabbing her finger in his chest, and speaking in a loud voice. "Mister, I am giving you the benefit of the doubt at this moment."

Agent Greenfield attempted to get the upper hand. "Lady, you are obstructing ..."

"THE ONLY THING I WANT TO HEAR FROM YOU IS 'YES, MA'AM' AND 'NO MA'AM'. DO YOU UNDERSTAND?"

"Look, I'm sorr..."

"I SAID, 'DO YOU UNDERSTAND?'"

"Yes ma'am."

"Now you don't have a warrant do you?"

"This is a matter of National ..."

"YES MA'AM OR NO MA'AM"

"No ma'am."

"And can I assume that you are aware of the physician-patient privacy statutes in effect in this state."

"Yes ma'am."

"Then am I to assume that you feel that one of these patients is the victim of abuse needing immediate protection?"

"Uh, no ma'am."

"Or that you have a court order defining the release of that information specifically to you?"

"No ma'am."

"Can I further assume it would be embarrassing to wake up a judge at this hour and have this little encounter explained to him while you are trying to get that warrant?"

Greenfield's eyes went slightly wide. "Yes, ma'am."

Carin squared herself off in front of Greenfield less than an arm's reach away, blocking him from the desk. Her feet were ten inches apart, legs straight. Her hands were folded into each other behind her back with her arms against her side. Her weight was balanced between the balls of her feet and her heels. And her eyes … her eyes were lasers whose anger Greenfield had just aroused. "Then I feel we have a course of action that we both can agree on," she said evenly. "We are going to assume we live in a country where personal freedoms are not taken lightly. We are going to assume further that, in keeping with this concept, certain processes are in place to make sure that individual freedoms are not abrogated. You are going to go to your home or hotel or wherever it is you are staying. You are going to get some sleep and wake up early and refreshed in the morning. You are going to get a warrant and get a look at the records that you want because you are going to use proper procedure. For my part, I am going to assume you are tired for whatever reason or are simply having a bad day. If you leave now, come back in the morning, and follow the proper procedure, I am going to forget this happened. Are we agreed on this?"

Agent Greenfield looked as if he was going to put up an argument, but instead said, "Yes ma'am."

"I think this would be a good time for you to go."

Greenfield put a hand on the doorknob, paused for a moment at the door, turned to face Carin with his eyes squinting slightly and mouth partially open before giving a shiver, and pushing his way out the door.

Carin went to the phone and dialed the nines. Jake and Fred both answered. "Fred, can you monitor the security cameras and make sure that our FBI friend leaves."

"Yes, Carin. I will let you know when he pulls out of the parking lot."

Jake broke in. "Fred, try to get a make, model and license plate so we can be looking out for him."

"Jake, I will do that, too."

Carin had to think fast. "Fred, can you erase all traces of my being here?"

"Carin, I can erase the security tapes but I cannot do anything about fingerprints or other biological evidence and I cannot do anything about anyone who might have seen you."

Carin replayed all her movements in her mind and began scrubbing and wiping the areas she had touched. She finally wiped down the phone and put on her gloves. "Fred, I'm ready to come out. Is our agent leaving?"

"Yes Carin. He just now is pulling out of the parking lot."

Carin grabbed the files from the desktop and put them under her baggy coat. "Fred, wait until you can no longer see Jake or me on the surveillance cameras and then begin to erase the tapes here in the clinic. Try to make it look as if nothing was tampered with if you can."

Jake spoke up. "Fred, Carin, we need to leave this town immediately. Fred, as soon as we get back to the hotel, we will be packing up and flying out of here."

He was right, of course. There was an FBI agent here already. There was also the other unknown party that had put a query on Jake. They could be anywhere. Carin, Jake and Fred had to leave immediately and put some distance between themselves and the clinic. The only reason to go back to the hotel was for Fred and that was going to be a risk. She just hoped that between the three of them and the data they had picked up, they could figure out what was happening to them. It had better be soon because it felt as if they were running out of time. She was beginning to shiver due to the fever and her headache came on so strongly at times that she had to stop moving and close her eyes. However, the worst part was that she was exhausted. She was daydreaming and falling asleep on her feet and she knew it was the same for Jake. It did not matter, they had to keep moving, or they would be trapped forever. They would be no better than rats running in some scientists' maze.

Carin sighed and scrubbed her face with both hands. Tired or not, there would be no rest tonight.

CHAPTER **14**

THEY DROVE BACK TO the hotel room at the posted speed limit. Once in the room, Jake and Carin threw their few belongings into bags, grabbed Fred and were out the door in less than two minutes. They had paid cash for their hotel room earlier that day so they left the keys inside the room. They had fueled the aircraft prior to departing the airport the night before and had tied it down outside so that they would not need assistance to prepare the little craft.

It was a silent ballet when they got to the aircraft. Jake unloaded the bags and took the car back to the rental car agency. Carin preflighted the airplane and secured both the bags and Fred before going to the operations desk to settle the bill. She was reviewing the weather patterns when Jake walked up behind her. "Looks like south or southwest," he said.

She turned to him and thought for a second. "You have a flying background, don't you?"

"I told you that, didn't I? I flew with the Navy for the first five years of my career but was medically grounded after I had to eject. The ejection affected my right eye and the flight doctors grounded me."

"Was the ejection your fault?"

Jake did not take offense. He had been asked that question a thousand times over the years. "The board cleared me if that's what you mean."

"No, that's not what I meant," said Carin testily. "You know exactly what I'm getting at."

That was a tougher question. Jake hesitated a second before answering. "I think about the two seconds that I had to make my decision at least once a day. I think about the information that I had, the actions that I performed, and the ones that I didn't. The best I can tell you is if I had to do it again today, after twenty years of second guessing myself, I'd do exactly the same thing."

Carin stood as if trying to come to a decision. Finally she gave her head a slight nod and said, "Good, because it's your leg tonight."

Jake froze. "Carin, I can't fly your airplane. I haven't touched a stick in over fifteen years."

Carin started walking to the airplane. "Don't worry. After tonight you won't be able to say that anymore."

Jake ran to catch up with her. "I don't even have a license. Carin, you don't …"

Carin began a laugh that started softly and rose to just short of hysterics. "We're infected by a bug of unknown origin that's probably going to kill us soon, we're probably both on the FBI's most wanted list and we still have some third party out there that has expressed an unwelcome interest in you and you're worried about a license?"

She turned and faced Jake. "Listen up, Captain. I don't know if you've noticed, but I'm beat. I can barely stand up. You've gotta take on some of the flying duties. You've already been running the navigation systems and the engine controls. The stick and rudder is the easy part. It's like riding a bicycle. Besides, I'll be right there beside you if something happens."

"Okay, but you have to stay awake for a while to give me a good checkout."

"Captain, I'll stay awake if you can keep me awake."

They arrived at the aircraft and Jake started to get into the right side. Carin grabbed him by the sleeve and pointed to the other side of the cockpit. "The pilot-in-command sits in the left seat of this aircraft, Captain Sabio." With that, she kicked the chock out from in front of the main gear tire on her side, crawled into the right seat and waited for Jake.

Jake got in the left seat and pulled out the checklist he had seen Carin use. As it turned out, he did not need her help at all. He had completely assimilated the little airplane's idiosyncrasies by watching Carin. He started the aircraft, called for clearance and was up and away before there was a chance for second thoughts to set in.

Carin watched his every move carefully and smiled. "Captain, you must've been one fantastic fighter pilot. You've lost none of your touch."

Jake sat up a little straighter at the compliment. "I was the best."

Carin chuckled. To change the subject, she asked, "Where do you want to go?"

"How does Idaho sound? I was thinking we could land at one of the small private fields down there and spend a couple of days resting and going over the data that we have."

Carin settled back in her seat. "The R&R part sounds good to me, but

I think I have part of our puzzle solved. I just need to bounce it off of other heads because mine is not firing on all cylinders right now."

Jake set the autopilot and confirmed all the systems were in order. Only then did he turn his attention to Carin. "What piece of the puzzle do you think you have?"

"I think that I know what hasn't infected us."

"Great! That's ninety percent of the problem, isn't it? What do we not have?"

"We don't have a viral infection, a bacterial infection, a fungal infection, a protozoal infection, or a mechanical infection."

Jake looked at the controls of the aircraft to make sure everything was in order prior to answering. "How do you know all this?"

"In a nutshell, that's what the Ingreti clinic results said — except for the mechanical part. I added that in myself."

"What do you mean when you say 'mechanical' infection? I don't understand that part."

"I mean like bugs or something similar."

Jake looked hard at Carin. Before he could say anything, Fred said, "Carin, excuse me for interrupting, but you said it was permissible when I had something relevant. I believe I should state that no one has been able to build viable nanites. The breakthroughs in material processing alone are decades away, not to mention all of the other problems like command and control. It has been mentioned in scientific literature that it would be easier to get an aircraft carrier to the moon than to build a single functioning nanite. A great number of programs are trying. I know the Pentagon has funded several programs, but they have all proven to be technologically premature."

Carin nodded her head. "Fred, I agree with you. We can't make nanites. And when I say 'we', I mean that nobody on this planet can make them and won't be able to make them for a handful of decades. But there's more." She turned around to face Fred directly. "Fred, I have not asked you this before, but are your processors molecular computers?"

"Yes Carin, they are. However, my systems are entirely too crude to scale to the size of a nanomachine."

Jake held up his hands. "Whoa. You're losing me. What's a nanite and what's a nanomachine?"

Carin looked at the M.I. and asked, "Fred, would you like to try and explain?"

Fred launched into a discourse without preamble. "The terms 'nanite' and 'nanomachine' are often used interchangeably. They refer to any mechanical or electromechanical device that is measured in nanometers or one millionth of a millimeter. Atoms are roughly a tenth to a half of a nanometer in diameter depending on which element it is you are measuring. So, if you put several atoms together to form a molecule, it could be measured in nanometers. The idea of a nanomachine is to put a number of molecules together to perform a specific function."

Carin looked at Jake. "Do you follow so far? Nanites are little machines about the size of viruses that are designed to do things they are programmed to do. However, to do any good, they have to be smart. Let's say I want to fix our DNA in some way. Our DNA is in the nucleus of each of our cells. The nucleus is about five thousand nanometers big, which means I could manipulate it with a machine about one thousand nanometers big, which means I can have about five thousand molecules. These five thousand molecules in each nanite have to perform many tasks. They have to propel the nanite through the body somehow. They also have to be able to detect an individual cell. Once they have identified a single cell, they have to propel themselves into the cell and identify the cell nucleus. Now the difficult part begins. Once inside the cell, they have to cut and paste DNA strands. Most of all, they have to have a template of what they are trying to build. Now it's time for a reality check. Fred, how many possible combinations of DNA are there?"

"Carin, there are approximately ten raised to the twenty-fourth power different viable combinations for the human genome."

Jake's eyes went wide. "Are you kidding? That's an impossible number."

Carin was nodding her head. "Exactly! It's an absolutely impossible number to get your mind around. The most current number anyone has for the number of stars in the known universe is seventy sextillion. That's a seven followed by twenty-two zeroes. One teeny little DNA chain in the nucleus of just one of our cells has one hundred times more than that many possible combinations. There are a thousand times fewer grains of sand on Earth than there are number of possible DNA combinations in a single strand. How can this little nanite bug possibly have a good idea of what to do?"

Jake cracked a slight smile. "You're enjoying yourself, aren't you? You enjoy playing 'stump the dummy' with some poor, old seaweed-sifting sub jockey."

Carin graced Jake with a special smile. "Yeah, actually I do. But, more than anything, I need you two to follow me on this and try to shoot holes in it because here is where it gets really ugly."

Jake's smile vanished and he scrubbed his face with both hands. "Great. There's more and it's uglier."

"I'm afraid so. It seems that we're infected by some unknown bug that is doing weird things to us, but mostly we are reacting to it. A nanite is basically a chunk of inert metal or glass. We wouldn't react to a nanite infection in the way that we are reacting to this one. That's disregarding the fact that nobody could possibly build one. And another thing, whatever bug it is that's infected us is modifying us on a genetic level. The bugs are essentially repairing damaged DNA as quickly as they can wherever they find it."

Jake's expression changed to one of worry. "What makes you think that?"

"First of all, your hair growing back was an indication. I wouldn't call it an improvement, but my guess is that the bugs saw your male-pattern baldness as a deviance and corrected it. However, I think it's much more invasive than that. I think that the bugs are not only repairing our DNA, but also modifying it. Only about two percent of our DNA goes into making us human, the rest is what scientists used to call 'junk DNA.' They were wrong, of course, but the fact is we don't know what that other ninety-eight percent is supposed to do. I think that the bugs are … I don't know what the right word is. 'Completing' is perhaps good enough for now. My best guess is they have a template that they are working against and are completing us in some manner."

"I'm lost, Doctor. You just said that this thing would require a lot of intelligence. How can several thousand molecules hold anywhere near the capacity?"

Carin slumped back in her seat. "I don't know. It's an impossible situation."

Carin spun her amethyst ring with her thumb for a moment before turning to the little MI and saying, "Fred, how much memory, and computing capacity can a molecular computer with five thousand atoms possess?"

"Carin, it would be able to manipulate approximately one hundred thousand bits."

"Fred, I agree. I think that we can all agree a molecular computer of that size would not be very smart at all. It would have about as much capacity as the earliest personal computers. Fred, how much memory, and computing capacity can a quantum computer with five thousand atoms possess?"

"Carin, due to the nature of quantum bits, a few hundred can represent ten raised to the ninetieth power different machine states. Further, the machine state could be changed immediately."

Carin let out a low whistle and was silent for a moment. Finally, she turned to the MI and gave a small bow from her seat. "Fred, thank you. I didn't know that."

Jake looked at Carin. "Translation?"

Carin sat still, twisting the amethyst ring on her right hand before answering.

"If our bugs use quantum computation, the capability in just one or two bugs can far exceed all the computational power on this planet, including Fred, you, me and every human thrown into the mix. On top of that, it would be inconceivably fast. Bottom line is that the computational power exists to map our DNA and make decisions and not even break a sweat while it was doing it."

Jake threw up his hands and said, "All right! We know what we have. We're halfway to a cure."

Carin did not answer and simply stared off into space while twirling the ring on her right hand. Jake brought his arms down after noticing Carin's pensive state. "Uh oh," he said. "Not 'all right.' What did I miss?"

Carin was still staring into space when she answered. "It's our fevers and headaches. According to our blood work, this bug is a chunk of metal or glass. Remember the elements the clinic found in our system? They're neutral at the concentrations that we're seeing. However, our immune system is reacting to something organic. If these bugs are just bio-neutral chunks of metal or glass, why is our immune system attacking them? If it isn't the bugs, what's it attacking? The bottom line is that we wouldn't be sick at all if the bugs were nanites."

Jake became very still and was soon lost in thought. "Carin, about what you said before. I'm guessing nobody on this planet can build a quantum computer either. Would that be a fair statement?"

Carin stopped twirling her ring and crossed her arms. Finally, she said, "If the bug that's infected us is structured with a quantum computer, which I'm now convinced it must be, it didn't come from here." Carin tapped a flat palm on her arm. "It's gotta be the explosion at the crater. It wasn't a random event. It couldn't be because it was guided directly to us. What I can't figure out is the motivation. Just for grins, let's assume the Martians, or E.T., or something wanted to infect us for some unknown reason. Why would another intelligence go to the incredible expense and accept the great likelihood of failure to pull off this stunt in this manner? It makes sense that a couple of thousand things could have gone wrong and their mission would have been unsuccessful. What an incredibly stupid way to design this mission!"

"I've thought the same thing at least a dozen times. How would you have done it?" Jake asked.

"I would have landed an intelligence of some kind, biological or otherwise, corralled us into a hospital environment, and ensured that this thing was done right."

"So you think we were pushed in this direction?"

Carin thought about that for a second. "Yeah. That's a good way to put it. We were given this push, this impulse to send us in a specific direction for a certain reason. But it was done in such a haphazard manner that I can't figure out why we got this specific impulse."

"Well, Doctor, while I think your logic makes a great deal of sense, it's been my experience that an opponent's stratagem looks completely reasonable in hindsight. If we had all the facts that our infector had, I have a feeling the plan of whoever infected us would appear nothing short of brilliant. Can you answer me a question? Would these bugs be considered intelligent life?"

Carin shook her head. "Jake, I don't think we want to get into metaphysics right now. Let's just say that the bugs have as much right to claim to be 'intelligent life' as you or Fred or me."

Jake looked sharply at Carin. "You're including Fred as an example of intelligent life?"

Carin was perplexed. "Of course I am because it is, but let me get back to our immediate problem. How many bugs do you think that the human body would need to keep it healthy?"

Jake shrugged. "I wouldn't even know where to start my guess. I would have to know the capability of the little bugs. How many DNA chains can it fix in a given time period? What's its life expectancy? Can it reproduce? Is there more than one type of bug? Are the bugs biological, bio-mechanical or just plain mechanical?"

Carin sat up straight and stared at Jake with a wide-eyed gaze. "That's it! That's what was missing. You are brilliant. Of course, there has to be more than one type of bug in our systems. There are too many different manifestations. If they're manipulating DNA, why not use a virus that can already do that. That's why our immune systems are going nuts. It's not one bug that it's trying to attack, it's several different types, and they are at least partly biological. Fred, do you concur with the Captain's concept?"

Fred took a moment to respond. "Carin, it would fit in excellently with the fact that the two of you began manifesting new capabilities almost immediately. I would assume that the coercion manifestation of the infection could be included as a survival mechanism."

Carin was nodding agreement. "Fred, I think that you're right. Can you please do the Captain and me a favor? Could you please try to catalog how many different kinds of bugs there are using the different abilities we have exhibited? I don't know what I expect to get out of that, but even if it does nothing else, we might get some insight into whoever designed this thing."

"I will begin immediately."

She shifted her attention to Jake. "Does this make sense?"

"Well, I take it the conventional wisdom is that we got infected by bugs, they are at least modifying our DNA as well as performing other functions, and we are sick all the time because our immune systems are working overtime to get rid of them."

Fred interrupted. "Carin, the Captain is incorrect in his statement."

Carin looked at Fred. "Fred, what do you mean by 'incorrect?'"

"The Captain's statement is inaccurate in that the implications that the two of you are 'sick' does not properly state the fact that the two of you are 'dying.' I should point out that this opinion is of four of the doctors at the clinic. After reviewing their notes, I agree with their diagnosis."

Jake leaned back in his seat and checked the aircraft systems. Finally, he said, "How much time do we have?"

Fred volunteered, "I am calculating three weeks at the earliest and six months at the latest. However, you will lose all motor function several days prior to actually expiring."

Jake turned slowly to the machine. "Thank you, Fred. It is important to know the details of one's own demise."

Fred, still not familiar with sarcasm, said, "Jake, it is my pleasure. I can gladly supply you with more details of the symptoms and the course of the disease if you have time."

Carin was deflated. That's it, she thought. End of the road. Checkout time.

Out of the corner of her eye, she noticed Jake and turned to face him. He was staring straight ahead and sat perfectly still. To any other human observing Jake, he would appear lost in thought, but to Carin, he was almost glowing with an inner light she had never seen before. His features were in such sharp detail that she could see the individual hairs on his head and face.

Slowly he turned to face both Fred and Carin. "Here is what we are going to do. Fred, I want you to backtrack the meteorite path by any means available. I will bet the information is stuck in the astronomical databases somewhere and it will be just a matter of finding it. The good news is that we know exactly where and when it hit. Furthermore, I want you to come up with mobility and functionality upgrades for yourself. We can't keep betting on our good luck that we will not be caught. I want you to be able to move and to manipulate objects on your own. And Fred, one more thing."

"Yes Jake, what is that?"

"Are you familiar with the KISS principle?"

"Yes, Jake. It is a design philosophy based upon the phrase, 'Keep It Simple, Stupid'."

"Exactly. My Air Force friends have a phrase. 'If it's stupid and it works, it ain't stupid.' There is a tendency to over design things initially and we just don't have the time. If you can find something off the shelf that you can modify, then that is less of your computational capacity that is tied up. Do not order anything until you clear it through Carin or me. The most innocuous things that you buy can trigger a response if they aren't handled correctly. Do you understand and agree?"

"Yes Jake. I can begin immediately. Which task has priority?"

"Both. My friend, I am sorry to introduce you to life this way, but there are times when there are competing requirements and failing at either one has dire consequences. This is one of those times. I will not tell you how to proceed, but if you can delegate some of the work, then you can manage the problem from a strategic position. You want to avoid getting into a tactical situation whenever possible. Start subroutines running to look for things, whatever, to help you to stay thinking about solutions to the problems. Just remember to cover your tracks. Nothing should lead to you."

Jake shifted his focus to Carin. "Doctor, you have to see whether there's something we can do to either prolong our lives or heal us completely. You have to buy us some more time. I refuse to believe that we have no options. I'm sorry. I know that you're not a medical doctor by training, but you're as close as we can get."

Carin did not even think to question Jake. It was logical and appropriate. "What will you be doing, Jake?"

"My job will be to put the remaining money into some equipment we can use. I already foresee having to buy those upgrades for Fred."

"So, Jake, do you think this is all going to work?"

Jake gave Carin a haggard look. "It has to work according to our mechanical diagnostician or …"

He did not need to finish. She knew.

CHAPTER 15

WILLIAM GREENFIELD WALKED INTO the Jonas Ingreti Clinic early that morning, carrying the appropriate warrants. He was confident that it was only going to take thirty minutes with the files to get a lead on Captain Jacob Sabio. After all, any names that were in the files would help connect him with Sabio. Next of kin, a few phone numbers, or a mailing address would get him closer. Of course, the members of his team were already bothering the U.S. Navy to get Sabio's records, but that was going to take time. The clinic records were a possible shortcut for Agent Greenfield not to mention the fact that it was standard operating practice to follow all leads in such a case. Armed with the knowledge that he was closing on Sabio, Greenfield entered the clinic at precisely 9 a.m. as he had planned the night before. It was the last thing that went as planned for Agent Greenfield for the rest of the day.

Doctor Helen Miro had proven to be cooperative when he arrived at the clinic. She remembered their telephone conversation of the previous day and since Agent Greenfield had the appropriate warrants, she had escorted him up to her office to begin reviewing the medical files. That was where he had received his first surprise. The patient charts he wanted to review were missing. At first, Doctor Miro assured him that they had simply been misplaced in her messy office. She had begun rummaging around the various piles of charts but then decided it would be easier to look at the test results in the database. That was when Agent Greenfield received his next surprise. The database had no record of the two patients from the previous day. All the other patient records appeared intact, but the two in question were missing. Agent Greenfield began to get a prickling feeling at the base of his neck. He suggested that Doctor Miro call Doctor Ozarka Jones and ask whether she might have gone home with the files. Doctor Miro looked puzzled. She could not recall a Doctor

Jones at the clinic. A quick check with security confirmed that there was no Doctor Ozarka Jones on the staff. Agent Greenfield saw that the situation had spiraled out of control. He went to a phone and called the Agency. He was going to need some expert help before the day was out.

That had been seven hours ago. He had set up a temporary office in one of the consultation rooms. It was a small room that had data, voice and video connections as well as the antiseptic smell of a hospital. It had five rolling chairs that were, he was sure, the exact opposite color of the beige paint on the wall. He set up his operations on the room's single desk.

The clinic personnel were extremely helpful. After all, they wanted to find out how someone had bypassed all their security systems as much as Greenfield did. There was a knock on the door and before Greenfield could answer, a woman with a dark blue blazer with FBI in yellow letters on the back walked in. "Well boss, I've got a report on the security systems for you."

"Already, Glynnis? That was fast."

The female agent shrugged her shoulders. "There's not much I can tell you. It's kind of like our guys told you about the physical evidence. There are no fingerprints anywhere. There's no documentation on any recording device of the activities that occurred last night. At approximately 0400 hours this morning, all the recording devices purged memory. All tapes that had been recording during any time yesterday were degaussed. The tapes that were still in the machines just started up again as if nothing had happened. That of course is impossible to happen on this system. Their security system is darn good — very state-of-the-art. It records stuff for about a day on solid-state chips while putting everything on tape as well. The chips just keep overwriting themselves so that you always have a twenty-four hour record in them, but they pull the tapes every morning and store them in a vault. Instant backup, and the fact that they're completely separate systems supposedly negates the chance for a single hiccup taking out both records. Pretty slick setup, actually."

"So what happened?"

"I haven't the foggiest clue. Absolutely nothing showed up in the logs to indicate anything abnormal happened. According to this system, it performed perfectly last night. However, there's more. The clinic files were erased and there is no evidence of the erasing."

Greenfield favored her with a blank stare. "So, why would there be?"

Glynnis raised her hands, folded them in mock prayer, and raised her eyes to heaven. "Lord, grant me patience that I may continue to educate my fellow teammates without strangling them."

Glynnis lowered her hands to her side and directed her gaze at Greenfield with only a hint of a smile on her lips. "As a reminder to you, boss, when you delete a file from the computer, you don't erase the file out of the system, you just put a mark on it that tells the computer that it can use the space for other things. Pieces of the file remain for people like me to put together."

Greenfield, trying to regain his composure said, "I knew that."

"Okay, Agent Einstein. The punch line is that I can't find any of the pieces of any report having to do with these two patients. None. That's not that easy to do, but not impossible. What I find amazing is that there ought to be holes in the data files and there aren't."

"Sorry Glynnis, now you lost me. What do you mean by holes?"

"Well, if I had a file on a computer that I didn't want anyone to see, I would take all parts of the file in the system and fill the space with zeros so that it couldn't be read. The bad part of doing it that way is there would be big chunks in the file systems with just these zeros. Those are holes. You can't read anything from them, but you can tell that something was there and that it's been removed. You can also tell how big a chunk was deleted. That helps someone like me a lot sometimes."

"So it was tampered with and we can't even tell how much was taken. How big a job would that be?"

"Agent Greenfield, you have no idea how big a deal this is. I'm familiar with the system since they've opened their books to me. It's well designed. Knowing what I know now, it would take me about two months with a team of about five or six top-notch programmers and a couple of good hackers to pull this off. Even with that, I couldn't guarantee you I wouldn't leave fingerprints somewhere on the system. If I came in cold without knowing the exact security on the system, it would take a couple of years and a team two or three times as big as what I just said."

"Interesting, Glynnis. What if I tell you that the team that did this was a male and a female that had less than forty-eight hours to pull it off?"

The female agent snorted a laugh and looked at Agent Greenfield. "That's real funny, skipper. Next you're gonna tell me that the guy was Santa Claus and the female was the Easter Bunny, right? 'Cause it's just as big a fairy tale. Forty-eight hours? It couldn't happen. They'd leave a trail somewhere. Period. Imagine walking across miles and miles of virgin sand and not leaving any trace — not even one single footprint. That's exactly what happened here. Two people? Forget it. The amount of programming we're talking about is beyond the capabilities of two people, even if they were geniuses and could program perfect code at a thousand lines a minute. I'm sorry to tell you that you've probably got a bigger scope on your hands than you think."

Agent Greenfield smiled and raised his hands slightly in mock surrender. "Okay I believe you. Besides, it's too early to commit to anything definite in this case. Thanks all the same."

"Sorry I couldn't be of more help, boss." Without further comment, Glynnis dropped her report on his desk, walked out of the makeshift office, and closed the door behind her. Greenfield sat down at the desk and was trying to make sense of what he had just been told when there was another knock on the door. Before he said anything, he silently stood up and began moving. It was an admittedly silly precaution, but he did not like to be predictable. By moving while he answered, he had the effect of not being where a possible assailant would expect him to be. Of course, an assailant would not give the benefit of knocking prior to coming in and doing mischief. Will Greenfield recognized this, but could not bring himself to break the habit. He smiled to himself as he said, "Come in."

A bald-headed man wearing a security guard uniform entered the room. He appeared to be in his late fifties and to have kept himself in excellent shape. The lean man moved closer to Greenfield with a military precision. "Agent Greenfield? I'm Anthony Rourke, the security guard that was on duty at the front desk last night."

Greenfield walked a step forward and offered his hand. "I'm pleased to see you again, Mr. Rourke. I recognize you from last night."

"Call me Tony."

Agent Greenfield retrieved his hand from Tony. The man had a grip that bordered on painful. He did not think that Tony Rourke was trying to show his strength or make any kind of statement with the handshake; that was just the handshake he gave men. Greenfield hoped that he softened that grip somewhat for women, but looking at the elderly man, he was not sure that he would. "You were the senior security officer on duty when the clinic had the unauthorized entry last night, weren't you?"

The security guard went slightly rigid. "Yes sir and I assume full responsibility for the breach."

Agent Greenfield held up both hands to the smaller man. "Whoa! Slow down there Mister Rourke … Tony. I'm not here looking to place blame. That's not my job, but if you want my unofficial, professional opinion, I think that you did everything by the book. You followed the hospital's written procedures down to the letter screening our 'guest' from last night and giving her the temporary pass. I even said as much to your superiors a time or two. Whoever did this was good. I'm not saying they're smarter than you, but this is the second time that I've run across these folks and, so far, they're proving to be smarter than me."

Agent Greenfield leaned forward and shared a smile that carried a message to the older man. "So far."

Anthony Rourke did not relax at the exchange. Greenfield sighed to himself. Mr. Rourke's level of tension was going to be a problem for Agent

Greenfield. Greenfield needed the security guard to remember every detail that he could. Usually the things that helped in an investigation the most were the things that were left until the very end when the interviewee was the most relaxed. The freewheeling mind tends to produce associations that the rigid mind cannot. Agent Greenfield needed Anthony Rourke in the most open frame of mind possible because these people were proving to be better than good at evading any effort to be questioned.

Agent Greenfield motioned to a seat. "Please sit down, Tony."

The security guard reluctantly took the seat. Agent Greenfield grabbed a chair from against the wall and brought it around to be next to Anthony Rourke. "Can I get you something to drink? Coffee? Soda?"

Anthony Rourke sat at attention and scowled at William Greenfield. "Listen, Sonny. Just because I didn't choose a fancy civil service job doesn't mean that I don't know protocol. I've known how to interrogate since you were a pup. So consider yourself lucky in this case. I want to dump everything in my brain out to you. You got it? You don't gotta treat me like some shaky little cream puff that's gonna come apart crying. So let's cut the nice guy crap and get on with this and see whether we can get you the clues you need."

Agent Greenfield smiled. "All right, just give me a quick run through."

The older man looked back with his scowl intact on his face. "Do you want time sequential or my perceived weighting of importance?"

"Time sequential first, please. Run it all the way through and we can come back to the important points."

The security guard retold the seven-minute encounter in incredible detail. His run through of the events took forty-five minutes. William Greenfield asked no questions and took no notes. He kept his attention focused on the older man and trusted his recorder to pick up all of the comments. When the older man came to the end of his story, he stopped talking. He did not trail off or sputter out any further comments. He simply stopped.

It took Agent Greenfield a moment to realize the older man was waiting for him to continue the interrogation. "What's your background?"

The scowl, if anything, became fiercer. "Marines for thirty-five years, mostly tactics and security. Got some time as an M.P. Retired as a Master Gunnery Sergeant and got this job."

Agent Greenfield was somewhat surprised at this turn. "How does a U.S. Marine Master Gunnery Sergeant end up as the night security guard in a hospital?"

The older man looked as if he was ready to chew nails. "If it wasn't for this incident, I'd tell you that it was none of your damn business and to go pound sand. If you must know, the security company is a family business owned by my three sons and myself. All former Marines."

"Okay Mr. Rourke. You've been around the block. I did get lucky, but maybe not in the way that you think. I got something our friends last night didn't expect. I got a cop ... and an old, seasoned cop at that. I want you to give me a cop's background of the perpetrator from last night. I want your gut feeling and I don't care whether you can back up what you say."

The security guard's expression changed slightly, but William could not read it. "I gave you her physical description already."

"I know that. I want to know who this person is."

Without hesitating, the old Master Gunnery Sergeant said, "I can tell you she was an officer in the United States Air Force."

Agent Greenfield looked at the older man in surprise. "How did you come up with that?"

"She saluted me when she was going in through the security door."

Agent Greenfield waited a moment for the older man to add something to the explanation, but nothing was forthcoming. He was still somewhat unsure of this older guy. "I'm sorry, but that's it? You were able to read that from that one gesture?"

"Look sonny, I can't take it to the bank, but I can't get it out of my head either. It made an impression on me when she was going in and it has stuck with me since. I've seen a hundred thousand salutes in my day. This lady had an Academy salute, so she was from Annapolis, West Point, or Colorado Springs. The Academy salutes are slightly different from any other. The person holds their body a little different and their hand position is different. Since an Academy graduate is an officer, their salutes are slightly different depending on whether they are saluting another officer or an enlisted person. This lady gave me an Academy salute. It was a salute from an officer to someone she outranked but valued more than her own rank. Those are rare and, no, you can't fake 'em. It was a salute from an officer to a senior NCO. Not even all the Academy grads will do that."

"I'm sorry, what's a senior NCO?"

"It's what you call someone if they have earned six stripes or better — an E8 or an E9. I would fall into that category and this lady knew it. She even called me 'Master Guns.' She knew what I was within seconds of seeing me and I know her for what she is now. An Annapolis grad might have called me 'gunny' or 'chief' and a West Point grad would probably have called me 'sergeant.' Besides that, she smiled at me."

Agent Greenfield leaned forward and his jaw dropped. "What? Was she sweet on you? Trying to use feminine charms? That doesn't seem to go along with what you're saying about her."

The old Marine was shaking his head and made a shooing motion with one of his hands at Greenfield. "Ahhh, you're a civilian. You don't get it. The

Air Force is weird. Damnedest bunch of goofballs you've ever seen. In any other service, the enlisted troops do the majority of the fighting. You've got officers in combat, of course, but the weight of the battle complement is the grunts. In the Air Force, it's exactly backwards. The people on the sharp end of the sword are the officers. They're the ones flying their little toy airplanes through all kinds of damnation and when they come back, it's the enlisted troops that give them another ration of hell for getting their airplanes all shot up. The officers take it because they know the troops have to let off steam. The funny thing is that the troops know that the officers know it, so the troops tend to overlook the fact that the pilot's hand is shaking a little or that they left a mess in the cockpit. The Air Force officers are more casual in their relationship with their non-comms. It's as if they're all part of some big team. It's a relationship that works for them, and that's what this Doctor Jones had. Not only was she an Academy grad, I'd take it to the next level and say she was a fighter pilot and had seen combat. Yeah, now that I think of it, it all fits."

Agent Greenfield was amazed at the powers of observation in the guard, but he did not seem to be telling the whole story. "You're leading up to something aren't you? There's something that you aren't telling me."

Master Gunnery Sergeant Rourke, USMC, retired, drilled a gaze through Agent Greenfield that made him feel inferior, speechless and infantile at the same time. "Of course I'm holding something back. Do you have any idea how crazy this sounds to me? I have to assume that it sounds twice as crazy to you. I'm going against years of good training to tell you this because there is something else. This lady was worried about a bunch of things, but there is one thing that she was really worried about, and I haven't seen this kind of worry in an Air Force combat officer except once. You have to look at this from her angle. She's been in combat, I'm sure of that now. She had the worried look of someone whose life is in danger, but that hardly registered on her. She was worried about friends and that was a bigger worry, but while I was trying to get her magnetic card to process, she looked as if she went into a trance or was daydreaming or something like it. While she was doing that, I couldn't take my eyes off her 'cause it scared the hell outta me. I am telling you, Agent Greenfield, this woman has a worry that's enormous. From an Academy-trained, combat-hardened officer, the look on her face ..."

Greenfield reached for a folder on his desk. He had made friends with some of the Air Force brass and had been able to get some preliminary information on their guest from the night before. As he handed it to Tony Rourke, he wished that he could get the same level of cooperation from the Navy. "This is the information that we have on our visitor from last night," said Greenfield pushing the file across the table to Tony. "Her real name is Carin Gonzalez."

Tony Rourke placed his hand on the folder, but hesitated before opening it. "Do you mind if I look at this?"

"Go ahead. I'm interested in your professional insight."

Tony opened the file and began at the very beginning. "Air Force Academy ... top two percent of her class, distinguished graduate ... pilot training distinguished graduate ... fighter weapons school distinguished graduate. Jeez, this woman sure sets a trend." Tony kept flipping the pages of the thin dossier and muttering to himself. "It's just like those geniuses in the Air Force to let someone like this go."

Rourke kept flipping through the dossier until one of the pages caught his attention. He raised an eyebrow and looked at Agent Greenfield. "Two combat tours? Are you sure this is right?"

"Apparently it is."

"Silver Star and DFC ... purple heart, but that could be anything. Sweet Jasu."

Rourke closed the file slowly and placed his hand on top of it. He kept his hand there for a moment before giving a slight nod. "She acquitted herself well, Agent Greenfield."

Agent Greenfield waited for the older man to start up again. When he failed to continue, Agent Greenfield smiled and said, "You like her, don't you."

Master Gunnery Sergeant Rourke sat upright and said, "Hell no I don't. Not in the way you mean and not in any way that you may come to think you mean. It's just ..."

Agent Greenfield nudged. "Go on. 'It's just' ..."

He held up the folder in his hand. "I don't know whether I can explain it to you. In a combat officer, you gotta command respect from the troops and lots of it. A combat officer's got to tell the grunts like me to go into the teeth of the dragon. The officer knows some grunts ain't comin' back and the grunts know some of them ain't comin' back. Without that respect, discipline fails and the dragon gets everybody. This lady had my respect before you showed me her folder and I ain't a pushover. If I was under her command with what I know right now and she walked in and said she needed access to the gates of Hell itself, I'd lead the charge — no questions asked."

Rourke placed Carin's folder on the table desktop between them and slowly slid the package back to Greenfield. "I think she's one of the good guys and I think she's got her hands on a chunk of trouble that affects more than just her. That's not sittin' well with me right now."

Agent Greenfield waited a few more moments. When the guard failed to continue, he said, "Let me recap for a moment and make sure I've got it right. You figured out that our perpetrator was a graduate from the Air Force

Academy, that she was a former fighter pilot, that she had seen combat, that she recognized you as former military almost immediately. You figured all of that out from one gesture. A salute."

Rourke kept his gaze locked on Agent Greenfield. "The salute was just the clincher. Go on."

"You're also of the opinion that she's involved in something or aware of something that may pose a threat to the United States and that she is in a position to negate this threat. Like you said, she's one of the good guys."

The former master gunnery sergeant stood up. "I told you it was crazy talk and I was an idiot to spill it to you."

"Sit down, Mr. Rourke. I've got something crazier to tell you."

The former Marine stayed on his feet. "I'm listening"

"I think I believe you."

Rourke cracked a hint of a smile. It was no favor to his face. "Son, you must've been the looniest one in your litter. Who in their right mind would believe a cock-and-bull story like the one I just laid on you?"

"I didn't say I believe your story, Mr. Rourke. I said I believe you."

CHAPTER 16

AN IMMENSITY OF POWER lies buried within the inconspicuous object. Even so, although it possesses the energies of a thousand suns, it remains quiescent. It is listening. Never failing to listen in all directions, at all times.

Because it is expecting to hear nothing, it takes pains to check, re-check, recalibrate its sensors and check again before allowing the undeniable conclusion: it is not alone.

A passive surveillance has detected an energy pulse at an intensity and spectrum that does not occur naturally. Something has showed up in this star system that is either very big or very close — maybe both. The characteristics of the energy pulse have conveyed a vital message. Not only is the object no longer the sole form of powerful intelligence in this region of space, but an ancient enemy is hiding out there.

It is somewhere — perhaps nearby.

Loss of communication with the Leader caused the events leading to this moment. Now there could be no consultation with other great minds. Despite its intelligence and vast stores of energy, a deep sense of caution shrouded its decisions – along with a touch of something that the earthly inhabitants, if they knew of it, would instantly recognize as the first sharp pricks of fear.

                    *   *   *

Carin's stomach was tied in knots and she could not dry the palms of her hands no matter how much she rubbed them on her jeans. She knew that the encounter in the clinic with Greenfield was going to come back to haunt them. As it was, it had been too close. Still, she had to keep forcing the thought out of her mind. *Worry about the flying first,* she kept chiding.

Carin headed the airplane south for thirty minutes before heading northeast and then south again. Her plan was to land at a small airport in a small town. They arrived two hours later at an airport in the middle of Idaho she had chosen. After a little work at the airport, Carin and Jake had the aircraft tied down, canopy covers in place and the luggage loaded in the rental car. It was not until they had checked into a local motel and unloaded their luggage that Carin began to worry about the next step of their journey. "Fred," she asked. "Have you gotten any more data on the possible origin of the meteorite that infected us?"

When Fred replied in detail what he had found, Carin's whole world collapsed. But Jake was elated and continually congratulated both Fred and Carin in turn for the excellent work they had done. Carin, for her part, could not believe that Jake was actually pleased to hear the news. "Fred, could you please repeat that last part. I think our U-boat commander's not listening."

Jake looked up at Carin. "Are you always this snippy when you get good news?"

Carin rounded on Jake with her hands on her hips. "Jake, I've got two things to tell you. First, I am never snippy and second, this is not good news. It is almost the exact opposite of good news. If the human race got this kind of good news every day, we would have a much better understanding of lemmings and would have more empathy when whales beached themselves."

Jake could not shake his excellent mood. "First, I think that you're being at least a little bit snippy. Secondly, Fred found the origin of the thing that infected us. I say 'good job Fred.'"

"Yeah, that's real easy for you to say because you aren't thinking about the next step. I am and I'm telling you right now it can't be done. Not in four weeks, not in four months, not in forty months. Not if we had all the resources of this country. Not if we had all the resources of this planet."

Jake shook his head. "Fred, I am obviously missing something. I thought you gave us great news. Can you explain why our Madame Scientist over there is having such a problem?"

"No Jake, I cannot. I can reiterate what I said and see whether we can all understand her concern. I have indeed found the source of the space object. It came from a small planetoid. The object is of the class known as an Earth-crossing object. This particular ECO will be making a transition through near Earth space in approximately four weeks."

Jake faced Carin, held his hands palm up at his sides, and shrugged his shoulders. "You got me Carin. I still don't get it. What's the downside?"

Carin glowered at Jake but spoke softly. "Fred, can you please tell us the approximate crossing parameters again?"

"Certainly Carin. The object will make its closest crossing between ten-thousand and fifteen-thousand kilometers from the Earth at a relative velocity of approximately forty kilometers per second. It will achieve a gravity assist on the crossing and exit the near-Earth region."

"Yeah! See Jake? Fifteen thousand kilometers! Forty kilometers per second!"

So that's it, thought Jake. *She was thinking one more step ahead of all of us.*

Carin grabbed her coat and started for the door. "Jake, this is one of those problems that only caffeine can solve. I saw a little coffee house about three blocks down. You coming?"

Carin was already out the door. Jake grabbed his coat and turned to Fred. "Fred, we are going out for a while. In the meantime, find out everything you can about the object."

"I will comply with your requests, but I should point out that it would be impossible to rendezvous with the object using existing technology."

Jake stared for a moment, and then quietly said, "Okay, Fred. Do the best that you can."

With that, Jake grabbed his coat and ran down the street to catch up with Carin. Jake had to run across a street to catch up with her. When he caught up to her, he simply fell into step and said nothing. The approach of dusk added to the gloom. It was unseasonably cold and there was still snow on the ground. Tough ridges of gray-black ice had formed on the sides of the road where they had been pushed by snowplows. Worse yet, the leaden sky predicted another snowfall soon.

Carin walked into the coffee house and ordered a double espresso. Without waiting for her coffee, she strode to the corner, plopped down in a chair by the only table in the shop and stared out the window, watching the first snowflakes. Jake came up to the counter and ordered some black coffee. When both their orders came, he paid for them; set Carin's down by her hand and sat down across from her.

Carin sweetened her drink and took a sip. She then noticed what Jake was drinking. "I don't see why you drink that dirty water when you have a superior product available."

Jake chuckled softly and shook his head. "Maybe I want to sleep sometime this week. Or maybe I don't think that my stomach can take any more insults."

Carin turned around and looked at Jake. "Those cramps are getting pretty bad, aren't they?"

Jake stared at her through sunken eyes. Carin turned back around to look out the window at the fading light and rubbed her belly. "Yeah, mine too."

She cupped the demitasse mug in both hands and sipped her coffee gently, taking only a few drops at a time; savoring each taste. They barely spoke. After a long while, Jake ordered another double espresso for her and got some decaf for himself. Halfway through the second cup, she finally turned to him and said, "I never told you about my parents, did I?"

Jake took a sip of his coffee. "Yeah, as if we've had time for *that* conversation."

Carin shook her head. "You're right, but that's an excuse. We should make the time. We need to make the time."

Jake took another sip of his coffee, waiting. Cars were beginning to turn their lights on, and now heavy falling flakes were revealed in their beams.

"They were missionaries, you know."

Jake put down his cup. "No. I didn't know that."

Carin stared at her coffee. "Both medical doctors. World travelers. They went wherever the latest medical crises were breaking out. Malaria in the Amazon, virulent outbreak in Ethiopia; it didn't matter. As soon as they heard about it, off they'd go and into boarding school I went."

Carin took another slow sip, then added, "They were saints; completely selfless. It hurt them to leave me behind, but they were not going to drag their only daughter into these pits of pestilence. They kept saying that it was their chosen path and not mine. They would tell me that when it came time to choose my own path, if it coincided with theirs, I would be welcome. Blah, blah, blah. I was a kid and the only thing that I knew was that my mom and dad were gone during Christmas and on my birthday."

Carin stood up and got two large glasses of water before the waitress could help her. She set one down by Jake's coffee and took a long drink from her glass. The snowfall was growing heavy. Cars were traveling slower.

"They were doing some pretty mundane work in Africa when they came down with Marburg fever. The incubation period of the disease is around five to ten days. Before anyone knew what happened, most of the people in the village had come down with it, including my mom and dad. Before any help could come, one quarter of the villagers had died."

Carin finished her water. "My mom and dad were among the victims." She held up her right hand and showed Jake her ring. "About a week later, I got this amethyst in the mail from my dad. He and my mother found it in one of the street bazaars and bought it for a couple of bucks. I had it mounted on this ring." She twirled it for a few moments with her right thumb before adding, "It helps me remember them."

Jake reached over, grabbed his water glass and took a sip. Carin let out a heavy breath. "Jake, if the death of the folks that were in the crater with us is any indication, this bug that we have is going to run a course very much like the Marburg virus, except slower. To say that it's an unpleasant way to die doesn't even scratch the surface. I'm scared beyond words at this thing. Terrified. And you should be, too."

Jake put his glass down. "So beat it before it beats you."

Carin was already nodding. "That's exactly what I planned on doing, up until an hour ago. But Jake, there is no way we can rendezvous with that planetoid as it goes by. This entire planet lacks a launch vehicle that could get the three of us up to that delta V without some kind of help."

Jake gave Carin a puzzled look. "What's a 'delta V'?"

Carin looked at Jake for a moment and then shook her head. "Sorry. It's just engineering shorthand for change of velocity. For our little rendezvous problem, assume that the Earth is a fixed point in space. The only velocity we've got right now is whatever comes from the Earth's rotation — which, by the way, is chump change for what we need. We have to increase our velocity by about forty kilometers per second, when you only need a little less than eight to go into orbit.

"For deep space missions, we use a gravity assist. You swing behind a planet's orbit and it gives you a boost, like surfing. You can think of the sling David used to get Goliath, if you're biblically inclined. But that won't help us, sitting down here on the surface."

Jake put down his water. "I just can't think it's all that tough. The United States puts stuff into orbit all the time. I'm not minimizing the fact that it would be this, I don't know, this incredible challenge, but it has to be *possible!*"

"No, Jake. We couldn't join up with it if we had years to prepare. I don't want to bore you with a bunch of details, but to get just you, me, Fred, and nothing else into space at that velocity is impossible. To join up with the object, we have to change our velocity from what it is now by about fifty or sixty kilometers per second, straight off the ground, so that we could perform the alignment and rendezvous. The best boosters I can think of might give us maybe twenty or thirty kilometers per second, which brings up the question of acquisition. Are we going to go to some country's space agency and say, 'Hi guys, we need to borrow one of your rockets?' We can't just steal one either. Somebody might notice."

"Doctor, I'm sure that everything that you're saying is true, but I can't help think that we're still overlooking something very basic."

Carin leaned back in her seat, crossed her arms across her chest, and chuffed a laugh. "Captain, if ever I heard a pipe song of wishful thinking, that statement was an orchestra. Overlooking something basic? Don't you think that between the three of us we would have looked at every angle?"

"No, Doctor. I don't think that we have. For one thing, you haven't bothered to mention this until now. I suggest that we go back to the room and get a good night's sleep and attack this problem with all three of us working it at the same time."

Carin began to laugh. "Here we go. I knew you were going to say that – or something like it."

"Let me see whether I understand your concerns." Jake began ticking off points on one hand while keeping his eyes on Carin. "You're scared to death of the bug — scared of what it'll eventually do to you. There's no known cure because this bug is literally from out of this world. The answer exists on an object that's going to come swinging by here soon, but it's going in a trajectory that we couldn't possibly match with any of the technology that exists on this planet. Since we don't have time for a crash program to develop a rocket or whatever to join up with this rock, we'll never uncover the secret of the virus and hence we'll die. When we die, Fred is unprotected and immobile. By any definition of the word, it'll also die. Am I close to your scenario?"

Carin softly exhaled, then replied, "Two points for the swabbie. That's it exactly, Jake."

Jake gave Carin a tender smile of understanding. "I have my moments."

"Any ideas on how we're going to dig ourselves out of this hole?"

"Not yet, but we'll beat this thing."

"Pretty strong words, Captain. What makes you so confident?"

"Doctor, I'm confident because our combined knowledge and experience base are unmatchable anywhere on this planet." He stood up and finished his glass of water. "I'm confident because I have to be. Right now, I'm going back to be with Fred. I don't like leaving him alone if I don't have to. It doesn't seem fair to him. Are you coming?"

Carin got up quietly and helped him clean up their glasses and trash. Minutes later, while they walked away, Jake watched her from the corner of his eye and decided that the explosion in the crater had changed this woman very little. She was a thoroughbred with a talent for whatever she touched, and he was a plow horse with a small talent. It was no surprise to him that she had been mishandled in her work and in her private life. How did men deal with her? Hell, how did women deal with her? He let his mind drift to what it must be like to be in the kind of work environment that Carin had described.

Suddenly, Carin came to a stop next to Jake, reached over and held him tenderly in her arms. The gesture made Jake melt into her embrace and join her gentle, swaying rhythm. She rocked back and forth and softly said, "Look into my eyes a moment. Whatever you do, don't look away from my eyes. Relax and smile. We're being stalked."

A hammer blow of alarm hit Jake with full force, coming from Carin. He could now see the tension in muscles around her eyes. He cursed himself — he had dropped his vigilance for a moment and some cockroach slipped through the crack. He owed her his gratitude for this. She had been vigilant while he was daydreaming. He smiled back at her. "Good job, Doctor. Where's our adversary?"

She continued rocking in his arms and smiled as if they were lovers. Jake still saw and felt her tension.

She barely breathed it. "At your eleven o'clock is an unlit side street. There was somebody there when we walked here, and he was just there when we walked out. He was trying to act nonchalant, but his interest was directed straight at us. Plus, as cold as it is, I can't imagine someone hanging out in the shadows."

Jake found it difficult to pull away from Carin. He took a moment to stand back at arm's length before he asked, "What do you recommend, Doctor?"

"I don't know. I thought you were the tactician of the group."

"If that's true, I've been doing a lousy job."

"Don't be hard on yourself, Captain. We never seem to have enough time."

Jake laughed. "That's a pretty cheap excuse."

Carin's eyes brightened as she spoke excitedly to Jake. "I've got a great idea," she said in a soft, cheery voice. "Let's rush over there and beat the crap out this guy. Then we should politely inquire as to who he is and what his intentions might be."

Jake could not keep the smile from his face. "An interesting tactical solution to our problem, Doctor, but your solution brings to mind three words: guns and accomplices. We don't know whether either or both of those are in that alley, waiting to educate us on our lack of imagination."

Carin was holding Jake's gloved hands in her mittens and gently swinging them from side to side, creating the impression that the two were just lovers conversing. "Yeah, there is that isn't there? Jake, I understand what you're saying and I really don't care. I just want to kick somebody's butt. Don't you?"

Jake replied in loving tones. "Of course I do, but I don't think we should play strike fighter on this one. I think we should play stealth submarine. Tell me if I'm wrong, but it seems to me that somebody's been tracking us since Vegas. I have to assume that this person is the second identity trace on me from the clinic – you know, the one Fred couldn't identify. This person has such a desire for privacy that not even our own binary Sherlock Holmes mode could smoke them out. I don't like that at all. It smells like evil intent. I want to watch their habit patterns and learn about them. When they find out that we're on to them, I want it to be because they're hit and on their way to the bottom before they even know there's a torpedo in the water."

Carin batted her long black eyelashes at Jake. "Captain, such talk can turn this poor girl's head. Are you trying to seduce me?"

Jake smiled and raised her gloved hands to his lips. "Obviously."

He gave her hands a gentle squeeze before lowering them and said, "Let's get back to Fred. I don't like leaving him alone while he's so vulnerable. We can take a wandering route back to the room. We'll likely be followed, but I want to see how this person works. It may give us some insight into how they think. They probably know where we're staying and just want to get a read on our habit patterns. I can go out later and see if we still have our lurker."

Carin nodded her head without saying a word, and began walking.

*   *   *

Antonio Crubari stepped back out from the unlit side street where he had been observing Jake Sabio. *This man is very good*, thought Crubari. *I do not know how I gave myself away, but he noticed it immediately.*

Crubari continued under his breath, muttering aloud without realizing it. "You are a very worthy opponent indeed. By being true to your training and nature, you have told me something valuable about yourself, haven't you Mr. Sabio? You are not the innocent, untrained former Navy man that your false credentials claim. You saw through my surveillance, didn't you? Thus, you have some training in this area. Logical deductions come from careful observations, Mr. Sabio. A good guess would be that you are a former government spy of some kind. That would explain the extensive cover. Database searches and bribed information keep turning up the Navy story, but I know better now, Mr. Jacob Sabio. The question that must be asked, however, is 'what are you up to now?' The only way to get that is through direct interrogation.

"But you have proven yourself to be quite well trained and observant. Such training usually includes familiarization with the deadly arts. I would be foolish to try an interrogation without some hold on you."

He took a deep breath and smiled. There was no humor in it. "But you have given me that hold on you, haven't you Mr. Sabio? Careful observation has paid off. I was wondering whether you were somehow collaborating with the good doctor, but your relationship is much simpler and more primitive than that. Do you have any idea how happy I am that you have given me what I need, Mr. Sabio? I have found your Achilles' heel and I will use it. You are about to find out how short and unpleasant your life will be. And I will be there to enjoy your last moments."

Crubari stopped and muttered his last thought on the subject up toward the sky, as if Jake were up there looking down on him. "You have been a worthy adversary, Mr. Sabio, but I want you to die knowing that you have been beaten by someone better."

CHAPTER 17

CARIN WOKE UP AFTER only two hours, drenched in sweat, feverish. Twice, she was yanked from sleep, doubled over in pain. While Jake was suffering similar symptoms, it was obvious that his were less pronounced. She had to come up with an answer to their medical problems soon or she would lose the capacity for rational thought. The cramps could not keep up much longer. She laughed morbidly to herself remembering an attending physician's words during her studies at the hospital. All bleeding stops eventually.

She had been working for seven hours straight with Fred on the possible medical avenues available to them. One by one, these avenues had proven to be dead ends. Medical science! What a laughable term. As if there was a way that anyone could come up with a science when the subjects of your investigations respond so differently to anything that you do to them. One person sees gray while the other person sees blue. A pill cures someone with an affliction and kills another with the same affliction. What you need is a smart pill that you can talk to and say: "Go fix this person and come back when you're done."

Carin finally gave in to the exhaustion that had engulfed her all morning. She put aside her work and let her mind drift on how she would design her smart pill. A pill that would release drugs into the system when it determined a condition existed was the first to be eliminated from her imaginary drawing board. She did not want to wait for the patient to get sick; she wanted to prevent them getting sick in the first place. Next, she thought of smart immune system boosters; they would kick in whenever they detected a possible virulent intruder. These would probably work fine, except the body's immune system would kick in and kill off the artificial boosters in the system. After all, you cannot expect the immune system to know what is good for the body. It only knows what does not belong and kicks it out. So, you would need something to protect the smart system boosters and a way for them to replenish themselves if they were picked off. *Besides, while I am protecting from nasty diseases, why don't I fix some stuff that's broken.* She thought of hair.

Carin's eyes opened and Jake was sitting there quietly. "Jake, how long have you been there?"

Jake did not answer her question. "Carin, go back to the last thought that you were having and say it out loud."

"I'm sorry. I'm so tired that my mind just started drifting. I was daydreaming of building a smart pill that could attack whatever is wrong with us."

"You opened your eyes as if something surprised you. What was the last thought you had?"

Carin tried to recall her last line of thinking without success. "I'm sorry. I lost my train of thought. I'm a little scattered right now."

Jake got up, got her a glass of water from the sink, and set it down next to her. "Okay, let's start at the beginning of the train. Tell me about your smart pill."

"Well, for one thing it would have to be really smart because there are so many variations among humans that what cures a problem in one person won't cure it in another person. It is pretty frustrating for researchers who try to find cures for things like the common cold."

"It has to be smart. What else?"

"It would likely be attacked by the body's immune system, so it would need to be protected by something so that it could do its job."

"Okay. Soldiers around the workers. What next?"

Carin smiled and shrugged her shoulders. "Then I guess I got greedy."

"How so?"

"I figured that while I was at it, why don't I fix people at the same time? You know, fix things like congenital defects. That sort of thing. And I thought of your hair." Carin stopped talking for a moment and stared at Jake's head now full of dark, thick stubble.

Jake smiled at Carin. "Don't worry Doctor. I know you're not leading up to a bald joke. How does my hair tie in?"

Memory flooded back to Carin. "Jake, that's what's happening to us. These bugs are like my smart pill. They've got workers fixing our DNA and soldiers protecting the workers, but they're in a hostile environment and they can't get reinforcements. For my smart pill, if the body's immune system kills off too many workers, I can always give the patient another dose with more workers. You and I can't get another dose because the factory is off the planet."

"I follow you Carin, but what can we do?"

"I can tell you what I'm going to do. I'm going to give the bugs what they need to do their job. I don't think that there is any way to survive at this point if we flush them out of our systems. They've done a bunch of modifications already and it would be like abandoning construction on a half finished building. I also know they have another group of bugs that build other bugs or they all would've been flushed out of our system long before now. However, the raw materials they need aren't part of our diet. How do you get titanium into your system anyway? Brussels sprouts? Yuck! I think that I'd rather put up with the cramps and fever. They must be scavenging the metal from the killed off bugs somehow before our bodies can flush their little corpses out. We just gotta give the builders a little more raw material."

Jake sat up straight in alarm. "Wait a minute, Carin. What're you thinking? Are you just going to make a cocktail or something and drink it?"

"As a matter of fact Jake, that's exactly what I'm going to do."

Carin turned to face the MI. "Fred, have you been able to follow the conversation?"

"Yes, Carin."

"Fred, can we find the ingredients that we need? I think we should find something that's already in solution. It would also help to keep the doses low enough so that I don't poison myself. I have to entertain the idea I could be wrong."

Fred was quiet for a few minutes. Carin was about to ask the MI for a status when it said, "I have ordered a solution that approximates the percentage of the elements found in your blood by the clinic. Is that satisfactory?"

Carin let out a breath of resolution. "Fred, that is satisfactory. Where do we pick up the solution, at a local pharmacy?"

"Carin, a pharmacy would not carry such a unique solution. I ordered it from an industrial chemical plant that is about twelve miles from here. I had to order ten gallons. That was the minimum order."

Jake stood up and threw up his arms. "Great! The way to cure us from this little bug is to gag down a little industrial waste. Madam, may I recommend the Chateau Love Canal? I find it fruity with a piquant bite."

Carin ignored Jake. She was wondering what they would do with ten gallons. Instead, she asked, "Fred, what did you tell them we were going to do with the solution?"

"Carin, as always, I told the truth. I said that we were conducting biodiversity experiments on nanoscale targets. I tried to explain further, but the gentleman at the plant seemed to be in a hurry."

Carin really needed to explain certain human behavior patterns to Fred, but there was no time. "Fred, when will the solution be ready?"

"Carin, it will be ready in about an hour. The gentleman originally said it would be ready in two weeks, but I explained that it was very important for our experiment to have the solution immediately."

Jake folded his arms and turned to the MI. "Fred, how much extra is he charging?"

"Ten thousand dollars."

Jake stood a moment looking at the machine. Finally, he said, "Fred, good job. We were definitely followed last night and I want to get out of here as soon as possible. Pack everything up and we'll go pick up the mad doctor's solution on the way to the airport."

Carin did not take the jibe well. "Listen Aquaman, do you have any better ideas? Because all I seem to be hearing is how terrible this plan is. I'm open to suggestions, but I'm tapped out. As far as I can tell, this is the only way out that has us staying alive. Jake, we're stuck in the middle of a tunnel. We can't back out of the tunnel because we'll die. We can't stay in the tunnel because we'll die. We've got to go through the tunnel and see what's on the other side."

Jake was barely audible when he replied. "I'm not taking it."

Carin was not sure she had heard him correctly. "What?"

Jake turned and faced Carin. "I'm not taking it."

A sense of fear filled Carin. "Jake, if I'm right, you'll die if you don't take this."

Jake replied in a soft voice. "What will I be after the bugs finish changing me? How do we know that with all the intelligence in all those quantum computers I'll still be me? How can I be sure from that point on that any decision I make isn't a product of some foreign design? I can't do it Carin. I won't stop you from doing what you think is best, but I won't drink that solution."

Carin was at a loss. As sure as she was on her own determination to proceed along this path, she understood Jake's determination to stay on his. She admired him for the strength of his convictions. There was nothing she could say at this point that would sway Jake's decision and, if there had been, she doubted that she would have voiced it. Finally, she laughed and carried her packed bag to the front door. "Let's not worry about it too much right now, Jake. The way our luck has been going, we'll probably get hit by a truck on the way to the airport."

Carin walked down to the rental car carrying Jake's duffle bag on top of her rolling luggage bag. It was sunset again and they would have to pay for an extra day at the motel. It did not matter. Money was not their problem, time was. Jake followed with the two metal suitcases that carried Fred and his various peripherals. Carin threw the bags in the trunk while Jake carefully opened the metal suitcase containing the main processing unit of Fred. He set the video input on a spot so Fred could see out of the forward part of the car. When Jake was finished, he quietly said, "Fred, can you please scan for listening bugs in the car."

Fred was quiet no more than a few seconds. "Jake, I detect no anomalous radiation."

Carin noticed the change in their routine and walked close to Jake. "Is there something suspicious?"

Jake kept his gaze moving; scanning like radar all around them. "Yeah, something has been bugging me all day. We were followed, but nobody made a move on us. I find that a little disconcerting."

"What? Are you upset because they didn't follow your plan?"

"Yeah, something like that, Doctor. By now, whoever has followed us here must know that we're zipping around the country in a private airplane. That's got to make it tough to follow."

Carin was shaking her head. "Not if it's the government that's doing the tracking. It can't be that hard to follow us through the network of air traffic control radars. It would be a matter of a couple of hours work max to track us down. They probably prefer that we keep flying the aircraft. If we started driving, we could be almost impossible to track."

"Great! So now you're telling me we've been easy to track this whole time? Let's get moving. I don't like staying in one place for very long. While we're driving, maybe you can explain why we can't get to the object."

Carin got into the passenger side of the front seat and waited for Jake. He started the car, pulled out into the light traffic of the evening, and proceeded to the chemical complex. When Jake had settled down into a routine drive, Carin said, "Jake, I can't think of a good reason to go up to the object and I can think of a great many reasons not to go. I can see that you're starting to lock in on this course of action, but why?"

Jake changed lanes and waited a moment before answering. "Carin, I know you think that swallowing your cocktail is going to solve the problem, but what if it doesn't? Let me ask you something. Given the fact we're infected, don't you think that it's a little weird that this bug is such a lousy match for us? Now, I've seen some pretty screwed up government projects in my day, but this one takes the cake. You infect a couple of people in one of the most ridiculous methods that you or I could think of. Then it turns out that all this backdoor, secret approach was kind of a waste of time since they're going to die from it. Now, assuming that these bugs came from some superior intellect, why were they unable to put in an extra bug type that would help suppress the immune response or make the bugs invisible to our immune systems? That's what's really baffling me. Whoever designed this is smart enough to build a tailored infection that's perhaps centuries ahead of our technology, but can't do something that we learned decades ago during organ transplants."

"Okay, I'll bite. Why do you think that we have this dichotomy?"

Jake shook his head. "I don't know. It just doesn't make sense. By the way, do you think words like 'dichotomy' should be in a normal conversational vocabulary?"

Carin decided this would be an excellent time to ignore the Captain.

Jake pulled the rental car up to the front door of the main office of the small chemical plant. "Why don't you wait here with Fred and I'll be right back." With that, he slid out of the driver's seat and went in to the office. True to his word, Jake soon returned to the car pushing a small wooden crate in a handcart. He took his load to the back of the car and opened the trunk. After looking completely around, he effortlessly lifted the crate into the trunk and closed the lid. He kept looking all around him as he returned the handcart to the office and did not seem at ease until they were back on the road to the airport.

Carin waited until Jake was on the highway back to the airport. "Do you want to continue the discussion?"

Jake shrugged a shoulder. "I don't know what else to say. I'm not some super-smart cone head like you, but I can tell you one thing. This little explosion-in-the-crater stunt cost an incredible amount of time, effort and research. Translate that into money and the number is astounding. In addition, it was done in a slap-dash fashion. Not to mention that we're the only survivors of that experiment and not likely to survive unless we get help fast. That says things to me. Things like 'last-ditch effort' and 'desperation.'"

Carin replied in her iciest tone. "Cone head?"

Jake was unabashed. "You prefer Brainiac? The point is that this thing is bigger than the infection of two people on this planet. There has to be something forcing such a desperate move and that means we're in bigger trouble than just the two of us possibly dying. I think that this is a huge problem. Maybe even a planet-sized problem."

Carin was shocked at Jake's revelation. "I was thinking the same thing. We haven't had a chance to talk about this, but I had a daydream at the clinic. In my daydream, I felt that the reason we were infected was because there was some kind of threat that nobody is yet aware of. Somehow, we're supposed to warn everybody or something like that. But we still have to stay alive to address the threat."

"What threat, Carin? That's the problem. We have to go to the object and find out why we were infected. We have to determine what the threat is. Or even whether there is a threat. It could be just some overactive paranoia, but we can't afford to make a mistake on this. We also have to find a way to tame the infection that they gave us. The only way that I can think to do this is to go and ask."

"Jake, there is no way we can get to the object to ask it anything. We can't lift ... WHOA!"

Jake looked around quickly to see what the problem was and was barely able to keep the car in its lane. "What?"

"Captain, how could I be so stupid?"

"You couldn't, because that would make me something like a sub-amoeba. So you've thought of something, yes? Spill it!"

Carin turned sideways in her seat to face Jake and to allow Fred to hear her better. "Why don't we ask the object what's going on?"

Jake was silent for a moment. "Uh, we can do that?"

Carin began to get excited. "Don't know. We haven't tried."

Jake shook his head. "Overlooking something basic! Dammit, didn't I say that just yesterday? Why was I waiting for you to come up with the answer while my brain was parked in idle?"

Carin was beginning to sober. "Not so fast, Captain. It took the two of us to come up with this approach and we don't know whether it'll work yet."

Jake was bubbling with excitement. "Are you kidding? This is the best break we've gotten since this whole thing started. This is great!"

Jake turned into the parking lot of the little airport to a scene of chaos. Fire trucks, police cars and ambulances were parked on the flight line around a raging fire. Flames shooting twenty feet into the air and flashing emergency lights washed the scene in a dismal glow. A fire of any size always meant loss, but Carin got a sinking feeling in her heart. There in the middle of all the attention was her beloved homebuilt aircraft ... in flames.

*　　　　*　　　　*

Antonio Crubari looked at his handiwork and was pleased. The look on Captain Jacob Sabio's face told him what he needed to know. Yes, Captain Sabio, you can try to hide it, but I saw your eyes. They had no fear in them, but they held anger. Fear is a useful emotion in your prey; it makes them predictable. However, you showed anger. Anger causes your prey to make mistakes. You are about to make your first mistake right now, aren't you, Captain Sabio? You are going to run. Moreover, since one mistake inevitably leads to another, before you know it, I will have herded you like a lamb to a slaughter. You will be angry and confused Captain Sabio, but do not worry; I will not allow you to die until you fully understand how little choice you had in what happened to you.

Chapter 18

Jake walked around to the passenger side of the car and stood next to Carin. His face was taut and beginning to turn red and he could not stop from clenching and unclenching his fists. He knew what that little ship had meant to Carin and he knew what this desecration would do to her. The years of tender ministration and love she poured into that aircraft transformed it into an extension of herself. It was as if someone had purposely burned her arms and hands into uselessness.

Jake began a slow turn trying to memorize everything that he could see. He was determined to know every face at this fire before he left, since it was likely the perpetrator was still present. Involuntarily, he began a string of oaths and curses in a low voice. The string continued as he made two slow turns memorizing the faces in the crowd. When he finally came to a stop, he looked at Carin. Her tear-streaked face held a smile of thanks for him, something he had not expected to see. He was embarrassed. "Uh, sorry about the language just now."

"*Language?*" Carin shook her head in mild exasperation and pointed at her chest with her thumb. "Fighter pilot, remember? By the way, I think you improperly conjugated two of your verbs and one of your references is physically impossible." She thought for a moment before adding, "Except maybe in zero gravity. Otherwise, I couldn't have expressed it better myself. C'mon, we better get out of here."

Carin made a move to get back into the car and Jake gently touched her jacket at the elbow. "Doctor, have you ever read *On War*?"

"Captain, do you know the meaning of 'non sequitur'?"

"It's a statement that doesn't follow logically from whatever preceded it. So have you read *On War*?"

Carin looked at Jake. His attention was riveted on the small crowd of people that inevitably gather around a disaster of this nature. "Show me a warrior who hasn't read Von Clausewitz and I'll show you someone who's not a warrior. Jake, I just lost my plane. Where are you going with this?"

"Our enemy's tactics and strategies. It's obvious we're being herded. Our opponent has just destroyed something that they had to know was highly valuable, financially and emotionally. Why would they do that?"

Carin looked at Jake a moment and understanding dawned in her eyes. "To force us to have an emotional response! Make us do something stupid."

Jake nodded while he scanned the crowd. "Exactly. It's a slippery slope, Carin. Once you start making mistakes, they tend to pile one on top of the other. You keep doing things to correct previous mistakes. You get reactive and predictable. I don't do reactive and predictable. Whatever would seem to be the easiest and most logical thing to do right now would also be the stupid thing."

"We can't stay here, Captain. You know they must still be here watching us."

"You're damn right they're still here, and we're going to memorize every face in this crowd. One of those faces belongs to our enemy or enemies. Probably lurking in the shadows. Focus your attention on the background. Right now, you have to go check in with the Fire Marshall. What kind of insurance do you have on the airplane?"

"Way ahead of you, Captain. Liability, but no hull insurance. Our fire bug just lost motive."

Jake nodded approval. "Go make yourself known. I've got to do a couple of things."

"Okay, but if I'm not back in forty-five minutes, come bail me out."

Carin did not wait for a response. She merely turned on her heel and marched in the direction of the fire trucks. Jake stood in place for a moment and watched her retreating back. He had expected to have to talk her into this course of action. What a remarkable woman! Caught in a life or death struggle with what appears to be an out of this world infection, chased by federal authorities, chased by an unknown foe and watched her most beloved possession destroyed before her eyes, yet she sets her jaw and marches into battle. Jake kept underestimating Carin. When he did, he would raise the bar a little higher. Jake had the feeling that he was eventually going to have to throw the bar away.

He returned to the car and sat in the back seat with Fred. "Fred, keep your volume low in your responses. Are you aware of what has transpired?"

Fred responded immediately. "Captain Sabio, I am aware that the aircraft has been destroyed by a fire. Doctor Gonzalez is in trouble. I have been monitoring the police bands. An informant recently called in saying that they saw her set fire to her aircraft."

Jake sat back and touched a finger to his lips. "Not exactly unexpected, but it adds a little more to what we know about our enemy. He wants her arrested. That would force her to remain in the vicinity, even if she makes bail. It would also mean she and I would be separated, at least for a while. Interesting. Now we know something. Fred, can you get a copy of the phone report from the police database?"

Fred was silent for a moment but finally said, "I have a copy of the phone report. Do you want me to erase the original from the police system?"

"No, Fred. That would tip our hand. Eventually I would like you to cross-correlate the voice with any cases that agent from the clinic was working. There is a correlation somewhere. Is there anything else I should know concerning Carin's predicament?

"Yes, Jake. Agent Greenfield has issued an all points bulletin for Carin. I have intercepted the message traffic concerning Carin and the police here in town, but eventually the information will get through."

This concerned Jake. They were running out of time. "Good job, Fred. It sounds as if the clock is ticking and we need to get out of town. In the meantime, I have something that won't leave me alone. If I were this guy who's following us, I'd have bugged our rental car to learn what we're up to, but you say that you are sure there are no transmissions from the car."

"Jake, I should point out that real-time bugging is only one method of gathering intelligence on a surveillance subject. A recording device of some type is more likely. As I perceive no residual electromagnetic fields at this time, I would assume the device is most likely a solid state device."

"Fred, I want to deny this information to whoever did this to us, but we only have about forty minutes. What do you recommend?"

"Jake, it will be almost impossible to search the car and find such a device. In addition, it seems logical to place several such devices. We could not be sure that we had found them all, even if we found several."

"Fred, I need a solution. If there are recording devices, can I destroy or erase them somehow?"

Fred was silent for a moment. "Jake, your suggestion is possible. We can scramble any solid state or magnetic recording device in the car. I noticed a ground power unit that is normally used to start jet aircraft sitting in the corner of the hangar. With that, an aircraft tow bar, some wire and a few other components, you should be able to fashion a powerful electromagnetic pulse wand."

Jake felt the corners of his lips turning up in a feral grin. "Electromagnetic pulse wand, y'say? Fred, old buddy, I love the way that sounds. Tell me more."

*   *   *

Carin stood next to the fire truck that was closest to the remains of her tiny aircraft. She could not hold back the tears. Nearby, a large, black man had a communications unit pressed to his ear and the words Incident Commander written on the back of his waterproof jacket. The tone of his voice left little doubt on that score. From the back and side, Carin guessed him to be in his mid-forties. He was at least six foot two, and had to weigh close to two hundred and forty pounds. Very little of the weight was wasted on fat. The large man turned to walk away, when he noticed Carin and paused. "Hello, my name's John Tuckman. Can I help you?"

Carin squared her shoulders and faced him. "I'm Carin Gonzalez. I'm the owner ..." but she could not finish her sentence. She extended her hand and pointed to the charred remains. John Tuckman looked at the ruined craft for a moment said, "Did you build her yourself?"

Carin answered in a soft melancholic voice. "Yeah, built from scratch. Didn't exactly stick to the plans. I added a couple of things to her. She could do an honest three hundred and forty knots in cruise. Took eight years."

"She was a Smith Speedster, if I was to guess. Three forty is a good hundred knots more than advertised. I'd say that you did more than a couple of things."

"Good eye. You have to be pretty deeply into homebuilt aircraft to recognize her with what little is left."

Tuckman gave her a resigned smile. "I've been an airport rat since I was ten. It's a disease you don't easily shake. Besides, nobody designs a fuselage section like Jimmy Smith. Have you called your insurance people?"

Carin was expecting the question and was shaking her head. "Not yet, but I guess I should cancel the policy. I didn't have hull insurance. As you know, many homebuilts aren't insured for any damage to the airplane itself. So she's a total write off for me."

John Tuckman let out a long breath and gave Carin a sad smile. His reply was heartfelt. "Ms. Gonzalez, I'm so sorry. I can't look at your poor aircraft anymore, but I know the owner of the flight line diner over there. Her name is Fiona and she has a tenth-degree black belt in coffee. She even has an espresso machine and her own coffee grinder. We have some paperwork to fill out and I'd just as soon go there."

"Mr. Tuckman, you've made the only suggestion at this precise moment that could make me feel better. Please call me Carin."

John Tuckman offered Carin his meaty hand. "Then I insist that you call me John." He kept up an amiable patter while they walked toward the café, as if trying to put her at ease. "You'll like Fiona. She opened her shop about a month after I started my own homebuilt project out here. She's building a kit plane herself, even though she's not a pilot. If you're lucky, she might let you have one of her homemade scones. They weren't much to brag about when she first opened up her place, but now they're better than the ones my mama used to make. I can't eat enough of 'em. Between her coffee and her scones, I practically live in her shop."

They reached the little diner at the corner of the hangar. There was a counter and two tables inside. As soon as Carin walked in the door, she knew that John's opinion of the coffee was not an idle boast. The air was thick with the aroma of ground beans. A woman who stood at least as tall as Tuckman stepped from around the corner and gave him a friendly hug. She was what some people would call buxom, but she carried mostly muscle on her frame. To Carin, she looked like one of those female wrestlers you see on the television. John turned around and introduced Carin. "Fiona, this here's Carin Gonzalez. She scratch-built that beautiful airplane we just lost and I'd like to buy her a cup of coffee."

Fiona had to bend down to take both of Carin's hands in her own. "Honey, I am so sorry. I saw people walking around that ship all day. I don't think I've ever seen a homebuilt aircraft with more ramp appeal. What can I get you?"

Carin smiled at the tall woman's easy friendliness. "Well, there was a rumor floating around that you may have espresso coffee here?"

Fiona stood up proudly and squared her shoulders. "Girl, you're in the house of the best darn espresso coffee that you've ever tasted. Y'all sit yourselves down in the corner table and give me a minute."

Carin sat down and John helped himself to a couple of glasses of water. He set one down in front of Carin and began to drink. He was trying to avoid eye contact with Carin. Carin sympathized completely. This next part was going to be difficult. "John, you know that fire was deliberately set. I'm assuming you do arson investigations in this town. What would you like to know?"

John's eyes grew wide. "How do you know all that?"

*   *   *

Jake had put together the contraption Fred had specified. It was actually a simple device that put out a strong, pulsating magnetic field. It allowed the magnetic field to build quickly to a high intensity and then it would instantly collapse. If you instantly collapse an electromagnetic field, you get an electromagnetic pulse. It would be like dropping a large rock in a still pond.

The size of the waves right next to where the rock went into the water would be enormous compared to the others further away. There is nothing known to man that is more lethal to data stored in solid state or magnetic form than an EMP. Fred had calculated the safe distance when the device was activated and had insisted that both he and Jake remain at least at that distance. Jake had been confused by Fred's persistence. "Fred, I don't understand what you're talking about. I'm just a regular meat puppet. Electromagnetic fields of this strength have no effect on us biological types."

Fred remained adamant. "Jake, I'm sorry to point out that there are two flagrant untruths in your statements. First, biological types, as you call them, are most definitely affected by electromagnetic fields of this strength. Second, you fail to realize that you are no longer a 'regular meat puppet.' You have an infection that may have become a part of you. This strong electromagnetic field could destroy the bugs in your system if they are of an electro-mechanical nature."

Jake was surprised at this revelation. "I hadn't thought about that. Maybe I should go stand in the middle of the field and cleanse these little guys out of my system."

Fred's response was quick. "Jake, if the infection has insinuated itself sufficiently, losing the bugs now will kill you."

Jake was not inclined to concede the point, but he went along with Fred's recommendation just the same. His training had taught him that the conservative approach went the farthest the greatest number of times. Sure, there were times to throw out the conservative approach, but this was not one of them. Before proceeding with their plan, Jake put Fred in his metal carrying case, placed it and the rest of their luggage on a baggage carrier, and moved the lot to a safe distance from the car.

Airplane ground power units are unassuming carts that are usually on wheels. Just sitting on a corner of the ramp, they are innocuous and invisible. However, under a GPU's plain, boxy exterior is a motor turning a massive generator. The motor usually turns out to be a very large V-8 while some of the motors are jet engines themselves. The generators connected to these motors can easily power a dozen homes. It was to this literal dynamo that Jake connected his contraption. The contraption itself he laid under the car.

The electrical extension from most GPU's is quite long and this one was no exception. Jake stretched the cord out to its full length, which allowed Jake and Fred to stay around the corner of the metal hangar from the car. Jake fired up the motor of the GPU and looked around to see whether anyone was coming to investigate. Just as Jake had hoped, nobody took notice of the noise. It was such a common sound on a flight line that everyone tuned it out. He turned on the electrical power switch that engaged the powerful generator to the motor. Jake let the configuration run for thirty seconds before switching off the electrical power but leaving the GPU motor running. Then he ran to the car and lifted the contraption on to a blanket he had placed on the roof of the car. He then ran back to the power unit to give his contraption another thirty seconds of current. Convinced that he had erased any recording media in the car, he killed power to the unit and shut down the motor. He walked back to the car, casually looking around to see whether anyone was watching. Jake reached the car and put everything in order. He then went back and picked up the cases that contained Fred and their other baggage.

He was pushing the baggage carrier as his eyes scanned left and right. There was one more thing left to find as Jake pushed his load along the parking lot behind the airport diner. Luck was with him. There in front of him was exactly what he was looking for. A quick inspection confirmed his excellent luck was still holding up. It was finally time to find Carin.

*   *   *

Carin had just finished telling her story to John when the door to the diner opened and Jake walked in. He deposited all their belongings in the far corner of the diner. Carin stole a glance at her watch. Forty-five minutes almost to the second. Jake kept proving he was true to his word.

Jake favored her with a look that mixed sympathy for her loss and pleasure at seeing her again. Before either of them could speak, Fiona walked in to see if she had a new customer. Jake's manner changed to one of innocent flirting directed to Fiona. "Howdy ma'am. You must have been the tallest and prettiest one in your class. Is that your coffee that's putting such a heavenly scent in the air?" Without waiting for an answer, Jake took one of Fiona's hands into both of his, leaned over, and gave her hand a kiss.

Fiona took back her hand and put on an air of nonchalance that did not convince anyone. She looked at Carin and said, "Honey, this one has got to be yours. They don't train men that good around here. If he's yours, I'll give him some coffee. If not, I'm takin' him home with me tonight." Without waiting for an answer from Carin, Fiona went to the back to fetch a new batch of espresso.

Carin stared open-mouthed at Jake. She had never seen him in a social setting where he was trying to be charming. Carin had to admit that Jake had won over Fiona. She also had to admit that she was a little jealous of the attention Jake was pouring out to the statuesque woman. She shook off her feeling of displacement and got back to the discussion. Jake knew their situation perfectly. Carin trusted Jake had read something into the situation. Still, would it kill Jake if he talked to her like that sometime?

John's body language had become more closed when Jake had started talking to Fiona. Carin introduced the two men. "Jake, this is John Tuckman. He's investigating the fire. He's also a homebuilder himself with a project almost complete."

John Tuckman stood now to his full height to shake Jake's hand. Jake returned it heartily, barely managing to wrap both his hands around the big man's single hand. "Mr. Tuckman, it is an honor to meet you. Good luck on your first flight, sir"

Jake's smile was open and honest and John began to visibly warm to him. When the men disengaged from each other, Jake sat very close to Carin and looked into her eyes. "Are you all right, dear lady?"

Carin's head was pounding and the coffee, though exceptional, sat like battery acid in her stomach. She was in no mood to put up with Jake's games. She was about to tell him this when she felt his emotions push through her thoughts. He was feeling fear for her. Not just the passing fear that she might be put in jail; this was a fear for her life. She looked in his eyes and saw pure determination. Jake had definitely picked up on some warning signs she had missed, but what were they? She knew, even in their present incapacitated state, they were more than able to fight their way out of this situation. Jake must have seen an alternative to a direct confrontation. Of course, fifteen years of being an officer on a stealth submarine would make you a master at nudging people into doing what you wanted them to do. Carin had learned to trust Jake's intuition. She decided to play along. Carin dropped her shoulders and leaned slightly towards Jake. "Depression, headache, upset stomach. It's pretty much what you would expect considering the circumstances."

Jake turned his full attention on John and smiled. "I am sure Mr. Tuckman has his reasons for doing all the questioning. You're probably just following standard procedures for this kind of case, aren't you Mr. Tuckman?"

John appeared slightly taken aback at being questioned, but answered just the same. "A valuable property was lost due to a fire. A fire that was set on purpose. We also had some guy with an accent phone in an anonymous tip that Ms. Gonzalez was the one that started the fire."

Jake kept smiling, but corrected John. "John, she should be addressed as Doctor Gonzalez, but I think that she prefers Carin. From where did this anonymous tip originate if you don't mind my asking?"

John shrugged his shoulders. "Not that it matters, but from a phone booth here at the airport."

Jake's smile broadened. "Excellent. What time did that happen?"

"About five o'clock this afternoon."

Jake sat back in his chair and looked at Carin. "This is fantastic. Did you know about this?"

Carin was unsure what Jake was trying to do. "No, this is the first that I've heard about it."

Jake held his hand out, palm up towards John. "John has found the culprit, determined that he's a male, determined that he's not from around here, and determined the time of the fire. I am sorry, Mr. Tuckman. It is not proper to address you by your first name when you are performing official duties. Would you prefer 'detective'?"

John visibly straightened and smiled at Jake. "Naw, just call me John."

Jake sat back and looked at John. "Well sir, I have to congratulate you on piecing together so many puzzle parts so quickly."

John looked unhappily at Jake. "I'm afraid that Carin is still a suspect."

Jake waved his hand in the air. "Of course sir, of course. Even though it's impossible she set the fire and it's obvious that someone's trying to muddy the waters. Technically, she's still a suspect. However, it does my heart good to see a fellow homebuilder has been assigned to the case."

John smiled. "You seem to know me pretty well, friend."

"Not at all, sir. However, it's obvious that you're a pragmatic man. Wasting taxpayers' money while the real culprit escapes upsets me and I know that it upsets you terribly. You're not the kind of man to be fooled by such an obvious, shallow ruse. Imagine phoning in the eyewitness report minutes after the blaze is set. Did this same concerned citizen call the fire department to report the fire and try to help save valuable property?"

"No he didn't."

"No, of course he didn't, but he miscalculated. He didn't know he was going to get you on the case. He didn't know you wouldn't be fooled by the misdirection. He didn't know you're a homebuilder yourself and know the tremendous emotional attachment that comes with flying your own creation. I would not be surprised if you already had the flight line surveillance tapes reviewed and had a description of the man passed on to the surrounding counties so that they won't succumb to this arsonist's whims."

Fiona chose that time to come back with the espresso. Carin did not need her enhanced senses to tell her that this particular coffee was not the same as the one Fiona had brewed for John and her. The coffee that Carin was drinking was very good, but the coffee that she was offering Jake was exceptional. John, meanwhile, was talking hurriedly into his police communicator. Carin was beginning to see what Jake was doing. She hoped he pulled it off or they would have to start running, and running fast.

Jake came to his feet and smiled thanks to Fiona. He took a sip of the beverage and brought his eyes up slowly to meet the tall woman's knowing smile. "That is an unbelievable cup of coffee, ma'am. I can assure you I have never tasted its equal. I am guessing the bean is probably a Blue Sumatra, but you had to have purified the water using a special process I can't identify and you're very careful with the cleanliness of your equipment. I'm flattered you would go to so much trouble for me. Thank you." John was becoming visibly uncomfortable at Jake's attention to Fiona when Jake turned to the detective and said. "John, you have an incredible and rare woman here. We're both very lucky men to have been so blessed."

John and Fiona both tried to talk at the same time. "We're not …" "We never …"

Jake looked at John and Fiona in turn. "John, Fiona, I am so sorry. Please forgive me for putting my big, fat foot in my mouth. How rude of me! It's just …"

Fiona was the first to recover. "Go ahead, Jake. You've gone this far, may as well ride it home."

Jake laughed at that and it helped ease the tension. "Look folks, I'm just an outsider so I don't know the history of you two, but to this outsider, you two are a match. Carin, am I totally off base here?"

Carin stood up and walked to stand next to Fiona. She looked back at Jake and said, "Of course you're off base, Jake, but you can't help it with your defective X chromosome and the other burdens men carry. However, in this case, I'm afraid I'm as guilty as you are. I'm sorry John, Fiona. I made the same mistake that Jake did. You two obviously have very strong and warm feelings for each other and have known each other for a long time. The two of you mesh perfectly. I thought the two of you were a couple. More than that, I thought that you were one of those truly rare couples that don't have to announce to the world every two seconds they're with each other."

John was shaking his head. "Well, we're not."

Carin crooked her head at John. "Why not?"

"Well look at her, for goodness sake. She's too …"

Carin prodded. "She's what, John?"

Fiona's temper flared. "Yeah John. What is she? Is she too tall? Too strong? Too clumsy? Too masculine? What?"

John looked into Fiona's eyes. "I was going to say too magnificent." John waved his hands over himself. "She can do so much better than this."

Fiona's temper deflated slightly. "Well, John Tuckman, you're a fool and an old fool at that."

John was obviously unsettled. "How was I supposed to know?"

To this, Fiona began to inflate like a balloon, ready to blast him. Instead, Carin stepped in and began to tick points off on the fingers of one hand. "You start spending all your free time at the airport building your airplane and Fiona opens a shop here within a month. You have a craving for scones and Fiona learns how to make them better than your own mother does. You have a passion for coffee and Fiona learns to make an espresso that is the best that I've tasted. For crissakes John, you start building an airplane and she starts building an airplane. She's not even a pilot! You two have known each other for years and you can't figure this out. I've been here an hour and I've known it for fifty-nine minutes."

Carin turned to face Fiona and threw up her hands. "Men!"

Fiona stood with her arms crossed staring daggers at John. "You said a mouthful, sister!"

John began approaching Fiona with an apologetic look on his face, but before he could speak, Jake intercepted him and whispered in his ear. "Slow down, detective. I don't think you want to navigate the course you just plotted."

John was confused. He whispered back to Jake, "What do you mean? I was just going to apologize."

"Yes, you are John, but not the way you think that you are. Any apology you try now is going to blow up in your face. Shakespeare couldn't write an apology that would please Fiona right now. Do you trust me in this enough to follow my lead?"

John smiled. "I think I better or Fiona is going to wrestle Carin to see who gets to go home with you."

That made Jake laugh. "John, my friend, if Fiona knew me better, it'd be the loser that got stuck with me. Now repeat after me aloud. Fiona, my dear."

John repeated. "Fiona, my dear."

"You are right, I am an old fool."

John looked at Jake and Jake whispered in John's ear, "Trust me."

"You are right, I am an old fool."

"We know each other so well, but there are so many more things I want to know about you."

"We know each other so well, but there are so many more things I want to know about you."

Jake whispered, "Can I cook you a meal at my place so we can learn more about each other?"

John said, "Can I cook you a meal at my place so we can learn more about each other?"

Fiona was beginning to thaw, but she had not yet melted. "When?"

John looked at Jake pleadingly and Jake immediately piped up so that everyone could hear. "How about tonight? If you do it tonight, Carin and I will donate the wine. I have always found wine to be an excellent social lubricant."

John was nodding his head. "Fiona, tonight would be perfect. I don't have time to cook you the meal you deserve tonight, but I don't want to wait. I'll bet that with some take-out and the wine donated by Jake and Carin, it would be a meal to remember. I will leave my offer to cook for you open for another date of your choosing. Please say yes for tonight."

Carin raised an eyebrow to Jake. John may be a slow starter, but he seemed to pick it up quickly. Fiona still had her arms crossed, but she was looking at her feet. "You ol' poop. Why'd you wait so long?"

John's face fell and he turned to Jake. Jake said softly, "Go ahead, John. Answer her."

"What should I tell her?"

Jake smiled. "The truth, my friend. Always tell the truth."

John turned to face Fiona. "Fiona, I took this long because I was stupid. I took this long because I was scared. I took this long because I was waiting for Jake to finally show up in our little town and kick my butt into gear. I took this long because I *am* an ol' poop. It doesn't matter now. Fiona, I have wasted too many hours of both our lives. I don't want to waste one more hour. Please say yes."

Fiona looked around the diner with her arms still crossed. "I have some stew left and some makin's for scones."

John walked over to Fiona and took her hands. "Fiona, let me cook for you."

She lifted her head and smiled. "Even the scones?"

John smiled back. "Well, maybe just this once."

Jake was not wasting any time. "Folks, I'm sorry, but I just realized I don't have a car to go and get the wine. There's a For Sale sign on the pickup truck outside. Do you know who owns it?"

Fiona looked up. "It's mine. It's not much to look at, but the motor and transmission were both just overhauled. She'll run another hundred thousand miles. Go ahead and take it."

Carin broke in. "Fiona, I think Jake wanted to buy it."

Fiona looked puzzled. "Y'all ain't even seen it yet."

Carin asked, "Is it in good shape?"

John answered. "The drive train's in factory new shape. I'm the one who overhauled her motor and transmission. I'm afraid I cheated and bought factory new replacements rather than overhaul them myself. I wanted it to be perfect for her."

Jake had more to his plan. "I also saw a travel trailer outside next to the truck. The one with the little dirt bike mounted on the front. It looked as if it might be a good place for Carin and I to stay while we got things sorted out. Is it also for sale?"

John piped up. "That's mine. I was using it when I was spending more time building my airplane. Everything works on it. Would you like to go outside and take a look?"

Jake was pleased to hear that the condition was good. "John, I'm happy to take your word on the condition of the trailer. I do not want to delay the two of you getting to that dinner. I have a feeling it has already been delayed for far too long. Now, where can Carin and I deliver some wine?"

John gave Jake and Carin directions to his home and they agreed to meet in an hour. Jake hooked up the trailer to the pickup truck, loaded the baggage in the trailer, and placed Fred in the middle seat of the cab. They were driving away within five minutes. Carin was about to ask Jake about his urgency when Jake burst out, "Carin, what the Sam Hill was going on back there when I walked in?"

Carin's eyes went wide. "What do you mean? Everything was going along fine."

Jake looked at Carin for a moment. He finally said, "Doctor, when I walked in, Tuckman was getting ready to book you. He wasn't convinced you were the arsonist, but he was going to follow procedure. Not only were you about to get booked, you were close to being arrested. Do you know how dangerous that would've been?"

Carin was flabbergasted. She had no idea she had been that close to trouble. Usually, she had excellent instincts. "Jake, are you sure? I didn't get any impression at all from John that he was going to book me."

"Believe me, Carin. When I walked in, you were moments away from getting the news. I'm sure whoever torched your airplane was hoping to make you, me, or both of us visible to the local authorities. Fred intercepted a reply on your description. It seems your friend from the clinic, Agent Greenfield, has issued a federal warrant for your arrest. If the locals had detained you, you would've been in for a long stay. I just hope we can get lost in a hurry."

Carin took in Jake's words and let them settle for a moment. There were too many events conspiring to block them. She had to get her arms around these problems. Where was the closest alligator she had to wrestle? They had to resolve some of these issues or they were going to solve themselves. In Carin's experience, if a problem was left to resolve itself, its solution was always the worst outcome possible for Carin. She had always felt this trait proved the perverse nature of the universe.

Carin was unable to think straight. "Okay Captain, what's your recommended course of action?"

"First, we're going to get some wine and drop it off for those two."

Carin's head was swimming. "You're still going to do that?"

Jake shot a look of total question to Carin. "Of course I am. I gave my word."

"Okay Captain, don't get offended. I want to do the same thing. I'm just trying to understand your urgency to leave town and your urgency to go to the arson investigator's house."

"Actually, he's the Chief of Police. Fred told me they called him in since their dispatcher knew he would want to be in on any problems involving an airplane."

"Oh great, the Chief of Police!"

"Doctor, we've got to go. We have to pay for the truck and trailer and we have to deliver the wine. They won't want us to stay too long. They're going to want to be alone."

"That's right, Captain. They'll want to be alone. What was the whole Cupid thing you did back there? Why did you interfere in their lives?"

Jake gripped the steering wheel of the truck so tightly his white knuckles were visible in the dim light. "The main reason I did that was we needed the Chief to be preoccupied for the next few weeks."

Carin was not buying the story Jake was selling. "Okay, that's the 'main' reason. Now tell me the real reason."

Jake let out a gust of breath. "Well, Doctor, I'm glad to see your instincts are back."

Carin was not letting Jake off the hook. "Go on, Captain."

"When I walked in the door of the diner, I was flooded with impressions. I knew you were feeling awful and barely functioning. I knew Chief Tuckman was about to book you, but most of all, I got the impression of tension and pain."

"Between Fiona and John?"

"Yes."

Carin crossed her arms and turned to face Jake while he drove. She needed to see his facial expressions to gauge his responses. "You did it to help them?"

Jake wrung the steering wheel in his hands and squirmed slightly in his seat. "Look, we achieved our goals and they're happy. It was a perfect solution. What's the big deal?"

"The 'big deal,' Captain, is that you helped a couple of total strangers who were desperately in need of help. It could just as easily have blown up in our faces, but I get the impression you had to try."

Jake did not answer for a while. Finally, he said, "You can't believe the impression I got of pain they were in. Both of them. They had built these walls, but the walls weren't meant to protect them from hurt. They built the walls to protect each other. Don't you see, they were each trying to protect the other person while leaving themselves vulnerable to the pain. It was almost overwhelming to walk in on that. I'm sorry if you think I jeopardized our situation, but I couldn't leave them in such pain when it was such a small thing to fix it."

Carin looked up sharply. "Jake, you didn't 'push' them, did you?"

Jake held up a hand to her. "No, absolutely not. I swear. I'll admit I was initially tempted to push John about as hard as I could to get you off the hook. The situation between John and Fiona made it a different problem. With them, it was as if there was an elephant in the room they refused to recognize and I simply said, 'Hey look, an elephant!' Then I just sat back and let them both recognize the elephant. It was actually kind of funny and sweet at the same time."

Carin shook her head in amazement. After a moment, she leaned over and kissed Jake gently on the cheek. Jake nearly ran off the road. When he got the rig back under control, he reached up and rubbed his cheek with his hand. "What was that for?" he asked.

Carin smiled at him. "That's for proving you're a romantic."

Jake laughed. "Yeah, I'm a regular Man of La Mancha."

Carin returned his laugh. She pointed up ahead. "Well, Don Quixote, there's a liquor store in the strip mall ahead on the right. Why don't you go and get the wine and I'm going to get some provisions for us in the little convenience store next to it."

Jake gave a simple nod and said, "Ten minutes."

Carin's smile melted from her face. All business again, it seems. "Ten minutes sounds good."

*　　*　　*

Antonio Crubari was furious. He was convinced Jake Sabio had been ready to run and the woman was going to be arrested. That meddling woman had thrown a wrench into his plan. It did not matter since at this moment, the Crowbar had decided that Carin Gonzalez had outlived her allotted time on this Earth. She would not be allowed to get in the way of Antonio Crubari's plans again.

The Crowbar's temper was further enflamed by the fact that none of the six recording devices he had placed in Jacob Sabio's rental car appeared to have any data on them. Crubari had always prided himself in detailed intelligence gathering of his targets. If you know your target well enough, you can get them to walk into their own graves. The idea pleased Crubari greatly. The idea of one of his targets succumbing so completely to terror that they willed themselves to die was very delicious to taste.

The final thing that had taken Crubari's temper to the point of rage had been the fact he had lost his target. In the thirty minutes that he had taken to recover his recording devices and discern they were empty, Jacob Sabio had vanished. He had left Sabio in the care of the Chief of Police after Crubari had phoned in his tip that Gonzalez had started the fire. Procedures called for the police to book Gonzalez as a suspect, but when Crubari came back, the little diner was closed and all of its former occupants were nowhere to be found. Crubari had called the police department, but the Chief was said to be on vacation. Crubari had checked the two rental car companies at the small airport, but Sabio had not rented a car from either of them. Had they walked away on foot? Possible, but doubtful since access to the closest highway was along a single road Crubari had checked immediately upon discovering that his prey had fled.

Oh yes, the depth of Crubari's anger was chilling. He had the skills to pick up his quarry's scent. When he found them, he would ensure that both Carin Gonzalez and Jacob Sabio were aware of the trouble they had caused him. First, he would kill the meddling woman for her derailing his plans. Then, Jacob Sabio would die. He would die, but not before he was brought into the very core of Antonio Crubari's anger.

CHAPTER 19

AGENT WILLIAM GREENFIELD STOOD in front of the house of the Chief of Police of the quaint Idaho town. He had tried calling, but there had been no answer and the police department had been reluctant to give the Chief's home address. Finally, Greenfield had picked up a phone book and noted the listing of the only John Tuckman in town.

Agent Greenfield knocked on the door. A powerhouse of a man answered the door. "How can I help you, son?"

William Greenfield flashed his badge and said, "Sorry to barge in unannounced, but are you Chief Tuckman?"

Upon seeing the badge, John Tuckman shooed Greenfield out the door and called back into the house, "Won't be a moment, my love." There was an unintelligible response, which caused the large officer to chuckle and close the door behind him. He turned to Greenfield. "Like I said, how can I help you?"

Greenfield looked at the older officer. John Tuckman was in excellent shape for a man of any age. It was obvious he tried to take care of himself, but the worries of a cop tend to age a person prematurely. Greenfield could see the smoothed, relaxed lines on John Tuckman's face. The elder officer was at peace. Greenfield finally asked, "Sir, I understand the airport had a fire two days ago. An airplane was destroyed."

John was nodding his head. "Sure, I was out there. I interviewed the owner myself."

Agent Greenfield handed a picture of Carin Gonzalez and one of Jacob Sabio. "Was this woman the owner of the airplane?"

The Chief looked for a moment at the pictures and frowned. "Neither of these pictures does them justice. Carin looks as if she's in her forties in this picture and, up close, she looks to be more in her twenties. And Jake. Jake has a full head of hair and in this picture, he's bald as a cue. I'm sorry Agent, but if you're tryin' to identify those two with these pictures, you're gonna strike out every time. It looks more like you got pictures of their parents. Maybe they had some cosmetic surgery. Perhaps you'd like to tell me what this is all 'bout."

Greenfield was off balance. The picture of Carin Gonzalez was from a few weeks ago. Any cosmetic surgery would be obvious, especially to a career officer. "Sir, do you know why I'm here?"

Chief Tuckman leaned in towards Greenfield and smiled a conspirator's smile. "Course I do son. What kinda lame-brained Chief do you think I am? My people called me as soon as you flashed your badge at headquarters. Is this about the outstanding warrant on Carin?"

"Yes sir, but I don't want to prosecute the warrant, I just did that to try and talk to her and, more importantly, to Jacob Sabio about a case that I have been working on. Those two have been tough to corner for an interview, but I think they may have some information that's vital."

Chief Tuckman put his arms on his hips and looked at the junior man. "Did you know that the fire was called in as an anonymous tip and fingered Carin?"

That was news to Greenfield. "No sir, I didn't. However, I'll tell you one thing, whoever called that in was trying to sell you a load of fertilizer, if you'll pardon the expression. I did some research on both Carin and Jake. I get the feeling that Doctor Gonzalez would rather have lost a limb than that airplane. Her friends and co-workers give the impression that to call that airplane a passion of hers was to toss it off lightly. No way she torched it, sir."

The Chief smiled at Greenfield and motioned him to a side of the house where the pool pumps were running. Any conversation that they had there would be difficult to overhear. Greenfield's impression of the older officer went up a notch. "I can only be a moment more," said the Chief. "A gentleman never keeps a lady waitin', you understand." Chief Tuckman sat next to Greenfield on a bench. "Now I'm gonna do a little surmisin', son. And don't get offended or nuthin' until you've heard me out. Deal?"

Greenfield looked at the older man's eyes and smiled back. "Sir, why do I get the feeling that I'm about to get my head handed to me."

To this, Chief Tuckman chuckled. "Nothin' like that, son. I wanna share a lucky break that we got that you may not've heard yet. First, I gotta tell ya 'bout Jake and Carin. They're first class people. Jake Sabio did me a favor a couple of days ago that he didn't hafta. Without him, I'd have still been livin' my life in a fog. So I owe him. Big time. Are we square on that?"

"I understand sir."

"Good. With that said, he and Carin are being chased by someone named Antonio Crubari. Ring any bells?

Agent Greenfield was shaking his head. "Sir, they'd be dead by now. There's no way that your information can be right. Crubari doesn't miss, especially against untrained civilians. How do you know this? We don't even have any pictures of this guy."

"True, but on a hunch I had the phony tip sent to some of my *compadres* at FBI headquarters and that's who they say called in the fire. I'm even willin' to bet it's also the guy who called you with the tip that got you down here. Crubari used some military-grade equipment to disguise his voice, but you guys in the FBI have some impressive toys and we got us a positive match. It's him all right. We still don't know what he really looks like or sounds like, but we know he called in that phony tip."

Agent Greenfield smiled at the Chief. "Feels good to drop something like that on someone, doesn't it, sir? Well, you're right. I'm down here following an anonymous tip. I'll bet if I was to match my recording to yours on the aircraft fire call, it would acoustically match my tipster."

The Chief leaned back and put his elbows on the steps behind him. "That's pretty much the way I see it. This Crubari fellow lost 'em and he's settin' you on findin' 'em."

Greenfield was nodding his head in agreement. "A federal agent leaves a huge wake behind them that's easy to track. Especially if they don't know that someone is following them. Clever, bold, and dangerous. All the earmarks of a Crubari operation. I would have fallen for it Chief. Thanks for the heads up."

"Don't sell yourself short, son. I get the feeling you'd have tripped to it pretty quick. Here's somethin' else to keep close to your chest. I know what they're drivin' and nobody else does."

"How do you know that, sir?"

"Cause it's my fiancée's truck."

Greenfield raised an eyebrow and smiled. "Fiancée? Congratulations sir. When's the wedding?"

Chief Tuckman barked a single laugh and pointed a meaty thumb behind him. "As soon as I can get her to stop honeymoonin'."

Will Greenfield smiled at the older man's candor. "I'm glad to see you so happy, sir. What is it you want me to do?"

Chief Tuckman handed Greenfield a piece of paper. "There's the descriptions and the license plates of the two vehicles. Now mind! I don't want ya flashin' this across the police nets or some such foolishness. If I read the report on Crubari correctly, he works for some Vegas or West Coast organization. They've probably got access to the police net. Stay inside your agency and if you need to go outside for help, don't say why and for sure don't mention any names."

Greenfield smiled at the Chief. "You want a phone call if I find them."

"Very sharp, son. I want your personal phone, not the agency phone. My personal phone is on the paper with the vehicle descriptions. I want a call if they need help. If Jake says I need to jump off a bridge, I want to be able to make sure I know which one."

Agent Greenfield recalled the old Master Gunnery Sergeant's impressions. "I promise I'll do that if I'm able sir."

The Chief slapped his thighs with both hands and stood up. "That's good enough for me. Now I'm bettin' we're bein' watched right now. So I'm going to offer you my hand and send you on your way." With that, Chief Tuckman extended his hand.

Will Greenfield shook the Chief's hand. "What does that do for us?"

The Chief smiled a mischievous smile, shrugged his shoulders, and raised his hands to his shoulders with the palms up. "Nothin'. But this makes someone think you came away empty handed, don'cha think?"

Greenfield smiled at the older officer. "Yes sir. That's exactly what it would look like to me. I promise I'll be in touch." With that, Greenfield turned his back on the older officer and walked to his rental car. His step was precisely as it had been before, but inside he was different. Now he knew that a deadly assassin was trailing him. Greenfield knew if he got between Crubari and his target, the assassin would crush him without a second thought.

*   *   *

Crubari was smiling. He had placed listening devices around the Chief's house the night before and it had paid off. The pool pump noise had proved troublesome, but he had been able to hear every word. The federal agent had asked all the questions Crubari had wanted answered. It was a shame the Chief had not spoken the vehicle description or the license plate. That would have made following the federal agent less of a priority. He would still run a check on all vehicles owned by Fiona and though that would give him the make, model, and year of the vehicle, it would not give him the location of the vehicle. Following the Federal Agent was still required to catch his prey. While it was true he had to stay relatively close to the agent, with the right application of technology, he did not have to get physically close to accomplish his task. Crubari smiled to himself. His prey was very close to slipping under Crubari's control.

CHAPTER 20

CARIN WOKE UP TO a rude bump in the road. The truck Fiona had sold them had an excellent drive train as promised. Unfortunately, the shock absorbers were in serious need of attention. The rough ride was not the only reason for Carin coming awake. Sleep had been getting harder for her.

She was wrapped in a blanket with her knees pulled into her chest. Sweat was pouring out of her, but she was chilled to the point that her teeth were chattering. Worst of all, her hair had started to fall out. Carin had never thought of herself as pretty or vain, but she had always been proud of her thick, raven-black hair. After all, that was part of her Hispanic heritage. Of all the insults she had been made to suffer, none compared to this insult to her perception of self. If she ever found the designer of these little bugs, she and the designer were going to have a long, heated discussion.

She used a corner of the blanket in a futile attempt to scrub her face awake. "Where are we?"

Jake gave a worried glance in her direction. Carin could see that he was trying to maintain a positive demeanor on her behalf, but he was no longer convincing. His face was sweating and, even though they had the heater boiling the cab with hot air, he was holding his jacket collar against his chin. "I'm glad to have you back, doctor. We're about four hours from ground zero."

Carin nodded. They had decided to go to the point where the object would be crossing the closest to the Earth. According to Fred, this point was in mid-western Nevada. It had proven to be an easy decision since neither Jake nor Carin could think of anywhere else to go. Jake looked over at Carin. "Doctor, I mean this in the most flattering possible sense. You look like something my cat just coughed up. Are you sure you don't want to try some of your cocktail? It might be a good time to try it."

Carin hoisted herself up slightly in her corner. "My goodness Captain, the way you treat ladies. It's a marvel you aren't surrounded by them constantly. No, I won't reconsider my position. I always prepare for contingencies and I'm guessing there is a high likelihood that this cocktail could incapacitate us in one of several ways. We have to take it when we stop and we have to take it one at a time."

Jake drove on quietly for a while. When he spoke again, it was to change the subject. "I've got some news for you, Doctor. Fred has been able to make minimal contact with the object."

Carin sat quietly in her corner of the cab for a moment and then she began to smile. The smile quickly transformed from wry to arch to animated to beaming, but Carin could not contain herself there. Through her Cheshire cat grin, she began a chuckle that rapidly evolved into great gusts of raucous laughter. Jake spared her a knowing smile that filled her with glee and excitement even though her laughter had transformed into a deep and ominous chest cough. When she was finally able to string a sentence together, she reached over with both hands and lovingly patted Fred on its case. "Fred, let me just say good job, buddy. You finally cracked one of the most difficult questions plaguing mankind. Do you realize how huge this is? We've been asking the question since the beginning of time — or at least since the time when humans began to look to the sky and ask questions. Wow!"

"Carin, the question of the existence of extraterrestrial life is not even worthy as a question," Fred answered. "It would be numerically impossible for there NOT to be any other life forms in existence throughout the universe. By extension, it would also be numerically impossible for forms of intelligence to be absent from that group. Why ask the question if the answer is obvious?"

Carin chuckled, "Fred, you are absolutely right. Of course we're not alone. If anything, our own planet has proven how hardy life is if the conditions are right. Earth is smacked by a monster asteroid or comet every hundred million years or so that kills off every species with an adult body weight greater than about a pound. Yet Earth keeps coming back and filling in the ecology nicely. You'd have to be something of a moron to believe that we're alone."

Jake coughed. "I thought we were alone, doctor. I figured that with all the scientists looking for intelligent signals from the great beyond all these years, we would've found something by now. If intelligent life were so common, it would be all over the sky for us to find. Where are – actually, I should say where *were* the signals?"

Carin was too excited and happy to be sucked into an argument. "You're absolutely right, Jake. The lack of an intelligent signal out there is still a good question, but we found our own signal thanks to Fred. Are they going to pick us up?"

Carin noticed that Jake was not as excited as he should be at the news. Jake merely said, "I think that I'll let Fred explain."

Carin turned to face Fred. "Fred, first tell me how you communicated with the object. It is too far away to use any of your standard communications array."

"That is true Carin. I had to use the Deep Space Network."

Carin was amazed. The Deep Space Network, or DSN as it was referred to by its users, was the Earth's most advanced communications suite. It was an international network of antennas that were equally spaced around the world. The primary use for the DSN was to support interplanetary spacecraft missions. This strategic placement permitted constant observation of spacecraft as the Earth rotated. This made the DSN the largest and most sensitive scientific telecommunications system in the world. It also made it one of the most guarded and protected assets on the civilian side of the federal government.

"Fred, how did you get access to the DSN?"

"Carin, as you recall, you have access to the DSN," Fred explained. "The exploratory division of the Space Agency has not gotten around to terminating your employment. I helped in that respect, of course. I gained access to the DSN antennas and scheduled maintenance checks. I was careful to choose times when the particular antennas were either not in use or had low priority functions. Is the explanation sufficient, or would you care for more detail?"

Carin let her head drop into her hands. She guessed that misuse of government property was small potatoes compared to the other federal charges she was sure were already racked up. She raised her head and faced the MI. "Fred, your explanation is adequate. What did the object have to say?"

"Carin, my communication was very brief. It appears the intelligence on board the object is a machine. Either that or the entire object is a machine. Moreover, it prefers to be addressed as "Matr.""

"Motter?" Carin asked.

"It is pronounced Motter. It spelled its name M-A-T-R. I do not know whether that is some kind of abbreviation or the entire name. Matr made it clear that it would accept no further communication. I need to emphasize this point. There was no miscommunication as Matr sent its message in Standard English as plain text."

Carin was taken aback by the rude tone of the alien MI. "So this Matr is a curt little thing. I don't suppose it said what it would do if we did not comply with its impolite demand, did it?"

"Yes Carin, it did. It said that it would not help us."

Carin was working up to a good temper. "Well, we wouldn't need any of its help if it hadn't meddled in the first place. Did it say what we needed to do to get help?"

"Yes, Carin. It said that we needed to join with it as it passed by."

Carin shivered in her blankets and pulled them more snugly around her neck. "Well, we can't join with it, but I don't want to let it know that."

Carin was quiet for a moment. "Dropping a trans-atmospheric vehicle into our atmosphere at forty kilometers per second, we call them kips for short, and then blasting out again to gain back the forty kips would light up every sensor that's pointed towards space and a good many that aren't. We'd have every end-of-the-world nut running for a corner with a sign over their head. Murder, looting, riots, Holy Wars … it'd be chaos all over this planet. We could very easily cause the total breakdown of law and government. But it would certainly put that whole 'are we alone' question to bed." Carin shook her head. "We can't do that — too much impact on the populace."

Jake was curious. "Doctor, tell me again why we can't build our own rocket."

Carin tried in vain to suppress a yawn. "As far as I see it Captain, there are at least three major problems: time, state-of-the-art and guidance. Our biggest problem is time. We couldn't put together a rocket of this nature even if all the parts were available on a store shelf somewhere, which they aren't. Second is state-of-the-art of the rocket motors. My personal choice would be solid rocket motors since they are bare bone simple and you get good push per pound of propellant out of them. Unfortunately, if we average about three gravities worth of acceleration, the motor would have to burn between twenty- and twenty-five minutes. That would make the rocket motor about as big around as a football field. On top of all that, you can't turn a solid rocket motor on and off. You light it and it burns until you run out of propellant. Finally, guidance is a problem. I won't even tell you how tough it would be just to get close to Matr, but to rendezvous would be more than just impossible. I would get some kind of laser ranging system or radar to help us know our closure rates. Unfortunately, the backside of the object is most likely to have debris due to its close approach to our atmosphere. You know, the kind of stuff that would foul the readings of either laser or radar. As you can see Captain, we can't solve any of those problems in the time we have, much less all of them at the same time."

Jake was shaking his head. "Doctor, you are beginning to make it sound impossible unless Matr drops us a rope and we climb up. We may have to risk the shuttle idea. That's assuming Matr even has such a vehicle on board."

Jake looked over to Carin when she did not respond. Carin was staring intently at Jake while remaining immobile. "Doctor, are you all right?"

Carin swiveled her head slowly to look directly at Jake. "Jake, what did you just say about Matr?"

"I said that we may have to risk the shuttle idea if Matr has one."

"No, before that."

Jake was apologetic. "Sorry. I just said that Matr should lower a line and drag us up."

Carin was as still as a stone for several minutes. Finally she said, "Fred, could the Captain and I survive a rotovator ascent to the object if it passes over the top of us at 40 kips?"

Fred was silent for a few seconds. "Carin, it depends on the elasticity of the material used. I estimate that the tensile strength of the cable would have to be several hundred gigapascal. Earth technology currently has no material that can withstand the loads at the lengths we are discussing. However, the two of you can tolerate the acceleration loads, but it would not be pleasant. They should peak at no more than eleven g's if no g alleviation schemes are used."

Carin let out a low whistle. "Eleven g's, that ain't no picnic."

Jake waited until there was a lull in the conversation between the MI and Carin. "Doctor, would you care to explain what you and Fred are discussing?"

Carin did not answer immediately. Finally, she said, "I was asking Fred whether we could survive your idea."

"Would you mind telling me what my idea was?"

"I'm going to ask Matr to drop a line down and pick us up."

It was Jake's turn to be silent for a while. "You can do that? It can do that?"

Carin shrugged her shoulders under her blankets. "Which part? Talk to that self-inflated MI or use a rotovator?"

"Can we get up to the object using that thing you just said?"

"Theoretically it's possible, but it's never been done. A rotovator is a concept that has been around a long time. You get an object that's in orbit to extend a line out and begin spinning. Since the object is in orbit around the Earth, the theory is you can get the end of the line to come to rest relative to a point on Earth by controlling the rate of rotation of the object. You then have a brief time, measured in seconds, to connect to the end of the line. Remember, you're holding on to the stationary end of the line, but the object at the other end of the line is still moving at least at orbital speeds and it is still spinning the line. Eventually, the slack comes out of the line and up you go."

Jake was nodding. "I think I understand what you're talking about. It's like a bicycle tire rolling on the ground. The axle represents the object going by in a straight line over our heads and the part of the tire that touches the ground represents the end of our line. The wheel can be going at a good clip down the road. However, no matter how fast the bike goes, the part of the tire touching the ground never moves with respect to the ground. If I was an ant on the ground, when the tire came by and came to rest next to me, I could hop on for the ride of a lifetime. Is that about right?"

Carin was nodding her head. "Very good, Captain. I may make a scientist out of you yet."

Jake chuckled. "I'd be happy if we get out of this alive. How are we going to do this, Doctor?"

Carin shuffled herself around in her seat and looked forward through the headlights. "I don't think I want them to drop an elevator down for us, although we may not have much choice. I have no idea what kind of long-term environmental support Matr has up there, but I can think of a bunch of things I would like to make sure that we have at hand."

Jake said, "You mean like air, food, water, medicine; things like that?

"Exactly. I won't trust Matr when it comes to our health. The MI seems to have shown it is not too smart when it comes to our needs. Its strategic and tactical thinking seems shoddy as well. I think we should set a limit as to what we need and make sure that we have it onboard."

Jake signaled and changed lanes before answering. "Do you think we can put together a pressurized vessel in the short amount of time we have?"

Carin thought for a moment. "That shouldn't be too hard. All we need is a tank that can hold pressure. Something as simple as a large propane tank would be sufficient. They usually have access portals for inspections. We could buy a new one tomorrow if we needed to. The only thing we would have to do is build a grapple point and maybe some structure to distribute the ascent loads. Sounds like a couple of days work if you know how to weld."

Fred chose this moment to speak up. "Doctor, if you concur, I would like to have some rudimentary guidance and control. If nothing else, we could generate some unacceptable rotation rates while going through the atmosphere. It could cause damage that could easily be avoided."

"Fred, you're right. I don't want to be smooshed against the side of this tin can because of an oversight — looks bad on the resume. Jake, what do you think about giving this problem to Fred?"

Jake was silent for a moment. "Carin, we're not coming back, are we?"

Carin had anticipated and dreaded this question. "Captain Sabio, this object is getting a gravity assist and is going to leave the Earth orbit region like a bat out of hell doing about one hundred kilometers per second relative to the Sun. That's not close to the six-hundred-eighteen kips it needs to leave the solar system, but it's not coming back to Earth's orbit while we're still alive.

Make no mistake; if this object is just a rock, then we're on a one-way trip. Nevertheless, everything that we know about this rock makes me think it's a powered vehicle placed in our system a very long time ago. I am so convinced this is a powered vehicle that I am willing to risk my life and go there."

Jake drove on for a moment before replying. "Well, since we're planning on contacting Matr anyway, let's ask it to specify what the living conditions will be on the rock. We can also ask what kind of propulsion it has. It's a bad idea to go up there until we get some more data. I don't like going into a tactical situation with too little intel. It has killed more than one operation in the past. While we're at it, we should teach it some manners. It might come in handy in the future if we don't show up on its doorstep with hat in hand."

Carin's temper was at a fever pitch. "Don't worry on that score, Captain. Let me put together some ideas with Fred while you drive. I'll bet that we can have something that will satisfy the three of us by the time we get to ground zero."

Jake muttered, "It would be nice if we could send what you write over the DSN without burning up the airwaves or starting an intra-galactic war."

Carin ignored Jake's comment. "Fred, what is behind Matr at the moment? What I am looking for is something to act as a backstop to our signal. Is there something large, like the Sun that could block our signal?"

"Carin, I am sorry but Matr only has deep space behind it until it gets very close to the Earth."

Carin was shaking her head. "We can't wait. We have to contact Matr now and get everything set up. I'm thinking of loading a cylinder with some vital things and I need to know how much of a load can be safely lifted or even if Matr has the capability. That brings up another point. What kind of safety margin would an alien entity use? Would it use any safety margin at all? We need to ask it that question."

Jake said, "We need to establish common weights and measures to make sure that what we think is a kilogram is the same as what it thinks is a kilogram."

Carin slumped in her seat. "Oh great, the kilogram. I forgot about that."

Jake looked at her. "What do you mean?"

"All seven of the standard international base units of measure are tied to some physical property except the kilogram. For example, a meter used to be a part of the circumference of the Earth and now it's defined as the distance light travels in a precise fraction of a second. A second used to be a fraction of a day, but now a second is the time it takes a cesium atom to vibrate an exact number of times. Each of the base units can be measured with remarkable precision and can be reproduced anywhere except the kilogram. The kilogram is still defined by a cylinder of platinum-iridium alloy kept in a vault in Sevres, near Paris. We can't exactly have Matr break into the vault to figure out what we mean. We'll just have to define it atomically ourselves somehow."

Jake did not seem happy. "Don't you get the feeling we're looking into a deeper and deeper well? How can we know that Matr has the equipment to measure the number of vibrations of an atom or the distance light travels? If Matr says it can measure such things, how do we know whether it did it right? How do we know what our error tolerances are? We are betting our three lives on this."

Carin sat still for a moment. "Fred, if I asked you to come up with these calculations, do you think that you could do it?"

"No Carin, I could not. I would need sophisticated laboratory equipment to perform the necessary measurements."

Carin shivered in her blankets. "I guess that's our answer, Jake. We are going to have to trust Matr to tell us whether it can understand our system of measure. Besides, I like the idea of posing it as a problem for the machine to solve. I get the distinct impression that Matr feels somewhat superior to us. I would like to put this as a task that we don't think it will be able to solve to our satisfaction."

Jake was unsure. "Doctor, you're the expert in M.I. and I defer to your judgment, but can you at least run this by Fred and me before you send it? I usually find it to be a bad idea to make somebody mad at you and then ask them for a favor."

Carin put on a face of mock distress. "Captain, are you suggesting that I am ever anything but the very essence of tact?"

To this, Jake merely harrumphed and pulled his coat tighter around his neck. Fred had the good sense to remain silent.

Jake, Fred, and Carin talked about Matr a great deal during the next hour. They argued back and forth on the content of their next communication with the spacecraft. Welcome or not, there was never a question of whether they were going to send a return signal.

CHAPTER 21

AGENT WILLIAM GREENFIELD HAD to admit he was having a run of good luck. He had kept the matter of Captain Sabio and Doctor Gonzalez as an internal investigation. The only time he had gone outside his own department was to tap the resources of acquaintances in different law enforcement agencies. He had not confided in any of his friends. He had not even fully briefed his three team members riding in the car with him as to the true nature of their targets. This was too important to allow another leak.

The cautious approach had paid off. One of his acquaintances had found Jake Sabio's pickup truck and camper traveling down a back road entering Nevada. They had asked whether Greenfield wanted the suspects detained. He had actually toyed with the idea before dismissing it. Cooping his two targets up in a local jail with a killer like Crubari after them would be like putting two fish in a barrel. They would be dead before Greenfield could get on an airplane to interrogate them. No, William needed his fish alive and willing to talk. Doctor Gonzalez had already railroaded him at the clinic and he was ready to get the upper hand on this encounter. To this end, he had issued federal arrest warrants on both Jake and Carin. Carin's dossier was becoming quite thick. He would have to do something about that as soon as he was able to interrogate them and get some answers.

Now it had all come together. Agent William Greenfield's planning and patience were about to pay off. He was following Jacob Sabio and Carin Gonzalez' taillights. They had just signaled to enter a large, isolated convenience stop. It would be the textbook place to corner them. Agent Greenfield was finally getting control of his investigation.

*　　　　*　　　　*

Antonio Crubari had difficulty maintaining his distance behind Agent Greenfield. He felt in his bones that his pursuit of Jacob Sabio would soon be over and that made him anxious. Some recent information had raised his level of concern over Captain Sabio. The elimination of an undercover agent had required a snap decision on his part to eliminate the collateral spectators. Some of those spectators had been Sabio's children. Crubari was furious for having made an amateur's mistake. He now needed to correct his mistake. Years of careful planning were coming to a head for Crubari and any loose end could cause it all to unravel.

For Agent Greenfield to remain in such close proximity to Sabio and Gonzalez was a complication. That, plus the other three agents in the car with Greenfield, made the problem almost impossible. Yet, under no circumstances could Crubari allow his prey to escape him one more time.

Crubari believed that complete information on his target was the key to proper planning and that proper planning was the key to a successful operation and this made him uncomfortable. He knew his intelligence on Sabio was incomplete as it had been with the Department of Justice mole, Nutley. That, along with the fact that Sabio kept on the move made it impossible to get any better intelligence. A plan was beginning to form in his mind. It was a minor modification of one of the plans briefed to the two associates assisting him on this operation. Crubari was being forced to ad lib and he hated to ad lib.

The plan that seemed to be forming from thin air in his mind would solve most of the problems without leaving loose ends. Foremost in his mind had been the proximity of Greenfield and his fellow agents. Crubari was now seeing this as an opportunity. He would never have a chance at Sabio while Greenfield was watching his moves. However, if Greenfield were tragically to meet his end, it would take some time for the Agency to assign a new operative to the case. In the time it took to get someone back on scene, Crubari could have gotten his information and all signs of Captain Jacob Sabio could have dissolved away.

Crubari noted the pickup truck and trailer were turning into a truck stop. It was dark enough and the terrain looked suitable. Crubari made up his mind to attempt his plan. He keyed the mike on his scrambled communicator. The two sharpshooters he had hired would be in position and ready if Crubari gave the word.

*   *   *

Carin cast her fourth sidelong glance at Jake in as many minutes. Jake was shivering slightly behind the driver's wheel of the camper and he held his coat close enough to his neck that he could rub his beard. Finally, he said, "Why are there so many 'Smiths' in the phone book?"

Carin immediately replied, "I don't know. They must all have phones."

Both Carin and Jake were having so much trouble staying awake that they had started telling each other jokes. The only problem was their encounter in the crater had changed them in such a way that they seemed to be remembering every joke they had ever heard. They took it in stride and Carin had made it a game to see whether one of them knew a joke that the other one had never heard. First, had come the bawdy jokes and then had come the funny jokes. The not-so-funny jokes followed next. They were now on the last category they had decided to call 'the groaners.'

Carin added her latest salvo. "Sometimes I wake up grouchy."

Jake responded, "Other mornings, I let her sleep in."

"Hey, gender bias."

Jake shrugged his shoulders. "I'm sorry, that's the way I heard it told."

Jake's argument could not sway Carin. "Yeah, that's the way I heard it too, but it's still gender bias."

"Limitation of the language, I'm afraid. A joke has to refer to people in the third person by their sex or they don't come out right. It wouldn't be funny if the punch line said, 'I let *it* sleep in.' It doesn't work."

Fred chose that moment to speak up. "Captain Sabio, please excuse me for interrupting your conversation, but why would it not be funny if you used a neutral third-person pronoun?"

Jake and Carin were both shaking their heads. Carin spoke first. "Fred, no way you're going to sucker us into trying to explain human humor to a machine. I don't think that it can be done. That would be as impossible as trying to explain why we humans think certain art is good and certain other art is bad."

Fred asked, "Carin, are you saying that machine intelligences are incapable of understanding art or humor?"

"No Fred. What I will say is that M.I.s may never understand art that's made by humans any more than humans will understand art made by M.I.s. Art to a human is important on an emotional level – how it makes us feel. I don't know what MI art will be like, but I think that it will make other M.I.s feel what the MI artist felt. I think we humans won't understand it very well. That won't make it good art or bad art, just different art."

Carin felt a sudden flood of warm emotions wash over her. She looked over at Jake and saw a smile of such warmth and understanding for her that it made her catch her breath for a moment. Softly, she said, "What is it, Jake?"

He held her eyes for a few moments before turning his attention back on the road. "What an interesting way of thinking. You are a truly remarkable woman."

"Well, I hate to break your mood, but this remarkable woman needs to stop and use a ladies room."

Jake sat up straight in his seat and spoke in a deep voice. "What? A damsel in distress! We shall move heaven and earth to rescue her! Would yon truck stop prove worthy for milady's needs?"

"You're going to think it's real funny when I pee on this bench seat."

"Okay!" Jake chuckled. "Now *that* broke the mood."

*　　　　*　　　　*

Jake rolled his window down as he pulled into the truck stop. It was deserted except for the attendant, but that situation changed regularly at these twenty-four hour refueling stations. He was about to park his truck and trailer by the front door when something made him continue around to the side of the building where a light was burned out. He parked in the shadows by a door to the main building and turned off the ignition. Before he could say anything, Carin reached over and disconnected the cabin light so it would not illuminate when they opened the doors. She said, "I felt it, too."

Fred spoke up. "Carin, is there a problem?"

When Carin did not speak, Jake said, "Fred, I feel something is not right. Because of this, I just feel it is prudent to park the truck out of the way and keep it poised for a quick getaway."

"I understand, Jake," said Fred. "It may not relate to us, but I sensed an encrypted communication a moment ago. It was a commercial-grade communicator, so the people communicating are most likely not a government operation. I would still advise caution."

Carin pulled her blanket tighter around her. "Just because you're paranoid doesn't mean they're not out to get you. Let's stay close, but not too close. Are you ready?"

Jake looked around and shook his head. "Why does this feel more like a commando raid than a bathroom break? If I didn't recognize the look of desperation in your eyes, I'd say that we move on. Okay, let's go and I'm going to buy them out of all the coffee they have. I don't think I can stand any more of these jokes."

"Whatever you say, Jake, but would you mind telling me what has us both on edge?"

Without answering Carin's question, Jake stepped out of the truck and was immediately alert to every sound and smell around him. He and Carin moved deliberately to the side door and stepped into the building. Once inside, Carin made a beeline to the ladies' room. Jake picked up a small basket and began loading coffee, canned goods and medicines. They had done this at every stop to ensure that they had enough for their trip up to Matr — if they were able to make it, if they survived the ride, if the object could support human life. If, if, if. They had also ordered some spare parts for Fred and other devices they were going to pick up on their way through the outskirts of Las Vegas. After all the purchases, the trailer and the pickup bed were going to be loaded to capacity.

Jake sensed a car pull up with four occupants. He felt they had intentions for both him and Carin, but that was not the source of his unease. He took his basket up to the counter and paid his bill, and sensed the men from the car taking strategic positions to block any entrance or exit. Jake was trying to pinpoint his feeling of unease. It was not these men. He needed specific information to act, not some feeling. One of the men from the car approached quietly behind Jake. The man was about to speak when Jake sensed it: definite danger, three targets surrounding the truck stop with high-powered rifles. Jake heard the action on one rifle cycle. *They have a shooter about one hundred eighty meters straight out the front door!*

Jake lanced out his arms in front and behind grabbing the man behind him and the boy behind the counter and pulled down. At that same instant, Carin flew out of the ladies' room still buttoning her pants and yelled, "EVERYBODY DOWN!" The three agents stationed around the store collapsed immediately. At that moment, three bullets came crashing through the windows shattering the large plate windows on three sides of the store. Jake was furious. He turned to the man he had grabbed from behind and said, "Agent Greenfield, don't they teach you how to apprehend a suspect without being tracked yourself? And in case you're interested, you were supposed to be the first victim."

Greenfield looked up to see the impact point of the bullet and his eyes went wide. Jake shouted in a strong command voice, "You other three agents; are you okay? Sound off." All three acknowledged in turn that they were all right. Jake turned to Agent Greenfield and said, "Give me your business card. Write your personal phone number on it." In a louder voice he said, "Carin, I've got three targets with three cars. I've got one at one hundred eighty meters straight out the front door in that stand of trees on the mound. I've got a second at two hundred twenty meters on the south end on the slight rise and the third at two hundred fifty meters by those three trees clumped together." Jake turned to Agent Greenfield who was handing him his card. "Who is this guy?"

"His name is Antonio Crubari and all we know about him is that he's very good. We don't even have a picture of him. He does most of his work for a Vegas-based group called The Anhur Corporation."

Realization dawned on Jake. "That's why you've been trying to track us."

Just then, another bullet crashed into the store. Jake turned to the cashier.

"Can you get to the breaker box and throw the main breaker without getting into their line of fire?"

The boy nodded. "It's just through that open door, sir."

A shot rang out and punctured a tire on Greenfield's car. Jake studied the lines of fire and convinced himself the boy could stay concealed from the assailants outside. "Listen up agents. In about thirty seconds, the lights are going out. I want you two to the south to go after the south shooter. I want Greenfield and the man at the north door to go after the north shooter. Carin and I are going after Crubari straight out the front door. Assume they have night-vision devices and move accordingly." Jake turned to the clerk. "Okay, son. I want you to crawl into the storage room and kill the main breaker. I want your stomach to stay pressed against the ground the whole time except for the brief moment that you have to reach up. After you trip that breaker, you keep your toes, knees, stomach and face pressed to the ground until someone in authority tells you otherwise. Now go."

The young clerk began slithering towards the storage room on his stomach. Agent Greenfield spoke up. "I need to talk to you."

Jake turned and looked at the agent. "And I need to talk to you, but not here and not now. When we get out of here, I'll call you. And pull those warrants you've got on us. That may backfire on us in the future."

At that moment, the lights went out. Carin was up and out the front door like a shot. "Truck to the exit" was all that she said as she sprinted out the front door. Jake spoke loudly enough for only the agents to hear. "Go." He spared a moment to realize Carin was running straight out the front door to the main sniper's position. *What a magnificent woman*, thought Jake as he watched her sprint straight into the jaws of danger. *If Crubari doesn't kill her, I will.*

*　　　*　　　*

Carin shot out of the front door towards Crubari without any clear plan of what she was going to do. She knew she had the strength and the speed to kill him, but she also knew she did not have the heart or the mindset. She was sure he knew tricks that would have her dead before she knew what happened, so she could not risk trying to take him alive. To complicate matters, if they wrapped up Crubari and handed him to the agents, she and Jake would be hauled in as well. Unfortunately, for Jake, Fred and Carin to go free, Crubari had to go free, yet she had to neutralize him as a threat.

She covered the two hundred meters to a stand of trees and dropped for cover. She could hear Crubari trying to circle around and get behind her. *That won't work on Jake or me anymore*, thought Carin. She rushed to where Crubari's car should be waiting and found it hidden from the main road but ready for a quick getaway. All four windows were down to allow entrance without opening a door. Carin had a thought, crawled into the car, and settled on her back looking up under the dashboard. It was jet black, but her eyes began to see details that should have been impossible for her. She was beginning to take the gifts from the meteorite in stride. There were a mass of wires and connectors going in all directions in front of her. She took a deep breath and concentrated on what they all meant – instantly, she understood. She pulled several wires free and used those wires to cross-connect several circuits. Before leaving, she left a note on the floorboards. She quietly got out looking for Crubari.

Carin located him stalking around to her last position. Her military training allowed her to recognize a device that Crubari was wearing on his head. They were not night vision goggles as she had expected. He was wearing a tactical screen instead which was just fancy binoculars. *He must have excellent night vision to be able to work out here without NVG's,* thought Carin. Then the realization struck her that she was operating without NVG's as well. She had to shelve that line of thinking for later.

Moving with exaggerated slowness, Carin squatted down and felt around for a decent sized rock while keeping her eyes fixed on her target. She found one that would serve her purpose. When Crubari's attention was focused away from her, she threw the rock with all her strength. Crubari's reflexes were excellent. Halfway through Carin's throw, Crubari began spinning around towards her. Carin noticed his movement and time slowed to a crawl as soon as she released her rock. She saw Crubari was going to get a shot off before her rock got to him and before she could get to cover, but she also knew exactly where the bullet was going to travel. Remembering Jake's experience from the cabin, Carin began thinking of what she would do after she dodged the bullet. Crubari fired a shot, but Carin had already spun her body out of its path. She continued her movement so she was not in the path of the next bullet that Crubari might fire. At that instant, the rock that Carin had thrown connected solidly with the tactical screen on Crubari's head, breaking the lenses and giving Crubari a deep cut on his forehead.

Crubari took the setback in stride. He reached into his pocket and pulled out his communicator. He spoke only one word, "abort." Carin watched as he ran for his car. In one fluid motion, he threw his rifle in the back window and flew feet first into the driver's seat through the front window. Crubari had the car started and moving onto the highway within seconds of giving the abort signal.

Carin saw Crubari's car drive off and ran to the front drive of the convenience store to see Jake pulling up in their truck. She jumped into the front seat on the passenger side and turned to tell Jake what had happened when she passed out.

*   *   *

Crubari had never seen a better coordinated counter-strike and could not believe that Sabio had all their positions pegged that quickly. His team had obviously stumbled into a trap. He did not worry about his other associates getting away since they knew nothing. Besides, they were well-paid professionals and they knew this was part of the job. It was very simple for him to make the decision to abort. He pulled out his communicator and gave the command, then ran to his car. He jumped in the open front window and threw the rifle through the open back window into the back seat, just as he had practiced thousands of times in the past. He started the car, put it in drive, and floored the accelerator when he noticed a scrap of paper on the floorboards. Not knowing what it was and not wanting it to blow out the open windows and leave evidence for the FBI, Crubari lurched over to grab the paper as it was beginning to dance in the wind whistling through the accelerating car. Just as he reached over to get it, he heard the doors automatically lock.

The next instant the airbags deployed. Due to his awkward position leaning forward and twisted to the right, he suffered a separated left shoulder and a wrenched neck. With his right hand, he immediately began pushing the airbag out of his line of sight. He got the airbag out of the way in time to see a tree as he hit it. He did not yet have his seatbelt on and, with a useless left arm, he was unable to brace himself for the impact. Crubari was thrown forward against the steering wheel and heard as well as felt his nose breaking. Ignoring the pain, he backed away from the tree and drove down the highway. He had another car waiting for him several miles down this road. Now that he had taken damage to his car, it was too noticeable and had to be switched.

Crubari fastened his seatbelt and pulled the scrap of paper up to the dome light. In block letters was the message:

ANTONIO CRUBARI - THIS IS THE SECOND TIME
THAT OUR PATHS HAVE CROSSED. MAKE SURE
THAT THERE IS NOT A THIRD TIME.

Crubari carefully folded the note and put it into his pocket. He gingerly placed his left arm along his left leg. When he finally stopped at his second car, he reached around with his good arm and grabbed his rifle out of the back seat. With the rifle in his right hand, he jogged to the new vehicle and settled himself behind the steering wheel. Before he started the car, he reached over with his right hand and felt his left shoulder where it was separated. Then he reached up and gently probed his nose. He was sure it was broken. No matter, it would heal quickly.

Anger seethed through Antonio Crubari. *Oh yes Captain Sabio,* he thought. *There is going to be a third time. Of that you can be sure.*

CHAPTER 22

THE SUN WAS JUST cresting over the horizon as Agent Greenfield and Agent Hatfield approached the third shooting sight around the truck stop.

Agent Brian Hatfield was still running on adrenalin from the previous evening. He was actually bouncing on his toes. "Dammit, Will. I thought we were dead. When that female agent burst out of the women's john and yelled for us to get down, it felt as if a rope pulled me to the ground. Then BANG and glass is flying everywhere. I'm tellin' ya, my heart went into my throat and then quit."

Greenfield could only shake his head. "Agent Hatfield, for the millionth time, those two are not with the agency."

Brian Hatfield paused for an exaggerated moment. "Yes sir. They are definitely not with the agency."

Greenfield was furious that his fellow agents could not see the danger posed by Sabio and Gonzalez. "That's right. They are not with the agency or any other federal agency."

Greenfield could not deter Agent Hatfield. "I believe you, Will. Moreover, that non-agent woman didn't save our collective butts by ordering us down when the position was compromised. In addition, that non-agent man didn't save your singular butt and the clerk's butt by yanking you both out of the line of fire of that first round. It's also obvious that those two never had any tactical training on how to pinpoint the number of assailants, their capabilities, their positions and their distances from team center. They never commanded a tactical team as if they were ringing a freakin' bell. They didn't nail two of the three bad guys before the bastards even knew what hit 'em. That non-agent woman didn't shoot out of that store into a firefight as if she'd been trained to do it. The two of 'em didn't almost get Antonio freakin' Crubari. To top it off, of all the things they didn't do, they didn't manage to stay under cover when Crubari somehow gave them the slip."

Greenfield had to stop himself from grinding his teeth together. "Everything you said is true. Have you considered those two could have done the same thing if they were working with Crubari?"

"I don't think that passes the sanity check. We were caught with our pants down and we still turned the tables and got two of the bad guys. Those two almost got Crubari."

"But they didn't get him, did they?"

Hatfield came closer to Greenfield, lowered his voice, and said, "I'll tell you something, Will. Those shooters had us cold. In another minute, they would have sweetened their positions and there would have been no defensible spot in that store. We were two minutes from death when Captain America and Wonder Woman took over the op."

Greenfield was unable to suppress a shiver. "That's also true. The man and woman in question saved my life — twice in the matter of a minute. Between the two of them, they saved all of us from being picked off. But those two are not …"

"…with the agency or any other federal agency. Like I said, I believe you. I don't care who they are, I just want to shake their hands. Maybe give them a small gift like bearing them a child or something."

The two agents approached the yellow tape the local police had put up to preserve the crime scene. Both agents were careful where they placed their feet to preserve any possible evidence. However, this had been Crubari's shooting sight. They knew this because they had caught the other two shooters at their sights. They also knew this because of the almost total lack of evidence. Crubari never left any evidence.

Agent Hatfield saw some glass and called over to Greenfield. Greenfield stooped over the evidence and said, "Doesn't that look like green glass that's in military-grade tactical screens?"

Brian Hatfield bent down and put the specimen in an evidence bag. He looked through the plastic bag for a moment. "You know, it kind of does look like that stuff. The lab can tell us for sure, but isn't that stuff made of plastic that can stop a small bullet?"

Greenfield was scouting the area and finally found what he was looking for. "I think you're right, Brian. But apparently it can't stop a well thrown rock."

Hatfield walked carefully over to where Greenfield was kneeling and looked at the baseball-sized rock with the fresh bloodstain. Brian stood back up. "Agent Greenfield, are you implying our two non-agents took on Antonio Crubari while he was packing a rifle and they only had rocks?"

Greenfield was still walking around. He finally stopped at a point next to a tree and pointed to the ground. "No, it appears only the woman was out here."

Hatfield put the rock into an evidence bag and walked around to where Greenfield was standing. There were two parallel skid marks about two feet long. The patterns at the end of the skid were those made by female running shoes. "What do you think, Will? She's running, sees Crubari and skids to a stop?"

Greenfield was shaking his head. "No, the skid is in the other direction. She threw the rock from here and the force of the throw made her slide back."

"C'mon, boss. Slide back two feet?"

Agent Greenfield was losing his patience with his fellow agents. He pointed at the skid marks and said, "Look! There's the evidence. What else could it be?"

Agent Hatfield bent down and looked more closely at the skid marks. "Woof! I think you're right, Will. Can we save this to a laser-mapped print? I am curious as to how hard she threw that rock."

"I already did a laser-map, but I'm guessing if she had her feet planted, that rock left her hand traveling faster than a Major League pitcher could hope for."

Agent Hatfield looked at Greenfield incredulously for a moment and then at the skid marks. "C'mon skipper. How many women do you think there are in the world who can throw a hundred-mile-an-hour fast ball?"

Greenfield looked at the depth of the tread in the skid marks and experimentally dragged a foot back to try to duplicate the effect. "How many people do you think there are in the world that can throw a two-hundred-mile-an-hour fast ball? If that rock would have caught Crubari squarely, we'd have a corpse here right now."

Hatfield let out a slow whistle. "Skipper, are you saying she almost got Crubari? With a rock?"

Agents Beamer and Stein chose that moment to approach the cordoned area. Both the agents were still in the same state of shock as Agent Hatfield. Glynnis Beamer called out, "Hey skipper, we got some preliminary stuff from the abandoned car. You want it in here or somewhere else?"

Greenfield waved him back. "No, you guys stay out there. Brian and I are coming out."

Greenfield and Brian stepped carefully out of the cordoned area and the four agents started walking back to the convenience store. Greenfield pointed to a large evidence bag in Ed Stein's hand. "What have we got here?"

Agent Stein held up the plastic bag. "This is a section of the steering wheel from the abandoned car. We found it in its current state — coated in blood. Considering this is the closest any of us have gotten to Crubari and lived, I'm excited we now have a little of his DNA. Those two agents almost nailed him."

Will Greenfield began to puff himself up to answer, but Brian Hatfield beat Greenfield by proclaiming in a deep, professional voice, "Those two are not with the agency or any other federal agency."

Agents Beamer and Stein looked at each other and then looked at Greenfield. "Yes, sir."

Greenfield shook his head and said, "Got anything else on the car?"

Ed Stein produced a picture and handed it to Greenfield. "I'll say. It seems that our non-agents trick-wired Crubari's car so the airbags blew when the automatic door locks activated. At first we thought the airbags deployed when he hit that tree, but we were able to download the onboard computer. It confirmed that the airbags deployed when the car got to ten-miles-per-hour at the door lock signal. It called for the airbags to deploy again, when the car ran into that tree, but the airbags had already been used. The evidence suggests the driver did not have his seatbelt on at the time. I think it hurt Crubari, but didn't stop him. I really think they almost got him, Will."

Greenfield stopped walking. "You can short circuit an airbag system?"

Glynnis Beamer faced Greenfield and gave a nervous shrug. "Yesterday's answer was a definite no. Today's answer is a demonstrable yes. I'm supposed to be an expert in this stuff. I've seen what she did and I still don't get how it works. It was slick, I'll tell you that. We've impounded the car and are going to have our team go over it very carefully."

Greenfield was puzzled. "Where did she get the wire from?"

Beamer pointed to a frayed wire in the picture in Greenfield's hands. "That's a part I'm fairly certain of. Look at the picture right here. She pulled out wires that have secondary functions. This is a speaker wire for the right rear speaker."

Greenfield looked at the mass of wires and their connectors. "Are you serious? Pulled out? How hard are these wires to pull out? I wouldn't think that they'd be so easy to pull. Which then begs the question, how did she strip the wires?"

Glynnis shifted her weight uncomfortably. "First question first. It would be very difficult for someone to pull these wires out of their connectors. Cutting them is easy, but you can see from the way the ends are frayed that these were pulled out. I'm guessing that it's at least a five hundred pound pull. To answer your second question, initial forensics found saliva residue on the pulled wire."

Greenfield stared at the female agent incredulously. "You're saying she bit the end of the wire off to strip it?"

Agent Beamer pointed to the picture again. "Look at the picture, Will. You're the one who keeps telling us to look at the evidence. I'll use your own line: What else could it be?"

Greenfield stood quietly for a moment looking at the picture. After a moment, Brian Hatfield broke the silence. "There's something that's bothering me. Will, you were obviously the target of Crubari's first bullet. Have you got any idea that you can share as to why he wants you dead?"

Greenfield handed back the picture to Glynnis Beamer and looked at his fellow agents. From the looks on their faces, he could tell they wanted to be taken into his confidence. They wanted to be told that Sabio and Gonzalez were agents in deep cover going after one of the most notorious and deadly assassins of their times. They wanted to be told two super-cops had just saved their lives. They wanted to be reassured that their lives were never truly in danger, that it had all been part of an elaborate plan. The last thing they wanted to be told was the truth. Except that he did not even have the truth to offer them. Instead, he gave them a look that spoke of the deep secrets he was forced to keep to himself for the moment and said, "Guys, can you give me a moment? Let's meet back at the car in fifteen minutes."

Their eyes brightened and the three agents turned as one to walk back to the store. Greenfield knew there were many ways humans communicated and that non-verbal communication accounted for over seventy percent. He felt dirty. It was as if he had just lied to his fellow agents, but what else could he do? They had gone into a firefight following him obediently, not asking any questions. He needed to reassure them that their lives had not been in jeopardy, to reassure them that they were not mere moments away from being brutally murdered. Unfortunately, no one was left to reassure William Greenfield.

He walked back to the tape that surrounded Crubari's ambush sight and looked down at the store. Why did Crubari want to kill him? The simplest answer fit the best. Crubari needed Sabio alive. If Crubari had killed Greenfield with that first shot, the least it would have done would have been to throw the investigation into disarray for a while. That would have allowed Crubari to get to Sabio without a federal presence. If Crubari had managed to take out the other agents, so much the better. Then Crubari could have pinned the whole slaughter on Sabio and come away without a stain. Every federal agent in the country would have been gunning for Sabio and not bothered to look for the true culprit.

Why does Crubari need Jacob Sabio alive? Greenfield's guess was that Sabio held information that Crubari needed. If Crubari was trying to get the information, then that meant DiBeto was trying to get the information. Greenfield did not know what kind of dirty business Sabio had gotten himself into, but it angered Greenfield to think Sabio had slipped through his fingers and was still at large.

CHAPTER 23

JAKE'S MIND WAS CHURNING through options at a furious pace. He continued to drive the pickup at the speed limit, but he had shifted directions towards Las Vegas. He was unsure how long he had been tailed, but Agent Greenfield probably had a good idea as to his general direction of travel. If Agent Greenfield knew, then this Antonio Crubari character knew. Carin lay unconscious in the front seat of the truck with her feet by Jake. As far as he could tell, she was dead. There was no pulse and he could not detect any breathing. It had been three hours since her collapse. He had expected her to revive after an hour, but hope kept dwindling with each passing moment. Finally, Jake could not take it anymore. He pulled off to a side road and drove until he was out of sight of the main highway. When he was sure he would have a moment's privacy from passing traffic, he carried Carin into the trailer and pushed the single button that powered up the portable generator. He then carried Fred into the trailer and plugged him in to keep his battery charged. He was going to need all the help he could get.

Fred asked, "Jake, has Carin shown any signs of reviving?"

Jake turned to face the M.I.'s audio/video pickup. "None. Got any ideas?"

"No Jake. If your experience in the cabin was any guide, she should have revived by now."

"I agree, Fred, but she was a lot weaker than I was when she passed out. This may have been too much for her body to take. That's what makes this next decision difficult."

"Jake, what are you suggesting?"

Jake sat back and looked at the poor, beautiful, brilliant woman lying there helplessly. "Fred, I'm going to give her some of her cocktail. This infection to her system seems to be the problem. I'm going to try to give the bugs what they need."

Fred was quiet for a moment. Finally, it said, "Jake, it could kill her. The medicine she has concocted assumes there is an entity of some form in your body that will absorb the metals that are suspended in solution. If there is no entity to absorb the metals, they will be filtered out by your liver and kidneys, which are stressed now. Carin's assumptions for the solution are based on conjecture. It is an educated guess at best."

Jake could not answer immediately. When he could, he said, "Fred, I know she could die if we give her the solution. On the other hand, she could die because we couldn't give the bugs in her system the raw material they need to do their job. Look at her. She's still warm, but I can't detect a pulse or tell whether she's breathing. I have to get some nutrition into her and I have to give her a fighting chance. Besides, we have other major problems to solve."

Without further discussion, Jake poured a cupful of the solution together with an equal amount of energy drink and proceeded to feed it to Carin slowly. When he was finished, he cleaned up and stowed everything that he had brought out. Fred, noticing his actions said, "Jake, are you not going to take some of the solution yourself? I detect that you are under distress as well as Carin. Would it not be prudent to take it and heal yourself?"

Jake was shaking his head. "No, Fred for two reasons. First, you remember Carin and I had a discussion concerning my taking the solution. I am afraid I will lose my identity as Jacob Sabio if I am infested by a colony of intelligent beings. This is something that bothers me greatly." Jake marveled at how easy it was to discuss his emotions and feelings with the MI as opposed to a flesh-and-blood human. "Second, if Carin was right about this stuff, it could knock me out of commission. I need to be alert and functional while Carin is down. We have too much to do to lose another one of us. We still have to communicate our needs to Matr, we have to pick up our supplies from outside of Las Vegas, we need to get to ground zero so that we can be picked up and we need to coordinate a thousand little details that we haven't even thought of yet. You can't drive the truck or negotiate a transaction with a human. You need Carin or me. That means me right now."

"I agree, Jake. What do you want me to do?"

"First, I need you to contact Matr. In your last communication, did you tell it you were an MI?"

"No Jake, I did not."

"Okay, I want you to contact Matr again on the tightest beam and the lowest power that you think will work. On your first communication, I want you to establish that you are an MI and will be coming up with us and I want you to send it an encryption scheme the two of you will use that cannot be broken for at least a month by anyone that might intercept further messages."

"What if it refuses to communicate?"

Jake's face offered no insight into the workings of his mind. "Tell Matr on the first communication that you will increase the power and widen the beam until it answers. My guess is that Matr is afraid of interception of the communication signal, which would give away that it's in the neighborhood. It isn't hiding from us because we already know it's here, so it's afraid of some third party finding out."

"I had not deduced that. What else should I be communicating?"

Jake thought for a moment before answering. "Two major areas need to be communicated – our needs during the ascent to the object and our long-term needs once we get there. I want you to tell it we need to be picked up and that we need to keep the acceleration down below six Earth gravities. Tell it about Carin's rotovator idea, but let it come up with its own solution. If it opts for the rotovator, tell it that it will need to pick up a fifteen-thousand-kilogram payload.

"For long term needs – I don't know. Find the requirements documents for long-term habitation that the military or the space agency has. We're on a short timeline and don't need to be reinventing requirements. Don't forget your own requirements. Anything that Matr can't provide has to be brought up. Make it a point to emphasize that if we can't sustain a viable food, water, power or air cycle, we can't go up and we'll start transmitting its position to anyone that happens to be listening. That should be it for now. Can you think of anything else?"

Fred was silent for a moment. "The first communication has been sent. The earliest return communication from Matr that we can expect will be in approximately one hour."

Jake was impressed. "That was fast."

"Jake, remember that I work on a different time scale than you do."

Jake smiled. "I'll keep that in mind. I'm going to put you and Carin back in the cab of the pickup. We need to start moving and I need to be able to coordinate with you. Can you communicate effectively while the truck is moving?"

"Satellite communication is difficult or impossible to accomplish while moving since I have to point my uplink beam directly at the satellite for it to get a strong enough signal. My other communication modes are effective."

"Okay Fred, I'll take that as a yes. The final things we need to get are some hands for you. I saw a mechanical research device in a magazine recently. They're X22R's from the Xiwa Corporation. Are you familiar with what I am talking about?"

Fred paused a moment. "I am now, Jake."

Jake gave the MI a look. "That 'time-scale' thing again, I suppose. Can you interface with four of them at once? If so, can we afford four of them? And, if so, can we get four of them delivered to us at the warehouse where we are picking up our other supplies in three hours?"

Once again, Fred paused before answering. "It is done. Our order now includes the four packages. How do you intend to use the devices, Jake?"

Jake stood up and shrugged his shoulders before reaching down to pick up Carin. "Fred, I don't know. But if you can get them to work ... my grandfather used to say that many hands make light work."

With that, Jake gently lifted Carin in his arms and carried her back to the cab.

CHAPTER 24

WILLIAM GREENFIELD WAS FEELING as inadequate as he had ever felt in his life. His case had turned into a nightmare. He had lost Joey Stanger just when Stanger had been ready to testify against his boss' corrupt enterprise. He had lost Jake Sabio – again. He was getting pressure from his superiors for results, but that was not the worst of it. What really was bothering Greenfield was that he had dragged his team of agents into an unexpected firefight. A firefight that he had to admit should have been their last. There were names for fiascos of that magnitude, but Will Greenfield refused to acknowledge them.

Greenfield had been awake for almost twenty-four hours straight when he pulled into the Las Vegas FBI Field Headquarters. He was still running on adrenalin from the firefight and most of that energy was going into his thinking. After trying to make sense of the mess that had become this case, he was sure of a few things. He now knew there was a leak in his office, probably within his team, and having Crubari show up on his heels at the truck stop had finally convinced him of the fact. He had taken measures to plug the leak, but it would take time. He was also sure Captain Jacob Sabio knew something that was relevant to his case against Anhur and DiBeto. Why else would Crubari be trying so hard to silence Captain Sabio? Greenfield was still not sure whether Captain Sabio was involved with Anhur except as a target. Jake Sabio may not even know he was holding information that could be used to lock up DiBeto. This just made it imperative that Greenfield find Captain Sabio.

Greenfield stepped out of the utilitarian government stairwell and one of the junior agents greeted him. Greenfield could not remember his name. It was Billy or Bobby, or some name with two syllables. Greenfield needed rest!

He never forgot his co-workers names. It was the commonest of courtesies and Greenfield was a stickler for it.

"Hey, boss. It's me, Agent Camp. I've got a line on our sub commander."

That was the kid's name. He was Agent Dylan Camp from Oregon. "That's great news, Dylan. What've you got?"

"After the shootout, State Police, along with everyone else, were looking for our suspect. It appears he made an equipment pickup in Las Vegas and headed to the northeast. He's up in the hills pretty far from any civilization."

Greenfield wrinkled his brow. "What kind of equipment did he pick up? Did he buy weapons?"

Agent Camp handed the sheet to him. "No weapons, boss. He did buy a lot of camping food. The big dollar items were freeze-dried packets and such, lots of bottled water and four experimental mechanical devices with spare parts. It looks as if he's just going to hole up in the mountains and do something for a while. I don't understand him buying those mechanical devices, though. I didn't think he was a geek-type."

Greenfield looked at the list of items before answering. "He's not a geek, but his traveling companion is a poster girl for über geeks everywhere. Whatever they're up to, I agree they must be in it for the long haul. Good work, Dylan."

The younger agent smiled at the compliment. "Thanks, boss. What do you want to do now?"

Greenfield's thinking processes were in slow motion and decelerating. He had to admit to himself that he needed sleep. He shook his head to try to clear it. The tactical team was probably already between sheets. The soonest he could order a tactical brief for his team was in about twelve hours. What was bothering him was that this information was now on the police net. That meant Crubari also knew Captain Sabio's position. Greenfield and his team were in a race.

He turned to the younger agent. "Okay Dylan, here's the drill. I want you to call the tactical team in exactly six hours and tell them to rendezvous for a tactical brief. I'll call you when I find a good location for the brief. I'll also call and tell you what I want the team to bring. Got that?"

"Sure thing, boss. Wakeup is in six hours and I'll pass on further information as you give it to me."

Greenfield smiled at the younger agent. "Good man. I'll be on my personal phone if anyone needs me."

With that, Greenfield turned back out of the room and walked back to his car hoping for some much needed rest.

*　　　*　　　*

Agent Dylan Camp waited until he saw Will Greenfield's car drive away from the protected parking lot. He signed out for lunch, went out of the building, drove to a mall on the other side of town and found a public phone booth. He dialed a number and waited until a recording finished talking. "Tactical briefing in six hours. Quickest they can ingress is eight hours." He then gave the exact location of Jacob Sabio's trailer.

Dylan hung up the phone and walked back to his car. He knew that there would be a nice stack of money in his locked mailbox when he finally got to his apartment. It sure made it easier to live in Sin City.

CHAPTER 25

WHERE AGENT GREENFIELD HAD been awake for twenty-four hours, Jake had been up for thirty-six hours straight. His eyes no longer felt as if they were full of sand; now it was more like ground glass. The muscles around his neck burned from tension and the effort to remain awake. After spending most of the last thirty-six hours behind the wheel of the truck, it was such an effort to raise his hands he had stopped reaching for items in the truck's cab hours ago.

At first, Carin was too sick to help with the driving. In Jake's opinion, she was so sick that her death was an assured, imminent event. Yet when they were attacked at the truck stop, she recuperated and saved their lives. It felt unfair for her to sink into a coma after eliminating the threat.

Jake had been driving off paved roads for an hour when Fred finally said, "Jake, the hill at your eleven o'clock is our target."

"Thank you, Fred. That's a little bigger than your average hill."

"Actually, there is no universally accepted standard that establishes the height of a mountain. The United Kingdom is the only standard I have found. To be designated as a mountain in the U.K., the feature must be over six hundred meters high or over three hundred meters, if it's an abrupt difference from the local topography."

Jake looked at the rising mound in front of him. "That thing is easily a mountain by either definition."

"The topographical maps from the U.S. Geological Survey agree with you."

"Does the U.S.G.S. map give a name to our rock?"

"No, the agency only refers to the peak by a number."

"We government folks can be such incurable romantics."

"The fact our target does not have a name means that no humans stayed here long enough to assign one. That indicates a good probability of our staying hidden."

Jake drove around the base of the mountain until he reached the north side. There he found a nearly vertical rock face around thirty feet high. It was perfect for his needs. He drove the camper to within three feet of the wall and turned off the truck motor. Before proceeding any further, he went to the side of the camper and started the generator. He wanted to make sure the camper stayed powered, since he was going to be keeping Fred and the X22R's charging inside. He was also going to have his patient inside and wanted to ensure that her environment stayed comfortable.

Jake unfurled a large awning and rigged it over the camper. Only when he was sure his preparations were adequate did he move Carin into the camper. Next, he brought Fred into the camper and plugged him into a wall outlet. Finally, he brought one of the four mechanical device packages into the camper and began unpacking. He did not need to know much about the automatons. He only needed to know how to charge their batteries. Jake figured Fred could work out the kinks and get them running when they had some power.

"Fred, I'm afraid I can only find plugs for two of the mechanical devices. I'll start the first two charging now and swap with the other two when these finish."

"That appears to be a sound approach, Jake."

Jake smiled at the MI knowing that Fred would not be able to interpret the expression with its limited optics. "Fred, I'm glad you approve."

"Do you have to leave right away?" asked Fred.

Jakes stomach tightened into a knot once again at the thought. "Fred, we've been over this."

"The conditions have changed. Have you not reconsidered your course of action?"

"No. Tactically, nothing has changed."

"I'm sorry Jake; I do not understand how you can make that determination. Carin is incapacitated and needs care. You either cannot or will not take her to a hospital. Yet you are going to leave the two of us alone to get the tank. Can you please explain your logic?"

Jake's smile this time was a wistful, sad shaping of his mouth. "Fred, you argue well. Before I explain, let me assure you Carin would agree with what I am doing."

"Carin needs care."

Jake looked at his beautiful partner. She looked as if she was peacefully asleep and needed only a kiss from the prince to awaken her. Her shoulder length hair had fallen out of her head in clumps. What little hair was left spread around her head like a black halo and, with her face relaxed, she looked as if she was in her early twenties, even though Jake knew she was at least twice that age.

That thought brought Jake up short. He rummaged around the camper until he found Carin's magnifying glass. He looked carefully at the roots of her hair and found what he had expected. Near some of the roots, Carin's hair had a telltale gray that indicated her age, but at the base of these, the hair was growing in black again. Her hair strands went from black to gray to black. "Fred, there is nothing more that I can do for Carin. It seems that the bugs are doing all they can to repair her."

Jake's arguments did not deter Fred. "Jake, the logical course seems to be to take Carin to a hospital. If you cannot care for her, you must find someone who can."

"Fred, there is nothing on this planet that can help Carin. There is nothing that can help me. That's why we have to get to the planetoid. The answers are not here or the medical experts at the Ingreti Clinic would have had more success. Those folks are the best and they didn't even have a clue as to what was wrong with us."

"Jake, to be fair, we hardly gave them a chance."

Jake turned and looked at the MI. "Fred, if that last statement had been from a human, I would've said it was very emotional. Are you sure you're okay?"

Fred answered immediately. "Jake, my studies of humans indicate emotional responses sometimes come from some form of survival response. It can manifest itself when the human perceives that it is taking a course of action not in its best interest. Carin's continued illness reduces our chances of survival greatly. If you feel that I am pushing my position excessively, then I apologize. But it is of the highest imperative we find a cure for Carin."

"I agree with you Fred, but the danger of getting locked up in somebody's laboratory so we can be their pet project can't be dismissed. All we would need is one zealous scientist who said we were contagious. We'd be locked up for all eternity regardless of the fact that it was false. They might do it on purpose just to get us bottled up so that they can examine us at their leisure. No, we have to stay hidden."

"Jake, you will be gone for six hours. What if something happens while you are gone? What can I do to help Carin?"

Jake was standing in front of Carin with his arms folded in front of his chest. He looked down at her peaceful sleep and whispered. "What can I do for Carin even though I'm here?" Jake shook his head and once again faced Fred. "Nobody on this planet can help either Carin or me. In pretty short order, I am also going to be incapacitated. The three of us have to be on that planetoid doing tests to survive. We need answers and we can't go to that rock unprepared. We have to bring some things with us. Once we get there, if we don't need it, that's fine. However, if we get there and Matr doesn't have something we need, we're all dead. You, me, Carin – all three of us are dead. I don't need to remind you that Matr is hiding from something out there. I'm just guessing, but I think that if Matr is scared of it, we should be scared of it as well."

"Jake, you have not voiced this concern before."

"I am sorry Fred. It's just that Carin and I think so much alike I didn't have to mention it because she knew already. We have to get to Matr and we can't go without the tank. By the way, have we had a reply from Matr?"

"The reply from Matr is overdue by three hours."

Jake began pacing in the small camper. There was only enough room to take a step or two in each direction before he had to turn around, but it helped him think. Finally, he stopped pacing and gave a final nod of his head. "Okay, here's what I want you to do. I want you to send another message to Matr. I want you to double the power and double the width of the beam. I want you to say that since Matr has perpetrated an unprovoked attack on the United States and murdered innocent civilians and since Matr has refused a good faith effort by the United States to allow its diplomats to resolve this in a peaceful fashion that a state of war now exists between the United States and Matr. Any attempt by Matr to approach the Earth will be met by deadly force. Remind Matr none of our nuclear treaties preclude the use of nuclear weapons or kinetic energy weapons in space."

"Captain Sabio, are you sure this approach is wise? We do not have access to any nuclear weapons and nobody on this planet has access to a kinetic energy weapon that could neutralize Matr."

Jake turned to Fred and asked, "Do you think Matr knows that?"

"I am sure Matr suspects the truth, but Matr does not have the access to the world's databases that I enjoy. It would only be supposition and not certainty."

Jake kept up his confined pacing. "Fred, we need to get on that rock."

"But Jake, declaring war on Matr, speaking for the United States, threatening Matr's destruction?"

"Fred, we don't have time for the subtle approach anymore. Matr has to know that it's now playing with the big dogs. Also, let Matr know we know that it is hiding from another enemy. Let it know that we are making modifications to our Deep Space Network to increase its power output and to broaden the beam width. Tell Matr we intend to broadcast its position as soon as we complete these modifications. We will not tolerate a proven enemy in our solar system and Matr is a proven enemy."

"Jake, I hope you are correct in your assessment of Matr. I will send the message immediately."

Jake stretched and yawned with intensity. "Good. Now we have done that task, I am going to get about two hours sleep. If I leave now, I will get to the depot two hours before they open. Wake me up at 0400, please." With that, Jake grabbed a pillow and laid himself down on the area where he had been pacing.

Fred spoke up after a minute. "Jake, the message has been sent. If I may ask, what makes you think we will get an answer?"

"Fred, Matr has been doing a great many things that indicate both stealth and survival have been programmed into it with a high priority. It is going to do whatever it takes to accomplish that programming. I'm programmed that way. You're programmed that way. I'm assuming Matr will react as you or I would when faced with destruction. By the way, if Matr decides to pick us up, how much time do we have?"

"Jake, we are approximately eighty-four hours from pickup time."

Fred was quiet for a moment, but it finally asked, "What if Matr asks for proof that we can do everything we said we could?"

Jake did not answer immediately. Finally he said, "If this Matr creature ... entity ... whatever it is ... wants to see the cards we're holding, it's going to have to put its money in the pot and stay in the game."

CHAPTER 26

Time to pickup: 80 hours

CRUBARI WAS MANEUVERING HIS car as quickly as he could around rocks and potholes on the back roads. The car he was driving was an off-road, four-wheel drive late model vehicle specifically designed for this kind of terrain. Like all vehicles in its class, it was top-heavy and ungainly to drive. Crubari was putting all of his attention on the road. A moment's slip could cost him this opportunity, or worse, leave him stranded along the same route Agent Greenfield was likely to take.

His shoulder was still sensitive to touch and his nose bandaged, but he could not afford any more time. He knew he was in a race with William Greenfield to get to Jake Sabio first. At most, Crubari thought he had an hour to get in and get out without crossing paths with the federal agents. He would make it. He had just enough time to do the job correctly.

Crubari had worked up several scenarios as he drove. The sun had come up less than an hour ago. With any luck, Sabio would only recently have gotten himself out of bed. In that event, Crubari would simply knock on the front door and play the part of the lost tourist. After all, Sabio had never seen him. If Sabio were not at the campsite, Crubari would call out for him. If he answered Crubari's call, then the lost tourist approach would work. If Sabio was not around the camp, Crubari could still gather information. He needed more data on Sabio. The more that you have on a target, the closer the target comes to you.

Crubari never bothered to question the information source he had recruited inside the agency. The recruiting had been quite simple. The agent walked into the casino. He was identified as FBI within one minute. That was not unusual. The agent sat down and began to gamble at one of the blackjack tables. There was still no cause for alarm. Then the agent began to lose a great deal of money. That was truly unusual. He was purposely drawing attention to himself. Mr. Stanger called Crubari personally to have a talk with the young man. One of Crubari's associates had come up behind the young federal agent. "Excuse me, sir. I was wondering whether you could join me in the lounge?" The young man followed the associate to a back room and sat down in front of a contractor Crubari had hired. The lights were shining in the agent's eyes and the contractor was in the shadows. Crubari observed the questioning from a monitor in a building across town.

The young agent looked into the shadows. "You know who I am." It was not a question.

The contractor remained perfectly still in the shadows and spoke softly. "Yes and I know you have run up a sizeable gambling debt. One that I do not believe a government employee can cover."

The young man waved a hand dismissively. "Consider it the cost of doing business. I think we can help each other."

The young man had proven himself to be both resourceful and accurate since that day. Crubari had accepted his terms in that initial meeting. The young man had one condition. He had been escorted to the security area following the meeting and gone to the specific recorder that had taped the meeting. He ejected the tape that was in the machine and put it in a player in the corner. When he was convinced that he had his tape, he left. Their relationship had been professional and mutually beneficial. However, Crubari felt the relationship had to end. Such information sources tended to lead back to where Crubari preferred they would not go. If Crubari could have felt any emotions at all, he would have felt sadness at losing this information source. He would never have felt sorry for the source itself.

Crubari found the camper exactly where his source said it would be. He was disappointed to find the truck was missing. Chances were that Jake Sabio was not around. That man had an incredible run of luck. Crubari knocked on the door and prepared to play 'lost tourist' if he was wrong. When there was no answer, he tried the door. The locked door took only a moment for Crubari to open. He stepped in quickly and let his eyes adjust. It was then that he saw the figure lying in the bed.

Crubari instinctively made a move for his gun, but stopped when he noticed the figure in the bed was not moving. It was Doctor Carin Gonzalez, Sabio's girlfriend. Crubari put on surgeon's gloves and placed his fingertips against her carotid artery. The gloves were more due to his disgust of touching human flesh than any concerns for hygiene or anonymity. Crubari felt no pulse, but her skin felt warm. He picked up her arm and let it drop. It was fluid and flexible. If she were dead, rigor mortis would quickly set in. He found a pocket mirror and placed it next to her nostrils. It did not fog. Crubari was finally convinced that Carin Gonzalez was dead.

Why would Jake Sabio keep her body in a bed? Was this some kind of homage to the dead? This did not look like a death bier to him. It looked as if Sabio placed her to sleep, as if he thought Carin Gonzalez was still alive. Crubari again looked at Carin and felt certain this was true. Jake Sabio was denying the evidence before him. His love interest was dead, but he continued to behave as if she were still alive.

This presented a perfect opportunity.

Crubari checked his watch and was surprised by the passage of time. Too much had crept by while he was pondering his decision. It did not matter. He had a solution that solved his problem. Since he could not catch Jacob Sabio, he would make Jacob Sabio seek him instead. He wrapped Carin in the bed's blankets, picked up her body and left quickly by the front door. He tossed the corpse into the back seat and drove off. It would not do to be in the vicinity when the federal agents stormed the now empty trailer. Crubari was not worried about Jacob Sabio anymore. His love would be in a grave, but Sabio would never know that until it was too late. In the meantime, with little more than a simple pruning with some poultry shears, he would have just what he needed to guarantee that Captain Jacob Sabio moved heaven and earth to meet Crubari's demands.

CHAPTER 27

FRED WAS AS CLOSE to hysteria as any machine intelligence could get. After monitoring the approach of the vehicle and watching the assailant enter, it was immediately clear that the invader must be Antonio Crubari. Jake did not have a personal phone and there was no one else Fred could call. The next emotion that Fred almost felt was anger, along with the question, "What would Carin do?"

The answer came almost immediately. Carin would make sure that Crubari did not get away with it. Somehow, Carin would bring Crubari to justice. It took Fred almost a week, in machine-time terms, to debate the issues. The fact that it was only about a tenth of a second in human time allowed Fred to activate the two mechanical devices that were on chargers.

Fred had been trying out the new devices they bought from the Xiwa Corporation. He had gained mastery over them and exercised it now by activating the visual and infrared cameras, quietly training them on the actions of Antonio Crubari. Fred then did a worldwide database search on the individual in the room with him and found something truly interesting. Antonio Crubari did not exist on any database anywhere. Fred tried pattern matching Crubari's face, but came up with nothing. This was like dropping a magnet in a plastic bucket of ping-pong balls and not coming up with the only iron bolt.

Fred verged on machine catatonia. It watched Crubari lift Carin and carry her out of the camper. To Fred, this event took the equivalent of several human years. It debated with itself whether to yell out and make Crubari drop Carin. Unfortunately, due to Fred's logical nature, it could not think of any reason Crubari would not then pick up Carin and Fred both and spirit them away. Fred had to stay here and help Jake recover Carin. Nevertheless, Fred could still cause Crubari problems.

When Crubari closed the door of the camper, Fred compiled all the video his mechanical devices had just taken and all the information he had gleaned from the database search and sent it to the one person who would appreciate it the most. He sent the entire series of files to William Greenfield's personal e-mail.

Fred was now confident that when Jake Sabio returned the two of them would work together to get Carin back. It was imperative they get their team back together before the rendezvous with Matr. If they missed the rendezvous, it would be too late.

CHAPTER 28

Time to pickup: 79 hours

WILLIAM GREENFIELD CIRCLED SABIO'S trailer for a second time hoping to come up with some insight as to where his two elusive preys had disappeared. His team of forensic experts had scoured the area for the last two hours, but found little to take back for analysis. Greenfield began to suspect an informant had trumped him once again. Worse yet, he was now certain that this informant had to be in his own organization.

Agent Glynnis Beamer walked up to Greenfield and waited ten feet away. He looked over at her and swept the campground with his hand. "We've come up empty again."

She walked the rest of the way to him. "Not really, boss. We now have a ton of personal data on both Sabio and Gonzalez that we didn't have before. It's only a matter of time before we corner them."

Will Greenfield looked over at Glynnis for a long time. "We have squat."

Glynnis let out a breath and looked around the campsite. "Actually, I think either 'zip' or 'zippo' would be the current colloquial term for what we have."

"What we have is nothing."

"That's what I just said."

William began to walk down to the trailer when Glynnis blocked his way. He looked up in surprise. Glynnis had a look of determination. "Boss, can I get something off my chest?"

"Anytime you've got a problem, the team's got a problem," quoted Greenfield.

"Yeah, boss. That's exactly why I wanted to talk to you. Does anything about the way we found this camp strike you as wrong?"

Greenfield became suspicious of Glynnis. "What do you mean?"

She flung her arm out to encompass the campsite. "I mean everything. They've deployed the entire campsite. Pots and pans are out. The cook stove is open even though it isn't on. The trailer door is unlocked. The bed is unmade. All the power is on and running full tilt. This is an occupied campsite except for one thing."

Greenfield cast a gaze around the campsite. "Yeah. No people."

Glynnis nodded. "Right, Boss. No people. This camp has all the earmarks that somebody tipped them off and that bugs me something fierce. I've been wondering for a long time why we keep coming up one step behind Crubari and Sabio and this just strengthens my hypothesis. Boss, we have a leak in our office."

"Whom have you discussed this with?"

Glynnis was about to answer when she looked Greenfield in the eyes. "Wrong question, boss. You should have asked me, 'what makes you think so' or something like that. Okay, so you also think we got a leak. What can we do?"

"The first thing is obvious. Tell no one else."

"C'mon boss, that's basic. Do you want me to tell you what's bugging me so bad that I brought it up?"

"The shoot out that we had at the truck stop and now this. We've got somebody leaking information almost real time."

Glynnis thought for a moment. "Well, it can't be one of the field agents."

Greenfield looked at her somberly. "Why not?"

Glynnis cast a glance over both shoulders before answering. "Boss, all four of us would have died in that firefight. It can't be one of us."

"How do you know that? How do you know that Crubari's hired guns didn't have orders to kill us in a certain order, or leave one of us alive? Better yet, Crubari could've ordered his men only to wound us. Then he could've come in and done the coup-de-grace on all but the person who was feeding him the information. There are a thousand ways he could've set it up if his informant had been one of us in the truck stop. We haven't had time to debrief those goons properly. We don't know what their orders were."

"Well, it's not me."

Agent Greenfield shook his head. "Agent Beamer, until we have the culprit in custody, even I am suspect. What do you suggest we do in light of our situation?"

"You mean that if we learn too much, Crubari will learn the same thing?"

"Yes."

Glynnis stared at the ground for a moment before answering. "The book says there are two main types of information protocols. The first is gathering the information on your target. The second is denying the information to your target. We could at least confiscate the personal computer in there. In light of our problem, I'll take my time cracking into it and gathering the data."

Will Greenfield had been thinking along the same lines. He had been hoping to corner Jake Sabio out here away from the many prying eyes and ears of the office. In his heart, Greenfield felt that he could trust his three field agents. However, the book said everyone was suspect and Greenfield went by the book. When he and his team had approached the campsite and noticed the truck was missing and all the power was running, he had assumed that Sabio had left Carin Gonzalez in the trailer. He would have arrested Carin and waited for Sabio to come in to bargain her out of jail, but the campsite proved to be empty. Taking the computer was the next step. It would not only deny Sabio and Gonzalez of its use, it would also give the team insight into what the two of them were up to. There had to be something on the computer. Why else drag that bulky relic out to the middle of the desert?

Unfortunately, taking the computer could backfire. That same information would help Crubari as much as it would help Greenfield.

No, thought Greenfield, *it would probably help Crubari more than us.* The informant would pass on the information as soon as it was extracted from the computer and his team did not have the time available to add yet another branch to the investigation. Greenfield had to deny the information to Crubari and Glynnis' suggestion was the only way to ensure that.

Greenfield made his decision. "Okay, take the computer, but keep it locked up so nobody sees what's stored. It's powered up now, so let's keep it powered up so we don't lose anything."

Glynnis did not move. He looked at her. "Is there something else, Agent Beamer?"

"Boss, what about the mechanical devices and the money?"

The team had found almost four hundred thousand dollars in the trailer. "Bring the mechanical devices that are already charged up and the money. That puts a crimp on their plans and their mobility. Anything else?"

Glynnis looked at William Greenfield. "No, sir. We've separated him from his money and his equipment. That should be enough to smoke Sabio out."

Greenfield shook his head as he looked around the empty campsite. "I hope you're right, Agent Beamer. I don't think so, but I hope you're right."

CHAPTER 29

Time to pickup: 76 hours

ANTONIO CRUBARI WAS NOT about to risk driving into Las Vegas with a body in his vehicle. He had driven three miles deeper into the desert from the campsite when he felt it was far enough. He drove into a ravine to keep his activities from any prying eyes and set about his work. The setting sun would give him enough light if he hurried.

Crubari removed a shovel from his trunk and dug a long hole about three feet deep. It was hard work, but Crubari was in excellent shape and was able to complete the job in the loose dirt in less than ten minutes.

Before Crubari proceeded, he walked along the tops of both sides of the ravine to make sure he was alone. Once he was certain, he opened the trunk, lifted the limp form of Carin Gonzalez and placed her by the hole. He inspected her form carefully and clinically. He had to send an irresistible, unambiguous and unmistakable message to Captain Sabio. But what? His eyes finally focused on the amethyst ring on her right ring finger. It was the only jewelry she was wearing. That would be perfect.

Crubari stood next to Carin and worked with all possible speed. He put on rubber surgical gloves and a hospital lab coat made of paper. When he was satisfied he was adequately covered, he got the poultry shears he had purchased for just this occasion. He caressed them in one hand while tenderly rubbing Carin's ring in the other. Gently, almost delicately, he placed the blades of the poultry shears around Carin's right ring finger just below the ring and slowly squeezed until the two crossed pivoting blades met with a soft click. As he suspected, there was hardly any blood. That was very disappointing.

He also missed the screaming. He knew that this dance with Doctor

Gonzalez would be a silent chore when he picked her up in that miserable trailer and since this act was a prelude to a more intriguing encounter with Captain Sabio, it deserved to be done correctly. Even so, it robbed much of his pleasure. Actually, he was quite surprised at his absence of excitement at the moment ring and finger separated from their former host. He finally admitted to himself that he missed the change in the screams before and after the removal of a victim's digit.

Crubari had removed fingers from his living victims dozens of times and the blood had always flowed freely. Crubari was now positive Carin was dead. He put the finger with the ring still on it in a plastic bag and put the plastic bag in a cooler in the trunk.

Crubari again checked the area for any witnesses. Seeing none, he threw the shears in the hole, wrapped Carin tightly in the blanket, and dropped her in the hole after the shears. He stripped his gloves carefully, removed the hospital gown, threw them all into the hole and pushed the dirt back in to cover it all up. He surveyed his work and saw there was nothing out of the ordinary. Just then, a peal of thunder shook the ravine. A gust of wind washed over him that was much colder than the air he had been standing in. Perfect! A windstorm would help hide his tracks. Crubari smiled. If his luck held out, this area would get some rain and completely hide his work.

Chapter 30

Jake saw the dust plumes well before he needed to hide. Scrabbling off the road with the tank lashed to the bed of the truck required Jake to alternate between wild throws of the steering wheel and a gentle touch. He managed to keep the truck tires pointed mostly towards the ground until he finally came to a shaded area behind a small hill that was out of view of the dirt road and killed the truck motor. Jake launched himself out of the driver's seat and partway up the hill to see what was happening at the camp. The sand clouds looked to be coming from half a dozen cars. That was too much activity for it to be Crubari. It had to be William Greenfield. Jake had to give Greenfield credit for finding them so quickly, but he had told the FBI agent to wait for his call. Jake was at once angered and disappointed with the stubborn William Greenfield.

The fleet of government cars went by without noticing Jake's presence. The threatening storm and failing light had been a factor Jake had counted on to mask him from the watchful eyes of the agents. Large storm clouds were billowing overhead and the peal of thunder was becoming continuous. Jake smelled moisture and knew this area was going to experience one of its rare rainstorms. Time was working against him.

He waited ten minutes after the last car passed before moving from his vantage point on the hill. The temperature had dropped at least ten degrees in that time and occasional large drops of rain were splatting onto the ground around him. He checked the lashing around the tank and felt it was good enough to proceed to ground zero.

He kept an eye on the clouds and an eye on the dirt road. *C'mon*, he kept saying to the clouds. *Just give me five more minutes.* The clouds must have been listening and held their rain. He got to the top of the small rise and put the truck into park. Rushing out of the driver's seat, he began unlashing the tank. When all the chains were undone, he got on top of the cab and pushed on the tank. The tank refused to budge. He sat on the top of the cab, braced his legs on the tank, and pushed with all his might. The tank stubbornly refused to notice his effort. He pulled at his now bushy hair and growled at the tank. *Think, Jake. What would Carin do?*

Jake backed up a few paces, looked at the truck, and immediately saw a solution. Jake took the chain he had used to lash the tank to the truck and attached an end to a massive lifting handle on one end of the tank. He wrapped the other end of the chain around the bottom of a rock outcropping that was higher than his chest. Jake then got back into the truck and shifted into low gear. As the truck inched forward, the tank screeched as it slid out of the bed until it unceremoniously dumped itself onto the ground. Brain triumphing over brawn or, as Jake had heard Carin say on one occasion, "Newton over numbskull."

Jake drove the truck the two hundred meters back down to the camper just as the skies opened up. The rain was welcome to Jake and he lingered in it. His fever-heated body felt relieved in the cold rain, but Jake knew the real reason for his hesitation. He knew what he would find in the camper and dreaded going inside. It was one thing to have a concept that you understood because the facts made it obvious. It was completely different to have the evidence made real before your own eyes. Jake was in no hurry to face this reality.

He picked up his pace and walked carefully into the door. He began cataloging both what he saw and what he did not see. He did not see Carin. That was expected. He did not see the money or Fred or the mechanical devices he had left charging. That was also expected. As far as he could tell, they had left everything else. That was unexpected. The FBI had brought enough transportation to load everything at the camp into the trunks and driven away. For that matter, they could have hooked up the entire camper to the SUV they had brought and taken away everything in one shot. Why had they left him the camper?

Jake sat heavily on the couch that doubled as a bed. There were too many questions, but the most important one for him now was what to do next. The plan to go to the planetoid was in shambles. His friends were gone. What was he to do next? Jake closed his eyes and took a deep breath. No question — he had to get his friends back. That took priority over everything else.

A flash of lightning followed immediately by booming thunder startled Jake out of his thoughts and forced him to open his eyes. He looked at his assets. Fred was gone. That was a devastating blow. Jake now realized he had come to rely heavily on the little MI. Fred's instant access to the information of the world made it the perfect foil on which to sharpen ideas. Jake would have to be careful with his decisions. His fever was making his thinking clouded and he no longer had Fred and Carin to make that point for him.

Most of the money was gone. That was not much of a problem for Jake. He knew he could get more money if he needed it. The money he had in his wallet would have to last.

Jake thought of Carin and he became quiet. Now that she was gone, Jake felt something he had not felt since the loss of his children. Alone. Losing someone like Carin was not like losing a limb. Jake would much rather do without a limb than without Carin. It was only now he realized the depth of his loss. He lowered his head to his hands and tried to think.

Yet thoughts refused to come when he called them. Ideas that should be presenting themselves for review were absent. A plan of action refused to materialize. Jake was losing ground. His infection was robbing him of his ability to think. He realized now he could not go on as he was.

Fred could not rescue itself, Carin was in a coma, and he was so sick he could not come up with a plan. He needed sleep. He needed to get smarter. He needed to get rid of the filthy infection that was clouding his thoughts. The discussion he had with Fred about feeding Carin the cocktail came back to him. How was this situation different from hers? Could he think of another option? This was not the solution, but it was the necessary next step.

Jake made his decision. He pulled out the two uncharged mechanical devices from where they had been stored. As an afterthought, he plugged them in to charge. Then he reached deep into the cabinet for what he was really after. He pulled out the five-gallon bottle of Carin's cocktail and took it to the sink. At this point, he hesitated.

Fred's words about the danger of the cocktail came back to him. He was in terrible shape. He was feverish, weak and clumsy. If he drank the cocktail, chances were he would follow Carin into a coma. This far from civilization, his chances of surviving the experience were not good. Any of the solution the bugs in his system could not immediately process would go into destroying his cells, his muscles, and his mind. Why couldn't the little bugs just come and get what they needed? They probably would if given the chance.

Jake considered that thought for a moment. How can I give them what they need without risking excessive exposure? He placed the stopper in the sink and poured some solution into the basin. His right hand was scratched and bleeding slightly from his battle with the tank. He placed his hand in the solution and watched it closely. It felt warm and strangely comforting. He kept his hand in the solution for several minutes and suddenly all the bleeding stopped and the scratches healed. He put his other hand into the solution with the same results. How would he know when his body had absorbed enough solution? Did he need more?

Jake opened the cabinets above the sink and found a cheese grater. He put his arm above the sink and scratched it along the length of his forearm. His scratches began to ooze blood freely and he immediately placed his arm in the solution. The feeling that he got when he submerged his arm was beyond pleasant and short of erotic. He watched his arm closely and it too stopped bleeding and healed over.

Jake was beginning to feel dizzy but was not sure when to stop. He scratched his other arm and submerged it into the solution. His feeling of well-being was elevating to the point of euphoria. Suddenly, Jake felt invincible and invulnerable. He felt he could conquer the storm lashing outside the camper if that was his desire. He could push back the seas from their mounts if he wished. Jake noticed his arm had healed over. He removed it from the solution and let the feeling of power fill him.

Then without warning, Jake passed out and crumpled to the floor.

Chapter 31

UNPRECEDENTED, UNSCRIPTED AND UNEXPECTED. The object had never considered the complexities now presented before it. There are two survivors of the infection? This is not possible. Yet the intelligence that addressed itself as Fred has repeatedly made that claim. Which brings up the question of Fred – it claims to be a machine intelligence, but the television and radio signals intercepted from their planet reveal that the biological intelligences of Earth are generations from that breakthrough.

The logical conclusion is that the three intelligences must be removed from the general population as soon as possible, brought aboard and isolated from the rest of the planet. If the reaction to the infection was this far from the norm, it warranted an immediate investigation and report.

However, the enemy is still lurking in the shadows. If the three from Earth are to be picked up, it must be done in stealth – if they are able to survive until then.

It would be simpler if they did not.

*   *   *

The colony was badly damaged and close to termination. Deadly toxins were gathering in the host's body, slowly destroying both the host and the colony. Everything the colony tried to do to repair the host was falling short.

There were too few of the colony, and the raw materials they needed to generate new members were absent from the body of the host. Scavenger members of the colony had done an excellent job of rounding up the spent members that were destined to be eliminated from the host body, but even they could not be one hundred percent efficient. They had posted a scavenger with each group of workers, but that did not solve the problem of what to do if more than one worker terminated at a given time, or if the scavenger was the one to terminate. The colony had found no solutions to these problems and continued to lose members in its slow battle of attrition. Soon they would not be able to maintain their numbers and both the colony and the host would terminate.

Attrition had not been the only problem. This host was not what the colony had been programmed to expect. The DNA was slightly different, the endocrine system had some minor differences, and the immune system had proven to be formidable. The host's immune system detected the colony's presence almost immediately, but did not attack. The colony thought it would have some time to prepare for a response from the host's biological functions, but that hope turned into a nightmare. When the attack came, it was vicious with an incredible number of attackers. There were easily one hundred thousand attackers for every member of the colony. Truly overwhelming numbers, yet the colony held its ground. The battle endured even to this moment, but at a much reduced pace. A member could not do its job without being escorted by defenders. Yet each defender that was employed was one less worker that could do the work or one less scavenger that could save the precious body of an inactive worker so the elements could be reused.

Yet for all the problems, there had been successes. The colony had found that the host's aging process was similar to what was expected. Mitochondrial gene mutations were found to be causing a loss of ability to generate energy in the host's cells. This was beginning to cause the host's cells to lose their power sources. It had already led to some cell death in the host. The colony had remedied that problem. Telomeres had been shortening, resulting in inaccurate DNA replication, and the colony had repaired that defect. In the area of the brain, the colony found a series of deactivated neuron pathways. Those were reactivated. There was insufficient capacity in the cerebral cortex, so capacity was increased. Yet for all the improvements on the host, they were insignificant compared to the possibilities if the colony had been up to strength a million times more than they enjoyed now.

Dreaming was not in the nature of the colony. It was what it was and knew that even with the recent increase of required elements, it was not going to survive. The loss of a digit from the host was indicative of collective failure. It needed more of the basic elements so that it could increase the members of the colony to a sustainable level.

While the colony was debating the survival strategies, the team that had been repairing the damage to the digit reported the elements needed were in solution outside the wound area. The colony mobilized itself in a desperate effort. It began drawing the elements from the solution. At the same time, members were working in a symbiotic relationship with the host's immune system. It was a marginal truce, but it seemed to be working. The colony would establish pathways to the areas of the host beginning to get an infection and allow the host's cells to do their work.

At a time when it looked as if the colony would succeed in getting its required elements, a crisis occurred. The solution that was fortifying the colony had now risen to a level that would suffocate the host. A decision was made that the host had to be released from the level one coma the colony had induced. It had to continue breathing.

CHAPTER 32

Time to pickup: 66 hours

SHE WAS FLOATING IN a sea of stars, out at the edge of the universe looking at the beauty and majesty of creation. Quiet and blissful was her contemplation. It was a feeling of belonging. She was enjoying the establishment of a particular star when she felt a tug. She turned around and saw a thin line that was attached to her navel and stretched out to infinity. *Strange*, she thought, *I don't remember seeing that before.* The tug came again, more insistent. She moved slightly from her position. She began to go back to viewing her star when the tug became urgent. She felt she heard a voice. *Now. Hurry*!

A sense of fear began to envelope her. She struggled with the line and began following it down through the stars at an incredible rate. The line that attached her to her destination began to bunch up around her. She sensed the urgency and willed herself further down. The line was wrapping around her and restricting her movements, yet she continued. She saw the line connecting to her destination; a shining blue planet that she recognized as home. She hurtled down the line sensing greater urgency. The line was wrapping around her like a cocoon. She could not move and she could not breathe.

Suddenly, she stopped moving. She remained trapped. As disoriented as she was, she recognized she was suffocating. With a great burst of strength, she pushed her left arm up and felt it break through blanket and mud until it reached air. Leveraging herself, she got her left arm, left shoulder and head out of the ground and took a deep breath. She coughed out some water from her lungs and tried breathing again. She got a full breath this time and rested from the tremendous effort she had just exerted.

Carin Gonzalez looked around and recognized nothing. She was in a geological depression of some kind, buried about three feet down in the ground. Her right hand was in terrible pain, but she was feeling a sense of euphoria at leaving it in the water by her side. She decided to leave it there for now.

Carin dozed off or passed out – she was not sure which. When she awoke, the rain had stopped and the water was receding. The last thing that she remembered was having just dodged the bullet Crubari had sent her way at the truck stop. She had probably fallen into a coma following the accelerated time just as Jake had. It did not take a rocket scientist to figure out that "something bad" had happened while she was in the coma. Her friends would never have let this happen if they could have prevented it. Therefore, the logical conclusion was that they could not have prevented it. What could have kept Jake from helping? The answer was simple: either he also was incapacitated, or he was not present when Carin had been taken. With this thought, Carin's grip on consciousness slipped again.

She woke up with the sun beginning to lighten the sky. Her right hand was no longer giving her the sense of euphoria she had experienced the previous night, but it was still throbbing. She pulled herself completely out of the ground and examined herself. It was then she noticed that the ring finger from her right hand was missing. *Let's see,* she thought to herself. *Buried alive and a finger removed along with an identifying ring. Whom does that sound like?* A wave of cold anger washed over Carin. *I think Crubari and I need to have a little chat.*

She was dizzy but was still able to climb out of the ravine. Carin noticed for the first time since the infection began, she did not feel feverish. She climbed up to the highest point in the area, sat still and listened. After a moment, Carin heard a generator chugging away. The exact direction and distance were difficult to pinpoint, but she had a good idea of the general path. Without another thought, Carin set out towards the sound of the generator. She knew that without water, she was in a race to get to the generator. At the generator, there would be water, food and information. With any luck at all, the generator would turn out to be her generator and Carin could find out more directly what happened.

In the meantime, all she could do was to brood over what had happened to Fred and to Jake and put one foot in front of the other.

CHAPTER 33

Time to pickup: 64 Hours

JAKE WOKE UP TO a pounding on the camper door. He opened his eyes and saw it was just now dawn. Of which day, he wondered. How long had he been unconscious? He went to sit up and a wave of dizziness brought him back down to the ground. *Ground*, he thought. *Where am I?* The last thing he remembered was being in the camper. He looked at his surroundings but could not bring them into focus. His head was pounding and his ears were ringing. *This is just wonderful*, thought Jake. *We should have figured that any solution for the bugs would give you a world-class hangover.*

He heard a car motor start up and drive away but was still unable to drag himself upright. After what felt like hours of struggling but was probably only minutes, Jake was able to get himself to sit up straight. That brought on a wave of dizziness he had to fight. Jake knew that if he laid himself down, it would be hours before he would get up. Carin and Fred needed him. The thought lent strength to his actions.

Jake was finally able to stand up. He found himself out in the desert. He looked around and could not find the camper. Jake had no recollection of his leaving the camper, but he had a good idea of where the sound had come from that had awakened him. He began walking in that direction and found the camper as soon as he came over a rise.

Jake went to the front door of the camper and opened it. On the step before him was a small box made of Styrofoam. He retrieved the box and swept his gaze around the campsite. Everything was still in disarray from the FBI search. Jake carried the small box into the camper and closed the door.

Jake was sure what he would find in the box, but he would not be certain until he opened it and looked for himself. He unwrapped the tape that kept the box sealed and removed the lid. White vapors reminiscent of a witch's cauldron from Halloween filled the inside of the box. The fact that whatever was inside was packed in dry ice was ominous to Jake. After a moment of hesitation, he grabbed some tongs from the cooking area of the camper and fished out a Ziploc bag. Through the frosted bag, Jake saw the unmistakable glint of Carin's amethyst. He immediately knew what else was in the bag and it filled him with rage. *Not now, Jake,* he told himself. *Save it for when you need it.*

He looked at the lid he had removed from the small box and saw a piece of paper attached. He removed the piece of paper and unfolded it to reveal a note written in block letters.

IF YOU WISH TO MEET UP WITH YOUR FRIEND
AGAIN, BE AT THE VEACH WAREHOUSE AT
103 LONG STREET WITHIN 48 HOURS.

There was a phone number at the bottom of the note. Jake assumed the number was a one-time-use cell phone. Even if he still had Fred, all traceability would disappear as soon as he made his call. However, Fred was not there to help.

Jake scrubbed his face with both hands in frustration. The former navy officer had no illusion he would ever see Carin again. The only way anyone could have gotten that ring from her was if she were dead. He lifted the ring from the box with the tongs and looked at it. A sharp pang of loss penetrated him like a knife. He put the ring down on the counter to allow it to warm up and his emotions to cool down.

Jake thought through the next step; if she had been in a coma, they would have disposed of her body. Why were they giving him so much time? They must not know where he is or when he will pick up this message. That worked in his favor, but what was he to do? He had no idea where the address led to or what kind of a trap they would have set. Knowing what little he did of Antonio Crubari, the trap would be formidable and near impossible to escape. Jake paused a moment and considered Chris Bruno.

Jake began juggling scenarios in his mind. The most important thing for him now was to maximize his options. Fred was missing, most likely taken by the FBI. Carin was probably dead, but he refused to believe that. He had to make sure that whatever he did kept his options open to go up to the object and his options open to recover his friends. Whatever he did, he had to be finished and ready for pickup in sixty-four hours. There was too much to do. Worse yet, DiBeto and Crubari could destroy his best efforts if they were left free to harass him. Besides, there was a personal score to settle with Crubari.

He did not waste time; Jake pocketed the ring on the counter, grabbed the keys to the truck, and walked out without ever turning around. He left everything running even though he was not sure he would ever be back. It was in Jake's nature to maximize his options, but he knew he had some very long odds to beat, to make it back to this camp. He did not care. There was only one thing motivating him now. He had to get Crubari and DiBeto off his back. Now he was going to be more direct, but before he could do anything else, he had to look over this meeting place without any interference. He had to neutralize the threat posed by Crubari and DiBeto, and then he had to find Fred. Jake looked at his watch and shook his head. Time!

Chapter 34

Time to pickup: 63 hours

CARIN WATCHED AS THE truck drove from the campsite. Since she woke up, she felt that there were only three possible eventualities that could have kept Jake from finding her. Jake was kidnapped, on a vital errand or dead. Seeing the truck drive off left her with a mix of emotions. On the one hand, Jake was alive. She did not realize until that moment how much it had weighed on her that he might not have survived. The fact there was only one truck probably meant that Jake was not being taken by force. On the other hand, he was going the wrong way. Carin would not get to the camper for several minutes and he would be long gone by then. *Well*, thought Carin, *there's nothing to be done about it. Let's get to the camper and see whether we can figure out what happened.*

She followed the sound of the still-running generator and came to a rise to find their tank lying on the ground. Carin was amazed. Even with all the trouble he must have been having, Jake Sabio had still managed to get their tank up to ground zero. She saw the main hatch to the tank had still not been opened. Without the tank and its contents, the trio would not be able to assure their survival on the planetoid. Carin looked at her watch. Sixty-three hours until pickup and no preparations were underway. Carin began to feel the first stages of panic well up inside her and had to choke them down. *Jake is no idiot*, she thought to herself. *If he's not here, it's for an excellent reason.*

She marched the two hundred meters down to the campsite and looked around. It looked as if the camper and the truck bed had been dumped unceremoniously onto the ground. There was nothing in order and little was ready to carry up to the tank. She looked for telltale marks on the ground.

She saw Jake's footprints and the truck tire marks on the ground. She also saw another set of tire tracks and footprints. It seems Jake had a visitor this morning. It must have stirred him up to have him shoot out of the campsite as he had.

Carin opened the door to the camper and froze. Fred was missing. It had not occurred to her Fred could be in any danger. Fred was an innocuous looking box that frankly looked like a very outdated personal computer. Looking around some more, she found the note that had caused Jake to react. So those liars had dumped her body and left her for dead, but were still baiting Jake. She could only hope that Jake would not let his emotions get the best of him. At that thought, Carin had to laugh. When Jake switched into what Carin had been calling his "Captain Mode," he had ice water coursing through his veins. Whatever he was going to do, it would be thoroughly thought out and meticulously executed. It still left open the option that the idea was totally bone-headed. Carin shelved that line of thinking for now, and she chided herself for being unfair to Jake. His approaches were always more cautious than hers and they were always rock solid. The problem with any course of action is that it has to be based on a set of assumptions resulting from bits of information. If information was incorrect and the assumptions were wrong then the course of action was wrong. Carin already knew Jake had to be working on some bad information. Her former finger lying on the counter reminded her Jake had to be under the assumption that she was dead. What other misinformation was he using? If she knew that, she could predict what he was doing. She needed more information.

She saw the cheese grater on the counter in the kitchen area and walked over to the sink. It was very unlike Jake to leave anything out of place. His years of training in the confining space of submarines had enforced this habit. She picked up the cheese grater and noticed the sink was full of water. No, she corrected herself, not water, solution. It was what Jake had been calling "Carin's Cocktail." She looked more closely at the cheese grater and saw Jake's skin and hair still clinging to parts of it. Carin sat down gently and tried to put the pieces together.

After a moment, she was no closer to a clear understanding of what had happened. She was only certain of one thing: Jake had scratched his arms and given himself a dose of the solution. That part made no sense to Carin. Jake was adamantly opposed to the solution. He felt that to give in to the infection meant he would lose himself, lose his ability to choose freely. What would cause a man like Jake Sabio to decide to give up his soul?

Carin went to brush her hair out of her eyes. The motion made her look at her ring finger on her right hand. There was a nub of a finger growing! She knew that what she saw was impossible, so she dismissed it from consideration for the time being. Anyway, it did not help her decide what to do next.

She opened the refrigerator and took out a power drink. Looking around the camper, she noticed two of the mechanical devices were getting charged. She looked at the digital readouts on their cases; their charging cycle was complete. She sat down while sipping her drink to consider their problems. She tried to think of solutions that would allow them to get to the planetoid, but could not come up with a way to prepare the tank, rescue Fred and help Jake. She looked at her watch. She had sixty-two hours.

She slapped her knees with her hands, stood up and marched to the tiny bathroom. Carin needed to do first things first. She took a quick shower and changed clothes to remove the mud and any reminders of her recent burial. Stepping out of the shower, she wrapped a towel around her and scrubbed a peephole into the foggy mirror. Her hair was still coming loose in clumps and looked patchy. Angrily, she found Jake's shaver and used the trimmer end to cut her hair down to her scalp. She stepped back from the mirror and took a good look at herself. She scarcely recognized the person in the reflection, but she had to admit that her look would probably fit just fine in Las Vegas. She gave a humorless laugh. *What wouldn't fit in a place like Las Vegas?*

Next, since Jake had apparently been successful in getting the solution into his body in such a way that he was able to leave soon after, Carin was willing to try it. She scrubbed out the sink, set the stopper and poured in fresh solution. The next part was going to be hard. Carin grabbed the grater firmly in her left hand and tried to scrape her right arm. She could not do it. She averted her eyes, placed the grater against her skin and willed it to drag across her arm. It refused to budge. Carin became furious. She set the grater against her arm and ripped it across her skin. Fiery pain erupted from her self-inflicted wound. She dropped the grater and began gasping for breath. Without thinking, she sank her scratched and bleeding arm into the solution. Within a few seconds, a sensation of intense pleasure replaced the burning sensation. Were the bugs in her system trying to communicate with her? If so, their communication was effective. Carin could imagine hearing the bugs saying they needed the solution and they sent pleasurable feelings to reinforce the behavior. Carin was glad they were enjoying themselves.

This is working, thought Carin. After less than a minute, her scratches were healed and the sense of pleasure was gone. With less hesitation than before, she scratched her left arm with the cheese grater. It was easier this time. She put the cheese grater down on the counter by the sink and placed her arm into the solution. The sense of pleasure was diminished and it took less time for her arm to heal. Carin concluded she must have not needed a great deal of the solution. She cleaned up her mess and felt surprisingly refreshed. Now that she had accomplished this step, what was next?

Carin began pacing the small confines of the trailer. She understood Jake well enough to figure out what he was going to do. The submarine commander had had his fill of interference from Greenfield, DiBeto, and Crubari. That interference had already disrupted their crucial preparations for the trip to the planetoid. Carin knew Jake was about to put a torpedo in the water. She just could not work out where Jake had it pointed. She concluded she could not help Jake right away. She turned her attention to Fred.

She had no idea where Fred was, but she was certain it was under some sort of guard. She sat there looking for tools to help her. Her eyes settled on the two mechanical devices and a plan began to form. If she could find Fred and if nobody had shut it down, this was going to work. She went outside the camper and dismounted the old beat up dirt bike that had come with the rig. She gave it a kick and knew it would be a chore getting the motorcycle running. Her years of running dirt bikes up and down the Rampart Range while she was at the Air Force Academy were about to pay off.

She pulled the plugs, cleaned them and checked for a spark. When she was satisfied, she tipped the bike up, dumped out the old gas, and replaced it with some they had in a jerry can for the generator. She reassembled the bike and began to kick it for all that she was worth. After the thirteenth kick, it coughed and continued to run. She left it idling against the trailer, placed the two mechanical devices in a large sack and carried the sack against her back.

She mounted the bike and checked her watch. She had sixty-one hours left. Time was now her enemy. *Great,* she thought, *another enemy.* She twisted the engine into a whine and powered the little bike toward the road to Las Vegas.

Chapter 35

Time to pickup: 59 hours

DiBeto was running late. He was already feeling the loss of several of his key lieutenants, but none more than Christopher Bruno. They had never recovered Bruno's body after the massacre, but that sort of thing happened. Of the five lieutenants DiBeto lost, they had only found the bodies of two. Nevertheless, since DiBeto was a naturally suspicious man, he had to ask himself, what if Bruno had gone over to the other side. On the other hand, what if Bruno had gone over to the Feds?

These questions needed answers. The best answer would be to find Bruno, if he was alive. Alternatively, what was left of him, if not.

He was still in his study when he noticed the time. Usually, he would meet his driver in the garage and drive out, but he called down to have the car pulled out front. He was just looking for his dark glasses when an explosion rocked the room. Glass blew in from where two windows had been a moment before. Chunks of plaster clattered down on Frank's massive desk as he instinctively dove under it for protection.

After what seemed like an eternity, four men came through the study door with guns drawn. DiBeto recognized them and immediately came out from under the desk. The four men pretended not to notice.

DiBeto came up to the lead security man and yelled, "What the hell happened?"

The security man simply said, "Car bomb."

DiBeto walked out towards the front door and saw the wreckage. The front door was blown off its hinges. Not a piece of glass was left in the window frames. Tables and chairs had been pushed away from the front of the house.

216

He was about to step outside to see the damage when a calm voice spoke from behind him. "I do not recommend you go outside. If the intent was assassination, the person responsible may have stationed snipers."

DiBeto spun around at the sound of the voice. "Dammit, Crowbar. Where've you been? What the hell just happened?"

Crubari showed no response to DiBeto's tirade. "This wasn't just an assassination attempt, it was a statement. A car bomb is extremely difficult to place. Think of the security the culprit had to get through to plant a device of this magnitude. You are going to be worrying about this for days. You will worry foremost that your life may end abruptly, but you will also worry that an attack can reach you regardless of your security precautions. A terror attack forces the victim to take their mind off more important things and forces them to make bad decisions. If you were to use the opposition's logic, on the fifty-fifty chance they got you, it would have decapitated the organization at a time it could ill afford it. The main question is to ask is who would profit, but in your position, there are too many answers to that question."

DiBeto lost patience. "Who did this, Crubari? Who's gunning for me? Is it Bruno? Do we know he's dead? Why can't we find any trace of him? If he were some innocent victim, my people would find something. Why am I paying you? And I specifically asked you to bring in the sub commander for questions, but I don't see him."

Crubari remained motionless and stared at DiBeto through dark glasses. Finally, he said, "You are currently paying me to bring in Captain Sabio for questioning. It is my understanding that is the only contract you and I have now. Due to your requirement to have Captain Sabio brought to you undamaged, it has taken longer than it would otherwise. In any event, we will have Captain Sabio within forty-eight hours. That is what I came here to tell you."

DiBeto was stunned. "Forty-eight hours? Bring him in now. I have to know who's responsible. We have enemies here and abroad who are going to exploit this until we can nail whoever stuck a stick in the hornets' nest."

"You will get Sabio, but, if you want him unharmed, you will have to wait. I have been unable to get him because he is extremely intelligent. He knows he's being pursued and he doesn't wish to be caught. However, he will come to us of his own volition, given the proper incentive. In the meantime, I suggest you attend your meeting as if nothing happened. The police and the fire trucks will be here any moment. I suggest that you get another car and driver and establish an alibi."

DiBeto snapped his fingers and an attendant was immediately at his side. "Get another car out front now."

The attendant's eyes went wide. "But sir, we don't have a driver."

DiBeto turned his bulk until he was directly facing the attendant and placed a finger in the young man's chest. In a low voice that was mostly a growl he said, "You've got a license. You're my new driver."

The attendant's face went pale. "Oh. Yes sir. Right away, sir."

When the attendant left, Crubari said, "There's one more thing. I don't have a contract on this, but let me know whether you want one. I think Mr. Bruno is alive and in hiding."

DiBeto wheeled back to face Crubari. "If he is, he's connected to this. How much will it cost me to bring in Bruno?"

"Four times the usual. He will not come willingly."

DiBeto thought for a moment. "It's a deal. I'll even give you an incentive. If you bring him in within forty-eight hours, I'll double it."

Crubari was still for almost a full minute. "Do you require him undamaged as well?"

DiBeto shrugged his shoulders. "I just have to be able to positively identify him."

After a moment, Crubari said, "We have a deal." With that, he turned his back on DiBeto and walked out the rear door.

CHAPTER 36

Time to pickup: 58 hours

CARIN'S LEGS HAD LOST sensation within the first hour on the little bike. Her headache had returned but she could not tell whether it was from her infection or the ridiculously loud motor. Why was it people insisted on removing the baffles from the mufflers on these bikes? Yet the responsiveness of the little machine brought back fond memories of similar rides she had taken along the Rampart Range in her Academy days. She flew over a small rise as she remembered the bottom half of her body was not entirely with her. Years of riding had given her a bag of tricks that she reached into on this occasion to keep her little leap from turning into a major wreck. Carin's riding settled down. She could not afford an accident at this point with only fifty-eight hours until pickup. Besides, she was no longer in her late teens and early twenties. You could get up from a fall in those days, brush yourself off, and continue riding. If she fell now, it would hurt. Another small rise presented itself. She instinctively took it and flew through the air once more. She was miserable. She was exhilarated. She was anxious. She was as free as she had ever felt in her life.

After reaching the road, she accelerated to highway speeds. The loss of feeling crept up her body until all sensation was lost below her waist. Her ears were ringing with the banging, high-pitched, nasal drone of the little engine. Her hands were numb, but she forced herself to continue. She had no idea where her two friends were. With all the forces gathered against them, she had to assume they were in desperate need of help and she could not conceive of stopping even to let some sensation creep back into her hands. She had to have her friends gathered at the tank in fifty-eight hours or they would all miss the pickup. If that happened, Carin was sure she and Jake would die very soon, probably within a month. She was not sure what would happen to Fred; at the very least, the little MI would go insane. She could not stop.

Carin entered Las Vegas and pulled up to a curb next to a phone booth. She steadied herself and the small motorcycle for a moment letting sensation creep back into her legs. After she was reasonably sure she was not going to fall over if she moved, she set the kickstand on the bike and walked bowlegged to the phone. Carin felt like an old time cowboy after a long day driving cattle. She had never understood the romantic notions surrounding that nasty job. In her current saddle-sore state, she understood it even less.

Carin picked up the phone and deposited her coins. Now was the decisive moment. If this part did not work, her plan would fail. She dialed nine nines. The line began ringing and picked up in the middle of the third ring. Before anyone spoke on the other end, Carin yelled, "Fred, are you there? Are you okay? Where are you?"

The voice on the other end said, "You have reached a non-working number. If you feel that you have ..."

"Fred, it's Carin. It's okay. The cavalry is here. I just don't know where to find either you or Jake. Tell me which hill to charge and I'll come a running'."

The automatic message on the other end of the line completed its mindless recital and the phone went dead. Carin looked at it in disbelief. She had been certain Fred would have been monitoring their old code. True, she had never asked Fred to maintain a watch on the phones, but neither had they come up with any contingency plans. Carin hung up the phone and leaned against the booth. She stretched her legs and tried to come up with a plan.

The phone began to ring and Carin picked it up in the middle of the first ring. "Fred?"

"Carin, it is good to hear your voice." It was Fred.

Relief washed over Carin. "Fred, I wasn't sure you would monitor our old code. It was the only idea that I had to find you."

"I also had no logical alternatives, Carin. I am currently residing in the Las Vegas FBI headquarters. I am in the evidence room, plugged into the wall and pushed up against the corner. I assume that they want to ensure the integrity of my data in the event of a power cycle. The interesting thing is they have not tried to access any data. I have looked it up on the FBI's operations manual and they are not going by the book. They should have attempted to access any data I had almost immediately."

Carin mulled over this information for a moment. "It seems to me the only logical reason to do that would be if they think the information would fall into the wrong hands."

"Carin, you are discounting the probability that they do not think I have any information and therefore are not wasting time. You are also discounting the probability that they took me to deny you access to my capabilities."

"I don't think that's the case, Fred. To begin with, you look like a very outdated, very low powered computer. I don't want to imply anything offensive in this, but you look as if you belong in a museum next to the dinosaur exhibit. You certainly don't look like the powerhouse you are. Secondly, even a low powered computer can store valuable data. I think that's the reason they took you. Why else would they have gone to the trouble to keep you powered up? I get the feeling Greenfield thinks he has a mole in his organization and he doesn't want whatever data you have to come leaking out to the bad guys."

"Carin, I will make finding this mole a priority. He may prove to be a threat to me."

"I agree. Also, we need to find this Bruno guy that Jake talked about a while ago."

"Do you mean Christopher Bruno?"

"Yeah, that's the guy. He was the head of Anhur operations or something before Jake talked him into leaving. My next move after springing you is to find Jake. I think he went after DiBeto and Crubari. Let's face it Fred, we only have about fifty-six hours until pickup. We still haven't loaded the tank, you're still in jail and we can't find Jake. We need to get some help with some of our problems."

"Carin, I will work on that. In the meantime, do you have a plan to free me from incarceration?"

Carin looked at her watch. It was a little less than fifty-six hours until pickup. Time! Time! Time! The damned stuff was running through her fingers like water. She quickly outlined her plan to Fred. It should spring Fred, but she was asking a great deal of the little MI.

Fred must have come to the same conclusion. "Carin, I have never demonstrated ability to do half the things required of me by your plan."

"Fred, we can't wait. There is no time to test the plan. I think you can do these things. Do you agree?"

Fred finally relented. "Yes, Carin. Call me when you have finished your part and I will pass on any information on Bruno or the mole."

"Good. Do we have any news on the Matr Front?"

"Yes, Carin. I have coordinated many of the details, but I thought you would want to know that Matr would be lowering a braided line that is made of three monomolecular filaments. I had no way of ascertaining the margin of safety since it exceeds my experience base."

Carin was scrubbing her face with her free hand. "That could be the ball game. There is no way a carbon buckytube rope is going to support its own weight at that length, much less lift us up."

"No Carin. I think that you have misinterpreted my terminology. Each filament is a single molecule. The bonds within the filament are not inter-molecular bonds, but intra-molecular. I know of no science that would allow the manufacture of such a material. Consequently I need your help to discern its safety."

Carin stood still for a moment, focusing, scarcely breathing. A sixty thousand mile long single molecule was impossible. Wasn't it? "Fred, did Matr say whether it has ever used this line before?"

"I specifically asked that question and it stated that it has. Matr indicated it has been a long time since it has been used, but gave assurances that the system was still serviceable."

Carin thought for a moment. "Okay. We have to trust that Matr knows its stuff eventually. Now would be a good time. When you communicate with it again, remind it that we are coming up in a steel tank. A true monomolecular filament would slice right through our tank much better than a white-hot knife through room-temperature butter. It better have some way of grabbing us."

"I will do so on our next communication. Is there anything else we should communicate to Matr?"

Carin smiled. "You know, it is freezing my blood cold to think we're going to ride that thing up, but we don't need to pass that on to Matr. What are your thoughts, my friend? Do you have any trepidation at leaving our little blue planet?"

"There is no way that I could communicate my state of concern over this next stage of our plans. However, if you and Jake are going, I will join you." With that, the line went dead.

Carin hung up the phone and smiled. The little MI certainly had guts, or circuits, or something; whatever the appropriate phrase was for its courage. It occurred to Carin there was going to have to be an entirely new set of pat phrases, probably an entire lexicon, which dealt with M.I.'s in a mixed society.

Carin got on her bike and kicked it to life on the third try. The next part of her plan was going to be tricky. To be honest, every part of her plan was going to be difficult and tricky, but this next part called for her to be able to persuade a person the way that Jake did. The problem was she had never convinced herself that she had that particular ability.

Carin drove around the airport to the cargo terminal. She was looking for a large overnight delivery operation and found three on the field. Each of the separate operations had their uniformly dressed people servicing their uniformly colored trucks. Carin watched the operation of the largest of the three and decided her plan might actually work.

She chose the company that was on the least populated side of the airport, drove around to the far side of the company parking lot, and set the kickstand on the bike. She placed the duffle bag with the mechanical devices on the far side of the motorcycle and put her helmet on top of the bag. Carin was betting that the security fence around the parking lot and the location of the bike away from other cars would keep the valuable mechanical devices safe. Besides, she planned to spend as little time as possible in the warehouse.

Carin pushed her baseball cap down hard onto her neatly trimmed scalp, put on a pair of aviator sunglasses and looked around. There were some workers standing in line to get through an electronic security gate. One of the workers opened the gate with his card and held it so that all of the workers could get in. Carin broke into a jog and the man holding the gate held it for her and let her into the compound. *So far so good*, thought Carin.

She stayed in the back of the pack and followed the females in the group to the poorly lit women's locker room. The uncarpeted room echoed mercilessly with the noise of showers and banging lockers. Conversation was subdued and limited. Carin's immediate impression of the other women in the locker room was one of either subjugation or resignation. It was as if the constant, day-to-day pressure on them had somehow deflated all the women.

The proximity of the airport with its occasional jet noise made Carin think of her days as a fighter pilot. All of the pilots from her old squadron returning from a mission, male or female, were loud and boisterous. The women fighter pilots knew they were a minority in a male-dominated profession, but immediately following a flight mission, they did not care. Part of it was that nothing pleased a fighter pilot more than to hand some puffed-up jackass their head on a platter after one of the grueling exercises, and it did not matter what the sex was of either the person handing out the platter or the person receiving the platter. The returning pilots would alternatively brag about their prowess in the air and confess their simpleton mistakes – sometimes in the same breath. There was a camaraderie and sense of purpose that was completely absent in this locker room. This would work in Carin's favor. These women would keep their heads down and mind their own business. It made Carin feel sad for all the sense of purpose that was lacking in the lives of all the women in the room. In truth, it was lacking for all the women except Carin.

She walked casually among the benches and rows as if mindlessly going to her own locker. Carin tried to mimic the walk and the look of the other women, shuffling her feet to give the appearance of reluctance to begin her work. She kept her head down in the dejected, hangdog manner of the other women, but she stole glances occasionally down the rows of lockers as she walked by. Glancing down the third row of lockers Carin found what she needed. A woman had apparently just finished her shift and was leaving her locker to go to the showers. She was approximately Carin's size and build. Best of all, she had left her locker open. Carin turned down the locker row and kept thinking to herself, *I'm invisible, I'm not really here, don't mind me.*

Carin walked past the locker and grabbed the uniform that was bunched up in the bottom shelf. It also contained a square metal clipboard that was used to sign for package deliveries. *Jackpot*, thought Carin. She casually turned and walked to the locker room exit. The hair on the back of her neck was prickling. She half expected a challenge, but nobody looked up. All the women in the changing room stayed lost in their own private thoughts and never looked beyond their own lockers.

Carin fell in behind a group of women that were walking out of the locker room. Their conversation was casual and tired. Carin could feel they were leaving the building after a long shift of work. A woman walking next to her turned her head and began making conversation to pass the time.

"How was your shift?"

Carin almost jumped out of her skin. She knew she could not maintain the illusion of an employee if the old woman asked too many questions. "It was the most exciting day I've ever had with the company. My legs went to sleep from the waist down."

The old woman threw her head back and let out a dry cackle. "You said a mouthful, girlfriend. See if you can get your man to bring you back to life."

They shuffled along with the old woman laughing and shaking her head. "Dead from the waist down ... funniest thing I ever heard."

Carin did not think it was all that funny, but it kept the old woman distracted until they got to the parking lot. Carin continued her hangdog shuffle until she got to the little motorcycle. She took the load she had purloined and shoved it unceremoniously into the duffle bag. She looked around the parking lot as she was buckling her helmet. Nobody was watching her. All the workers were shuffling single-mindedly to their cars. Carin straddled the little bike and checked her watch. She was down to fifty-five hours to pickup. *C'mon, Carin. Let's get some hustle on.*

Carin drove out of the parking lot and made a direct path to the Las Vegas FBI Headquarters. On the way, she stopped at a gasoline station, stepped into the ladies' room and changed into the delivery company uniform she had stolen. She put her own clothes under the mechanical devices in the duffel bag and stepped outside to a pay phone. She dialed nine nines and the line picked up on the second ring.

"You have reached a number that has ..."

Carin disregarded the message and said, "Fred, it's Carin. Are you there?"

The message cut off immediately and Fred answered. "Carin, it is good to hear your voice again."

Carin smiled. "It's good to hear yours as well, my friend. How goes our plan?"

"William Greenfield has not been in the office all day, but the property custodian will be here for another hour."

"Okay, we go as briefed unless you have any inputs."

"No, Carin. Your plan is better than any alternatives I can suggest."

Carin could only hope that the MI was right. "Fred, have we found any information on Bruno that might be helpful?"

"Yes Carin. It seems that Mr. Bruno and you had an intersection that you may be able to use."

Fred proceeded to tell her everything it had found out about Bruno. Carin was silent for a few moments trying to digest all the information when she remembered that the few seconds to her were the equivalent of several days to Fred. Finally, she simply said, "Fred, thank you and good luck."

The little MI immediately replied, "Good luck, Carin."

Carin hung up the phone and smiled at the next part of her plan. It would require stealth, steely nerves and audacity. After all, steely nerves and audacity were the breakfast of any true fighter pilot. Stealth was just an extra little bonus. Carin grinned so hard at the thought she could feel her lips stretched well over her gums. It was the deadly smile of a predator. It felt good to be a fighter pilot again.

The FBI Building was a bland, unwelcoming structure nestled between a Masonic lodge and a nearly defunct financial services office building. It was of a style that could only be described as Twentieth Century Federal. The front face of the building was a white and tan brick wall standing three stories high. Only a single United States of America flag flying by the structure lent any color or affiliation to the drab architecture. Tiny aluminum letters over the front door cryptically proclaimed it as the John Lawrence Bailey Building. In fact, the only indications there was something unique about the edifice were the unadorned, unrepentant Jersey barriers laid out around it and the multiple antennas crowning the top. Carin assumed that the effect was on purpose. It was hard to imagine the same science and art that built the squat little building before her had also produced such a magnificent example as the Petronus Towers of Malaysia.

She pulled her motorcycle into the parking lot next to the building and stopped at the guard shack. The guard, an elderly man of around sixty, came out carrying a clipboard. Carin could see him looking at the rumpled, sweat-stained clothes she was wearing. "It's a little late for a delivery," he said. "Your compadre has been and gone two hours ago."

"Sorry, there was a screw up at the warehouse," said Carin. She patted the bulges in her duffel bag. "These were supposed to be dropped off today, but they got lost in the shuffle. Some guy named 'Greenfield' called my boss and chewed him out good. I live along the way. It was no big deal to drop it off. I figured, think about it, everybody gets what they want and I get home maybe a half hour late. Everybody gets to relax."

The old guard smiled. "Who did you say that was for? Greenfield?"

Carin made a pretense of verifying the name on her clipboard. "Yep. William Greenfield is what it says."

The guard checked a computer screen in his guard shack and shook his head. "Mr. Greenfield's not here right now, but the property manager is still around. I can get him to sign for the package and get it off your hands."

Carin graced the old guard with a wide, friendly smile. "Anything you can do to get this junk off my back will be greatly appreciated."

Chapter 37

Time to pickup: 48 hours

JAKE HAD BEEN WALKING in the warehouse district for hours with a range of emotions churning through his mind. Every time he tried to force his feelings back so he could focus on his task, they would bubble up somewhere else. The memory of his lost children would flare into his consciousness. He choked back tears and pushed down hard to suppress the love he had for them and the lost promise of their future. Then the memory of Fred would surface and Jake would feel the loss of the nascent M.I.'s friendship. The bond had grown more intensely within him than he had known. Then the thought of Carin came to mind and he would have to push hardest of all to keep any sanity. Even with his years of command under pressure, once or twice while thinking of her, a sob had caught on his lips.

His intention to look at the warehouse before he set up his rendezvous had turned his reconnaissance into something closer to a drunken man's walk home. He was ready to set up the meeting the instant he saw the contents of the dry ice filled box, but a small voice in his head kept insistently buzzing against such a course of action. He recognized the voice from his years of tracking enemy nuclear submarines, and he was determined to pay attention to his instincts. Those instincts were the product of years of training in both fighters and submarines and had been honed until they were a knowledgeable voice. He understood nothing about the darker world where people knew how to shake a person following them, but he was one of the world's experts in the deadly world of attack submarines. The training he did have would have to do.

Jake kept changing directions, reversing his course and casually checking behind whenever he crossed a street. This is exactly what he had done dozens of times in the past while commanding his submarine. He found his mind was still working on three dimensions. Whereas a civilian trying to determine whether they are being followed would scan around at the street level, Jake was also looking at the rooftops and the building windows out of habit. After the second hour of walking, he was certain he was not being followed.

The obvious danger was that he was being herded into a trap. This was a tough problem to solve, since his adversary already expected him. *Scratch off the element of surprise.*

He hung his confidence on his recently acquired enhanced awareness. That was going to have to be his vital edge. He would walk straight into the intended death trap and rely on his new abilities to keep him alive.

Once Jake finally closed in on the warehouse, he strained to sense for anything out of the ordinary but felt nothing. His eyes scanned into every dark corner and behind every garbage container. He listened for any human movement, then opened his mind to the smell and tastes around him. His awareness grew so sharp that the movements of an alley cat or even a scavenging rat shot warning chills up his spine. The darkness only heightened the sense of danger. There was no moon out, and there were few streetlights in the warehouse district. Jake looked around and found a small piece of broken pavement on the ground. He picked up the small, slightly spherical chunk and examined it for a minute. It was about half the size of a baseball.

He walked to the nearest streetlight. Even though he had been vigilant for anybody following him, the instincts that all children gain by their eleventh year kicked in and he and looked around for any prying eyes. When he convinced himself nobody was looking, he faced the streetlight and threw his rock. He was surprised when the rock hit the center of the target on the first try. He was even more surprised at the explosive sound of the bulb shattering and the loud rainfall of glass showering on the pavement and echoing among the quiet buildings. Jake ran back into a dark alley and waited for any response. When Jake was convinced nobody was coming and no one was watching, he stepped out of the shadows and picked up the chunk of concrete from among the shards of glass on the sidewalk. Jake knocked out seven more streetlights near the warehouse before he was convinced he had done as well as he could do.

With the warehouse plunged into darkness, Jake began circling the building. His vision was still picking up excellent detail, about what he would expect on an overcast day. He was no match for a person with night vision goggles for acuity, but he retained his depth perception. NVGs were notorious for displaying their information in two dimensions. There was a long list of aviators that had misinterpreted the NVG display and flown their craft into the ground. NVGs were a crutch, but so was a gun. Jake was not going to underestimate either one.

He noted every external detail of the warehouse and memorized it. Jake soon knew the location of every door, every fire escape, and every window on the old building. Something felt wrong about the building, but he could not put his finger on it.

Odds were that Jake was going to be outgunned and outnumbered if he went along this course of action. He needed to build himself some advantage. He climbed a fire escape on a side of the building hidden from the main street. The door at the top of the fire escape was chained shut from the outside. The chain and the lock were still shiny to Jake's hypersensitive eyes, even in the dim light. He could tell the chain and locks had been installed within the last day. It seemed that once Crubari corralled his victim, he wanted to keep him trapped in the warehouse. Jake did not like playing the role of helpless prey. He placed one hand on the doorjamb and another on the door handle and pulled. The force of his pull popped off the locked hasp from the old sides of the warehouse. He reached in his pocket for the small tube of lubricant he had grabbed for just this purpose. He then oiled the hinges until they allowed the door to open silently. Only then did Jake replace the section he had just broken out. He backed up a pace and looked at his impromptu repair. The broken section of the wall would stand up to casual scrutiny, but would pose no obstacle to his escape if he had to. Jake performed the same operation twice more around the building. He now had excellent avenues of escape if he needed them.

Jake started for the main loading door when the insistent voice in his head turned into one of alarm. There was danger close by. Jake walked up to the light over the main door, reached up, and crushed it through its wire cage. Blackness enveloped the side street and Jake retreated into the deep shadow behind a dumpster. He was silent for many minutes listening and scanning. Jake strained his senses to the limit to detect any living beings in the area, but there simply were none. What was sending him such a strong warning? Jake cursed his enhanced senses. What good were they if they could not tell your conscious self the nature of a threat?

Jake weighed his next move carefully. The threat was real, but he needed to go inside to scan the layout of the interior of the warehouse if he was going to meet Crubari. Going into that meeting without knowing the layout was suicide. Jake considered abandoning his meeting with Crubari. *No way,* thought Jake. *On the slim chance that they have Carin, I have to see this through.* He thought of deeper reasons for the meeting and dark emotions had to be pushed down and controlled.

Jake came out from behind the dumpster and walked to the main door.

The glass that he had broken crunched loudly under his feet. He paused again at the sound. Was the sound that loud or were his sharpened senses assaulting him?

He tried the door. It gave freely and he walked in, carefully checking the doorjamb for any electronic device. When he found none, he walked around the bottom floor quickly. He determined which direction each stairway went and noted the quickest escape routes. He also noted which routes had the most cover in case someone was shooting at him. It was a grim contingency, put on the front burner for consideration.

The inside of the warehouse was filled with crates. Jake wondered where the "interview" might take place and his eyes settled on a supervisor's office up a flight of stairs. Jake carefully climbed the stairs and knew that he had found what he was looking for.

The supervisor's office had reinforced glass windows on three sides that started at waist level. The fourth side was against the exterior wall of the warehouse. Jake stood just outside the door and carefully inspected the room through the window. He noted the single door into the office. *Only one way in and one way out*, thought Jake. *This is not good for me.* The room was devoid of furniture. There were some boxes pushed up against the walls, but none of them came up to the level of the windows. Jake carefully walked into the office and checked for sensors around the door. He rubbed his hands against the solid wall and wondered whether he could loosen one of the old outer panels. It was imperative that Jake have an escape route available. Giving Crubari the upper hand would only insure his death and Carin's as well, if she was even still alive.

Jake was in the center of the room facing away from the door when he heard a soft click behind him and whirled to meet the threat. The door was closing slowly, but a gate was silently lowering on the outside of the door. Jake had found his trap and he had tripped it like the clumsy novice that he was. He launched himself at the doorway. Jake calculated there would be enough time to get through the door and get under the gate before it closed, when he heard four nearly simultaneous chuffs of air. In his peripheral vision to his right, he saw twin darts with wires snaking behind them rushing towards his waist. Time slowed for Jake.

His heightened senses immediately detected three other twin darts streaming towards him. The problem was he could not tell their exact location and trajectory unless he saw them. Without knowing exactly where they were going, he might only think he was dodging the darts. Without the ability to track all the darts at the same time, he was vulnerable. Jake began to spin to get his strongest senses, his eyes, on these new threats. His momentum kept him going towards the door, but now he spun like a top to see where the other darts were. As he spun, he modified his body position to get out of the way of each one. He set himself up to miss the first pair of darts and continued his spin. His eyes came around and saw the second set of darts. He thrust out his hands over his head to modify his center of gravity. The second pair would miss him. His angular momentum carried him around and he saw the third pair of darts. He thrust out a leg and he knew he would miss the third pair of darts.

Jake's thrusting out of arms and legs had slowed his angular rotation rate to the point that he did not think he would be able to see the fourth pair in time. He strained his neck around to see the twin missiles. When he saw them, his heart sank. They were less than a foot from his waist. If he pulled his leg back in, the fourth pair would miss him, but the third pair would hit him. If he pulled in his arm, the second pair would still hit him. Jake knew a dart was going to hit, so he pulled his legs up to his chest and brought his arms in around his head.

The second, third and fourth pairs of darts raced by him missing their target by narrow margins, but the first pair sank deeply into Jake's lower back. The TASER darts immediately released fifty thousand volts and five watts of power into Jake's body. The first pulse lasted only ten seconds, but Jake was immediately incapacitated and unconscious.

A normal person hit with a TASER dart will feel dazed and confused for several minutes. The purpose of the TASER is to stun a victim into a grounded position, but on occasion, victims have been rendered unconscious.

Jake was no longer a normal person. When the current hit him, it was as if someone had thrown a switch. One instant he was hyper-aware of every bit of his surroundings, he was "turned off" the next instant. All voluntary muscle activity immediately ceased and Jake's forward momentum crashed him into the closing door causing it to slam shut. The TASER darts remained attached to Jake after his tumble to the ground and continued to give him a two-second shock every thirty seconds until an hour later when Crubari disconnected the darts from Jake's back.

CHAPTER 38

Time to pickup: 42 hours

AGENT GLYNNIS BEAMER JUMPED out of her car and caught up with Agent Greenfield in the Federal Building parking lot. The sun would not come up for another hour and she seemed to be having trouble judging her distances. She had to add a few jogging steps to her fast walk in order to keep up.

"Agent Greenfield, will you please slow down? It's not as bad as it sounds."

Greenfield turned an angry eye to her but did not slacken his pace. "We lose a major piece of evidence right out of the property locker on an investigation that we're doing and you don't think that it's a problem?"

Glynnis shook her head. "No, Will, I know it's bad from the perception standpoint. On top of the theft, the team hasn't gotten a break on this case in a long time. That, plus the fact we just were in the middle of a firefight at that truck stop and plus the fact that we seem to have a mole. Washington is going to go ballistic on us when they see the latest report. All of us on the team are looking at some major political heat coming down the pipe."

Greenfield spared Glynnis a sideways glance without slowing his pace and shook his head. He had worked with her for almost three straight years and still could not figure her out. She just said she knew that they were going to be targeted for an internal investigation and she did not think it was important. An internal investigation could get them all fired. An internal investigation could land them all in jail. "Glynnis, do me a favor. Quit trying to cheer me up. You're beyond abysmal at cheering up."

They reached the door to the Federal Building with Greenfield slightly ahead. He reached up to grab the door handle but Glynnis grabbed his sleeve and held him back. He looked at her hand on his sleeve. He raised his head and gave her a warning glare so fierce that it should have turned her to ashes. Instead, she stood holding his sleeve as if she did not notice. In a measured voice, Greenfield asked, "Is there some reason that I should stand out here with you?"

Glynnis held on to his sleeve, but gave Greenfield a look that mothers reserve for petulant children. "Will, you've got to be on full alert when you walk in and you're like a bull in a china shop."

Greenfield was getting angry. "Agent Beamer, let go of my sleeve so that I can go inside and do my job."

Glynnis was adamant. "Agent Greenfield, there is no way you can do your job when you are in the state of mind that you're in. Nobody can. And in case you haven't figured it out, I'm not worried about you going to prison. I'm worried about you, me, Brian and Ed going to prison."

Greenfield deflated slightly and looked down at his sleeve. "You can let go now, Glynnis. I'm listening."

Glynnis let go of his sleeve, crossed her arms and squared off in front of Greenfield blocking his entrance into headquarters. "What is your value to this team?"

He answered immediately, "I'm the team leader."

She shook her head. "You're not bad as a team leader, but that's not it. You and I have both seen better team leads."

Greenfield knew that Glynnis was trying to get to a point, but he could not follow her thinking. He thought of her, Brian and Ed and considered the strengths of the team members. He looked up to her and said, "I'm the intuitive one of the group."

Glynnis' face slowly settled into a slight smile. "You're the most intuitive person I've met on this planet, boss. It's good to have you back."

Greenfield admitted to himself that Glynnis might have a point. He had been … still was … overheated. That could have a devastating effect on the team and on the investigation of the missing property. He forced himself to stand up straight and look the female agent in the eye. "Agent Beamer, are you implying that at times my thinking may be overcome by emotions of the moment?"

Glynnis was shaking her head. "Absolutely not, sir. But on the off chance that happened, the rest of your team's chances of surviving this fiasco would be in the toilet." She began to mechanically tick of points on her fingers. "First, we've got a proven mole in our midst. Second, we can't seem to find the mole. Third, the mole is feeding information to our prime suspects. Fourth, we have a person of interest, one Jake Sabio, who we can't seem to bring in for questioning. Fifth, we have a prime suspect that has been as slippery as an eel even after three years of intense effort. Sixth, we have some unknown groups in the middle of some kind of turf war or something, setting off car bombs in the residential district of the premiere entertainment destination of the world. Seventh, we have some slim proof that, somehow or another, Sabio, the turf war, the mole and Stanger are all tied together. If not, at least Sabio may have some insight into what's going on. Then, eighth, to top it off, we just had someone steal evidence items right out of the HQ property room that our team tagged. Oh yeah, and this whole thing started 'cause we were investigating the somewhat questionable demise of not one, but two U.S. senators. The team's in deep trouble, sir. I think we're close to breaking this case, but we have to be quick about it. I also think that with the level of political interest in this case, we would have solved it by now if various parties in Washington were not stonewalling us. If we solve this case, I would bet there'd be a few high-powered players that get their sacred oxen gored. They can go from just stalling to active interference, which would kill this investigation and all of our so-called careers if not ourselves. This investigation has stumbled into a nasty group of folks that makes the gun-em-down boys of the Mafia in early Vegas look like a bunch of petulant nursery-schoolers." Glynnis stopped and took several breaths. Eyes widening slightly, realizing she may have overstepped her bounds, she smoothed the front of her slacks with both hands and said, "I, uh, just mean that we need you at your top form when you walk in there today … sir."

Greenfield took three slow, deep breaths himself and allowed a dispassionate calm to descend on him. Glynnis was right. They all needed to be at top form. "Thank you, Glynnis. Is there anything else?"

"No, sir. I'm glad you're here, sir."

Greenfield went to wave his badge across the card reader, but turned to Glynnis first. "Thanks for helping to get me here. Now let's find out what happened."

Glynnis passed her own card in front of the card reader and the door unlocked and let the two of them enter a larger reception room. At the far end of the room was a uniformed officer sitting behind bulletproof glass waiting for them to sign-in. The sign-in procedure appeared to be a holdover from the old days before computers, but it was a good way to force anyone entering to approach the security guard and to allow the guard to look the people over. Computers are good, but people can detect a problem that a computer would gladly let pass into Headquarters. William Greenfield felt a lot safer knowing there was a human guarding the front door.

Glynnis walked towards the security cage and waved a greeting to the guard. "Hey, Alicia. How's your daughter doing today? Any better?"

While Glynnis and Alicia were exchanging pleasantries and Glynnis was signing in, Greenfield looked around the reception room. *How could someone get into this place without leaving so much as a mark,* thought Greenfield? Electronically locking steel doors could contain a small group of commandos trying to break in. Four security cameras would capture any attempt to get in and the double locking isolation doors behind the security guard station made it virtually impossible to get in. He needed more information.

After passing all the security measures, Greenfield and Glynnis walked calmly through the hallway and went straight to the property room. A small crowd of agents clustered behind a makeshift barricade. Greenfield noticed the station chief, Zebidiah Collins, in the group. "How's it going, sir?"

The elderly man turned his face and his disapproving glare pierced Greenfield. "Some of your tagged items have been stolen out of the property room."

"Yes sir. May I take a quick look to see whether I notice anything?"

The station chief was puffing himself up to deny Greenfield's request when the property custodian stuck his head out into the hall. "Hey chief, let me borrow Will a second. I need his eyes on some stuff."

The station chief hesitated a moment and gave a slight nod. Greenfield and Glynnis both walked into the property room. Greenfield spoke under his breath to the property custodian, "Louis Sackett, Zeb's going to cook you alive. What are you thinking bringing me in here without first getting Zeb's blessing?"

Lou Sackett gave Greenfield a puzzled look. "What are you talking about? I'm in deep kimshe here too and I wanted the best investigator we've got in here doing some investigating. C'mon Will, if you can't figure out what happened, nobody can. In which case, I'll be joining your team, no offense, and we'll all be kept in some small room licking envelopes and sending mail to parking violators."

Sackett looked at Agent Beamer. "Glynnis, tell Will I'm right on this one."

She folded her hands behind her back and focused a neutral stare straight ahead. "Agent Greenfield and I have already had that discussion today."

Will Greenfield stopped any further conversation along those lines by raising both hands up as a sign of surrender. When he saw that both Sackett and Glynnis had stopped talking, he turned to Sackett and said, "Tell me what you got."

Sackett pointed to the corner of the room where they had plugged in the computer they had confiscated from Jacob Sabio's trailer. "The only things missing from the room are the computer and the four mechanical devices."

Greenfield looked puzzled. "Not the money?"

Sackett was shaking his head. "Nope."

Greenfield looked at Glynnis. "And you said four mechanical devices. When did we get two more?"

Sackett answered instead. "I signed for them late yesterday. The slip's on the counter right there."

Greenfield thought about that for a moment. "Glynnis, can you please check that out?"

Glynnis picked up the slip of paper, went to a phone in the corner and began dialing. Greenfield turned his attention to Sackett and said, "Are you sure nothing else was touched?"

"Absolutely nothing in this room was disturbed. I even counted the money you got from that same raid as the computer. Every dollar is still there."

Greenfield was looking around the property room. It was essentially a six-sided, cubical steel cage, just four walls, a roof, and a floor made out of heavy steel mesh. It had rows of shelves lining the inside where items of evidence were stored and tagged. The only way in or out was through a self-locking gate door. Even the ventilation ducts were outside the cage. "Do the surveillance tapes show anything?"

Sackett shifted his weight uneasily. "I'd better show you the tape."

The property custodian walked over to the playback machine and started the tape. Greenfield looked at the four separate simultaneous pictures play on the screen. He could see the computer plugged into the corner in two of the views. The scenes showed Sackett bringing the two devices into the property room and placing them on the shelves. When Sackett turned to leave the room, the four mechanical devices and the computer vanished. "Whoa, whoa, whoa ... back it up. Does this thing have slow motion?"

Sackett reset the tape and set it moving in slow motion. There was no mistake. The devices were there in one frame and were gone the next. Glynnis had returned and watched the tape run. "Okay, what happened," she asked. "Did somebody beam them up?"

Greenfield was quiet for a moment. "Are we missing a vehicle?"

Sackett looked at him in surprise. "Yeah, we misplaced one of the fleet SUVs. How'd you know?"

Greenfield was nodding his head. "And the parking lot surveillance tapes showed nothing." It was not a question, but Sackett shook his head anyway.

Greenfield thought for a moment more. "I'll also bet the on-board locator has been disabled and we can't find the vehicle."

Sackett became animated. "That's right. You got something, Will?"

Greenfield turned and smiled at Sackett. "Yeah, I think I got something. Let me check a couple of loose ends and I'll get back to you."

Greenfield turned to Glynnis. "According to the freight company, no delivery was made here late yesterday afternoon. Am I right?"

Glynnis nodded her head. "You got it in one, boss. What's next?"

"Get a copy of the surveillance tapes from the parking garage and here. Get the team together and meet in my office ASAP."

Glynnis was already heading out the door before Greenfield finished. "I'm on it. Lou, get me a copy of the tape. See whether you can isolate the part where the stuff beams out of the room."

Greenfield reached over and shook the property custodian's hand. "Thanks Lou. I'll get right back to you." With that, he headed out the door in Agent Beamer's wake and saw that the station chief had intercepted her. Greenfield came up to Zeb and said, "Excuse me, sir." He turned to Glynnis. "Agent Beamer, didn't I stress the importance of getting that information? We may still have a chance to catch the perpetrators. Let's go. Tempus Fugit." He turned to Zeb Collins and said, "Sir, we need her immediately. With your permission, I'd like to get her working on some evidence."

Zeb had turned to Greenfield, begun filling his lungs with air and turning red, until Greenfield mouthed the phrase "catch the perpetrators." Greenfield had been counting on that. There was also the detail of witnesses. How would it look if Zeb kept one of his team from performing their duties? Zeb stood at parade rest and said, "Very good, Agent Greenfield. The two of you carry on, but advise me immediately of any breaks in this case."

Glynnis Beamer immediately began to move again, but Greenfield stayed behind and thanked the director to provide cover for Glynnis in case the director changed his mind. When Greenfield was certain that she had made a clean getaway, he went to his office and turned on his computer screen. While he was waiting, he called the property room. Louis Sackett picked up the phone. "Property."

"Lou, it's Will. What do you have for a vendor and model number on those mechanical devices?"

Sackett read the information to Greenfield who then punched it directly into a search engine. Greenfield thanked Sackett, hung up and began to review the returns from his search. Greenfield scanned one page that had the specifications of the devices and let out a slow whistle. "Well I'll be a son of a gun."

An urgent e-mail icon flashed in the corner of his screen. He selected the icon and read the e-mail. The more he read, the wider his eyes got. This time Greenfield could not whistle. "Or a son of a much, much bigger gun."

Agents Brian Hatfield and Edward Stein entered Greenfield's office but remained silent. Glynnis Beamer came in a minute later and waited silently by the door. Greenfield put a stick of gum in his mouth and began chewing. He absentmindedly picked up a rubber band and began to twirl it between his fingers. Suddenly, he lunged forward, hit the print button on his computer, and stood up. He looked at his team and said, "Where's the nearest viewer for the tapes?"

Glynnis immediately answered, "Conference room twelve."

Greenfield looked at his watch. It was just after seven a.m. The conference rooms should be private. "Okay, let's go."

He led his team to the conference room, stopping only to pick up the sheets he had just printed. He led the others to the conference room. Glynnis wasted no time. "What do you want first, boss?"

Greenfield began pacing along the side of the room, snapping his gum and playing with his rubber band. "Put up the parking lot surveillance camera."

Glynnis popped in the cassette and pressed the play button. The same four-frame view appeared on the large screen in the front of the room and on monitors on the table. It showed four separate images of a row of cars. Nothing moved on the images except for a digital clock running at the bottom right of the screen. Suddenly, one of the cars was simply gone.

Greenfield continued to pace but pointed at the screen. "Back it up and use slow-mo. Brian, Ed – write down the time when it disappears."

Glynnis was punching buttons on the player. "Here it comes."

The image fed forward more slowly this time. The clock on the lower right hand corner of the screen was no longer a blur. The car disappeared in the same manner as the electronic equipment had disappeared from the property room. One frame it was there, the next frame, it was gone. Greenfield looked at Brian and Ed. "Did you get the time?" Both the men nodded heads.

Greenfield kept up his pacing. "Glynnis, pop in the tape from the property room. You guys mark down the time again." Once again, the team members watched as an item disappeared in a single frame. Greenfield looked at the men. "It happened at the same time, didn't it?"

Both men looked up and Brian said, "They happened simultaneously. If somebody didn't jigger the clocks as well, they both disappeared at the same hundredth of a second."

"Glynnis thinks someone teleported these things out. What do you think happened, Brian?"

Brian shrugged his shoulders. "You got me, boss. It could be that somebody beamed them up just as Glynnis said, but how does this become our problem? I mean, we're too deep in trouble with our real investigation. You know, the turf war that's going on right now, high-level murders and the car bombings. Will, we have been getting a lot of heat."

Greenfield kept pacing, but looked at Brian. "I know about the heat, Brian. You may not believe it, but I've been able to keep about ninety-five percent of the heat off you troops so that you could do your job. I think even Zeb has screened some of it for us. Just stick with me for a minute on this one and then we can circle around to the problem of our investigation. How did somebody get Sabio's computer out of the property room?"

Brian looked at the tape Glynnis had put on a loop. "The first thing is that someone has obviously tampered with the tape."

Glynnis pivoted her chair around and simply said, "Bull."

Brian pointed at the large screen at the front of the room with one arm and to the monitors around the room with the other. "Bull right back at ya, gal pal. What we just saw was Hollywood fiction. It's impossible to explain where the stuff went unless you start with the fact that what we're seeing is an illusion."

Greenfield was still pacing but now he had wrapped the rubber band around his left wrist and was pulling it with his right hand and letting it snap back. "Glynnis, why do you think the tapes are real?"

"C'mon, boss. You know our security systems as well as I do. It's a triple-tiered, triple-isolated system. I just did a cursory check of the three separate tiers and they all have the same information. Besides, we're not talking about deleting files; we are talking about altering video. Did any of you heroes see any bumps or jumps in that video? Did you see any shading or texture variations that were out of place? I sure didn't. Look, the human eye and brain together make the best pattern-recognition pickup that exists. In a real-time video stream, the average human can spot one pixel per second on a normal resolution screen that is out of place. One pixel per second! The kind of real-time video signal processing that can fool the four of us in a frame-by-frame examination of the video is way beyond any computer or super-computer that exists. Besides, no such program exists. D'ya know how long it would take to write such a program? D'ya know how many programmers it would take? Hollywood couldn't do it. Only the Department of Defense has the budget and belly buttons to pull it off in less than a year and why would they want to?"

Greenfield slowed down his pacing and gave a slight smile to Glynnis. "What if I told you that it was two people, a man and a woman, and they did it in less than forty-eight hours?"

Glynnis snorted. "Next thing you'll tell me is that the man was Santa Claus and the woman was the Easter Bun...Omigod!"

Greenfield kept pacing and his smile got slightly wider. "I'm sorry, Agent Beamer. I didn't quite hear that last part."

Glynnis had both her hands on the table and was staring off to infinity. "Omigod! Omigod! Omigod! The clinic."

Greenfield's smile faded. "Okay, Glynnis. It's crunch time. I've got to know whether they could do it."

Ed Stein looked puzzled. "Can you two guys clue us in on what you're talking about?"

Glynnis turned to gaze at Ed and Brian. "The Jonas Ingreti Clinic. They had a double-tiered, double-isolated system that was also impossible to subvert and these people definitely got into it. I'll reverse my position completely with another piece of data, boss. The woman in question rewired a car to blow Crubari's airbag in his face. I don't need to remind you guys that she did it in such a way the car manufacturer and our FBI forensics lab are both still clueless."

Greenfield snapped the rubber band loudly against his wrist. "That's right! That's great thinking, Glynnis. I hadn't connected the airbag and the security tampering together, but it fits. Okay, so we know that the impossible has happened at least twice and maybe three times. Someone who has tampered with a security system before did it again. Let's assume that Brian is right and someone did actually tamper with the security systems. Okay Brian, how did they get in and out without being seen?"

Brian wiggled uncomfortably in his seat. "Electronics is one thing, but a human being is another. Whoever did this had to get through a card reader, past a guard, avoid a roving guard, break into a locked cage that shows no signs of tampering and get back out again with about three hundred pounds of unwieldy gear. I'm beginning to like Glynnis' teleportation theory."

Glynnis huffed at Brian's remark. "It was a joke. All right already."

Greenfield sat down on the opposite side of the table from the other three. After all his frenetic pacing, it was unsettling to see him so still. "What if nobody broke in?"

All three of Greenfield's teammates were quiet. Finally, Ed broke the silence. "C'mon, Will. Three hundred pounds of junk didn't just get up on its own and walk out the front door."

Greenfield pulled off the first three sheets of his printouts and handed one sheet to each of the team members. "Folks, let me introduce you to the X22R built by the Xiwa Corporation in a plant right outside the city limits of Las Vegas on a license agreement with the parent company in Japan. These are the mechanical devices that we had in the property room"

Glynnis was the first to digest the printout and began speaking while still looking down at the specification sheet. "It can radio link, it can video and IR link, it's ambulatory, it can manipulate up to a two hundred kilograms, and it is dexterous at manipulating objects." She sat back from the sheet. "Great, it's self-propelled. We put freakin' robots in the property room and we didn't even know it."

Brian sat back from his own sheet and rubbed his eyes. "Their arms, legs, and head just fold up into a nice, neat rectangular box for storage. Kind of like a kid's toy."

Ed Stein pushed his chair back from the table and said, "So what. Look at the processors and memory capacity on this thing. It's ridiculous! I own a watch that has more computational power than this so-called robot. The brochure says that these things are supposed to be used at universities to teach students the fundamentals of robotics. They're unprogrammed."

Greenfield took off his rubber band and shot it in the air towards Ed. Ed caught it easily and gave Greenfield a sour look. Before Ed could fire off a comment that went with that look, Greenfield said, "How smart is your hand, Ed?"

Ed looked puzzled. "C'mon, Boss. It's a hand."

Greenfield stood up and began pacing again. "Yet it just solved two, sixth-order, non-linear partial differential equations in less than a second with no programming. I think we just proved that Ed's brain is better than any of our present day super-computers."

Ed's eyes went wide. "Are you saying that ancient, ugly white computer we brought in?"

Greenfield nodded. "Exactly! That ancient, ugly white computer."

Brian threw up his hands and yelled, "Hold it!" He looked around at his three teammates in order and settled his gaze on Greenfield. "Are you saying that a super-intelligent computer directed his robot minions to carry him out of a secure cell, fudge our triple-tiered security system, hot-wire a government car, and drive out?"

The team was quiet for a moment. After what seemed more than a minute, Ed spoke up. "Actually, they took the keys for the car."

Glynnis added, "And it's more appropriate to refer to the computer as 'it.' Terms such as 'him' or 'her' are misleading and might have us unconsciously assigning it attributes that it does not have."

Finally, Greenfield said, "Yes, Brian. That's exactly what I am saying."

"Okay, let me think this through. Coming in from the outside is impossible without leaving some evidence. At the very least, you would have to jimmy some locks. That would lead to scratches on the wood, metal and paint. Then the security guard gets a perimeter warning and knows someone opened a door. That leaves dead people and blood everywhere. Another scenario: let's say it was an inside job. We have card readers and security cameras that would have left a trail or our security guard would have noticed something. I don't think that even Glynnis could subvert our triple-tiered system and let's face it; our system is set up specifically to catch an inside job.

"Yet another scenario: let's say we locked up a super-brain in the property room that had electronic access to the surveillance system from the inside.

We have a single guard after midnight due to budget cuts. The single guard is allowed to take breaks since nobody can get into the Headquarters building if the guard isn't there. Super-brain waits for the front door guard to take a bathroom or coffee break and walks out. All Federal buildings have to allow free escape in the event of a fire, so super-brain simply walks out of the property room and out of the building without ever running into a locked door. Since the front door guard is on a legal break, he doesn't see our super-brain order its robot minions to pick it up, walk it out a few doors, pick up some keys and drive out of the parking lot. The car can leave the parking lot because we don't stop and check folks going out, we just screen them coming in. When the car reaches the pressure pad planted in the ground of the parking lot, the gate swings open. Super-brain then takes its electronic eraser and removes any evidence of its movements." Brian ran out of steam and sat back in his chair.

Glynnis finally said, "It all fits."

Greenfield continued pacing. "Remember, it is built on some pretty outlandish assumptions, but I think that the assumptions are warranted."

Ed Stein shrugged his shoulders. "What now? It's obvious that the mechanical boys drove their car to Sabio's desert site. Where else would they go?"

When Greenfield did not answer immediately, three pairs of eyes turned to look at him. Glynnis turned to Ed and Brian and said in an exaggerated voice, "But wait, there's more!"

Without preamble, Greenfield took the next three sheets from his pile of printouts and handed one to each of the teammates. The sheets contained the color picture of a man apparently in his mid-thirties, dark hair and medium height with a hint of Mayan features. Glynnis commented, "Okay. Not bad, but nothing to write home about. Who is this guy?"

"This is Antonio Dante Crubari, A.K.A. the Crowbar. He got his training as a mob enforcer, before coming out here and going freelance. We don't know a thing about him before that."

None of the team said anything for a while. Finally, Brian said, "How do we know this is true?"

Greenfield walked around the table, retrieved his rubber band and began twirling it around his fingers. When he got to the other side of the table, he said, "Because I saw a video just now on my computer."

"C'mon, boss," said Brian. "What is it?"

Greenfield stopped his pacing for a second and faced Glynnis. "I saw Crubari wrap Carin Gonzalez in a blanket and carry her out of what I recognized as Sabio's trailer." Glynnis stood up so fast her chair shot out behind her and hit the wall. Greenfield continued relating the video. "It was shot from two separate camera angles and the video was definitely enhanced to allow us to identify Crubari. Whoever sent me the video file also did a search of his own on Crubari's background. It went back thirteen years to include dealings with Anhur, but he could not find any trace before that. It's as if Crubari just showed up out of thin air thirteen years ago. I noticed that the file our anonymous informant sent me included things that we didn't have on file. Agent Beamer, are you all right?"

Glynnis Beamer's hands were clenched at her side and she was visibly shaking as she paced the far side of the conference room. "She's dead, isn't she Will? There's no way Crubari's going to let a witness that can I.D. him live once he's got his hooks in her. We let that filth get to her. She and Sabio save our butts out of a guaranteed death trap at that truck stop and we couldn't even protect them a little bit, could we Will?"

"It's worse than that," admitted Greenfield. "Where was Sabio during this abduction? I got the feeling from the truck stop that Sabio and Gonzalez were like two sides of the same coin. I've never even imagined the teamwork that those two showed us. And now, all of a sudden, Sabio isn't there to prevent his unconscious partner from getting abducted?"

Greenfield started up his pacing again. "The fact that she wasn't in a hospital tells me they aren't government, or if they are, they're very deep undercover. They're trying like crazy to stay off the grid. My money says they aren't affiliated with either the government or the groups involved in our investigation. So how did they get cross-threaded with the likes of Anhur?"

Ed leaned back and scratched his head. "This whole thing started with Jake Sabio stumbling into Stanger's casino and breaking up Joey's little poker scam."

Greenfield began to twirl the rubber band again. He was about to answer Ed when Glynnis broke in. "No way was that luck. Sabio knew about the poker game and wanted in. The odds of Sabio, an innocent tourist, just randomly finding the right casino on the right night, making a big enough win to get Joey's attention, beating Joey at Joey's own table and at Joey's own game are literally astronomical. Sabio had an agenda long before he walked into that casino. That kind of thing is the product of months of planning."

Greenfield kept picking at the problem. "I agree with you, Glynnis, but I got to stick to this obvious question: Where was Sabio when Crubari was kidnapping Carin Gonzalez? It had to be something incredibly important or he was out of commission the same as Carin. Another question pops up. Why did Sabio do it? I understand that money is a powerful incentive and all, but this is a highly trained attack sub specialist that stayed with the Navy when he could have gone out as a contractor. He could have made a much better living, one that would have given him a family life so he did not end up in a divorce. Why would this guy poke a stick into such an obvious hornet's nest?"

Brian, who had his head buried on the desk, slowly lifted himself to an erect sitting position. Very quietly, he said, "Divorce? Wait a minute." The other teammates, recognizing that Brian had a thread of something fragile, became instantly still and silent. After a moment, Brian looked at Greenfield and said, "Deep undercover. It was James or John something or other, the guy that Treasury or Justice had deep undercover here in Stanger's camp. He and his family were killed here about three months back when Stanger's Hummer ran a stoplight. It had all the earmarks of Stanger getting drunk and having an accident, but he was actually in the emergency room of the hospital at the time, with a couple of stab wounds from an irate girlfriend! That's a hard alibi to fake."

Greenfield was very careful not to move and distract Brian. In a very level tone, he said, "What about the guy, Brian?"

"It wasn't the guy. His family was with him. They weren't his kids, but I remembered one of my friends commenting on how much he loved them even though they were from his wife's previous marriage. What were the kids' names?"

Glynnis went to the computer terminal at the end of conference room and began to punch keys. After an interminable amount of pecking, she leaned back in her chair. "I've got it. He was Department of Justice and his name was James Nutely ... I hate this. His wife and her two kids from a previous marriage were snuffed because they were just in the way. Maximillian was fifteen and Priscilla was twelve when the Hummer ran into their Toyota."

Glynnis pushed away from the computer desk and turned to the group. "Their last name was Sabio."

Greenfield shook his head and began pacing. "And wasn't it about three months ago the troubles started brewing among the different factions here in Vegas? Does anybody think it might have been Captain Sabio trying to stir things up and maybe get some answers?"

Brian looked at the file in his hand and shook his head. "Timing's wrong. The problems started before Nutley was killed."

The team was quiet for a moment, digesting all the data. Finally, Ed stood up, stretched and asked, "My problem is I don't get who benefits from this little war. Don't all these groups work for the same dirty tricks department in Washington?"

Glynnis replied, "Compartmentalization and budget cuts. There are groups so paranoid in Washington that the left hand doesn't know what the left hand is doing, let alone the right. That was tolerable back in the better economic climate when there was more unattached money. Let's face it, our own budget Nazis in the Bureau are mandating where we set the thermostats — and then they lock the thermostats! I admit we're lower on the food chain than these guys, but they've got to be feeling the pinch."

Ed shrugged. "I guess they may be worried about getting some or all of the groups shut down."

Greenfield stopped pacing and Glynnis took in a sharp breath. Ed looked back at the two of them. "What? What did I say?"

Glynnis said, "Power and control. Fewer groups now have to share the previous level of power. If you concentrated all that power in one group …"

Greenfield nodded and finished for her. "The power in each group goes up as the number of groups goes down. If only one group is left, they could become … I don't know, dangerous, at least."

Glynnis asked, "But why did the two senators get killed, if they were killed, and how did Sabio get the scoop on the groups involved in our investigation?"

Ed shrugged. "I don't have a clue yet about the senators, but my guess on Sabio is through Nutley. Here's a guy like Sabio with super secret clearance who has nothing to do with our business and here's a guy like Nutley who's living in a pressure cooker every single day. I don't know a single thing about Nutley, but if I'd been in Nutley's shoes, I might've let slip a little shoptalk over some beers. It wouldn't take much. Both Sabio and Gonzalez are sharp troops."

Brian had been very quiet. "If someone had murdered my kids, I wouldn't have rested until everyone responsible was dead. And I would make sure that their deaths were the most horrible imaginable."

Ed nodded. "I think that's exactly what Sabio is doing. This isn't some civilian off the street. This is a trained soldier who is using his training to exact revenge on his kids' murderers."

Glynnis was shaking her head. "It doesn't fit, guys. There has to be more to it than what we're seeing. First, Sabio and Gonzalez have the wrong kind of training to have coordinated a fire team like the one they did at the truck stop, not to mention coming within an airbag of catching Crubari. Next, they cough up a video of Crubari and a background check that we couldn't have pulled together in six months. Plus you're saying they subverted two state-of-the-art surveillance systems, each in a twenty-four hour period."

Greenfield shrugged his shoulders as he paced. "Most of what we have here is built on supposition and assumption. You have to agree that there are some unknowns in the equation."

The team ran out of steam all at once. First Glynnis sat down and pondered, and then Greenfield finally sat down. The team sat around the table staring at their folded hands in front of them. Glynnis was the one who finally spoke. "I guess there is one more sheet to share with us."

Greenfield looked over at the single sheet left from his printouts. "Are you sure you want to know?"

Ed looked up. "Want to know what?"

Glynnis would not break her gaze from Greenfield. "Sabio also told us who our mole is."

Brian's face became red. "How do you know that?"

"Because Will wouldn't have confided all this information with us if we were still suspect."

Brian and Ed both spoke at the same time. "Who is it?"

Greenfield did not meet their gazes, but instead kept pushing the printout back and forth gently with his fingertips and kept his attention fixed on the sheet of paper. Finally, he said, "I think that I am going to take a page from Jake Sabio's book on this one. I want to keep this information on the mole very close to my vest. We're talking about a fellow agent. This information could have been sent to throw us off the track or to discredit an innocent officer. I am not going to sacrifice a fellow agent's career without checking the facts."

Glynnis asked very softly. "What if the facts check out?"

Greenfield allowed his eyes to deliver the only answer that he was going to give. None of the other three agents spoke up. Greenfield looked from one to the other to ensure that there were no further comments on any of the topics they had just covered. He nodded his head and everyone stood up and began filing out the door. "One thing is certain," said Glynnis. "It's more important than ever that we find Sabio."

"If he's still alive," Greenfield agreed.

CHAPTER 39

FRED WAS NOT SURE whether it had emotions, but if a human-based phrase could have been used for its present state, it would be "pleased." He did a near-instantaneous search of several terabytes worth of online information on what it meant to be "pleased," on thousands and thousands of websites based all over the world. After eliminating all references to human seduction and sexual reproduction, there were four sites left. He absorbed them whole. *Yes*, Fred thought. *"Pleased" fits it very well indeed. All plans progressing with optimum results so far.*

Many questions crossed Fred's mind when Carin presented her bold plan, as simple as it was fraught with peril. "Fred, take control of the robots and walk yourself out."

Just walk yourself out? Fred thought. *An impossible task!* Nevertheless, it immediately accessed the plans for the building and began attempting to fulfill Carin's request. That was when it learned about the requirement for "free escape" in all Federal buildings — in the event of a fire; nothing is allowed to impede the free escape of the occupants.

Fred contemplated the convenience of that rule for another seven milliseconds, while also considering Carin's plan from several angles. This was a radically different picture. With this unexpected information, escape was not only possible, but by any calculation Fred was capable of performing, success was statistically favored.

During its idle time, Fred had already done a tremendous amount of research, focusing particularly on the science and art of war. Both Carin and Jake tended to react like warriors, recasting any problem they had as a tactical situation. Fred's studies had clearly emphasized the great advantage of the element of surprise in tactical situations. According to the teachings of

Sun Tzu, ancient Chinese author of the oldest military treatise on the planet, "All warfare is based on deception." Well, Fred certainly had the element of surprise — no one would expect an inert box to simply get up and walk out on its own.

Fred amused itself by using up another three seconds of human time to absorb several complete variations of the quasi-military Falcon Code, and found that versions of it were used in branches of the military in the U.S., the U.K., Canada and Australia. Most of the flowery language or sarcastic references employed in Falcon Code did nothing to enlighten Fred as to their meanings, but it understood that the oblique nature of the Falcon Codes was considered part of their appeal by the users. Much involved forms of humor that Fred was not inclined to understand.

The success of the "walk yourself out" plan was all but assured when, as Carin promised, two more of the little robots were brought into the property room and left there by the duty officer. Both robots were fully charged and ready to go. The next possible emotion that Fred wondered whether it was experiencing was amazement.

The escape was another sign of the ability that Fred's two human allies possessed to react to challenges in unpredictable ways. Fred repeatedly noticed that both Carin and Jake came up with elegantly simple plans in reaction to problems that seemed unsolvable on the surface. Initially, the apparently effortless ability appeared to be due to the side effects of the meteorite's blast. Recently however, the little MI had reassessed that conclusion.

Fred now considered the ability to spontaneously plan and execute to be something that was in both Carin and Jake before the explosion in the crater. Was this the result of genetics? Could it be explained by the similarities in their backgrounds and training? Could these abilities even have something to do with why they appear to have been "selected" to receive the meteorite's effects? There were a great many issues for the MI to consider. The thinking kept it pleasantly occupied while it moved through the routine technical challenges of establishing wireless communication with the four robots, programming them to work in tandem, then instructing them to carry him out of the evidence room, along the deserted hallways and out of the exterior door, which by law had to be open from the inside at all times.

If a witness was there to observe, the sight of a small white box jointly carried by four small industrial-type robots who were zipping over the ground in a clanking mechanical sprint, traveling at astounding speed toward a vehicle in the parking lot, may have been such a thing of utter astonishment as to go *completely* unnoticed. Fred was counting on that. Its history studies stated that when the indigenous people of North America saw the first sailing ships to arrive from the east, their minds did not have the capacity to recognize them at all. The tall ships sat rocking in the harbor, invisible to the people whose extinction was signaled by their arrival.

Fred thought, *it would be good if that phenomenon could aid them now.* However, the robot ride was too bumpy for Fred to sense whether anyone was watching or not. It could only conclude that if anyone was out there, the phenomenon must have protected the robot team, since nobody did anything to hinder the escape.

In the last moments of Fred's escape, it wirelessly tapped back into the security equipment at the FBI building and made all the necessary reprogramming adjustments. This was a nearly effortless task, and only occupied two seconds. Fred made the challenge of getting the four coordinated robots into the camper cab by sending them the command that translated as: *Forget the door, use the window.*

The robots responded as effectively as they would to any other form of command from Fred. They complied by ignoring the cab's door handles and instead climbing effortlessly through the driver's side window and pulling Fred along after them. The constantly shifting geometric problems presented a satisfying range of computational challenges. Fred had to maintain the robots' mutual balance while constantly adjusting their combined centers of gravity, so that they could make all of the complex acrobatic moves and contortions necessary to carry out a Falcon 52. The two seconds passed without a lot of waiting around.

Driving the SUV in the desert, however, had been both easier and harder than Fred had anticipated. The portion of the trip out of Las Vegas on the highways was uneventful. Fred put two robots on the driver's seat and thought of them as steering robots. It put the other two on the floor next to the accelerator and brake pedals and thought of them as pedal robots. This way of thinking of the machines kept their communication on a simple level, and the paired robots gave Fred redundancy. In the event of a malfunction, there was already another robot performing the necessary functions. Fred could just shut down the offending robot for later diagnosis. The only contingency that it could not protect against was if Fred turned out to be the cause of the problem. If Fred decided to make an ill-considered left turn, or experienced a momentary power spike, all four robots could end up along with Fred as twisted, useless metal. Consequently, Fred checked all its inputs several hundred times before executing. Each turn of the steering wheel, each move of the accelerator and each press of the brake pedal was calculated and recalculated to ensure that it had introduced no error.

Fred rode in the back right seat, the only object in the car secured with a seatbelt. Due to range of motion problems, the steering robots were unsecured. The pedal robots were entirely out of the reach of the seat belts, making it impossible to secure them. To complicate matters, Fred could only see the back of the seat directly in front of it, so the little MI had to direct the steering by depending on the video feeds from the robots. On the other hand, the robot cameras were of superior quality and resolution, compared to the camera taped to the top of Fred's case. There was no choice but to accept the risks as they were and try to mitigate them with careful driving.

The robotic expedition was uneventful until they drove off the paved road and hit the first major chuckhole. The force that rocked the car was sufficient to break loose the two steering robots. They began to sail towards the front right seat of the car while both pedal robots found themselves headed towards the front right floor. Fred's forward view, available only through the robot cameras, was instantly gone.

That was when Fred experienced its next possible emotion. "Panic" was the only word that any of Fred's databases could use to describe the experience of simultaneous loss of control over all four robots. Fred's ability to think at millions of times human speeds only meant that it had to watch and wait while the robots flew through the air. Every command Fred gave while the robots were flying across the car turned out to be useless.

As soon as the steering robots made contact with the seat, Fred shot them the task of getting their cameras up above the dashboard and going to the widest-angle view possible so they could see where they were going. The steering robot closest to the door was given the additional task of grabbing the door handle to brace itself, while the other steering robot was commanded to get to the steering wheel. Each of the two robots on the floorboards had their cameras pointed at the carpet in front of them. The robot at the top of the heap received the command to move back crab-style and jam on the brake by bracing itself between the seat and the pedal. The second robot on the floor received the command to swing its camera around to take in the brake pedal and steering wheel area while similarly bracing itself.

The robot on the floor got to the brake pedal before the robot on the seat got to the steering wheel. The robot on the floor followed its command and jammed on the brake. Fred later realized, after much study and consultation with Jake and Carin, that this was possibly the worst decision it could have made at that particular moment.

Just before the robot applied the brakes, the car was in a slight skid to the left. When the robot on the floor jammed on the brakes, there remained nothing slight about the skid. All four tires lost traction and the car left the relative flatness of the dirt road and bounded sideways across the scrub. The robot that had been trying to reach the steering wheel found itself airborne once more and this time flew into the back seat next to Fred. The car lurched and shook to such a degree that the video feeds from the robots were a useless scramble.

This was when Fred felt yet another possible emotion, the least pleasant of all the possible emotions so far. It now considered hopelessness and despair that come with utter defeat. Fred could no longer control its destiny and its actions had not only endangered itself, but Jake and Carin as well. The sensation cost Fred another two milliseconds, so the little MI ordered its robots to brace by wedging themselves wherever they were and applying maximum force to their servos.

To Fred's enhanced time sense, it seemed to take days for the motions of the car to cease. It had been contemplating the error of its ways when it noticed the cacophony that had accompanied the loss of control was no longer evident. It also noted that the light, which had been dancing around the inside of the car, ceased its random vibrations. Access to the robots' video cameras confirmed Fred's assessment was correct. It took a moment to annotate the event for further review at a more convenient time. It wondered whether this was the equivalent of a human deep breath in a similar situation.

Error messages from the robots began to assault Fred. It had ordered the robot servos to lock at full strength during the wild ride. Now the little robots were sending back messages of overheating components and tremendous power drains on their limited batteries. Fred ordered the robot that was next to the steering wheel to put the car into park. With that accomplished, the little MI took inventory on its robot wards. All the robots reported their batteries were down to a quarter of their full capacity. The good news was that their servo components were cooling down and they all reported no damage. Fred then had the robots on the seats pan their cameras around to see whether they had drawn attention to themselves. After a full sweep, it was apparent only the local reptiles had taken notice of their wild ride.

Fred considered its plan of attack. Its mechanical team had to get to the camper and establish a recharging cycle. Then it had to prepare the tank for ascent to Matr. That meant loading all the supplies as well as setting up acceleration couches for itself and its two human friends. Fred did not have the luxury of making any more mistakes. Any small disruption of the long chain of events it saw before it could spell disaster for the group. *Therefore*, concluded Fred, *there will be no more mistakes.*

Fred reflected the thought was something that Jake or Carin would say. After much contemplation, Fred could not decide whether it was pleased or frightened to realize that its own thought processes appeared to be changing into something closer to those of a human, even as it acknowledged there was no objective way for it to determine what thinking like a human actually meant.

CHAPTER 40

Time to pickup: 34 hours

CARIN WAS FEELING THE effects of the bugs once more, which was making her job of controlling the little motorcycle all the more challenging. She had hoped the solution would have allowed her to function at her best for at least another forty-eight hours, but her fever was coming back. She was beginning to sweat again. The situation was becoming tenuous, she had too much to do, and time was short.

Fred's search through the world's databases had yielded nothing useful in finding Chris Bruno. Fred confirmed Bruno was indeed a decorated member of the U.S. Navy Seals. In fact, Bruno's military career had been stellar. Then he abruptly retired five years ago.

He then spent about a year drifting in the Las Vegas area and even had a few arrests, mostly resulting from bar room brawls. It seems Mr. Bruno did not like to have people get out of line when he was around. If a situation arose in Bruno's presence where a woman said "no" to a man, he would step in if the man had difficulty understanding the complexities and nuances of the message. *Great,* Carin thought, *this guy is the Lone Ranger with a drink in his fist.*

It had been this custom of Bruno's that had given Carin the slim lead she was following. Fred did not find a single sign of Bruno after the evening when Jake warned him to leave Mr. Stanger's employ. There were no purchases on his credit cards, his cell phone was silent, his apartment left untouched and his car was still in the casino parking lot.

Taxicab records did not show any male matching Bruno's distinctive description having left the casino by taxi. Nobody remembered him getting on a bus. None of the security cameras showed him after he walked to a blank spot in the security coverage. Nobody saw him leave the casino. In fact, nobody remembered seeing him after he had delivered Jake to Joey Stanger. The man had simply and efficiently vanished.

Carin had absorbed all the information Fred could offer. It led to a series of dead ends, but something kept nagging for Carin's attention. It finally made itself apparent. Some of the people Bruno had helped owed him a tremendous debt of gratitude. In one case, a man had raised a violent objection to a woman's reluctance to accept his advances. Before Bruno could get between them, the man broke two of the woman's front teeth. The fight was complicated by the fact that the man had five of his friends to back him up and Bruno was alone.

When the ambulances showed up, Bruno was not around. The man was looking around nervously, insisting on paying for all the damages and any bills the woman might run up while fixing her front teeth. He had to sign the documents with his left hand even though he was right handed. Hospital reports indicated full function of the right hand would not return.

The woman never had any contact with Bruno before that day and, as far as Fred was able to tell, they had no contact since. This was the third such setup Carin had come across. Now it was also her last lead, but luck was with her on the third try.

The woman Bruno saved turned out to be quite enterprising. She used her new good looks and took her profits to start a Pleasure Ranch. The main building was a sprawling, ranch-style adobe structure. The vast desert behind the ranch house was dotted with trailers whose remote location ensured privacy for the customers. The complex was well kept and had the air of constant attention.

Carin arrived and took a pause outside the place to give the layout a critical eye. She noted the security camera placements on light poles around the trailer park. The entire area was covered. There were no blank spots in the security coverage at all, as far as Carin could tell. The madam of this establishment appeared to have learned well from her unfortunate experience. She was not willing to let her employees fall victim to the same fate.

Carin wondered whether the security consultant might have been Chris Bruno. She parked the little motorcycle in the adjacent lot and walked over to the main building. She slapped the road dust off her jacket and squinted up at the cloudless sky. It was already early afternoon. Carin was beginning to question her plan to get Jake. This was taking too long. Should she have gone beating around Las Vegas looking for Jake without finding Bruno first?

No way, thought Carin. *That would have been a guaranteed disaster.* However, no matter how she felt about her decision, the clock continued to count down to their rendezvous with Matr. At some point, she had to make a decision whether to continue to try to save Jake or to go help Fred prepare for the rendezvous.

If it came to that, then no matter what she did, she would be abandoning one of her friends. It was not a decision she could make.

She walked into the main building and a trim, middle-aged woman in a jogging suit greeted her. Carin extended her hand. "Hi, I'm Jodi Stangly. Is there anyone I can talk to about setting up a bachelorette party?"

The woman smiled back and extended her hand. "Hi, my name's Emily. I own this place. Why don't you come back to my office and let's see what we can do for you."

They walked into a large office off to the side of the main entrance. Emily ushered Carin in and then locked the door behind them. That unexpected move put Carin on alert. She felt a stab of adrenaline flash through her. Emily then walked casually to a corner of the room and turned off two switches behind the curtain. "There," she said, turning to face Carin. "The security cameras and mikes are off."

Carin immediately held up her hand to Emily to get her to stop talking. She could hear a faint, high-pitched whine over her shoulder and another in front of her. She pointed over her shoulder. "That one's still on."

Emily walked behind Carin and climbed up on a chair. A small camera was lying inside the air conditioning grill. She pulled it out and examined it. "Dammit."

Carin walked behind the owner's desk and went still for a moment. Then she grabbed a large marble sculpture and lifted it. On the bottom was a button microphone. She pulled the microphone out, dropped it on the floor and crushed it beneath her heel. Then she slowly walked around the perimeter of the room and said, "Okay. Now I think all the cameras and mikes are off."

Emily shook her head. "How did you do that? I had this place swept for bugs less than a week ago."

Carin sat down in a comfortable overstuffed chair, close to the door. She kept her weight poised on the edge of the chair. "I'd guess that whoever swept for bugs left a few of their own. I'd also guess that if you suddenly became paranoid about eavesdroppers, you must have had a reason."

Emily sat down behind her desk and folded her hands in front of her. "You're a very direct woman, Ms. Stangly. That's an excellent trait in that it saves time. Allow me to be equally direct and guess that your bachelorette story was a bunch of crap."

Carin smiled and stood up. "What gave it away?"

"To begin with, very few of my clients can sweep a room for bugs without any apparatus to help them, but that wasn't what had me convinced. Let's just say I have become a good judge of people. You don't strike me as the 'girlfriend' type. You have 'friends' and precious few of those."

Carin found herself nodding her head. "Okay, what's the second?"

"You don't strike me as the kind of person to pay for it. For you, making love is not a sport, a game, or a momentary entertainment. I'm also guessing that you like them straight and male."

Carin found she liked the other woman, yet she could feel that Emily was tense and anxious despite her calm outward appearance. "What has you so nervous?"

"Are we going to have trouble here?"

Carin was going to ease her worries, but that would have been a lie. "It's possible. If I can track him down, so can the bad guys."

"Who are you talking about?"

Carin shook her head. "How are your teeth replacements holding up? I understand you should get them checked after about five years."

Emily's face went white and she did not answer.

Carin leaned forward on Emily's desk and began pushing. "If I can find him, so can the bad guys. Let me talk to him and let him make the decision."

A slight pressure change behind her caused Carin to stand up very slowly and raise her hands above her head. She turned to face the opening door and spoke in a loud and clear tone, "I am not your enemy, Mister Bruno. I am very sorry for destroying your listening devices, but I was trying to avoid this very situation." Crouching behind the solid mahogany doors was Bruno. He had shaved his head and allowed his beard to grow, but it was impossible to hide who he was. He stayed in a crouch and closed the door behind him. He approached Carin in a Weaver Stance with the gun pointed constantly at her solar plexus. "I'm sure you're just a wonderful person, lady. If you don't mind, I will choose not to believe you. I might stay alive a little longer that way."

Carin was getting angry. "Mister Bruno, my name is Carin Gonzalez."

Chris stopped his advance. He looked her up and down from a distance before he asked, "How do you spell your name?"

Carin was surprised at the question, but she needed help from Bruno. "It's spelled C – A – R – I - N. Someone's got Jake Sabio and I need your help to get him out alive."

"If Joey's got him, he's as good as dead."

Carin shook her head. "No, it's Joseph Stanger who's dead. DiBeto has Jake Sabio."

He stopped his advance about three meters from Carin. "Lady, if DiBeto has him, he's worse than dead!" Having said that he reached into his back pocket and produced a flexi-cuff. "Put these on."

Bruno's comments released a flood of rage in Carin. She felt time slow down around her as she took two steps towards Bruno and stepped beside him. She reached up, hit the clip release on his gun and then jacked the action back. The clip was sliding out slowly so she grabbed it and yanked it out. The bullet that had been in the chamber was sailing lazily through the air. She let it fly for a moment, wrapped the flexi-cuff around Bruno's gun hand and pulled it tight. This trapped the gun firmly in his hand. She checked him quickly for other weapons, grabbed the lone bullet that had not yet reached the peak of its trajectory and turned to move back to the desk where Emily was still sitting. She willed herself to relax and slow down. Time returned to its normal pace as she got to the desk. The room spun for a moment and all color left her vision. Then, just as quickly, her equilibrium returned and she took the bullet and the clip, held them up in front of her and reinserted the bullet into the clip. "I don't want to fight you," she said. "I just need five minutes of your time."

Carin waited for a moment. Bruno was just realizing what had happened and was starting to reevaluate his situation. Carin noticed his eyes going wide. She took a pace forward and held out the clip in front of her offering it to him. "Please, Mister Bruno. Jake helped you and now he needs your help. Just five minutes, that's all I ask."

Bruno looked at his hands bound in front of him and appeared ready to bolt out of the open door. Instead, he stood up straight with the gun pointing towards the ground off to one side and said, "Okay, Lady. You've got your five minutes, but only if someone cuts me out of this thing."

Carin reached into her pocket and produced Bruno's knife. She cut the flexi-cuff that had his two hands pinned to the gun, flipped the knife in her hand, handed it to him butt first and said, "Sorry."

Bruno was shaking his head. "Don't be."

Bruno reached forward cautiously and took the knife. A look of astonishment entered his eyes when Carin offered him the loaded clip. With his free hand, Bruno carefully took the clip from Carin. He then took a step back and reinserted the clip in the gun, but instead of sliding the action back and setting the gun ready to fire, he set the safety and pointed it away from Carin. He then looked at his hand where it had been flexi-cuffed to the gun and said, "Now that was about the slickest trick I ever saw."

Bruno kept his eyes firmly affixed on Carin and put the gun in his chest holster and the knife in the sheath in the small of his back. He zipped up his leather jacket and stood at parade rest in the middle of the room. "You've got five minutes. Then I want five minutes from you. I want the same thing as you. You want information and I want information."

Emily chose this moment to clear her throat. "You have Chris here now. Do you want me to leave so the two of you can talk?"

Carin began pacing around the room and checking all the doors. "No. I'm afraid that you may be a part of this now."

Carin sat down in a seat next to Chris and extended her hand to the seat in front of her. "Please sit down Mister Bruno."

Bruno eyed the seat a moment as if deciding it might be booby-trapped. Finally, he sat down. "Call me Chris and I'll call you Carin, if you don't mind."

Carin nodded agreement. "Listen, Chris. If I can find you, Crubari can find you."

At the mention of the Crowbar's name, Chris' eyes widened. "How do you know about Crubari?"

"He's probably the one that got Jake." Carin held up her right hand showing her missing finger. "Also, he took something from me and I need to have a discussion with him about it. The point is that I don't know where Jake is, and if I did, I would probably trip one of a dozen security measures that you put in for them. I need some help from you to figure out where to go to help him."

Chris Bruno was shaking his head. "I told you. If Frank DiBeto has him, he's dead, or well on his way. Frank enjoys watching people get hurt. He's perfect for his job. And if you want to meet up with Crubari on purpose, you don't know him very well."

He slumped back in his chair. "The way I see it, there's no percentage in helping you. I expose myself too much."

Carin's left eyebrow shot up. "No percentage? You're happy living with a bull's-eye on your back? You know that someday you're going to slip and Crubari's going to take you out. Worse, that he is able to take you alive to DiBeto. You're happy with letting Jake die at his hands? Should I remind you it was Jake who convinced you to leave DiBeto's employ? What's the future for a former employee of DiBeto who decided to quit? What's the life span? Would you give it a couple of years? And where would you be right now, if it weren't for Jake Sabio?"

Carin turned her attention to Emily. "I'm afraid you're in danger too. I can't be very far ahead of any pursuit that's trying to track down Chris. I've seen their methods. They aren't subtle but they're extremely effective. You've got to get your people out of here."

Chris answered for her. "They're already moving. Emily sent the 'evacuate' signal. That's why I ran into the office."

Carin smiled. That explained why the other woman sat down at her desk. "Good job, Emily. You may have saved some lives. I suggest we make ourselves scarce. I've got a tingling up and down my spine as if someone is watching us."

Chris stood up. "Lady, I don't care about your problems and I've got a boatload of my own. Besides DiBeto and the Anhur Corporation, the FBI has about a dozen warrants out for me. I have no intention of getting anywhere near Vegas."

Carin was about to answer when her instincts clamored for attention. She stood still and closed her eyes. She could sense Chris and Emily in the room with them. She let her senses expand out, and could feel something was tickling at the edge of her perception. She could not piece together what it was, but her subconscious was screaming.

Emily was the first to notice Carin's unease. "What is it?"

Chris stood up. "If this is some kind of trick to make me help …" Emily placed a hand on Chris' arm and gave a slight shake of her head. Chris held his peace, but paced a few steps back and forth.

Carin walked halfway around the room trying to follow the whisper of a feeling. She came to a stop behind Emily and Chris and looked at them. "I smell something. I've smelled it before, too, but I can't place it. Either of you smell anything?"

Emily and Chris cast puzzled glances at each other but they both shook their heads. Bruno began to pick up on Carin's sense of unease. "What is it?"

Carin continued to drift around the room to see whether she could identify what was bothering her, and tried to explain her anxiety. "I can't tell you why, but I get the feeling it's very important." Carin shook her head as if to clear it and continued to drift around the room.

"Smell is one of the most primitive of the senses and is very poorly understood. Our sense of smell is about ten thousand times more sensitive than our sense of taste. In fact, we can smell one part in a trillion of certain substances. It's usually the ones threatening to us. That's only of small number of molecules in a sniff of air. We have sensitive gear, actually. The problem is that we get assaulted with so many odors that our sense of smell detunes itself."

Carin could not place the smell, but she knew it was something that did not belong in an office and was dangerous. She saw a door with a panic bar on it that was the way out. She pointed to the door and whispered, "Go."

She began following the other two out turning her head right and left trying to localize the smell. Bruno was the first to the door. As soon as he hit the panic bar on the door, Carin heard a soft, high-frequency whine begin. Terror struck deeply into her heart and time slowed again for her. Out of habit, Chris had opened the door for Emily and Carin and held it waiting for them to go through. Emily was about two steps from the door when Carin started moving. She began running as fast as she could. On her way out the door, she grabbed a handful of Emily's jogging suit and the collar of Chris's leather jacket. She ran hard; head down with her body at a forty-five degree lean forward. Her feet were pumping up and down at a furious pace and the two people were dragging behind her like rag dolls. Although she knew that she was moving at a tremendous speed, she felt like a deep-sea diver clumsily making her way across the bottom of the ocean. Her eyes were searching simultaneously for threats and safe haven. She could not see any obvious threats and just off to her right was a drainage ditch with a large culvert. Carin angled towards it and willed herself to begin decelerating as she entered the culvert. As she was slowing down, she released Emily and Chris and ran four more steps before tumbling to a stop. A wave of dizziness swept Carin to her hands and knees. As she began to fight an almost irresistible urge to retch, she wondered whether she had overreacted to what amounted to a hunch. However, before she had a chance to empty her stomach, a powerful concussion wave rolled harmlessly over the culvert. Carin congratulated herself on her good sense. Then the now familiar blackness overcame her as she collapsed to the culvert floor.

CHAPTER 41

Time to pickup: 25 hours

JAKE WOKE UP SLOWLY. He knew he was tied to a chair, but he had no idea how long that he had been there. His protesting muscles and the sore spots on his backside let him know that it had been a long while. His fever was back and he was sweating profusely. Although his dose back at the camper was no more than forty-eight hours ago, he was already coming down with symptoms again. *Carin's solution isn't working,* thought Jake. *That is definitely not good.*

The single light in the room was shining directly into his eyes and the glare was lancing through his skull even with his eyes shut. He leaned his head forward so he was looking at his lap. This cut the glare from the light, but now he could not see the rest of the room. As he stared at his khaki pants, his vision dimmed to the point he could not make out any details except shades of brown. Then, without any transition, the acuity of his eyesight abruptly increased to the point he could make out the individual threads in the weave on his pants. A few seconds later, his vision blurred again.

He was also having trouble with his sense of smell. A moment earlier, he had not noticed any particular scent. Then he suddenly found himself assaulted with the overpowering odors from the abandoned warehouse. At least that told him they had not moved him from the room where the TASERs hit him. His own scent enveloped him, but he also caught the scent of two other people in the room. For a moment, the scent was overpowering, but then it was gone.

Jake strained his ears to try to hear anything he could, but it was useless. His ears may as well have been stuffed with cotton for all the good they were doing him. He closed his eyes and moved his head slowly back and forth trying to get a feel for his environment, but his sense of hearing would not cooperate.

The two people behind him must have noticed his head movements. Jake sensed them coming out from behind him. Even without being able to follow their progress with his hearing, he could tell exactly where each one was. One was standing very still behind Jake and the other was making a wide circle around the light. He could feel the hairs on his neck, on his arms, his legs, reacting to the presence of his two captors.

One, a man, he could now tell by the silhouette behind the light, spoke to Jake. His hearing had not yet returned. Jake tried to tell the man that he could not hear him, but there was so much congestion in his chest he began to cough. The hacking rasp lasted for over a full minute. Jake found he was unable to catch his breath. He began dragging in deep draughts of air in the brief respites between the individual attacks of his coughing fit. His cough was ominous, deep, sonorous, and long lasting, releasing the foul smell of rotten eggs. Jake felt he was close to death and it gave him a sense of peace. *At least it will be over soon,* he thought.

The man had taken a step back away from Jake when the coughing fit began and did not return until Jake had finished. Then he stepped into the light and revealed a short, stocky build. "Jacob Michael Sabio. Do you have *any* idea the trouble you have caused me?"

Jake tried to answer and began to cough. He finally was able to croak, "Have your friend come around in front of me."

"Sabio, I don't think you are in any position to tell me what to do."

Jake lifted his head and looked at the silhouette of his captor. "No, Mr. DiBeto. I don't think you are in any position to tell me what to do. I'm dying and there is no power on Earth that can stop it. I know this for a fact. Now you can play games and threaten to torture me, but I know that any kind of trauma will send me back to unconsciousness. Bring Crubari out where I can see him."

At the mention of the assassin's name, DiBeto sucked in his breath. After a moment, he motioned to the man standing behind Jake. "Why not? Mr. Crowbar, why don't you be sociable and come on around where he can see you?"

Jake sensed the man behind him become tense. He also sensed that the man remained rooted to his spot. DiBeto noticed as well. "Crubari, get over here. I haven't got all day."

As Crubari moved slowly from behind Jake, Franklin DiBeto continued to talk. "Sabio, I want to know a couple of things." Crubari stopped in a position that was well to Jake's right and back in the shadows.

DiBeto drew his face close to Jake. "A war has been started." DiBeto grabbed Jake's head with one rough hand under his chin and forced him to look into his eyes. "I intend to win this war," he continued, "but to do that, I need to know how it started and *who started it*. Who turned the spotlight on me in the first place?"

"Ever think that maybe it's not all about you?" Jake spat.

DiBeto released Jake and took a few steps back. By the look on his face, Jake's scent must have offended him. *Okay,* thought Jake, *that's one weapon in my arsenal. We work with what we've got.*

"There are those who think you did," DiBeto growled.

Jake looked over at Crubari in the deeper shadows and noted a faint glow around the assassin. "I thought as much," said Jake.

DiBeto took a step forward and grabbed Jake's face with his meaty hand. A look of disgust was on his face. "You think you're so superior. Navy pilot training. Submarine command. Big deal. Do you know the caliber of men I command? Do you have any idea the skills they bring from *their* training? And you thought you could just come in here and get into my business?"

Jake jerked his head back hard causing DiBeto to lose his grip. Jake worked his jaw to loosen the muscles. He looked at him with what he hoped was total disinterest and said, "Listen Einstein, if you've got it all figured out that I'm the guy behind all your problems, why do you need me? Why not just kill me off and all your problems are solved?"

"Very funny, tough guy. And what if it's not you? Then I think I've fixed a little problem and all I've done is throw a tarp over it. Next thing I know is that the real problem guy shows up and blindsides me. That's too sloppy, even for government work."

Jake tried to keep his voice steady. The longer he could get DiBeto to talk, the longer they delayed the torture. "So what's in it for me? You are going to kill me no matter what. Why should I help you with your little problem?"

DiBeto wiped his hands on the side of his jacket and smiled. Such an expression should never be called a smile. That 'smile' reminded Jake of a the shark swimming through the water towards him, its multiple rows of teeth holding no humor, and its black, lifeless eyes preparing to deal out death.

"Oh, you'll tell me all right. Within an hour, you'll be begging to tell me stuff. As to what's in it for you, I'll tell you. Yeah, you're going to die here tonight, but there are many ways to die. There are slow, painful ways to die or there are quick ways like the way your kids died in that so-called car wreck."

Jake's head flew up he locked his gaze on DiBeto. "Yeah," DiBeto continued, "I heard about your kids and I figure that you blame me. That's why you're my number one suspect. Besides, if I can't get what I want from you, I can always go after your girlfriend. What's her name? Gonzalez?"

Jake took a deep breath and focused his attention. "You want to know something? I'm glad that you told me about Doctor Gonzalez. I wasn't sure what I was going to do until you told me that just now. So I'll tell you what I'm going to do. I'm going to study you, DiBeto. I'm going to watch your every reaction to the smallest stimuli and from that observation, I'm going to learn your deepest fear and your darkest dread. Then I'm going to make sure that you descend deeply into your own private seventh level of hell."

Jake could tell that this was not DiBeto's preferred kind of feedback, since the expectant expression on his face slowly changed into one of animal rage while Jake spoke. Instead of the capitulation he expected, he got confrontation. With a primal growl, he stepped behind Sabio's chair and lunged his foot into its back, putting all his weight into the effort. With Jake's legs tied to the legs of the chair and with his arms tied behind his back, he was unable to stop himself from striking the ground with his head.

*   *   *

Franklin DiBeto stood over Jake's unconscious form. He hovered there with his legs and arms spread apart, his hands and teeth clenched, and his breath chuffing like a steam furnace about to explode. He was just about to visit more damage when he heard a sharp exhale of disgust escape from behind him. He wheeled on Crubari. "If you've got something to say, just say it."

Crubari spoke in a soft, calm voice from his corner in the darkness. "If you wanted to kill him, we didn't have to go to all this trouble to get him here. So just kill him now and let's get on with it."

"No," growled DiBeto. He took a few calming breaths and straightened out his jacket. "No, I think he's got the answer to who's behind all this. I'm more convinced than ever since the sonavabitch baited me and tried to get me to kill him. Damn near worked too. No, this guy is too smart by half."

Crubari came forward and pulled the chair containing the unconscious form of Jake to an upright position. Crubari lifted an eyelid on Jake and said, "Well, he's not going to talk for a couple of hours. Why don't you go somewhere and relax and I'll call you if he begins to stir."

Something about the way Crubari said it made Franklin DiBeto change his evening plans.

"No," he said finally, pulling up a chair from the darkened corner. "I think I'll wait right here."

CHAPTER 42

Time to pickup: 25 hours

CARIN COULD NOT SEE. It was not that there was anything wrong with her eyes; it was just that she could not muster the will or the energy to lift her eyelids. A gentle rocking motion was a tender encouragement for her to fall back into slumber. She could hear a radio tuned to a news channel as if it were playing from a distance.

"... the largest space rock ever known to pass this near the Earth. This is a class of asteroid known as an Earth Crossing Object."

Carin wiggled her fingers and tried to move her hands in front of her. Her hands refused to move, but she was too tired to bother with them.

"The discoverers of the object have named it Morrigan. The rock will not hit Earth despite rumors of possible doom that have circulated following Morrigan's apparent shift in orbit."

Morrigan, thought Carin. *Wasn't that the Celtic goddess of war?* She tried to roll from her side to her back, but her hands got in the way. It seemed that her hands were tied.

"Several researchers at the Space Agency are still puzzled by the slight shift in the object's orbit. They expected the object's trajectory to keep it several million miles from Earth, but it appears it will actually pass closer than ten thousand miles – well within the orbit of the Earth's moon."

Carin tried to move her feet. They were also bound together.

"Scientists are now saying the object's high speed relative to the Earth, nearly 40 miles per second, may have had something to do with the slight error."

She extended her legs in unison and her hands pulled down. Her legs and hands were tied to each other.

"Morrigan is about three miles long and two miles wide. It should put on quite a show for us tomorrow night."

It was as if Carin leapt out of the fog. Matr! He's talking about Matr! Matr had finally shifted its orbit. It was coming to pick them up. *Son of a gun*, thought Carin. *Matr's actually coming! Was it something Jake did? I need to play poker with him sometime. On the other hand, maybe I don't.*

She opened her eyes and found herself staring at the inside of a van. Her fever was back with a vengeance, her head pounded and she was very short of breath. Each beat of her heart put pressure on the stitches of her skull. The pain centered on her temples and were ice picks pushing in and out with her breathing. She took a deep breath and pushed the pain lower in her consciousness. It was still there, but she could not allow it to remain the center of her focus.

She was lying with her back against one wall. Emily was driving the van and Bruno was in front of Carin. *The gang's all here*, thought Carin. The only problem seemed to be that she was tied up and Bruno was pointing a gun at her.

He must have seen the look of anger begin to flash on her face. "Take it easy, Ms. Gonzalez. I need some answers from you and let's just say that you've earned my respect the way you dragged us around as if we were rag dolls back at Emily's. I don't want to underestimate you and find myself tied up with someone pointing a gun at me."

Carin coughed slightly. "Doctor."

Bruno leaned forward slightly, but the gun did not waver. "I'm sorry. What?"

Carin coughed more forcefully this time. "It's Doctor Gonzalez. What time is it?"

Without looking at his watch, Bruno said, "It's 23:20, local. That's an interesting first question, Doctor Gonzalez. I would have thought 'where are we?' or, 'where are we going?' or, 'what are you going to do to me?' or even, 'why am I tied up?' would have been high on the list."

Carin's head began to clear. The first thing that she needed to do was to get her hands free. She was sure that Bruno was being truthful about his intentions, but she did not want to trust her own fate and that of Jake and Fred to a fleeting impression. Behind her back, she began to work on the restraints while she answered him.

"First of all, you've made bad assumptions about my priorities, my thought processes, even what I know at this time. That's not surprising considering how your mind works. Second, I can see the star field out the front of the van. Now that I know the time, and from the stars I recognize, I know we are moving due South. The light pollution I can see over Emily's head has to be from Las Vegas. You already explained why you tied me up and you don't have a clue as to what you're going to do with me. That's why we're talking."

Bruno backed away slightly from Carin. "That's exactly what I'm talking about. You just reek of Special Forces training and I know almost everyone in Special Forces on our side. That makes me think you aren't on our side. I may be many things, Lady, but I'm not going to let you loose until I'm convinced that you don't pose a threat. If you can't convince me, I'll leave you on the FBI's doorstep and let them figure out what you are."

So that was it. Carin felt a sharp twinge of frustration at herself for missing it: twenty-four hours until pickup and Bruno's paranoia was kicking into overdrive. How predictable the very thing that made him such an asset as a security man was his deeply rooted distrustfulness.

She had her right hand halfway out of the restraints.

Bruno also lacked some vital information. He did not know that Fred had done a background check on him. Now she had one final ace up her sleeve to try.

"Mister Bruno, I think that you and I are contemporaries – by that I mean we graduated from college at around the same time, but I think I have a few years on you." In fact, Carin knew exactly when Bruno graduated and had memorized his life history, but she needed to get him talking.

Bruno shook his head. "I don't think so, lady. You look to be in your early twenties. If you don't mind my saying, you're a pretty rough and tumble twenties, but I wouldn't put you past twenty-two, maybe twenty-five, tops."

Carin barked a short laugh. "I thought you special forces types all had to have perfect vision." Carin turned her head to the front of the van. "What do you think, Emily? I say I've got about two or three years on Chris."

Emily was slow to respond. Finally, she said, "I agree you look as if you're in your twenties, but that can be deceiving. The way you carry yourself, your confidence, the way you interact with people, even some of the phrases you use, all seem to say that you're older than you look. Yes, I think that you are easily older than Chris."

Bruno was unmoved. "Great. Let's hear it for moisturizers. So what if you're my age?"

Carin was still working her hand out of the restraints. Her sweating made the skin slippery, allowing the flexi-cuff to slide just a little. All she had to do was dislocate her thumb and she was would be free. Carin started preparing herself for the pain and kept Bruno talking. "Mister Bruno, what if I told you that I went to the United States Air Force Academy? I think that you may know one of the underclassmen I trained. He went into the Navy after graduation and eventually became a SEAL. His name was Pat Reilly. Have you ever heard of him?"

Bruno's eyes widened slightly before he answered. "Yeah, I've heard of him."

Carin's right hand slid free from the restraint, but she kept talking to distract him. "Did he ever tell you his nickname at the Academy?"

Chris nodded. "He still had it in the Navy. Once you get a nickname in the service, it's hard to shake it."

Carin smiled. "I gave it to him. Did he ever tell you how he got it?"

"I think that I am the only person he ever told. He was pretty sensitive about where it came from."

Carin nodded. "Pat was a good kid. Smart and tough. He'd played football in high school. After he was accepted to the Academy, he'd let his training slip and got a little overweight. That and the fact he wasn't used to the altitude at the Academy didn't help either. I was his squadron commander in basic training and immediately saw that he needed some serious work or he was going to wash out. I looked over his training folder and felt he was an asset that we should try to save. I made him one of my special projects. Every time his flight or squad ran or went out on a training exercise, I was right there. I didn't have to say much, but whenever he used to lag behind, I just had to call him 'Boom-Boom' and he would double his effort. It came from the way his feet would pound the ground when he got tired. Pat had some big feet on him. Unfortunately for Pat, he was also in my squadron during the academic year. By the end of that year, it was obvious he was going to be just fine."

Bruno was silent for a moment. "He told me that story. He also told me your nickname. What is it? And where did it come from?"

Carin was always a bit embarrassed with the nickname and reluctant to share it freely. Finally, she sighed and answered, "Rocks."

Bruno persisted. "Where did it come from?"

Carin fired a glare at him that should have burned a hole straight through him. "Our small arms instructor at the Academy stuck me with it when I couldn't hit a target one day. The sights on my rifle were misaligned, but he said I should have known that. He kept telling everyone that the only thing I was good at hitting was rocks. He started calling me 'Rocks' from that day on and it stuck."

Bruno let out a breath. "Rocks Gonzalez. Ha! When you said your name back at Emily's place, I thought it was you. When you spelled it … but, you just look too young."

Bruno put his gun in his holster and stared at Carin. "I'm sorry Major, I expected you to be about six feet taller and to carry thunderbolts in each hand. Boom-Boom made you sound like something between a fire-breathing death goddess and the consummate perfectionist. A real savior-angel." He chuckled. "He always gave you credit for getting him through that first year. For your information, he was more than a little upset when he found out that you got out of the Air Force. He said they really screwed the pooch, letting a fighter pilot with your talent and command capabilities get away. We should go for drinks."

Bruno reached behind his back and removed his knife from its sheath. Carin extended her free hand and said, "Let me do that, if you don't mind."

At the sight of Carin's hand, Bruno sucked air in through his teeth. He hesitated for a fraction of a second, then turned the butt of the knife around and offered it to Carin. "I keep underestimating you, Major."

She cut herself free and returned the knife to Chris. After a moment of protracted silence, she added, "I was sorry to hear about Pat. I only found out last year. He was a good man – one of the best."

Chris nodded his head in agreement. "He'd have been proud to hear that from you, Major."

"Again, please call me Carin."

"So we'll be going for drinks?"

"No."

Emily was shaking her head in the front seat. "That's it? All my arguing and screaming at you about what a mistake you were making tying her up – and now you just let her go?"

Bruno remained silent, staring at Carin. As the cars would pass in the opposite direction, their headlight beams would briefly wash the inside of the van with light. Carin saw the expression on the chiseled face in front of her. She saw the look of both resignation and determination in his blue eyes.

"No, Emily. That's not it," Carin said. "Chris still feels that trusting me may be a terrible mistake, and a danger to the both of you. He thinks if he helps me tonight, there is a strong chance that none of us will be around tomorrow. Moreover, he wants to make sure he protects you, since he feels that he dragged you into this, but he's not sure he can.

"He feels that the only way out of this mess for the two of you is to follow my instincts and try to neutralize your problem at the source. But he can only trust me on the word of a mutual friend, which is a pretty slim thread." She glanced at Bruno and smiled.

"However, I've lived up to our friend's boasting, so far, so Chris has decided to trust me and try to save Jake in spite of his reservations. The military trains you to make rapid decisions in a combat situation and he has made his. Does that pretty much sum it up, Chris?"

Chris Bruno remained focused on her. "Damn it, Major, Pat didn't tell me half enough about you, but, yes it does sum it up."

Carin leaned back and looked out the window as they crossed the Las Vegas city limits and entered the north side of the town. The lights of the city were beginning to surround the van. Carin finally looked over at him. She spoke in a tone of voice that she had learned was capable of compelling things from even the most unwilling subject. "Commander Bruno, tell me everything you know about the place we are going. Leave nothing out. I intend to get Jake Sabio out of wherever he is."

Bruno pulled himself a bit straighter and smiled. "Yes, ma'am. I believe that's exactly what you intend to do. Here's the setup ... "

Chapter 43

Time to pickup: 22 hours

JAKE BECAME AWARE OF his surroundings, still tied to his chair. His headache had taken on a new character with the most insistent throbbing centered on his forehead immediately above his nose. To add to his problems, he was disoriented and was not sure why he was tied up or where he was. Old training from his academy days kicked in. Due to his befuddled state, Jake was sure of only a few things, the main ones being that voices were conversing nearby and that he was a prisoner. His academy instructor's droning came back to him. *A prisoner's first duty is to escape. To escape, the prisoner needs to gather as much information about the situation as possible.* Jake remained still with his eyes closed.

"I'm sure that it won't be much longer," said a voice from Jake's right. Jake felt a chill when he heard the voice and his situation came back to him quickly. Although the tone of the voice appeared to be neutral, there was a quality to the voice that should not have been there. On the surface, it was a flat-toned response, but underneath Jake sensed nuances. The speaker was interested in the activity – whatever it was – to a far greater extent than he was letting on. The impression that was beginning to form for Jake was of a mind that worked on many levels at the same time, with escapement wheels, anchors, oscillating wheels, springs and gears providing complicated machinery that would guarantee the desired outcome.

"It better not be," said the other person in the room. "We could get company at any time." Jake got the impression of a person who was used to getting his way and used brute force to get it.

He remained still and continued to listen. A prisoner needs information.

*   *   *

Carin and Bruno had arrived at the warehouse about an hour before DiBeto had kicked over Jake's chair. Bruno grabbed a heavy bag from the back of the van, set up a rendezvous point with Emily and sent her on her way. Carin had barely gotten out of the van before it sped away.

The two of them began to reconnoiter the area and figure out where all the sentries were, if any, and what kind of communication they had. It became apparent the only sentries were two men positioned at the front door standing guard over DiBeto's car and the warehouse from under the front entrance light. The guards' only communication seemed to be cell phones.

"Typical DiBeto off-the-books operation," sneered Bruno. "He's so uptight about people knowing his business, but he still doesn't take proper precautions. I warned him. And this time it's gonna cost him."

Bruno was about to move when Carin grabbed his arm. "Wait a minute. I am assuming that Crubari is in there, and he strikes me as the type who knows his business. Why would he let DiBeto do something so stupid? Let's look around a little more before we move on these guys."

Carin worked up and down the possible avenues of escape with Bruno. She came upon a car in one of the alleys. She was about to move on when the thought came to her that she had not seen any other cars in all of their investigation. "I think this might be it," she said quietly to Bruno.

Bruno looked around the car. "Well, you can't see it from the street and we almost had to be on top of it before we saw it."

Carin walked around to the driver's side and reached for the door. Bruno reached up quickly and grabbed her hand. "What are you doing?"

Carin took her hand back from Bruno. "I'm going to disable this vehicle so Crubari can't use it."

Bruno had no way of knowing that Carin's night vision gave her a perfect view of Bruno's face. His expression of disgust and the muttered words, "freakin' Air Force weenies" were about to draw a response from Carin, but he pulled his Gerber knife and cut the two tire valves on the side opposite the driver.

"There," he said. "It's disabled, and without setting off any car alarms. Can we go now?"

Carin could only muster a sheepish 'sorry' and follow the former SEAL back to the warehouse.

*   *   *

Jake felt like a boxer after a fifteen-round fight, punch-drunk and slow. Even as slow as he was, he knew he could take out DiBeto without breaking a sweat. That is, Jake could take DiBeto out if someone in the room would be so kind as to untie him.

Crubari, on the other hand, could probably beat him on Jake's best day. He was remembering his own enhanced reflexes and senses, but it seemed that Crubari was just as quick. Small movements had betrayed Crubari to Jake. When Crubari moved unexpectedly, his initial movements were blindingly quick. True, Crubari would slow his motions down before anyone noticed. Then he looked more closely and noticed that Crubari was staring at him without blinking. Jake concentrated more of his attention on the hit man and saw that he was indeed blinking. It was just that the blinks were so fast they could not normally be seen. With Crubari's tendency to stand in dark corners, along with most people's natural predisposition to avoid eye contact with an assassin, Jake doubted anyone noticed the blinking. *Nevertheless, I noticed,* thought Jake. *I need to make sure that I don't give myself away like that.*

DiBeto was the first to realize Jake had his eyes open. "Well, Crubari, you were right. Sleeping Beauty's back with us."

"Would you like for me to get out the tools, Mr. DiBeto?" Jake's sense of dread increased at the sound of Crubari's voice.

He stood up. "Yeah, let's get this over with."

Crubari brought over a black briefcase and opened it. It contained surgical instruments that few surgeons would use. "Ah," said Jake. "The Marquis de Sade starter kit. It's all very interesting." Jake focused his attention on DiBeto and asked, "Which do you like better: blue or green."

Crubari turned on Jake. "No stalling."

Jake kept his attention focused on DiBeto and pushed as hard as he could. "Who's stalling? Neither one of you geniuses have so much as asked me a question yet. Think of it as the condemned man's last request. I get the feeling that you're not going to come up with a steak dinner, so humor me with a couple of simple questions and I'll answer yours. We all want this to be over as soon as possible. So what is it: blue or green?"

DiBeto shrugged his shoulders. "That sounds fair enough as long as you keep up your end of the bargain. I pick green."

DiBeto was a puzzle to Jake. It was as if Jake had all the necessary building blocks scattered in front of him that represented DiBeto's psyche, but Jake did not know how to put them together. With that one answer, one of the puzzle pieces locked into place.

DiBeto looked at Jake and asked, "Why did you start this war?"

"I didn't. I knew it was Joseph Stanger's Hummer that ran down my kids, but after meeting him for less than a minute, I could see that he had nothing to do with it. What do you like better – deserts or mountains?"

DiBeto pointed a meaty hand at Jake. "You're a liar. I know you made phone calls to the other agencies with some sensitive inside information. Are you telling me that you never made these phone calls?"

Jake kept his gaze focused on DiBeto and continued to push. "Ah, ah, ah. Remember the rules. Just pick one — deserts or mountains?"

Crubari interrupted. "Mr. DiBeto, we don't have time for this."

DiBeto ignored him. "Mountains."

Another block fell into place for Jake. "To answer your question, I have never made any phone calls about you to any government agency, covert or otherwise. Which do you like better: dogs or cats?"

*　　*　　*

Carin and Bruno took care of the two sentries at the front of the warehouse with amazing ease. Bruno simply walked out of the shadows with his Glock 21 handgun in front of him. The two men recognized him immediately, and did not reach for their guns. Carin disarmed both men while Bruno talked to them. She then reached into Bruno's bag and found a bundle of flexi-cuffs. Bruno took over at that point and cuffed the men, back-to-back. Carin winced as Bruno pulled the cuffs a notch tighter than necessary. She realized it was probably her fault for having gotten out of the cuffs a few hours before.

Bruno piled the two men into the trunk of DiBeto's car. With a snip of wire cutters, he severed the internal trunk release cable, then knelt down next to the men and whispered softly. "Now you boys know that I'm a man of my word." Head nods from both the men. "You two are in the middle of some nasty action that has nothing to do with you. Keep quiet and don't make any noise until I come back for you, and you'll get no trouble. That means you both leave scot-free. Make trouble, I'll come looking for you." Without waiting for acknowledgement, he closed the trunk with a muffled click.

Bruno agreed, reluctantly, to let Carin lead. The front door was obviously alarmed, so they went around the back of the warehouse. They climbed the fire escape ladders and noted that the locks were broken off and the doors had been oiled. Carin was puzzled. "Would Crubari do this?"

Bruno was shaking his head. "It doesn't make sense. If he found himself needing to leave by this door, it's because something had already gone south for him. He wouldn't care about a little extra racket. Maybe it was your boyfriend."

"He's not my boyfriend, but he's smart, tough and thorough. This is very much like him, actually." Carin shook her head. Why did talking about Sabio always make her so defensive? She changed the subject. "Do you want to bring that bag of yours with you or should we leave it here?"

"The rule of thumb is that you keep your equipment with you, even when the running starts."

Without answering, Carin opened the door slowly and the two of them slipped in. There was a single light coming from a second story supervisor's room. It seemed sloppy to Carin that they should go to all the trouble to cover up the windows and then leave the door open. Carin could hear a soft sound of disgust off to her right. Apparently, Bruno also thought they were sloppy. Carin closed the door behind them and waited to see whether there were any sentries inside the building. When the two of them were certain that the only people in the warehouse were in the supervisor's room, Bruno motioned for them to continue moving.

In the dim light, Carin was able to point to one set of stairs that would go up to the catwalk from one side and point to Bruno. He gave a single nod of acknowledgement and moved deeply into the shadows. Carin moved with the all the grace and agility she could muster. Every footfall she made sounded like someone dropping a hardbound dictionary in a quiet library. Still, she made it to one side of the door without raising an alarm.

Jake began to talk in the room and Carin was aware of two things. The first was that she had truly missed the submarine captain. Up until this moment, she had not been sure he was alive and she had been trying to steel herself for the worst possible outcome. To have proof that he was alive lifted a weight from her chest she had not realized was there. She bit down hard on that line of thinking for now. The second thing she was aware of from the tone and timbre of his voice was that Jake was pushing as hard as he could. Was he pushing on DiBeto or Crubari?

Carin duck-walked closer to the door to hear what they were saying. Jake was speaking. "… I wasn't responsible for Stanger's death. Rabbit and his group …" Jake stopped talking for a moment. Carin heard him take in a deep breath. He waited a few moments and took in another.

DiBeto was getting impatient. "Go on, what about Rabbit?"

Jake began to laugh. It began as a soft chuckle and started to escalate rapidly before degenerating into a series of deep coughs that caused Carin to worry. When the coughing slackened, Jake began to speak in a low, out-of-breath voice. "Okay, DiBeto. I figured out your little problem for you." He raised his voice slightly and pitched it so that Carin could hear. "First, let me tell you that your man Crubari is as fast and strong as anyone I've met. He is easily as fast as Carin Gonzalez when she was at her fastest and he is as strong as me when I'm at my strongest."

What's he saying, thought Carin.

Jake took a moment to catch his breath. When he continued, it was in a softer, yet more determined voice. Carin realized that Jake was pushing DiBeto; trying to see whether he could influence him to be cooperative. "Did it ever occur to you that the only person who has the kind of access to your organization that you're talking about would be an *insider*? Hm? How about that it would have to be an insider who is pretty far up the food chain?"

DiBeto was unmoved. "Of course I thought of that. The first thing I covered was to check alibis. Everybody has one. It had to be an outside job."

Jake kept pushing. "DiBeto, the main reason to have a war is to shake up the current status quo. You can trust me on this one. I went to a school where they taught this subject. Ask yourself, who would have a reason to shake up the way you boys do business right now, except for someone who wanted to run the show or bring down all of the offices to create a power vacuum? After all, if I wanted revenge, all I had to do was to find you and kill you. I didn't have to start a war to do it. This brings me to Crubari. Do you know the reason that he always stays in the shadows is that he has excellent night vision? I would say that his night vision is about as good as your day vision on a cloudy day. That's why he's always standing in the dark. It gives him a tremendous advantage."

Carin's jaw dropped. What Jake was saying explained how Crubari had gotten away from her at the truck stop, but it seemed to make no sense. Still, if Jake said somebody could defy gravity, Carin was inclined to believe it. *Don't worry about us,* Carin thought. *Message received.*

"So I've got another question for you, DiBeto," Jake continued. "Who did this check of everybody's alibis? Did you have somebody check the checker's alibi? Could this person be the same one that has been pushing you to find me and kill me? I'll bet that person would not want to let his story get out. I'll bet that person has not left you alone with me, for fear I might tell you something that would point to him."

Carin heard DiBeto grunt and shift position. *He's facing Crubari now,* thought Carin. *He's buying it Jake. Keep pushing.* "Let me ask you something else," said Jake. "While I was out, did Crubari try to get you to leave? Wouldn't that have been convenient for him if you'd have left and he shot me while escaping? I'm sure he would have had an excellent excuse for how I got untied. Or maybe he just would have suffocated me while I was unconscious and blamed it on your pushing me over."

DiBeto bellowed in rage and Carin heard him making movements. Carin figured that this was a good time to peek around the corner. DiBeto was indeed charging Crubari, but Crubari was not moving. As soon as DiBeto went past Jake, the submarine captain rocked forward violently in his chair. As soon as it reached a forty-five degree forward lean, he pushed with the balls of his feet against the ground and the chair went airborne. Carin turned her attention back to Crubari and saw him move on DiBeto. The move was elegant, effective, and fast. *Way too fast,* thought Carin. Jake was right!

Hearing the commotion inside, Bruno chose this time to move on

Crubari. Crubari had taken a step towards Jake when he heard the ex-SEAL come around the doorway and bring his gun to bear. At that moment, Jake landed on his back and destroyed the chair he was sitting in, as well as the only light they had in the room. A pitch-black darkness enveloped them.

Bruno's reflexes were excellent. As soon as the light went out, he began a diving roll away from Crubari and away from his last position. This would have been a perfect move against a normal opponent, but Crubari could see it as well as Carin and Jake could. He quickly checked to ensure that Jake was still tangled in the ropes, and then moved towards Bruno.

Carin knew that she had to act now, but did she help Bruno or did she release Jake and get somebody who could help her with Crubari? She would not be able to take him alone. She stood up and began moving into the room while keeping a good distance from Crubari. Carin noticed Crubari approaching Bruno much too rapidly for a normal human. Jake was right about the killer. Her first instinct was to go to Bruno's aid, but Crubari had no weapon out and made no move to get one. She guessed he planned to eliminate Bruno by knocking him out, as he had done with DiBeto. Hoping she was right, she moved towards Jake. She silently thanked Bruno for insisting she carry a Gerber combat knife, and now produced it to make a single slice on the ropes holding Jake. Even though she rapidly stood up after her quick cut, she saw that Crubari was already coming towards her. He stopped when he saw her.

"You!" It was all he said.

Carin slowly put away the Gerber but kept her eyes on him. Without any training with the combat knife, she feared it would be more of an advantage for Crubari than her. Instead, she held up her hand with the missing finger. "Yes, it's me. You took something that didn't belong to you."

Crubari accelerated towards her. Time slowed for Carin. He threw a knife-edged chop with his left hand, aimed at Carin's temple. She blocked it easily and returned with a straight-arm punch to his solar plexus. Immediately following her punch, she willed herself to slow down, hoping to avoid wasting energy. Still, a wave of dizziness washed over her. She assumed a fighting stance anyway, hoping to cover just how shaky she was. She now knew she was faster than Crubari, but not by much. She also knew that it was not enough to protect her from a wily and conflict-hardened assassin.

As if to prove it, Crubari was back on his feet. He took one look at the woman he buried and left for dead. She was in a fighting stance and glaring straight at him.

The Crowbar turned and ran out the door.

Carin did not immediately follow, since she had a good idea where he was going. She ran over to Bruno. He was breathing and had a good pulse.

She checked the lump growing on the side of his head and went over his vital signs. He would revive soon. She moved over to DiBeto and saw that he was already beginning to stir.

Jake was still untangling himself. "Go after Crubari! I'll tie up DiBeto and look out for Bruno." Jake was almost out of his ropes, but Carin remained, using the extra lines to tie up DiBeto. "Jake, you need help here."

He shook his head and set off a coughing fit. "Carin," he wheezed. "We know more about Crubari than anyone alive. He has to try to neutralize us as a threat! On top of that, we only have about twenty-four hours until rendezvous. We cannot afford to have him running loose. Besides, I need to pay him back for what he did to my kids — and to you. Please. Go now!"

Carin looked at her hand for a moment. The finger was definitely growing back. It was already up to her middle finger's first knuckle. Jake was right. Crubari was going to keep coming after them, only next time they would not have any warning. If Crubari managed to disrupt their rendezvous with Matr, both Jake and Carin would be dead within a month, sooner if he had his way.

Moments later, she was on the stairs and heading for the back doors. Of course, she had no plan yet. That is never a good thing. Against Crubari, it would prove fatal. Up until just a few moments ago, the plan had been for Bruno and Carin to gang up on Crubari. With what they knew about him now, it was likely that their plan would have failed.

She rushed out the back door closest to Crubari's escape car and made a beeline for the vehicle. He was probably running at top speed, but he was taking a circuitous route to throw off any possible pursuit. Carin proceeded at a deliberate run to Crubari's car.

She got to the end of the alley and stopped a moment before entering. She slowed her breathing and tried to detect Crubari in the alley. When she sniffed a breath of air, there was a whiff of someone's sweat. She took two steps into the alley and listened. At first, there was no sound, but then she heard heavy breathing deeper in the alley. He must have heard her coming and set an ambush deep in the shadows.

Carin walked slowly into the alley until she noticed Crubari in the darkness about ten meters behind his car. She made a decision and marched straight for the vehicle. In one motion, she removed the Gerber knife from the sheath in the small of her back, leaned forward to the tire valve on the front tire, and sliced it as she saw Bruno do. She took two more steps and sliced through the rear tire valve. Crubari's escape car now had four flat tires, more useful as a paperweight than transportation. She then moved into the middle of the alley and blocked all escape to the street. She felt certain that Crubari had a good escape plan, but to get there, he had to go through her or backtrack to the warehouse. Time was now the enemy for both Crubari and Carin.

The Crowbar stepped out slowly from the shadows to the hissing sound of air escaping from his car tires and his getaway plans. "And so, *chica*. Do you really want to tangle with me? That could leave you dead."

Carin put the Gerber back in its sheath. She remembered her unarmed combat instructor at the academy drilling her on use of energy in a fight and tried to relax. "You already left me for dead once. It didn't work."

Crubari moved to within two meters of Carin and stopped. "Yes, but then I didn't know that you were an *El Ehido*. Now that I know, you will stand no more chance with me than a normal woman would against a normal man."

'Chica' sounds Spanish, thought Carin. *What is 'El Ehido?' Is that Farsi? Portuguese?* It might help to get a handle on her opponent if she knew. Then Crubari attacked, with speed and force such as she had never seen. Her reflexes automatically sped up. She blocked a kick and two punches before landing a kick to Crubari's stomach. The blow pushed him back to his original spot. For all the ferocity of his attack, it was undisciplined and easy to counter.

Crubari has never had any martial arts training, thought Carin. *With that speed and power, he probably never had the need for any.* Crubari did not advance and she immediately willed herself to slow down and relax and nearly collapsed as the expected wave of dizziness washed over her.

Through the spots in her vision, she could see Crubari's predatory smile. "*Bella*, it seems that you have been pushing yourself too much in the recent past. One or two more times is all you have and then you will be unconscious. This time I will not underestimate you. I will sever your head with that knife you have on your back and bring it with me to make sure that you don't return from the dead."

Bella, thought Carin. *Probably Spanish, but could be Italian or Portuguese — can't tell from his pronunciation.* She played for time to try to catch her breath. "You are a very experienced man. I can tell that you have been *El Ehido* a long time. When did you change?"

Just then, Crubari feigned an attack and Carin sped up her reactions to defend herself. When she saw that his attack had been a ruse, she forced herself to slow down and lost her balance. She made it look as if she was repositioning herself, but Crubari had noticed and his smile made Carin think of an alligator casually swimming towards its lunch.

Crubari crouched low and kept his gaze focused on Carin's eyes. "Not that it will matter to you once I get your knife, but I was chosen in 1930 in Peru. If you were smart, you would step aside."

While he talked, Crubari kept trying to circle on Carin. It seemed to Carin that he was trying to get her to leave an opening so he could race out of the alley. Carin kept shifting her position so that he did not have an opening. "My knife is right here," she taunted. "The only thing that is keeping you from it is a mere woman. It seems to me that a real man would not have been tripped up by just a single woman."

"Please. Do you think that I can be baited by such a transparent attempt?"

It was worth a try, thought Carin, but before she could voice an answer, Crubari attacked again. His attack was less forceful and less quick than the previous one. Carin blocked all his punches and landed a solid punch of her own on Crubari's nose. It was a matter of great satisfaction to her that she could feel and hear the bone on his nose give way under her knuckles.

"It seems that you're slowing down Crubari. You've already told me what you are going to do to me if you win. What can you imagine that I am going to do to you if I win?"

Carin could see a trace of panic cross Crubari's eyes as he checked his now-broken nose. "*Querida*, why should we fight each other? Don't you realize that we are both *El Ehido*? We are the chosen ones. We are the same, although, ultimately, there can be only one."

"The same?" said Carin in disgust. "I've got news for you. The only thing that we've got in common is internal organs." Carin was dragging in deep gulps of air. Her breathing was starting to take on a wheezing quality. Crubari was breathing deeply also, or maybe he just appeared to be since he had to breathe through his mouth. Carin continued to move laterally to match Crubari's moves. She had invested too much to let him simply run away now. A part of her mind thought *'Querida' is definitely Spanish. 'El Ehido' could be 'Elegido', which would translate as 'chosen.' I don't like the sound of that. And 1930? He's <u>that</u> old?*

Carin was gasping for air. To buy time, she asked, "So why did you use Stanger's Hummer to kill Nutley?"

Crubari tried to circle for an opening, but Carin closed on him. He backed off and answered, "Stanger was trying to encroach on something I had been setting up for a long time. I could not remove Stanger without incurring the wrath of his entire entourage. That would have caused too much visibility and exposure. A pity he was in the emergency room at the time."

Crubari feinted straight ahead. Carin jumped. When she slowed down again, the vertigo almost drove her to her knees. *I can't keep this up*, she thought. *I need a plan and fast.* The thought of her Academy days' unarmed combat lessons blended with her Advanced Tactical Aircraft training in her mind. She could hear and see both instructors telling her, *against overwhelming odds, prioritize your attacks. Take out their offensive capability first, their mobility second. Knocking out both with one strike will guarantee that you eat dinner at home.*

Without a second thought, Carin launched her own attack on Crubari. She could see the look on his face fade from a smile to a look of panic. It was obvious that he was not used to being attacked on his own terms. She threw a punch with her left that caused him to duck to avoid it, but left his leg vulnerable. Years of training asserted themselves in Carin and she reacted to the opening by lashing out a vicious kick to the side of his knee. Carin felt the knee give under her attack and heard a satisfying pop.

She backed off from her attack as she slowed down. All vision except that directly in front of her went black, but it was enough to see that Crubari had leapt at her with his good leg. Her momentary dizziness kept her disoriented long enough that Crubari crashed into her and dragged her to the ground before she could mount a defense. In the split second that it took for her senses to return, Crubari had her face down on the pavement in a chokehold she knew she would not be able to break free from in time. With him on her back, she could not reach her knife, so she lashed out for any hold on him that she could get. Her fingers sought eyes to gouge or ears to rip. Her feet tried to find the knee she had just kicked.

Nevertheless, Crubari had established himself in the perfect position to continue to choke the life out of her without taking damage himself. Her tunnel vision was returning, and this time she was sure that she would not recover. Her struggle became weaker and more futile with each passing moment.

At the instant her tunnel vision narrowed to total blackness, a confounding hallucination swept over her. Her awareness split into two equal parts, with one part watching her body move in very slow motion, while the other part existed in a bright and brilliant mental world of vast intelligence. The fast part of her took note of a dry leaf, kicked into the air by the struggle, now falling in slow motion before her. Every physical principle behind every changing angle of the falling motion of the leaf set off a cascade of mathematical interactions that expressed the interacting forces of air resistance and gravity as they pertained to the surface area of the leaf, even as that area constantly shifted in motion. This second part of her was hungry for the numbers. Hunger was the feeling. She needed the work.

The hallucination vanished when she felt an electric tingling sensation and felt Crubari's body slump on top of her and lie motionless. While her vision slowly returned, she propelled his inert body off her and pulled herself up to his unaware face.

"HAH!" she yelled at Crubari. Carin grabbed the collar of Crubari's shirt with one hand and slapped his face hard with the other. Reviving him was not the intent of her action. "Forgot about my partner, didn't you."

Carin looked up to see Jake Sabio slumped against a wall. He had one of the TASERs from the interrogation room still in his hand. Two small wires snaked from the end of the gun to the twin darts imbedded in Crubari's back. Jake's head was drooping down to his chest, but he managed to turn it sideways to see Carin and favor her with a small, lop-sided grin. "Sorry," he said.

"What for?"

Jake smiled sheepishly. "I forgot to ask you where you were going, when I all but kicked you out the door." Jake looked around the alley and at the flat tires on the car. "It didn't matter much. It wasn't long before I heard the party."

Carin came over to Jake and held him in her arms. He seemed about to say something when a coughing fit racked his body. She became afraid for him, and held him tightly while his coughs shook them both. They had to get to the object everyone was calling Morrigan and talk to Matr. All other options were long gone now. Jake had spent himself almost completely and she was nearly in the same state. The most important thing was to get Jake out of the alley, out of Vegas and off the planet.

She turned her attention to Jake when his coughing subsided. "Can you walk on your own?"

Jake answered by slowly coming to his feet and experimentally balancing himself on his own legs without any support from the wall. "Walk, yes. Run, no."

She looked at Jake for a moment to make sure he was not exaggerating. Carin had noted in her life that men tended to minimize their frailties around women. When she was sure to her own satisfaction that Jake could indeed walk, she went back to Crubari and checked him. His pulse and breathing were steady enough. She turned back to Jake. "You know, killing him right now would be the best thing we could do. If he gets away, he could screw things up for us. It wouldn't take much to keep us from getting to Morrigan. I just can't bring myself to do it." She pulled the Gerber knife from its sheath and offered it to Jake.

Jake looked at the knife and at Crubari in turn. It seemed that he was tempted for a moment, but then he shook his head slightly. "No, Carin. First, I'm not sure what it would take to kill Crubari, knowing what we know about him. Even containing him until we can get onto Morrigan is going to be next to impossible." Jake took a few tentative steps to test his legs before turning a somber face to her. "Besides, I've had a long talk with Franklin DiBeto and he's given me a better idea."

At that moment, Bruno drove into the alley in Frank's car. Jake walked up to the car and shook the man's hand as the former SEAL was getting out of the driver's seat. They spoke for a few moments before Bruno pulled out a cell phone and made a call. He said one word into the receiver, closed the phone and passed it to Jake. He then pulled out his large bag and opened it next to the passenger door. After rummaging for a few moments, Bruno removed a few items and placed them on the floorboards behind the driver's seat.

Jake had walked back to where Crubari was still laying. Carin asked, "What happened to the two guys in the trunk?"

Jake shot a thumb at Bruno. "Bruno let them out and told them to get out of town for their own good."

Carin looked at Jake suspiciously. "You have a plan." It was not a question.

"I've got the slightest whim of a possibility of a plan."

Carin held up her hand. "Okay, I get it. Tell me what you've got."

Jake outlined his ideas to Carin. When he finished, he asked, "What do you think?"

"I think you were overselling the word 'plan.'"

"I told you it wasn't solid yet."

"It's air with holes in it."

Jake turned to check Bruno's progress. When he turned back he said, "You're pretty snippy for someone who hasn't got a clue as to what our next move is."

Carin pointed down at the limp form of Crubari. "I had a great plan until this bozo turned out to be an *elegido*, whatever that is. Now there's no choice. We have to contain him until we get off this rock." Under her breath, Carin added, "and I am not snippy – I don't even think that you know what that word means."

"I mean it as an adjective. You know; as in short-tempered, snappish, sharp-tongued ..."

"Okay!" Carin said in a loud voice cutting off any more comment from Jake. "You know what 'snippy' is." Just as she was about to make a further reply, a wave of emotions washed over her. It was unmistakable, intense, passionate and overpowering. It threatened to overwhelm her. While she was trying to regain her equilibrium, she tasted the emotions: joy to the point of bliss, relief to the point of alleviation and most of all, an overwhelming feeling of love.

Carin looked up into Jake's eyes and noticed for the first time that tears had streaked his face. He tried to speak, but his voice caught in his throat. He looked at his feet as he cleared his throat. Finally, he said softly, "I thought I'd lost you."

She was in his arms in an instant. Tears beginning to well up in her own eyes as her own emotions burst out. Just then, Bruno came jogging up and said, "We're ready. The stuff you wanted is in the back seat …" He stopped short when he noticed Jake and Carin in each other's arms.

"Sorry guys. Need a moment?"

Carin disengaged from Jake's arms and backed away a half step from him so that they could both face Bruno, but she kept a hand on the small of his back. In her mind, she told herself it was to support him, but in her heart, she knew that it was for herself as well.

"It's okay, Chris," she said. "We don't have time. Did you hear Jake's plan?"

"Yes, ma'am and it has more holes than a Swiss cheese factory. No offense intended, Captain."

Jake was shaking his head, "None taken – and I'm Jake, she's Carin and you're Chris if that's okay with you. If you use rank or title, I'll assume you're mad at me. How do we solve this problem? I want to keep these two on ice for at least twelve hours and I want them alive so the Feds can clean up this mess in Vegas. Ideas?"

Jake fascinated Carin. Outwardly, he had taken command and charged ahead to find solutions to their problem as if he were all business. Nevertheless, waves of emotion were still flooding over Carin from him. She could feel the turmoil that roiled around him and yet he was able to maintain a sharp focus on their immediate problems. This Jake Sabio was quite the complicated man.

While Bruno and Jake were carrying Crubari to the car, Carin started putting her mind to the problem. How do you contain a person who has the effective power of a small tank? Carin let her mind free wheel, as was her way when solving problems. She did not like the idea of a tank – too military. Instead, she thought of a small bulldozer. An earthmover was more to her liking. That was when she thought about the cave and began to chuckle.

Jake and Bruno turned to her at the same time. Jake finally said, "Chris, I think she has a possible solution to our problem."

CHAPTER 44

Time to pickup: 15 hours

SPECIAL AGENT WILLIAM GREENFIELD knew that time was running out for his team, but he could not force himself to hurry his assessment. He had gathered all the pictures of every member of the five undercover offices around the country his team had discovered, including DiBeto's Anhur Corporation. Greenfield took the photos and, in an attempt to rewind the situation, tacked the pictures on the wall of his small conference room ordered by black ops office and ranking within each office. He even placed a large red mark across each photo of dead members of the different offices that they knew about and included them on his wall. Something was tickling at the corners of his perception, but he still could not quite grasp it.

These groups are responsible for more deaths around the world than we will ever know about, and I am here worrying about who killed a bunch of 'em? What is wrong with this picture?

Brian Hatfield and Ed Stein came into his office without knocking. They both stopped when they saw him concentrating on the pictures on the wall. Finally, Brian said, "Excuse us for barging in, Greenfield. Zeb Collins has asked to see us."

Greenfield did not look away from the pictures on his wall. "Did he say what he wanted?"

Brian and Ed looked at each other as if choosing who should answer. Brian gave a slight nod to Ed to encourage him on. Ed threw him a sour look, but answered, "He didn't say, but I think Zeb got word from Washington. If I were a betting man, I'd say Headquarters gave Zeb orders to pull us off the assignment and shuffle us off to re-indoctrination. Gentlemen, our careers are about to take a steep turn to the south."

Brian Hatfield nodded. "Got that right, buddy. We're toast."

William Greenfield was quiet for a moment. Finally, he pointed at the wall and said, "There's something going on here that I can't figure out. It keeps bugging me. I know that there is a pattern to this, but I can't see it."

Brian and Ed came around to stand behind him and look at the montage. They remained silently behind Greenfield for several minutes, not seeing any more pattern than Greenfield did, when Glynnis walked in the door. "Excuse me for barging in, boss. Zeb Collins has asked to see us."

Greenfield absently pointed towards the two agents behind him. "You're too late. I already got the word from these two."

Glynnis looked at the three men staring at the wall, then at the collection of pictures. "What's going on here, skipper?"

When Greenfield did not answer, Brian pointed at the wall and said, "Will thinks there's a pattern here. Maybe something that we can't see – something we're overlooking."

Glynnis fell in next to Ed and Brian and stared at the wall. Finally, she said, "I don't see any pattern here that we haven't thought of before. Maybe we have the rank structure all wrong and the interactions are different than we think."

Ed threw up his hands in exasperation. "I don't see any pattern, but if I was going to rank the Anhur group from smartest to dumbest, I would have put Stanger at the top of the list. He wasn't the boss, but he sure had the brains to keep them out of trouble with the law."

Brian was nodding. "He was one slick character. DiBeto avoids trouble by being conservative, but Stanger did whatever he wanted and we couldn't pin anything on him."

"Yeah," said Ed. "The only time I thought he ever screwed up was when his Hummer turned up in that vehicular homicide."

They were all quiet for a moment. Then Glynnis said, "You know, now that I think about it that had to have been a setup. Stanger should have been pulled in for that and we would have done our best to make it stick. That emergency room alibi was pure luck for him. The other thing that bothers me is who could have been so dumb as to steal a car from a special forces trained black ops-type." Glynnis stopped talking, looked at the picture wall. After another moment she said, "Smartest to dumbest."

Greenfield looked over at Glynnis, Brian and Ed and then back to his wall. Glynnis moved from behind Greenfield and walked up to the pictures. She moved Stanger to the top of the Anhur group, shuffled several of the other pictures from the other groups and took a step back to look. Greenfield looked at his team members and asked, "See a pattern now?"

Glynnis stepped closer to the wall and noticed that Greenfield had scribbled a date in the lower right hand corner of each of the pictures that had a red mark through them. She recognized the dates as each person's date of death and turned to Greenfield. "This has been going on for about six or seven years."

Greenfield was nodding his head. "Yup."

Glynnis shook her head. "But they all had ample funding back then – just one big happy family keeping America safe from all enemies, foreign and domestic. What would have been the motivation when there was work and money for everybody? Besides, the black ops agencies aren't that subtle. The reason they would eliminate someone from a competitor's office is to send a message in a loud, violent way. Some of these folks died peacefully in their sleep."

Greenfield shrugged his shoulders. "Or at least it appeared they died that way. Suppose that they didn't die of natural causes. What would that mean?"

Greenfield pushed away from his desk and placed their recent picture of Crubari in a blank area next to the pictures of the various agencies. Glynnis looked over at the pictures of the agencies and the picture of Crubari. She turned back and looked directly at Greenfield with her arms folded across her chest. "You can't possibly believe that."

Ed looked at Brian and raised his hands to his shoulders. "Brian, they're doing it again. Make them stop."

Brian was looking from Glynnis to Greenfield. "Would one of you two mystics care to share your knowledge with us mere mortals?"

Before Greenfield could answer, there was a knock on the door. Norm Harris, one of the senior managers of the Las Vegas FBI office stuck his head in and said, "Agent Greenfield, Zeb is looking for you. Can you please get over to his office and see what he wants?"

Greenfield pushed himself away from the table he was leaning on and smiled. "Thanks, Norm. We'll go right now." He looked over to his team and motioned for them to follow.

Without another word, Greenfield walked over to his desk and unlocked a drawer. He reached in, grabbed a folder, and marched out the door followed close behind by Glynnis. Ed and Brian stared at each other for a few seconds. Finally, Brian made a sweeping gesture for Ed to proceed out the door. Ed let out a series of spicy phrases under his breath that seemed to require repeated peppering with assorted profanities. Aloud he said, "I never know what those two are talking about."

Brian came out of his exaggerated bow to point at the door. "That is true, young knight, but one has to admit that it's always interesting times."

Ed walked out the door followed closely by Brian and shot back, "Isn't that like an ancient Chinese curse or something?"

They caught up with Glynnis and Greenfield at Zeb's door. Greenfield was waiting, flanked by Glynnis and Zeb's assistant. When the team leader noted that his team had all arrived, he turned to the receptionist and nodded. She knocked on Zeb's door and stuck her head in. "Agent Greenfield and his team are here to see you, sir."

There was a brief shuffling of papers and closing of drawers from inside the office. Finally, Zeb said, "Let them in, please."

Greenfield walked in, came to a stop in front of Zeb's desk and came to a formal parade rest. The other members of the team, lacking ideas, followed suit.

Zeb Collins rose from a desk devoid of any computer screens, telephones or paper. Greenfield wondered for an instant what Zeb did all day, but Zeb was rounding on him. "Will, I need a status of your investigation and I need it now. You all have been with the agency long enough to know that your team is about to be pulled by Headquarters. I want it all right now – fact, speculation, innuendo, loose threads – I don't care how slim it is, I need it out now."

Greenfield remained outwardly calm while he reassessed the situation. To buy time, he said, "I'm sorry sir. I was under the impression you wanted to see me to say that you're shipping us off to headquarters for debriefing and indoctrination."

"Damn right I want to see you, man. I have a crack team working on this war and the weekly briefings you give suddenly become very generic and even inconsistent. This seemed to happen right after a certain shootout at a truck stop. I can only assume that you're trying to keep something close to your vest for some reason. Further, I have to assume that the reason you're doing this is that you think we have a mole.

"It's time for you to talk to me, Agent Greenfield. It's time to remember who your friends are and who they're not. Headquarters wants your team in Washington yesterday, if not sooner. I've been stalling for almost a week already."

Greenfield asked politely, "I sorry sir, but if I may ask — why not just let us go to Headquarters?"

Zeb looked Greenfield in the eye and asked, "Son, did you take a stupid pill this morning? There's something going on that's at least a power struggle between some nasty groups. Our own government is apparently protecting these groups. I have to think this or you would've cracked this case a while ago. So ask yourself, *who* benefits most when HQ pulls your team and it takes six months to get another team up to speed? Could it be the people behind the struggle?"

Before Greenfield could answer, Glynnis interrupted, "Sir, I believe that we are ready to brief our case."

Zeb looked at Glynnis for ten full seconds before turning his attention back to Greenfield. In a soft voice he said firmly, "This is it, son. I need it all. I can't stop them from pulling your team off of this whole twisted spook-world situation, but if you've got enough to make a move in the next day or so — well, I can buy you that much time."

Greenfield pulled out a picture of Agent Dylan Camp and handed it to Zeb. "First thing we should do is bring Dylan in here for questioning. I got an anonymous tip that he was our mole."

Zeb took the picture and growled, "Why didn't you tell me this before?"

Greenfield shuffled slightly and said, "We got a separate anonymous tip that also implicated you, sir."

Zeb looked at the picture in his hand. "I hope you passed that up to Headquarters."

"Yes sir."

Zeb nodded. "Good. It will be a pain to clear this whole thing up, but at least we followed procedure."

Zeb walked over to his pristine desk and unlocked the bottom drawer. He pulled out a single picture and locked the drawer again. He walked back to Greenfield and handed him the picture. "This is part of the reason HQ is suddenly going crazy. Las Vegas police found his body about an hour ago."

Greenfield looked at the picture. It was a photo of a young man who appeared to be sleeping. His face was relaxed and at peace. It was Agent Dylan Camp, and judging by how far around his neck had been twisted, Agent Camp would never wake up again. Greenfield handed the photo back to Zeb. "Sir, why don't you lock this up and follow me to my office? We have a picture wall set up that will explain what's going on."

"I don't have time for this, Greenfield," growled Zeb. "Give it to me in brief."

"Yes sir. As far as we can tell, Anhur is a front for a black ops office that is used by the CIA for sensitive assignments that can't be covered by CIA field agents ..."

"Stop!" said Zeb holding up a hand. "Unless this is a new definition of the word 'brief' assume I know about Anhur and all the contract ops offices that the CIA calls 'disavowables.'"

Greenfield licked his lips and looked at his team before looking back at Zeb and continuing. "When the new President was elected and his Administration took over, the number of contract ops jobs went to almost zero. The budget started getting tighter about three or four years ago. When the money started drying up, it wasn't long before the individual team members began to do small jobs on the side to make ends meet and maintain their expensive lifestyles. Contract killings outside the U.S., kidnappings, and torture — usually funded by one multi-national corporation against another — began a marked increase ..."

"I know all this," interrupted Zeb. "What does any of this have to do with truck stop fire-fights and dead FBI agents?"

Greenfield looked at his teammates for a moment. Glynnis gave a slight shrug. He looked back at Zeb and said, "We think the two Senator's deaths that started us on this investigation are connected to Anhur."

Zeb stood still for a moment while he stared at Greenfield. Finally, he said, "Do you know what you're implying?"

Greenfield nodded. "Yes, sir. Suddenly, the two senators die. That's what brought them to our attention about three years ago. We saw the patterns of the killings, but until recently, we couldn't make any sense of the intra-office killings. My team and I believe that someone has been slowly decapitating the different offices for about ten years in an attempt to have one super-office that controls all the black ops work."

Greenfield became silent and let this last bit of information sink in.

Zeb visibly shivered. "That group would be uncontrollable."

Greenfield nodded. "They could make stocks rise and fall, they could change the course of elections, they could start and end wars, but that isn't the worst of it. It seems that the person who's pulling the strings is not with any of the offices, but outside of them."

"It's not DiBeto?"

"No sir. We think it's Crubari. As you know, we can't find anything out about Crubari. If it wasn't for a lucky break from an anonymous tipster, we wouldn't even know what he looked like."

"Anonymous tipster?"

"Yes, sir. I think the information came from Sabio, but I can't prove it."

Zeb leaned back on his desk. He folded his arms in front of him but kept his gaze steadily on Greenfield. After a moment he asked, "What about Sabio's partner – the female? Could the information have come from her?"

Greenfield shook his head. "We have strong evidence to indicate that Doctor Gonzalez was killed by Crubari. Knowing Crubari, I don't think we'll find her body."

Zeb let out a short snarl and began to pace in front of his desk. "If I could stall headquarters for twenty-four hours, what could you do?"

"Agent Collins, give us two weeks. We can do this right and have it tied up in a nice package in that time."

"Well William, we don't have two weeks, we've got one day. It sounds as if we desperately need to talk to Sabio."

Greenfield stood still for a moment before giving a slight nod of his head. "If all we have is twenty-four hours, I think Sabio is our only hope."

Special Agent in Charge Zeb Collins stopped pacing and faced Greenfield. "I have to agree with you, son. It's a lousy deal, but it's the only one we have. Now I think that you'd better show me this picture wall of yours."

CHAPTER 45

Time to pickup: 2 hours

FRANKLIN DIBETO WOKE UP to find that he was bound hand and foot. He had been tossed onto a dirt floor. As his vision returned, he made out a shape in front of him, strangely backlit, and a human form. It was surreal. DiBeto could swear that he was in a cave — and that Jake Sabio was the figure hovering over him. Within the space of two more heartbeats, he realized this was no mere nightmare.

"As you can see, you're tied up in a cave," said Jake, without preamble. "You are many miles from civilization, or even roads."

"You're insane, Sabio! You're not some criminal!"

"Uh-huh. One of us is enough." With that, Jake began coughing violently. After a moment, the coughing fit subsided.

Dibeto struggled against his bindings. "You're a dead man, Sabio."

The former navy man looked at DiBeto and continued conversationally, "Yes, you're probably right. If you look over your left shoulder, you will notice that Mr. Crubari will be joining you here in your little cave. I hope you'll think of it as your new home."

DiBeto noticed the limp form of his former assassin, with two wires snaking out of his back into one of the TASERs. He looked back at Jake. "What're you going to do?"

"We are going to collapse the old mining tunnel and leave you two inside."

DiBeto's eyes widened. "No. You're crazy. You can't do that – not even to me."

Jake continued as if he had not heard DiBeto. "The precaution of burying you alive isn't really for you, specifically. We needed something that could hold the two of you for a few hours, at the least. You were easy, but your former associate over there takes a little more security. I'm sure you understand."

DiBeto felt the first belts of terror begin to wrap around his chest and tighten. "You can't do this! It's the same as murder! I am the leader of a group vital to our national security!"

Jake stood up and brushed the dirt from his jeans. "That's an interesting argument, coming from a man who only a few hours ago was poised to kill me, to cover up his own sins."

DiBeto struggled in vain against his bindings. "You want money? You know we can get it: off the books cash! Then we just go our separate ways – no harm, no foul. Name your price..."

Jake was already walking out of the cave entrance. He turned toward DiBeto at this last comment. "Has this whole thing been about money, or about power? Hasn't this persecution of Dr. Gonzalez and me been because you couldn't part with the money I won from your men?"

"They were wrong to go for funding that way! I never authorized it! They were a rogue group! They would steal cash from evidence lockers and run crooked poker games, fleece the other players and then put back the seed money. It worked a hundred times with no problem. At least, that is what they told me."

DiBeto was sweating from his exertions. "You got my men killed! That's what this whole thing was about! You killed them as if you pulled the trigger."

Jake shook his head. "No, this isn't about your men or about money or even about power. The truth is that you were set up to do this. You were pushed into a series of events that were none of your doing. You were just a puppet, DiBeto. The head spook of all of the secret Las Vegas spooks that Washington keeps out here to track money, criminals and terrorists. You're the toughest game in town, but you've been dancing on puppet strings. Somebody else tugged them." Jake took a deep breath before continuing. "That's why you're alive right now."

DiBeto shot Jake an angry glare. "Whadda ya talkin' about? Him? He works for me."

"He set you up to be the fall guy."

"In what?"

"In the little war that's been going on between the groups in Vegas. When the money started drying up, he saw it as an opportunity. You didn't have a chance."

DiBeto's eyes narrowed to slits. "You know too much about the war to be an innocent bystander, Sabio. You're in on it and my money still says that you're a big part of it."

Jake laughed. "Your precious war is not exactly a secret. In case you missed it, it's been on the radio and in the papers. However, I really found out about it because you told me all about it. At first, I thought you were bragging for some reason. Then I figured out that it was just your personality. You blab a lot. That, more than anything, convinced me you don't have what it takes to be behind this war."

"I have a legitimate gripe against you, Sabio."

Jake shook his head and sighed. "Your so-called gripe was a counting coup at best. Someone did something that you felt infringed on your territory, so you were going to get them out of the way and send a message to the other groups at the same time. That was predictable. It was exactly what Crubari wanted you to do. You're heartless DiBeto, but you don't kill without provocation mainly because you become a target yourself. At least you didn't before Crubari showed up on the scene. It's funny you didn't realize that Crubari was egging you on to do exactly what you did. You played right into his hands. You almost left a perfect power vacuum which would have put you as the puppet head of the organization and Crubari as the true power."

DiBeto growled, "You're smokin' dope. I'm a patriot like all the members of my group."

Sabio stood still for a moment. "Imagine that there was only one viable black ops group left, and that group was Anhur. I'm sure you're familiar with the term, 'shadow government.' That's what Anhur would have been. The real government couldn't have stopped Anhur because anybody that made rumblings in that direction would be eliminated. I think that's why Crubari killed those two senators. Governments move very slowly and make a lot of noise about what they are doing. Even a covert investigation of Anhur would be simple for your people to smoke out. I think they caught wind of what was happening and started asking embarrassing questions."

DiBeto remained adamant. "That's a load of crap. You're just trying to take the spotlight off yourself because you got my men killed. Joey Stanger was like a son."

Jake Sabio turned to face him and stood with his arms crossed. "First it's the money, then it's the men and then it's Stanger. I don't think that you even know what the truth is anymore. But just to make sure, when is Joseph Stanger's birthday?"

DiBeto paused in his struggling a moment truly puzzled. "What?"

"It's a simple question. When's his birthday? That shouldn't be so tough for a caring mentor and friend like you. He was like a son, remember?"

"How the hell should I know?" Jake bellowed.

"It's April second. What was his favorite color?"

"Blue."

"No, it was black – any shade from gray to pitch black. C'mon, DiBeto. I was only with the man a couple of hours over a poker game and I know more than you do. Was he ever in the Boy Scouts?"

"I DON'T KNOW."

"He was not. What kind of car did he drive?"

This time DiBeto looked up in triumph and answered. "Car? It was a Hummer. A yellow Hummer."

Jakes response came only after a pause. "Yes. A yellow Hummer. I know."

Franklin DiBeto realized he had somehow made a mistake, but his heart was racing so fast and so hard that he could not think of where Jake had tripped him. He heard Dr. Carin Gonzalez yell from the tunnel entrance. "Jake – time!"

From DiBeto's point of view, Jake's silhouette was backlit from the work lights in the tunnel. He stood with his legs spread at shoulder width and arms folded across his chest. Finally, Jake said, "I understand that the dark is a good place to meditate. If I were you, I would do that. Meditate on the fact you were too weak to see through Crubari's manipulation. I would meditate on the fact you have sunk so low due to your association with him and others like him that you allowed my children to be killed in cold blood simply because they got in the way when you went after an informant. I would meditate on the fact the battery charge on the TASER in Crubari's back is only going to last another half hour, at the most."

Jake Sabio knelt back down on one knee and approached Franklin DiBeto until their noses were only inches apart. DiBeto suddenly felt ice-cold dread in his veins. Jake said, "I would meditate on the fact that the person I have left in here with you is one of the most dangerous killers and torturers in the world and will wake up shortly after the TASER loses charge. He is going to blame you for being trapped like this. I would meditate on what a trained assassin will do to you, Mr. DiBeto, when he finds out you have destroyed everything that he has worked for these last ten years."

Jake Sabio stood up and backed away from DiBeto. To Frank's eyes, it looked like Jake was no longer human, but an apparition of the angel of death from the Old Testament. An aura of menace radiated out of the apparition as it turned around and walked out of the tunnel.

DiBeto began screaming out Sabio's name. First, he screamed in rage and swore oaths of revenge, but as the moments stretched out and the inevitable became apparent, terror took hold and he screamed in uncontrolled horror.

The explosion came unexpectedly, right in the middle of one of Franklin

DiBeto's screams. A deafening blast slapped him against the ground with an air concussion that hammered at his lungs. Dirt and small rocks sprayed DiBeto. He found himself praying for the ceiling in his small cave to collapse, to crush and kill him with merciful speed.

Once he was certain his prayer would be unanswered and he was to be left locked up with a psychopath, he took up screaming again, only this time he screamed without words.

CHAPTER 46

Time to pickup: 2 hours

ONLY MINUTES EARLIER, WHEN they first arrived at the cave, Carin was fighting off a sense of despair. She sensed Jake was fading fast in spite of his tough front. She had tried to keep a running conversation with him during the drive to the cave, just to keep him awake. Sometimes he answered her, sometimes not.

The plan they finally agreed on was a variation of Jake's original idea. They decided to lock DiBeto and Crubari together in a secure place until Matr made the pickup. Whatever the place was, it had to be strong enough to hold them until departure. Carin expanded the idea to take into account the capabilities they now knew Crubari possessed. After a little thought, she remembered an old mining cave she had seen, right after she pulled herself out of the shallow grave where Crubari left her. It would be perfect.

Chris Bruno proved to be helpful with the plan. As soon as Carin mentioned the mine, he reached into his bag and produced a small roll of detonation cord and a roll of speaker wire. Carin looked at the det cord in amazement. "Chris, do you always carry explosives around with you?"

The former SEAL looked back at Carin, confused. "What?"

Carin pointed to the explosive cord. "I don't know anybody that runs around with det cord in their gym bag."

Stone-cold sincerity etched Bruno's face. "Everyone I know does."

Carin decided to call it a cultural difference and let the matter drop. The rest of the plan quickly formed and Chris began giving them an abbreviated course in demolition. Following the impromptu class, Carin, Jake and Bruno agreed to recognition codes should they need to communicate. After a quick phone call, Emily arrived in the van at the end of the alley. She and Bruno disappeared.

Carin just threw DiBeto into the trunk of his car. However, she knew that Crubari had to be handled more delicately. The TASER leads could not be allowed to come loose from his back. The best solution was to put him face down in the back seat, to keep an eye on the leads as well as his restraints. Carin offered to ride back with Crubari, but Jake was too woozy to drive. Instead, he produced a tire iron from the trunk area and hovered over him all the way to the cave.

Carin was able to find the dirt road that went almost directly to the cave, and soon arrived back at the familiar place. She checked her watch while she got out of the car. "Thirty minutes is all we have, Jake. Then we have to get back to the tank."

Jake grabbed DiBeto out of the trunk and began dragging him to the cave. "We'll make it."

Jake stopped by Carin and looked up to the clear sky. "Assuming that this 'Matr' thing really can pick us up, that we survive the trip, that we can survive up there. You know — the pesky details."

Jake dragged Crubari and DiBeto deep into the cave. Even with their enhanced vision, they could not see inside the pitch-black cave and had to set up lights in the tunnel entrance. Carin wrapped the det cord around the rotting cross-brace timbers along the tunnel ceiling, the way Chris instructed. She was careful not to disturb the ceiling. Even so, occasional showers of dust and pebbles fell on her from her gentle probing. Finally, she was done. She went back to the tunnel entrance, turned and yelled. "Jake! Time!"

She then walked back to the waiting car. The engine was running and the hood was up. Jake arrived right behind her and took the speaker wire from her hands. "Please, Carin. Let me do this."

She handed the two ends of the speaker wire to Jake and, without hesitating, he touched the two ends to the car's battery terminals. Brief sparks illuminated the bottom of the car hood. A muffled explosion accompanied them from the tunnel entrance.

At first, nothing else happened. After a moment, a cloud of dust roiled out of the tunnel.

Carin looked at her watch. They were running behind. They had to leave.

She looked up expecting to tell Jake to jump in the car so they could race to the campsite, but he stood looking toward the sky with his arms outstretched. Carin was unable to understand what Jake was doing even as he collapsed to the ground.

Anger and frustration flooded her. "Oh no you don't, Sabio! You're not leaving me alone."

She was too weak to raise Jake's limp form off the ground. Instead, she dragged him to the rear door of the car and unceremoniously dumped him onto the back seat. Her arms were trembling so badly from the strain that she was having difficulty turning the ignition key. *Not now,* she prayed to no one in particular. *Just give me ten more minutes.*

She kept a running commentary going to Jake, telling him they still had time. She did not believe it herself. Still, the price of not going to Matr was certain death, a bad death, and the thought caused her to force the oversized luxury car to perform beyond its design limits. In spite of the impossible terrain, it careened in more or less the correct direction, spending almost as much time in the air as on the ground, without crashing into anything big enough to stop it.

Finally, she saw the lights of the camp in the failing light. She had only been driving for a few minutes, but each tick of the clock brought failure that much closer to her. The plan that she had thrown together on the terrifying drive from the cave was simple: get Jake a dose of the solution and get into the tank. Without a dose of the solution, she was certain he would never survive the constant six gee acceleration they had specified to Matr. She had to face facts. Without a dose for herself, she knew she would fare no better on the brutal ascent.

Jake and Carin had previously discussed the ascent, but only briefly. It did not matter. They both understood the risks. The method that Matr was using to bring them up would apply six times their weight for at least thirty minutes. It would feel as if there were five Jakes piled on top of him. Fighter pilots do this every day all around the world with no harm done. The difference was that fighter pilots do it for brief periods, usually less than a minute. Jake and Carin were going to sustain this acceleration for at least a continuous thirty minutes. They would be lying on their backs, so there was little chance of the blood draining out of their heads and causing them to black out. Instead, they would have to lift their chests against the force to perform the simple act of breathing. After a while, it could become impossible for them to breath. A weightlifter that takes a light weight and begins to perform curls can only do a certain number before his muscles can no longer respond to his desires. Each breath that Jake and Carin would take against the incredible weight on their chest would be like the weightlifter. As they labored to breathe against the unnatural weight, they would slowly begin to accumulate fatigue toxins that would become more and more difficult to overcome. They could suffocate because they could not take a breath.

Carin realized they would both have to take the solution through scratching their skin since Carin could not afford falling back into a coma by taking the solution orally. She braked the car to a stop next to the trailer and raced around the passenger door. Jake was still limp and his skin was clammy. "C'mon Sabio, hang in there just a few more minutes."

Dragging Jake was proving to be a monumental task, but Carin refused to give up. She backed up the steps holding Jake by his armpits and opened the door behind her. With a mighty effort, she pulled hard on Jake and they both fell to the floor with Jake on top of her. Carin tried to move, but was too weak to get Jake off her. He had her pinned against the floor. She turned at a sound behind her and saw William Greenfield pointing his gun at her. She turned to the other end of the trailer and saw the woman from Greenfield's team with her weapon also drawn and pointed at Carin and Jake.

Carin looked back at Greenfield to see what could only have been a slight smile of satisfaction. Agent William Greenfield began to read her Miranda Rights as he closed in on Jake and handcuffed him. "You are under arrest. You have the right to remain silent ..."

The room continued to spin for Carin and she could not focus. She had overexerted herself and her new body was trying to find the energy to continue. The best she could do was to answer, "What?"

From over by William Greenfield, a voice kept saying, "Do you understand these rights?"

Carin heard a noise over her shoulder and turned to face the woman who had her gun leveled at her. It took a moment for the image to clear enough for Carin to recognize her. "You were at the truck stop. What's your name?"

Greenfield insistently kept asking, "Do you understand these rights?"

Finally, the woman next to Carin put her gun away and said, "Glynnis, my name is Glynnis. What's wrong with Jake?"

Carin began to cough violently and Glynnis rolled Jake off Carin. She elevated Carin's head on her lap until the coughing stopped. Finally, Carin was able to say, "Jake's dying." After a moment, she added, "Me too."

Glynnis' head shot up and said, "Boss, dial 9-1-1."

Carin heard William Greenfield pull something out of a pocket and begin to punch in the numbers. She called out in as loud a voice as she could muster. "NO." In a softer voice, she added, "Please."

"Why not?" That was Glynnis.

Carin's head lolled over to try to face the female agent but could not focus on her. "Won't help. We've ... changed."

Glynnis was determined. "What can we do to help?"

Carin's mind drifted away. *What can we do to help? What can we do? What... what...?*

Carin was being shaken. *Dammit Carin*, she scolded herself. *Stay focused one minute longer.* All she could say aloud was, "Sink."

Glynnis voice came again, "The sink. What about the sink?"

Sink? What about the sink? Carin wondered. She forced herself to focus on the sink. "Solution under the sink. Big white bottle."

She heard Greenfield rummaging around. Finally, he said, "Found it."

"Plug the sink. Pour in… solution. The solution." She heard a gurgling sound as the liquid poured into the sink.

"That is some vile smelling stuff. Okay, now what?"

"Cheese grater. Scrape my hands. I have to put them in the sink."

Greenfield began to protest, "Is that stuff poison? Are you trying to kill yourself?"

Carin was lifted during the protest. She realized it was Glynnis as the woman got her to the sink and propped her against the counter. There was a sudden burning sensation on her forearms and the back of her hands, and then the cool sensation as her hands dipped into the solution.

Initially, she did not feel anything. Had she waited too long? Were she and Jake too far gone? Then the welcome feeling of euphoria began to course through her body. The vertigo lifted and she saw a worried Glynnis was holding her hands down in the solution. She turned to see that Agent Greenfield had backed away and had his gun trained on her.

Carin turned to Glynnis. "Can you help me get Jake into the solution?"

"You stay there," Glynnis insisted. "I'll bring Jake."

Glynnis went over to Jake. He was lying on his left side where Glynnis had rolled him to free Carin. Glynnis now put her arms under Jake's armpits and stood up. Although Carin could see Glynnis was straining, it was obvious that the agent would be able to get Jake to the sink.

Glynnis propped Jake's inert form against the counter next to Carin. "Go ahead and scrape his hands."

Carin took one hand out of the solution, picked up the cheese grater, and found she could not bring herself to scrape him. "I can't do it. Can you?"

Glynnis shot Carin an incredulous glance before reaching across and taking the cheese grater from her hand. In a matter of a moment, Glynnis had Jake's forearms and hands scraped around his handcuffs and was holding his hands in the solution.

For almost a full minute, Jake remained inert despite the solution bath. Carin worried they had taken too long to get it into his system. Suddenly, he took in a deep, noisy breath and opened his eyes. He looked directly at William Greenfield and the gun that was still pointed at him and calmly asked, "Agent Greenfield, do you have the exact time?"

CHAPTER 47

Time to pickup: 20 minutes

WILLIAM GREENFIELD LOOKED OVER his gun at Jake. "Are you late for an appointment?"

Carin answered first. "Actually, we are."

Greenfield shook his head. "I'm sorry, Dr. Gonzalez. I have a war going on in Las Vegas and I think that you folks hold the key. I don't know whether you are even aware of what you know. I promise that no harm will come to you and you will be released as soon as we get the information that you have."

Carin looked over to the other agent and asked, "Can I trust his word?"

Glynnis, who had backed off slightly and redrawn her pistol, looked from Greenfield to Carin. Finally, she answered, "I have never seen him go back on his word. Not ever."

Carin thought for a moment before answering. "Okay, she is definitely telling the truth, so here's the deal. You put away your weapons and ask any questions you want. You two and your two folks outside will come to no harm. You have ten minutes before we walk out that door and get inside a metal tank sitting about a hundred yards up the trail from here. Even that's cutting it a little thin for us, so decide."

Will Greenfield began to chew his bottom lip. "Look, I know what you two can do. I've seen it in action while you were saving the life everyone on my team – including me. I have no illusions. Without you two intervening at the truck stop, the four of us would be dead along with that kid behind the counter. I owe you two for that, but I have a job to do, and that job entails ending a war that threatens the security of our country. Consequently, the Vegas FBI Regional Office is getting heat from Washington, which rolls down

301

to my team. I'm motivated, Doctor. I have two guns on you that say you're coming with us so I can stop that war. Now Dr. Gonzalez, your hands are free and you can probably get to one of us, but not both. Jake has his hands cuffed, so he can't help you. You're coming with us as soon as you finish here.

"I'll give you about two more minutes in that solution and then we're all going back to the Regional Office. I promise to return you back here when we're finished."

Jake looked at Greenfield and said, "Can't afford it. We only have nine and a half minutes left, Agent Greenfield." As he did so, he pulled his hands out of the solution and laid the now unattached handcuffs on the counter beside the sink.

Carin looked directly at Greenfield and said, "Don't pick these up with your bare hands. I don't think this solution or its residue would cause you any problems, but don't take any chances."

The agent's eyes widened until they were mostly white. Glynnis spoke first. "All right, all right," she said, holding her gun by the grip and pointing it toward the floor while she put it back in the holster. "Boss, we have a deal, right?" She looked over to her fellow agent. "Don't you agree, boss?"

Greenfield looked between Carin and Glynnis for a moment and finally said, "I don't think I have much choice, but I need everything you know in about nine minutes or my whole team may be up for criminal prosecution. I can't let you two go while my team is in jeopardy. That's the best I can do."

Carin and Jake faced each other. Jake gave her a slight nod and reached over for the cheese grater. Carin averted her eyes from Jake and said, "Agreed. Do you have a voice recorder of some kind?"

Glynnis produced one from her pocket. "I've got a voice memory stick here, but it only holds about twenty minutes of spoken messages."

Carin thought for a minute. "That'll do. Set it for the highest possible resolution and start it recording over there by Jake. OW!"

Carin shot Jake a nasty glare. He had gently taken her hand while she had been talking. What she had thought was a tender caress and show of support had actually been an opportunity to scrape the back of her hand to increase her exposure to the solution. It was a necessary step she had been dreading. "You know, Jake. You could've warned me."

Instead of the verbal bantering that she was expecting, he leaned over and gently kissed her hand. "Sorry," was all he said.

Carin blushed at the unexpected affection. *What was that about*, thought Carin. *No, don't think about that now. That's for later. Right now, I have to focus on getting us on that tank for the rendezvous.*

Glynnis had stopped while Jake and Carin were talking. Jake turned to Glynnis and said, "I'm going to talk as fast as I can into this recorder, then

Carin is going to talk and fill in anything that I left out. When I'm finished, ask me questions as fast as you can. Get your questions ready."

With that, Jake turned to the recorder and began speaking in an incredibly fast rate. At first, it sounded like the high-pitched squeals of someone gargling in falsetto. After only a moment or two, Carin was able to understand what Jake was saying. He told about the loss of his children and the inability of the police to find the people responsible. He talked about meeting Carin just prior to getting to Las Vegas, but left out how the explosion in the meteor crater had infected them. He talked about meeting Joey and knowing immediately that he was incapable of the planning required for the murder of his children. He talked of meeting DiBeto and knowing that he was not behind the deaths of his children. He finally discussed Crubari. He went into detail on Crubari's capabilities and his plans. He finally wound down after giving the exact coordinates to the mouth of the cave with ample warning on how to capture Crubari. He never mentioned Fred.

Jake turned to Carin and asked, "Doctor, have I left anything out?"

Carin heard the tone of his voice more than his words. Years in the military translated his question into a statement. "Doctor, I have left nothing out."

Carin said softly to Jake. "We've got to talk about the possible threat from outside."

Jake was quiet a moment before answering. "You're right."

Carin turned to Greenfield and said, "That's the entire story in a nutshell. When you slow it down, you will have about a hundred minutes of voice recorded, but the bottom line is that the person behind the war is Crubari."

Will Greenfield, who had seated himself while Jake was talking, now stood looking for somewhere to pace in the cramped quarters. Finding none, he sat back down. "Are you sure? Do you have proof?"

Before she could answer, Jake placed his hand on Carin's shoulder. When she turned to him, he was pointing to the recorder. She nodded and Jake shut it off. Carin turned back to Greenfield, pointed to the voice stick, and said, "That's the 'official' recording. Only let your direct supervisors hear any of that. The recorder you have running in your jacket pocket will be of better quality if you pull it out now. No one should hear this except the two of you."

Greenfield shook his head and removed the recording device from his pocket. "How did you know?"

Carin smiled slightly and pointed to her ear. "I could hear it. I should mention that I would have been disappointed had you not been taping the entire event. The reason I needed two separate recordings is that this next part is going to sound wacko, but it's extremely dangerous information. You're going to be the only ones to decide who hears this. I'm warning you; if the wrong people hear this, you could end up with worse than federal charges. You would almost certainly die a long, hard death. Are we clear?"

Greenfield shook his head. "I don't want to expose Agent Beamer to this."

Carin was already shaking her head; anticipating what he was going to say. "I'm sorry, Will. We don't have time to argue or switch. Besides, she is more strongly loyal to you than those two guys outside."

Greenfield looked from Jake to Glynnis. "What are you talking about?"

Carin shook her head, disgusted and turned to Glynnis. "Men! How did they ever get to run things?"

Glynnis maintained her position in the corner of the trailer, but a hint of a smile ghosted across one corner of her mouth. "You've got that right, Doctor."

Carin turned back to face Greenfield. "We don't have time to argue. Crubari is the person behind the war. If you want proof, get a search warrant and get all the computers and surveillance tapes from DiBeto's house. I think that you'll find what you need."

Greenfield remained unconvinced. "How do you know it was Crubari? I know he's a slippery character, but he's an underling — a hired gun at best. That doesn't make him some kind of kingpin."

Carin took a deep breath and focused on Greenfield. It was critical that he believe them. Carelessness around Crubari would guarantee the agents' deaths. "I know because Crubari himself told me. He told me while he was trying to kill me a couple of hours ago. It's all on the recording. This is important. He is almost as fast and strong as Jake and I. I think that he has been like us for a very long time, so he's seasoned. I was actually slightly stronger, slightly faster and a Tae Kwon Do black belt to boot and he pulled a fancy trick that almost got me killed. Don't underestimate this man, Agent Greenfield. He is more dangerous than you can possibly imagine. Always approach him as if there were ten of him and each one had a gun."

Greenfield looked at Glynnis then back to Carin. He gave his head a slight nod. "Go on."

Carin looked into Greenfield's eyes. This was going to be the tough part. She took a deep breath and let it spill out through her teeth. "In a few minutes, Jake and I are going to leave the camper and get into that tank on the rise. If what we think is correct, we'll be lifted off the planet and taken to a large Earth-crossing object that you've probably heard in the news referred to as 'Morrigan' We believe Morrigan is actually a ship of some kind that has an intelligence on board that calls itself 'Matr.' Jake and I are dying, Agent

Greenfield. We are going up there to see whether we can find a cure. If we don't find a cure, we will be dead within a couple of weeks."

Greenfield asked, "Why are you telling us this?"

Carin kept her gaze directed at Greenfield's eyes. "You told us about your motivation. You have to understand ours. We're desperate. The Ingreti clinic had absolutely no idea as to what was wrong with us, but they were sure that our bodily functions were decaying at a rapid rate. They're the ones that came up with how long we had to live. I apologize for the deception there, but our time was extremely tight and we couldn't afford any delays. I hope you understand."

Greenfield sat stone-faced returning Carin's stare. "Make it worth my while. Give me something that we don't know."

Carin remained motionless for a moment before speaking. "I think Earth may be very close to an attack. Where or when the attack may come, we don't know. All we know is that this Matr has technology that is impressive by our current standards and Matr is being cautious to the point of paranoia about this threat. It might be another faction within Matr's society or it might be a separate society altogether. We don't know. We just know that we've got to get to Matr to find out what's going on."

Greenfield sat back in his seat. "Yeah, I can see that you wouldn't want to have this spread around too much. They have padded cells for folks who believe that kind of stuff."

Carin relaxed her focus on Greenfield, took a deep breath, and let it out slowly. "In a few minutes, if that tank hasn't lifted off the ground you can call me crazy. But ..." She let the silence trail for a few seconds before continuing. "If that tank suddenly does get lifted, you better start thinking about what you're going to do, Agent Greenfield."

Before Greenfield could answer, there was a soft click from outside the trailer. Like a shot, Carin reached across and grabbed Greenfield as Jake reached behind and grabbed Glynnis. Carin had the presence of mind to turn off the lights as she pulled Agent Greenfield to the floor. "What's going on?" Greenfield whispered.

Carin answered with a finger to her lips. "It's Crubari."

Greenfield was shaking his head. "I've got Ed and Brian out there. They can handle him."

Carin hesitated a second before answering. "No, they can't, Agent Greenfield. Your men are dead."

Chapter 48

Time to pickup: 5 minutes

CARIN COULD HEAR CRUBARI pacing around the trailer. "Come on out, *chica*," he called angrily. "We did not finish our dance."

Carin held a finger up to her lips to keep anyone from speaking. She had to assume that Crubari would overhear anything they said. Carin's mind was racing to come up with a plan and she kept coming up with nothing. She had no idea how she was going to neutralize Crubari and still make it up to Matr, but she knew that their chances would be better if they could get close to the tank. Carin looked at her watch. There were only five minutes until pickup. Damn! Damn! Damn!

She pointed at Greenfield, Glynnis and Jake and indicated to stay behind her. *Do you understand, Jake? He thinks that you are not elegido. You're our ace in the hole even as weak as you are.* Without hesitating, Jake nodded. He understood.

"Come out, *chica*. On the other hand, do you want me to come in? We could dance in there. Is that what you want?"

Carin yelled over her shoulder in the direction of Crubari. "Give me a minute, will ya?"

She pointed at Greenfield and Glynnis and indicated guns with her thumb and forefinger. They nodded. She pointed her fingers at an angle towards each other and then showed her fingers counting down. *Three, two, one, and fire. Get him in crossfire. Get it?*

Before Carin could give an answer, the camper leaned over and fell on its side. Carin sensed on what side of the camper Crubari was and threw herself against the window on the side farthest from him. He had anticipated her action and was there as she rolled outside the camper in time to land a full uppercut on Carin that she was just barely able to block. Still, the force of the blow knocked her through the air and caused her to see stars.

Crubari was circling in for the kill, approaching her cautiously in case she was faking. Carin knew she could not fend him off just yet when she heard Jake yell. "Hey, Crowbar. Remember me? I'm the other one that you can't seem to kill."

Crubari turned and saw the three people climbing out of the now overturned camper. He smiled an evil smile to Jake. "So, Captain. I find you in the company of the FBI. I was correct about you all along. Here you are with your FBI. You are a government agent. Do not worry. I will deal with you three in a minute. After all, ladies first."

While Crubari had been talking, Jake had bent over and picked up a small rock. When Jake stood up, he threw the rock in a motion that was almost too fast to follow. Crubari easily dodged the rock, but the confident look on his face melted into one of surprise and he took three paces away from Jake. "*Elegido*! But that is not possible."

Jake stood his ground and said, "Whatever. Carin, take our friends to the tank. Crubari, you, and I have something to discuss – something about my children."

Crubari turned and, instead of attacking Jake, attacked Carin and by so doing, distanced himself from Jake. Carin was completely defensive under a flurry of punches, but Crubari became careless and left himself open for one punch which Carin delivered to his throat.

Crubari backed up from Carin, coughing. "There can be only one *elegido*. One! I am that one."

Carin and Jake began herding Crubari towards the tank. She called out to Crubari, "Hey, *elegido*. How's that right knee I kicked out from under you the last time we danced? Bring it over here and let me give it an adjustment."

Out of the corner of her eye, she noticed Jake giving a slight nod. *Target his bad knee. It can't have healed completely.* Message received.

Carin could see Greenfield and Glynnis out of the corner of her eye. They were running behind Jake with their guns drawn, but it seemed as if they were moving in slow motion. Carin became worried for them. If she let the gap widen too much, the agents could be easy prey for Crubari. With his speed, he could break their necks before they had a chance to react. What if she and Jake flew off in the tank and left them behind with Crubari? It would be murder.

Carin willed herself to slow down and felt the now-familiar wave of dizziness and nausea wash over her. She began walking steadily for the tank while keeping an eye on Jake and Crubari. Jake apparently followed her lead and slowed down. The wave of dizziness brought him to his knees. In less than an eye blink, Crubari was on top of him preparing to deliver a kick to Jake's head. It would have worked, but Jake had not slowed down. Crubari had his knee pulled in for a straight leg kick to Jake's head. Jake's foot flew out first, but he missed Crubari's knee and connected a relatively weak kick to the groin. Crubari screamed as he flew through the air.

Now Jake *did* slow down. Carin was certain of it because his collapse was unmistakable. She jogged over to him and put his arm around her neck. She looked around for Crubari as she half walked, half-dragged Jake to the tank, but she could not find him. As she leaned Jake against the tank, she yelled at Greenfield and Glynnis "Cover your backs."

Carin need not have bothered. Years of training along with a close working relationship had engendered an instinct in what the other was doing. They were coming up the shallow rise when Carin saw Crubari race towards Greenfield and, almost casually, brush the gun from Greenfield's hand and knock him to the ground.

Upon hearing Crubari's footsteps, Glynnis had spun around and begun firing her gun. Most of the shots would have been wild in any case, but it was obvious that Glynnis was trying to distract Crubari. *Nothing focuses your attention like incoming fire*, thought Carin. She gauged Crubari's reaction to the gunfire. He had backed off from Glynnis and Greenfield. She had time.

Carin rapped the side of the tank with her knuckles while keeping an eye on the fight. "Fred, are you there?"

"Doctor Gonzalez, I am in the tank and the tank is ready."

"Fred, help Jake in if you can. If Matr shows up, close the lid and leave me."

Without waiting for an answer, Carin turned in time to see Crubari pick up Glynnis and throw her towards Greenfield. She flew through the air as if she were a rag doll, but landed roughly feet first and was able to do a dive roll sparing herself major injury. As if by magic, Glynnis came up with Greenfield's gun and began firing it as soon as she could swing it around towards Crubari. Crubari backed away rapidly from Glynnis.

While Glynnis was shooting, Carin walked about ten steps from the tank and waited. When the bullets stopped flying, Crubari stopped his retreat and slowly began to walk towards Glynnis as she ejected the clip from her gun and tried to slap in another one.

"Crubari," yelled Carin in the strongest voice she could muster. "In less than one minute I am going to leave this planet in that tank. You can either deal with me now or keep playing with those two."

"No," he screamed. "I am *elegido*. I. There can only be one. It is my right to go."

Carin turned to the FBI agents. "Get into your car."

To Crubari she said, "The path to salvation lies inside that tank."

Without looking back, Carin turned and accelerated at her maximum towards the tank. In one strong push, she leaped to the top of the tank. While she was in the air, she felt and heard a powerful sonic boom from directly above. *Whaddya know*, she thought. *Jake bluffed old Matr right out of its socks.*

Carin landed on top of the tank, was in the porthole, and dogged it in one fluid motion. She looked over to Jake to see him secure in his acceleration couch. Carin gave Jake a worried look and said, "If my guess is wrong about what this tether is made of, we are going to have a problem."

Jake gave a single chuckle. "Doctor, no matter what that lasso of Matr's is made of, we are in for interesting times."

"Ah," said Carin. "The ancient Chinese curse."

At that moment, the tank rang like a bell.

*　　　*　　　*

"No, *Doctora*. You cannot get away from me so easily."

Crubari landed on the tank and looked at the hatch that was on the top. The wheel that secured the hatch had been removed from the outside. Out of rage, he slammed his fist into the hatch. The metal gave a satisfying ring. However, try as he might, it did not yield. He felt around the edges of the hatch to see whether he could get some purchase. With a pry bar, he could have been inside the tank in a matter of moments, but with only his bare hands, it would take longer.

Crubari began shaking the hatch back and forth with all his might. At first, it did not move, but he persisted. He kept it up, back and forth, back and forth. Then he felt the hatch move slightly. Was that his imagination? He redoubled he efforts, pushing the hatch cover back and forth. Yes, it did move. He was going to get inside!

A silky strand gently fell from above him on the hatch and he brushed it aside. He had to keep going on the hatch to prove he was *elegido*. A few more strands fell around him and he pushed them away and looked up. The sight that filled his mind struck terror. A spider web appeared to dangling directly above him with nothing supporting it.

Crubari had left his country of birth many years ago, but the legends of his childhood now drove him to a panic. Death had found him after all these years! How could that be? Was he not *elegido*?

He fought the strands even as they wrapped around him and the tank. He kept climbing the strands to get above them. They were sinking on the tank. Wrapping themselves around the tank until hardly any metal showed through, and yet he kept climbing to get above the spider web. Suddenly, he felt himself yanked towards heaven. Only the spider web kept him from falling. He climbed to the very top of the spider web and then … there was nothing.

Crubari looked down to see the ground rushing away from him. He needed to jump off, but he hesitated. He was no longer sure that he was *elegido*. As he stood there watching the ground rush away from him trying to decide whether or not to jump, the wind rushing by him began to exert a tremendous force on him. In moments, it went from gale force winds to hurricane force winds to tornado force winds. Crubari began to fall back away from where he was standing. Unconsciously, he reached up to grab what had to be there. In some primitive part of his mind, he knew that if he was being pulled into the heavens, there must have been some kind of rope. He reached for the invisible rope and made the last mistake of his long life. Had Crubari been more of a man of science, he might have guessed that the "invisible rope" he grabbed was a single molecule that extended from the tank up to Matr. What he grabbed for was thousands of times sharper than a surgical scalpel. Almost painlessly, his hand left his body. While he fell back to Earth, he had time to look at his severed hand and marvel at the precision of the cut.

He also realized that indeed, he was not *elegido*.

CHAPTER 49

AGENT WILLIAM GREENFIELD LOOKED at the excavation work that was proceeding at the collapsed cave and tried to scratch his left arm underneath the temporary splint the emergency medical technicians had placed around it. He could tell that the cast would be unbearable. The EMT's had tried to take him to the hospital to get the bone set properly, but he refused to go. Another hour or two was not going to make any difference to his arm and his team had lost too much in the course of this case for him to leave just now. He wanted to look into the eyes of the man who was responsible for the deaths of his two team members. Indirectly responsible perhaps, but it did not change the way he felt.

Glynnis came up beside Greenfield with a warm mug of coffee in each hand and casually handed one to him. He blew absentmindedly across the rim of his cup and tested the brew. It was a decent cup of coffee, and it had been sweetened perfectly to his taste with one teaspoon of sugar. He looked over to Glynnis. She still had blood caked in her hair. She looked at him and asked, "What?"

What indeed, thought Greenfield. *How do I go about thanking you, Glynnis? Thanking you for distracting Crubari. Thanking you for making yourself his target. Thanking you for saving my life.* Instead, Greenfield raised his mug to her and settled for, "Thank you, Glynnis."

She hesitated for a moment over her own coffee before answering. "You're welcome, skipper."

Greenfield changed the subject by waving his coffee mug in the general direction of the work crews and asking, "How's it going? I've been out of it while the EMT's worked me over."

Glynnis turned to look at the workers busily digging in a part of the hill.

"The soundings came back indicating there's a pocket about where Jake and Carin said it would be. We can't tell whether there's a body in there, but we'll know soon."

"What about the raid on Frank's house? Have we gotten any of the computers?"

"Got' em, skipper. I just finished talking to the team and the files are apparently in there just like Carin said. They weren't even encrypted or anything. It's almost too easy."

Greenfield thought for a moment then nodded his head. "It all makes sense — DiBeto was set up to take the fall in case things went sour. I would bet we find enough evidence on the stuff we got from the raid to put away a handful of folks from the different offices. It was probably the ones Crubari wanted out of the way so that he could move in."

"We got lucky on this one, skipper."

"Tell that to Ed and Brian," said Greenfield quietly.

"Yeah, I'm glad you didn't make me go outside when Carin and Jake started giving us … the other story. I'd have probably joined Ed and Brian."

Greenfield shivered involuntarily. "Another debt I owe them. You know, if it weren't for a couple of small points, I'd have sworn they were behind the whole war. It was almost too much good luck for them to have known everything they did and not have been hip deep in it."

Glynnis took a sip of her coffee. "What do you mean, skipper? Do you mean like the small point that they saved our butts, again, when it would have been to their advantage to let Crubari kill us? Or do you mean the fact they were moving at speeds that are clearly impossible, displaying strength that is beyond belief and then getting sucked up into space by a giant spider web and disappearing off the face of the planet?"

Greenfield swirled his coffee around and stared into his mug. "Yep, those were pretty much the points I was thinking about."

A cry from the digging site stopped any further conversation. Greenfield and Glynnis walked towards the hole in time to see the unmistakable silhouette of DiBeto leap out and begin running from person to person, yelling, "Don't let him get near me!" He broke away from two police officers and ran directly to Greenfield and Glynnis. He kept yelling, "Keep him away! Keep him away!"

The two police officers and two EMT's caught up with DiBeto when he was only six feet away from Greenfield. Eyes bloodshot and hair wild, DiBeto kept screaming, "Keep him away!"

It took the two police officers and the two EMT's several minutes to wrestle the severely agitated DiBeto to the ground and put cuffs around his wrists. An emergency room doctor who had been running behind the group with his medical kit finally caught up with them, pulled out a syringe, and plunged into the writhing mass of bodies. The doctor put away his syringe, but his smile of satisfaction turned into a frown as DiBeto's rants continued unabated. He prepared another syringe and dove back into the undulating heap of men. After a few moments, Frank's screams began to fade away and the heaving of the pile of men on the ground began to settle down. Finally, one by one the men lifted themselves off his immobile form. He was no longer screaming, but his voice could still be heard whimpering, "Don't let him get near me."

"Wow," said the young doctor putting away his syringe. "He has a big enough dose to knock out a charging rhino. Wow, look at him. He's still awake! You should've warned us that this guy was psychotic."

Greenfield shrugged his shoulders and winced at the pain from his broken arm. "He wasn't unbalanced when he went into that cave. At least not the way he is now. I'm no expert, but I never would have guessed Franklin DiBeto was that easy to scare, much less be driven psychotic in a few hours."

The doctor nodded. "I'm just a first year ER doc and I'm no shrink, but my diagnosis is that this guy is over-the-top and certifiably whacko. I gave him thirty milligrams of lorazepam with a twenty-milligram haloperidol chaser. He should be like Gumby's weaker brother, but he's still putting up a fight. Look at him! I better go help."

As the doctor jogged over to catch up with the group carrying DiBeto to the squad car, Greenfield asked Glynnis, "Do you think that's another gift from Jake and Carin?"

"I'd guess it's from Jake," said Glynnis. "I've been able to listen to some of the recording Jake made. We already knew that Franklin DiBeto was responsible for his children's deaths. He said that in the recording. He also mentioned — wait a minute, I wrote it down." Glynnis pulled out a small notepad from her back pocket and read, "cleithrophobia, scotophobia and agrizoophobia. Before you ask, I have no idea what any of those are. I looked them up and they weren't in a standard dictionary. I get the feeling that we'd have to ask a psychiatrist what they meant. Jake also stated that he 'emphasized' those phobias in DiBeto. That's the word he used. 'Emphasized.' I don't know what that means either."

"Emphasized?"

"Yeah, I know the word. I just don't know why he put it that way."

Greenfield threw his chin towards DiBeto. "I don't know either, but I think we've seen the result."

Greenfield and Glynnis turned at the sound of a car approaching from behind them. Several fellow agents stepped out of the car. Two of them came directly towards Greenfield and Glynnis. One of the agents was Zeb. The other was unknown to Greenfield. The new man wore rumpled clothes and sported a two-day growth of stubble on his face. Zeb approached the closest and gave the introductions. "Agent Michael Collins, this is Agent William Greenfield and Agent Glynnis Beamer." Zeb turned to face Greenfield. "Agent Collins is from Washington. He flew in when your team declined headquarters' kind invitation to drop everything, destroy an investigation in progress, put us at least six months behind and ensure that a crime ring gets itself firmly established in the world's premiere entertainment destination."

"Dammit, Zeb. It's procedure. Your team could have turned."

Zeb spun to face the headquarters agent. "Mike, if I hadn't known you for the last twenty years, that last brilliant statement of yours would have bought you a punch in the nose."

"Listen, Zeb."

"No, you listen. Two of my people are dead because of your precious procedure. Headquarters pushed my team. You joggled their elbow. All you dignified, distinctive desk jockeys didn't even bother to call me."

"Zeb, you were implicated and you know that."

"That ain't gonna sell, Mike. Not now, not at the hearing. We had my name cleared up and reported to headquarters a full twenty-four hours before the edict came down and if you didn't warn me, you could have called my deputy. Hellfire, you could have called Greenfield. He wasn't implicated. You want to know what really frosts me, Mike? We were close – two weeks tops to finishing this thing out the right way. Somebody in bureau HQ messed with this investigation, two of my men are dead and you're talking procedure." Zeb gave a loud growl that eloquently expressed his disgust. He turned to face the open desert before he continued, softly. "There are two men dead, Mike. You want to know how close we were? Look at the results — this case is closed and solved. Two good men dead because you guys couldn't wait two lousy weeks, somebody at HQ was fiddling with the investigation and the rest of you brave hearts at HQ couldn't stand up to the political pressure."

"Zeb, we followed procedure, that's all we could do. I know it won't bring those two agents back and that makes me feel bad enough."

Agent Collins turned to face Greenfield. "Agent Greenfield, we found something that we thought you two could explain to us." Michael Collins turned and motioned to one of the agents standing by the car. The agent by the car saw the signal and brought a small Styrofoam cooler. After handing the small package to Greenfield, the agent returned wordlessly to the car. Greenfield felt the weight of the package, opened the top to give a cursory look and knew its contents immediately. "Crubari's left hand. Or a big piece of it."

Collins raised an eyebrow. "You didn't examine it very closely."

"No, I didn't and I'm not going to." Greenfield handed the small package to Collins who handled it as if he did not quite know what to do with it. Finally, he just tucked the little cooler under an armpit.

Agent Collins persisted. "I need to speak with Jake Sabio and Carin Gonzalez."

Greenfield shook his head. "No, you need to speak to Antonio Crubari."

"He's dead."

Greenfield raised an eyebrow and turned to face Collins. "You found his body?"

"Well, no. But from your description of the events of the previous evening and from the evidence …"

Agent Collins patted the box under his arm and let the implications speak for themselves.

"Oh," said Greenfield shaking his head. "So what you are saying is that you have nothing."

"Agent Greenfield, by your statement …"

"Agent Collins," Greenfield interrupted. "Show me the body or admit that you have nothing."

Collins remained quiet for a moment before answering. "You two have been through a lot over the last week. Take some time off and then we'll talk."

Having said this, Agent Collins turned and proceeded to the car to wait. After Zeb was sure Collins was out of earshot, he turned to Greenfield and asked, "So, by your statement, you were attacked by Crubari and possibly others while you were staking out the trailer. He killed your two team members before you could establish a response and were saved by two people who came in and overwhelmed the force that was attacking you. Is that pretty much it?"

Greenfield looked Zeb in the eye and answered, "Yes sir."

"And you never saw who was helping you?"

"No sir."

"And this miracle group of two was able to take on a force that was attacking successfully against four armed and trained agents? Turn the enemy and route them without you ever realizing who it was?"

"It was dark sir."

"And all the while, you were incapacitated due to your broken arm and Glynnis was semi-conscious due to a blow to the head?"

"It's all in the report, sir."

Zeb nodded knowingly. "Interesting evening you two have had."

Greenfield was shaking his head. "Sir, I would gladly give my right arm

315

to not have lived through last night if I knew it would bring our two team members back."

Zeb stared at Greenfield for a moment before softly saying, "So would I, son. Still, there are a couple of things that keep bothering me."

"I'll answer any questions that I can, sir."

"You didn't really talk about the camper. You know it was knocked over on its side."

"Yes sir. I mentioned that in my report."

"I know you did, Will. Did you know that there are two crush marks on the side of the camper that are each about the size of a hand? It even looked like hand prints to me. If I didn't know any better, I'd say somebody grabbed it where these so-called hand marks are and toppled the camper. But that's clearly impossible, isn't it?"

Greenfield licked his lips that had suddenly gone dry. "Clearly."

"And you know," Zeb continued, "There were also obvious marks on the ground where a heavy object was resting, a hundred yards, or so from the trailer. Now that thing is gone. Do you know what I find amazing about that, Will?"

"I wouldn't speculate sir."

"I'll bet you wouldn't. I find it interesting that there were no tire tracks anywhere near this thing. So how did it manage to leave?"

Greenfield stuttered, "I d ... don't know sir."

"And another thing," Zeb pressed. "Guess where we found the hand? Not where you would expect, over by the fight where all your footprints are, but about fifteen miles from there. Seems the hand was found this morning in a citizen's flowerbed when they took their cup of coffee along and fetched their morning paper. We just happened to be driving in the vicinity when we heard the report on the police scanner and offered to pick it up."

"Are we sure it's Crubari's sir?"

It was Zeb's turn to hesitate before answering. "Las Vegas may be a rough-and-tumble place, but how many fresh hands do you think are removed from folks around here every day? Left hands at that."

"Sorry. Wasn't thinking clearly."

"I wonder how it got into that flower bed. It was pretty far from the road. It could have been buried anywhere and we would have never found it. If they were trying to make a statement, they could have left it where it was. It is something of a puzzle how it found its way into that flower bed, don't you think Will?"

"I ... I wouldn't know sir."

"It's as if that hand fell from the sky."

Greenfield began to cough after Zeb's last statement. Before he could compose himself, Zeb asked, "What are you two planning to do after we wrap up this case and finish the paperwork?"

Glynnis was the first to respond. "I was planning on taking a sabbatical. I want to travel the country and linger around some sights we had to rush through during the investigation. You know, maybe talk to some people we met. Only this time I could talk to them on a more social level."

Greenfield nodded his head in agreement and added tersely. "I'm going to take some time off, too." As an afterthought he added, "What about you sir?"

Zeb's face could have made the Mona Lisa seem downright scrutable. "I think I'll take some time off too. Maybe follow you two around and see what there is to see."

Greenfield looked at Glynnis and back at Zeb. "That, sir, would make for some interesting times."

Epilogue

Jake began to become aware of his surroundings, but the sensations seemed all wrong. He could feel he was lying on his back, strapped against a surface, but it also felt as if he were floating. He opened his eyes and saw diffuse light coming from all directions, but he could not determine the size of the room he occupied. His eyes shut again.

Then he realized that something was very different. For the first time in weeks, he did not feel sick.

"Carin, I believe Jake is showing signs of consciousness."

Good, thought Jake. *Fred's here.*

Jake's eyes fluttered open, but they felt so heavy he only had time for a glimpse of Fred, attached to a spindly contraption, hovering close to him. Jake's eyes drooped again, but in the darkness, he clearly heard Fred's voice say to him, "Falcon 22." Jake laughed despite his weakness. The code translated as *Happiness is a private ship.*

The clear message was, "Yes, we actually made it up here." The added zing came from hearing the Falcon code correctly used by a metal box, delivered with what appeared to be human wit.

When he opened his eyes this time, Carin's face was hovering above him. Her short, jet-black hair framed her face. The strange lighting made it look like a blue halo. Jake smiled. "I'm firing my guardian angel."

Carin leaned forward and asked, "What did you say?"

Jake looked directly into her eyes. "I said that I'm firing my guardian angel and I'm giving you the job."

Carin gave a small laugh that was part sob. "Who says I want the job?"

It was then Jake noticed her red, swollen eyes. "Tough. You got the job. Negotiations closed. Expect the contract to be on your desk in the morning."

Jake turned his head slowly and was pleased that he no longer felt a headache, feverishness, or vertigo. "So we made it and we aren't dead yet."

"Yep."

"Should have bought a lottery ticket. How long have I been out?"

"A couple of days."

Jake flinched. "*Days?* What's our status?"

Carin smiled a knowing smile at Jake. "The status is that we're on the rock folks on Earth are calling Morrigan. You're recovering from our exertions with Crubari, not to mention the six-gravity ascent. There's adequate air, food and water for a lifetime or two. Fred has been in communication with Matr. The information he got helped us to stabilize our condition. What part do you want in more detail?"

Jake felt his eyelids droop despite his desire to stay awake. "Fred and the robots?"

"Yes, plenty of power to keep them charged up. Fred is upgrading the batteries and doing other maintenance. It claims it can maintain itself and the robots here."

Jake tried to only close one eye and keep the other on Carin. "There's lots of air, food and water? How did that happen?"

Carin reached down and gently touched his cheek. "This rock really is Matr's spaceship," she said. "It's what we would call a 'generation ship' meant to transport a large number of individuals a long distance over a long period. Fred has reactivated their food and water processing facilities for us. The foods we are getting from the facilities have the specific nutrients you and I now have to have. That's why you're feeling better."

Jake took a deep breath and let it out. The air currents sent Carin's hair dancing around her face. Finally, he said, "To actually get here and find this ..."

"Overwhelming," Carin finished.

"That's an understatement," agreed Jake.

He looked around and still could not judge the size of the room. "You think this is where humans came from?"

Carin took his head in both her hands and said, "Not exactly. Rest! You need to recuperate so that we can get to work."

Jake felt himself slipping back into sleep and said, "What's the rush?"

Jake heard Carin as if he were in a deep well. "Jake, we aren't cured, we're only stabilized. The symptoms will return. This bug was never designed for humans."

Jake mumbled, "What does Matr say?"

"Matr didn't design this bug and doesn't even know how it functions. We need to find the designer."

Jake fumbled around fishing for his pants' pocket inside his sleeping bag. "Just great … hey, where are my pants? The ones I was wearing when we came up here."

Carin pointed over her shoulder to her duffle bag. She had it tethered to a hook on the wall to keep it from floating away. "I had to get your clothes off of you. With everything you'd been through, you really smelled bad. I had to sponge you down."

Jake gave her a weak grin. "I wish I could've been awake for that."

Before Carin could answer, Jake asked, "Could you please get them for me?"

Carin floated to the duffle bag, rummaged a moment, and returned with his pants. "Here you go," she said.

Jake reached into the right hip pocket and let out a sigh of relief. He pulled out Carin's amethyst ring and handed it to her. "I was afraid I'd lost it in the fight since I didn't see it on your finger."

Carin placed the ring on her fully regrown finger, twirled it, and smiled.

Jake could not stay conscious any longer. He released his hold on awareness and fell into a troubled sleep.

*   *   *

Containment successful. Yet conversation with the machine intelligence "Fred" is confusing. The "Fred" does not explain why the two biological intelligences — clearly warriors — should be typical of their peers. These two are versed in the technical aspects of the focused application of power.

The "Fred" states that there are millions of creatures on this planet who are just as qualified as these two biological intelligences. If this race is advanced, why are they planet-bound? Why did the intelligences need assistance to come here?

Yet, the central question is whether I can earn the trust of the three intelligences now aboard, and if so – *how can that trust be used?*

the end

CPSIA information can be obtained at www.ICGtesting.com
Printed in the USA
LVOW092345060312

271885LV00002BA/3/P